Red Planet Blues

"Mars, like the sun-kissed streets of Los Angeles Philip Marlowe once patrolled, may sound like it's an exotic location, but underneath the glamour of being on another planet there's just as many dark and dangerous secrets as anywhere else. So it's the perfect setting for a private eye willing to skirt around the edges of the law. You'll have a lot of fun wandering the mean streets of New Klondike and over the surface of the Red Planet with PI Lomax, and he might even give you a few things to think about."

—seattlepi.com

"A wonderful Raymond Chandler–meets–Ray Bradbury vibe permeates *Red Planet Blues* . . . It's a genre mash-up that might have felt gimmicky in less capable hands; however, with Sawyer at the helm, it succeeds beautifully. A hard-boiled noir detective on Mars—the sort of character a guy like Sawyer was born to write . . . Alex Lomax is the good-naturedly tarnished soul of the story while the scientific detail that marks Sawyer's work is undeniably present . . . A ripping good read."

—*The Maine Edge*

"A new Robert J. Sawyer book is always cause for celebration. Even more so when the book is something completely different than he's been doing for the last few years. *Red Planet Blues* is a tour de force . . . It's a well-written, intelligent story with some unexpected twists . . . Sawyer makes New Klondike as real as the street in front of your house . . . To top it off, Sawyer obviously had fun writing this book, and that sense of fun comes through on every page. Definitely worth reading."

—*Analog Science Fiction and Fact*

"Sawyer has a lot of fun with the typical mystery-novel doings, always keeping one or two steps ahead of the reader's guesses. Dames and gats, treachery and MacGuffins abound—all of course flavored with a space-age ambiance . . . Sawyer introduces some deep backstory to complicate the plot, and zigs and zags in unpredictable fashion, always keeping the reader alert and entertained."

—*Locus*

continued . . .

BOOKS BY ROBERT J. SAWYER

NOVELS

Golden Fleece
End of an Era
The Terminal Experiment
Starplex
Frameshift
Illegal Alien
Factoring Humanity

FlashForward
Calculating God
Mindscan
Rollback
Triggers
Red Planet Blues

The Quintaglio Ascension Trilogy
Far-Seer
Fossil Hunter
Foreigner

The Neanderthal Parallax Trilogy
Hominids
Humans
Hybrids

The WWW Trilogy
Wake
Watch
Wonder

COLLECTIONS

Iterations
(introduction by James Alan Gardner)

Relativity
(introduction by Mike Resnick)

Identity Theft
(introduction by Robert Charles Wilson)

For book-club discussion guides, visit sfwriter.com

Red Planet Blues

ROBERT J. SAWYER

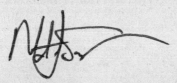

Incorporating the Hugo and Nebula
Award–nominated novella "Identity Theft"

ACE BOOKS, NEW YORK

THE BERKLEY PUBLISHING GROUP
Published by the Penguin Group
Penguin Group (USA) LLC
375 Hudson Street, New York, New York 10014

(Penguin logo)

USA • Canada • UK • Ireland • Australia • New Zealand • India • South Africa • China

penguin.com

A Penguin Random House Company

RED PLANET BLUES

An Ace Book / published by arrangement with SFWriter.com, Inc.

PUBLISHING HISTORY
Ace hardcover edition / April 2013
Ace mass-market edition / April 2014

PRINTED IN THE UNITED STATES OF AMERICA

10 9 8 7 6 5 4 3 2

Cover art by Tony Mauro.
Cover design by Rita Frangie.
Interior text design by Laura K. Corless.

The first ten chapters were originally published in a slightly different version
as the novella "Identity Theft" in *Down These Dark Spaceways*, edited by
Mike Resnick, published by Science Fiction Book Club, 2005.

For
Sherry Peters

ACKNOWLEDGMENTS

In February 2004, Hugo Award–winning author **Mike Resnick** approached me with an offer I couldn't refuse: write a "science-fictional hard-boiled private-eye novella" for an original anthology he was editing for the Science Fiction Book Club called *Down These Dark Spaceways*.

That story, "Identity Theft," went on to win Spain's Premio UPC de Ciencia Ficción, which, at 6,000 euros, is the world's largest cash prize for science-fiction writing. It was also a finalist for the Canadian Science Fiction and Fantasy Award ("the Aurora"), as well as for the top two awards in the science-fiction field: the World Science Fiction Society's Hugo Award (SF's "People's Choice Award") and the Science Fiction and Fantasy Writers of America's Nebula Award (SF's "Academy Award")—making "Identity Theft" the first (and so far only) original publication of the SFBC ever to be nominated for either of those awards. In a slightly modified form, "Identity Theft" makes up the first ten chapters of this novel.

In 2007, my wife Carolyn and I spent the summer at Berton House, the former home of Canadian historian and author **Pierre Berton**. One of Canada's most prestigious writers' residencies, Berton House is in Dawson City in the Yukon Territory—the heart of the Klondike Gold Rush. Although I'd already established the Great Martian Fossil Rush as the back-story to "Identity Theft," it was my time in the Yukon—living across the dirt road from **Robert Service**'s cabin, and just a block from **Jack London**'s old home—that made me want to really explore the madness and greed that drives stampedes of prospectors. My thanks to the Berton House administrator **Elsa Franklin**, and to **Dan Davidson** and **Suzanne Saito**, who looked after us in Dawson City.

For other help and encouragement, my thanks go to **Ted Bleaney**, **Wayne Brown**, **David Livingstone Clink**, **Paddy Forde**, **Marcel Gagné**, **James Alan Gardner**, **Martin H. Greenberg**, **John Helfers**, **Doug Herrington**, **Al Katerinsky**, **Herb Kauderer**, **Geoffrey A. Landis**, **Kirstin Morrell**, **Kayla Nielsen**, **Virginia O'Dine**, **Ian Pedoe**, **Sherry Peters**, and **Alan B. Sawyer**.

My working title for this book was *The Great Martian Fossil Rush,* but my American publisher wanted something that played up the noir angle. I asked for suggestions online, and hundreds of possibilities were put forth. **Jeffrey Allan Beeler**, **Nazrat Durand**, **André Peloquin**, and **Mike Poole** each separately proposed the title we ended up using, *Red Planet Blues*. My thanks to them, and to the more than one hundred other people who made suggestions. As it happens, the same title was used in 1989 by my great friend Hugo Award–winning writer **Allen Steele** for a novella he later incorporated into his terrific 1992 Mars novel *Labyrinth of Night;* I'm using the title with Allen's kind permission.

Finally, huge thanks, as always, to the Aurora Award–winning poet **Carolyn Clink**, who helped in countless ways; to my father **John A. Sawyer**, who encouraged my early interests in both paleontology and other worlds; to **Adrienne Kerr** at Penguin Group (Canada) in Toronto; and to **Ginjer Buchanan** at Penguin Group (USA)'s Ace imprint in New York. And, of course, many thanks to my agents **Christopher Lotts**, **Vince Gerardis**, and the late **Ralph Vicinanza**.

There are strange things done 'neath the Martian sun
  By those who seek the mother lode;
The ruddy trails have their secret tales
  That would make your blood run cold;
The twin moonlights have seen queer sights,
  But the queerest they ever did see
Was that night on the shore of a lake of yore
  I terminated a transferee.

ONE

The door to my office slid open. "Hello," I said, rising from my chair. "You must be my nine o'clock." I said it as if I had a ten o'clock and an eleven o'clock, but I didn't. The whole Martian economy was in a slump, and even though I was the only private detective on Mars this was the first new case I'd had in weeks.

"Yes," said a high, feminine voice. "I'm Cassandra Wilkins."

I let my eyes rove up and down her body. It was very good work; I wondered if she'd had quite so perfect a figure before transferring. People usually ordered replacement bodies that, at least in broad strokes, resembled their originals, but few could resist improving them. Men got more buff, women got curvier, and everyone modified their faces, removing asymmetries, wrinkles, and imperfections. If I ever transferred myself, I'd eliminate the gray in my blond hair and get a new nose that would look like my current one had before it'd been broken a couple of times.

"A pleasure to meet you, Ms. Wilkins," I said. "I'm Alexander Lomax. Please have a seat."

She was a little thing, no more than 150 centimeters, and

she was wearing a stylish silver-gray blouse and skirt but no makeup or jewelry. I'd expected her to sit with a fluid catlike movement, given her delicate features, but she just sort of plunked herself into the chair. "Thanks," she said. "I do hope you can help me, Mr. Lomax. I really do."

Rather than immediately sitting down myself, I went to the coffeemaker. I filled my own mug, then offered Cassandra one; most models of transfer could eat and drink in order to be sociable, but she declined my offer. "What seems to be the problem?" I said, returning to my chair.

It's hard reading a transfer's expression: the facial sculpting was usually excellent, but the movements were somewhat restrained. "My husband—oh, my goodness, Mr. Lomax, I hate to even say this!" She looked down at her hands. "My husband . . . he's disappeared."

I raised my eyebrows; it was pretty damned difficult for someone to disappear here. New Klondike was locked under a shallow dome four kilometers in diameter and just twenty meters high at the central support column. "When did you last see him?"

"Three days ago."

My office was small, but it did have a window. Through it, I could see the crumbling building next door and one of the gently sloping arches that helped hold up the transparent dome. Outside the dome, a dust storm was raging, orange clouds obscuring the sun. Auxiliary lights on the arch compensated for that, but Martian daylight was never very bright. "Is your husband, um, like you?" I asked.

She nodded. "Oh, yes. We both came here looking to make our fortune, just like everyone else."

I shook my head. "I mean is he also a transfer?"

"Oh, sorry. Yes, he is. In fact, we both just transferred."

"It's an expensive procedure," I said. "Could he have been skipping out on paying for it?"

Cassandra shook her head. "No, no. Joshua found one or two nice specimens early on. He used the money from selling those pieces to buy the NewYou franchise here. That's where we met—after I threw in the towel on sifting dirt, I got a job in sales there. Anyway, of course, we both got to transfer at cost." She was actually wringing her synthetic hands. "Oh, Mr. Lomax, please help me! I don't know what I'm going to do without my Joshua!"

"You must love him a lot," I said, watching her pretty face for more than just the pleasure of looking at it; I wanted to gauge her sincerity as she replied. After all, people often disappeared because things were bad at home, but spouses are rarely forthcoming about that.

"Oh, I do!" said Cassandra. "I love him more than I can say. Joshua is a wonderful, wonderful man." She looked at me with pleading eyes. "You have to help me get him back. You just have to!"

I looked down at my coffee mug; steam was rising from it. "Have you tried the police?"

Cassandra made a sound that I guessed was supposed to be a snort: it had the right roughness but was dry as Martian sand. "Yes. They—oh, I hate to speak ill of anyone, Mr. Lomax! Believe me, it's not my way, but—well, there's no ducking it, is there? They were useless. Just totally useless."

I nodded slightly; it's a story I heard often enough. I owed much of what little livelihood I had to the NKPD's indifference to most crime. They were a private force, employed by Howard Slapcoff to protect his thirty-year-old investment in constructing this city. The cops made a token effort to keep order but that was all. "Who did you speak to?"

"A—a detective, I guess he was; he didn't wear a uniform. I've forgotten his name."

"What did he look like?"

"Red hair, and—"

"That's Mac," I said. She looked puzzled, so I said his full name. "Dougal McCrae."

"McCrae, yes," said Cassandra. She shuddered a bit, and she must have noticed my surprised reaction to that. "Sorry," she said. "I just didn't like the way he looked at me."

I resisted running my eyes over her body just then; I'd already done so, and I could remember what I'd seen. I guess her original figure hadn't been like this one; if it had, she'd certainly be used to admiring looks from men by now.

"I'll have a word with McCrae," I said. "See what's already been done. Then I'll pick up where the cops left off."

"Would you?" Her green eyes seemed to dance. "Oh, thank you, Mr. Lomax! You're a good man—I can tell!"

I shrugged a little. "I can show you two ex-wives and a half dozen bankers who'd disagree."

"Oh, no," she said. "Don't say things like that! You *are* a good man, I'm sure of it. Believe me, I have a sense about these things. You're a good man, and I know you won't let me down."

Naïve woman; she'd probably thought the same thing about her hubby—until he'd run off. "Now, what can you tell me about your husband? Joshua, is it?"

"Yes, that's right. His full name is Joshua Connor Wilkins—and it's Joshua, never just Josh, thank you very much." I nodded. In my experience, guys who were anal about being called by their full first names never bought a round. Maybe it was a good thing this joker was gone.

"Yes," I said. "Go on." I didn't have to take notes. My office computer—a small green cube sitting on my desk—was recording everything and would extract whatever was useful into a summary file for me.

Cassandra ran her synthetic lower lip back and forth beneath her artificial upper teeth, thinking for a moment. "Well, he was born in Wichita, Kansas, and he's thirty-eight years old. He moved to Mars seven mears ago." Mears were Mars years; about double the length of those on Earth.

"Do you have a picture?"

"I can access one." She pointed at my dusty keyboard. "May I?"

I nodded, and Cassandra reached over to grab it. In doing so, she managed to knock over my "World's Greatest Detective" coffee mug, spilling hot joe all over her dainty hand. She let out a small yelp of pain. I got up, grabbed a towel, and began wiping up the mess. "I'm surprised that hurt," I said. "I mean, I *do* like my coffee hot, but . . ."

"Transfers feel pain, Mr. Lomax," she said, "for the same reason biologicals do. When you're flesh and blood, you need a signaling system to warn you when your parts are being damaged; same is true for those of us who have transferred. Of course, artificial bodies are much more durable."

"Ah."

"Sorry. I've explained this so many times now—you know, at work. Anyway, please forgive me about your desk."

I waved my hand dismissively. "Thank God for the paperless office, eh? Don't worry about it." I gestured at the keyboard; fortunately, none of the coffee had gone down between the keys. "You were going to show me a picture?"

"Oh, right." She spoke some commands, and the terminal responded—making me wonder what she'd wanted the keyboard for. But then she used it to type in a long passphrase; presumably she didn't want to say hers aloud in front of me. She frowned as she was typing it in and backspaced to make a correction; multiword passphrases were easy to say but hard to type if you weren't adept with a keyboard—and the more security conscious you were the longer the passphrase you used.

She accessed some repository of her personal files and brought up a photo of Joshua-never-Josh Wilkins. Given how attractive Mrs. Wilkins was, he wasn't what I expected. He had cold, gray eyes, hair buzzed so short as to be nonexistent, and a thin, almost lipless mouth; the overall effect was reptilian. "That's before," I said. "What about after? What's he look like now that he's transferred?"

"Umm, pretty much the same."

"Really?" If I'd had that kisser, I'd have modified it for sure. "Do you have pictures taken since he moved his mind?"

"No actual pictures," said Cassandra. "After all, he and I only just transferred. But I can go into the NewYou database and show you the plans from which his new face was manufactured." She spoke to the terminal some more and then typed in another lengthy passphrase. Soon enough, she had a computer-graphics rendition of Joshua's head on my screen.

"You're right," I said, surprised. "He didn't change a thing. Can I get copies of all this?"

She nodded and spoke some more commands, transferring various documents into local storage.

"All right," I said. "My fee is two hundred solars an hour, plus expenses."

"That's fine, that's fine, of course! I don't care about the money, Mr. Lomax—not at all. I just want Joshua back. Please tell me you'll find him."

"I will," I said, smiling my most reassuring smile. "Don't worry about that. He can't have gone far."

TWO

Actually, of course, Joshua Wilkins *could* perhaps have gone quite far—so my first order of business was to eliminate that possibility.

No spaceships had left Mars in the last twenty days, so he couldn't be off-planet. There was a giant airlock in the south through which large spaceships could be brought inside for dry-dock work, but it hadn't been cracked open in weeks. And, although a transfer could exist freely on the Martian surface, there were only four airlock stations leading out of the dome, and they all had security guards. I visited each of those and checked, just to be sure, but the only people who had gone out in the past three days were the usual crowds of hapless fossil hunters, and every one of them had returned when the dust storm began.

I'd read about the early days of this town: "The Great Martian Fossil Rush," they called it. Weingarten and O'Reilly, the two private explorers who had come here at their own expense, had found the first fossils on Mars and had made a fortune selling them back on Earth. They were more valuable than any precious metal and rarer than anything else in the solar system—actual evidence of extraterrestrial life! Good fist-sized specimens went for tens of thousands; excellent football-sized ones for millions. In a world in which almost anything, including diamonds and gold, could be synthesized, there was no greater status symbol than to own the genuine ancient remains of a Martian pentapod or rhizomorph.

Weingarten and O'Reilly never said precisely where they'd found their specimens, but it had been easy enough to prove that their first spaceship had landed here, in the Isidis Planitia basin. Other treasure hunters started coming, and Howard Slapcoff—the billionaire founder of the company that pioneered the process by which minds could be scanned and uploaded—had used a hunk of his fortune to create our domed city. Many of those who'd found good specimens in the early days had bought property in New Klondike from him. It had been a wonderful investment for Slapcoff: the land sales brought him more than triple what he'd spent erecting the dome, and he'd been collecting a life-support tax from residents ever since. Well, from the biological residents, at least, but Slappy got a fat royalty from NewYou each time his transfer process was used, so he lined his pockets either way.

Native life was never widely dispersed on Mars; the single ecosystem that had existed here seemed to have been confined to this basin. Some of the other prospectors— excuse me, fossil hunters—who came shortly after W&O's first expedition found a few excellent specimens, although most of the finds had been in poor shape.

Somewhere, though, was the mother lode: a bed known as the "Alpha Deposit" that produced fossils more finely preserved than even those from Earth's Burgess Shale. Weingarten and O'Reilly had known where it was—they'd stumbled on it by pure dumb luck, apparently. But they'd both been killed when their heat shield separated from their ship upon re-entry into Earth's atmosphere after their third expedition—and, in the twenty mears since, no one had yet rediscovered it. But people were still looking.

There'd always been a market for transferring consciousness; the potentially infinite lifespan was hugely appealing. But here on Mars, the demand was particularly brisk, since artificial bodies could spend weeks or even months on the surface, searching for paleontological gold.

Anyway, Joshua-never-Josh Wilkins was clearly not outside the habitat and he hadn't taken off in a spaceship. Wherever he was hiding, it was somewhere under the New Klondike dome. I can't say he was breathing the same air I was, because he wasn't breathing at all. But he was *here,* somewhere. All I had to do was find him.

I didn't want to duplicate the efforts of the police, although "efforts" was usually too generous a term to apply to the work of the local constabulary; "cursory attempts" probably was closer to the truth, if I knew Mac.

New Klondike had twelve radial roadways, cutting across the nine concentric rings of buildings under the dome. The rings were evenly spaced, except for the giant gap between the seventh and eighth, which accommodated agricultural fields, the shipyard, warehouses, water-treatment and air-processing facilities, and more. My office was at dome's edge, on the outside of the Ninth Circle; I could have taken a hovertram into the center but I preferred to walk. A good detective knew what was happening on the streets, and the hovertrams, dilapidated though they were, sped by too fast for that.

When I'd first come here, I'd quipped that New Klondike wasn't a hellhole—it wasn't far enough gone for that. "More of a heckhole," I'd said. But that had been ten years ago, just after what had happened with Wanda, and if something in the middle of a vast plain could be said to be going downhill, New Klondike was it. The fused-regolith streets were cracked, buildings—and not just the ones in the old shantytown—were in disrepair, and the seedy bars and brothels were full of thugs and con artists, the destitute and the dejected. As a character in one of the old movies I like had said of a town, "You will never find a more wretched hive of scum and villainy." New Klondike should have a sign by one of the airlocks that proclaims, "Twinned with Mos Eisley, Tatooine."

I didn't make any bones about staring at the transfers I saw along the way. They ranged in style from really sophis-

ticated models, like Cassandra Wilkins, to things only a
step up from the Tin Woodman of Oz. The latter were easy
to identify as transfers, but the former could sometimes pass
for biologicals, although you develop a knack for identifying
them, too, almost subconsciously noting an odd sheen to the
plastiskin or an unnatural smoothness in the movement of
the limbs; *paydar,* it was called: the ability to spot a bought
body.

Of course, those who'd contented themselves with sec-
ond-rate synthetic forms doubtless believed they'd trade up
when they eventually happened upon some decent specimens. Poor saps; no one had found truly spectacular remains
for mears, and lots of people were giving up and going back
to Earth, if they could afford the passage, or were settling
in to lives of, as Thoreau would have it, quiet desperation,
their dreams as dead as the fossils they'd never found.

I continued walking easily along; Mars gravity is just
thirty-eight percent of Earth's. Some people were stuck here
because they'd let their muscles atrophy; they'd never be
able to hack a full gee again. Me, I was stuck here for other
reasons—thank God Mars has no real government and so
no extradition treaties. But I worked out more than most
people did—at Gully's Gym, over by the shipyard—and so
still had strong legs; I could walk comfortably all day if I
had to.

I passed a few spindly or squat robots—most of whom
were dumb as posts, and none of whom were brighter than
a four-year-old—running errands or engaged in the Sisy-
phean tasks of road and building repair.

The cop shop was a lopsided five-story structure—it
could be that tall, this near the center of the dome—with
chipped and cracked walls that had once been white but
were now a grimy grayish pink. The front doors were clear
alloquartz, same as the overhead dome, and they slid aside
as I walked up to them. On the lobby's right was a long red
desk—as if we don't see enough red on Mars—with a map
showing the Isidis Planitia basin behind it; New Klondike
was a big circle off to one side.

The NKPD consisted of eight cops, the junior ones of whom took turns playing desk sergeant. Today it was a flabby lowbrow named Huxley, whose blue uniform always seemed a size too small for him. "Hey, Hux," I said, walking over. "Is Mac in?"

Huxley consulted a monitor then nodded. "Yeah, he's in, but he don't see just anyone."

"I'm not just anyone, Hux. I'm the guy who picks up the pieces after you clowns bungle things."

Huxley frowned, trying to think of a rejoinder. "Yeah, well . . ." he said, at last.

"Oooh," I said. "Good one, Hux! Way to put me in my place."

He narrowed his eyes. "You ain't as funny as you think you are, Lomax."

"Of course I'm not. Nobody could be *that* funny." I nodded at the secured inner door. "Going to buzz me through?"

"Only to be rid of you," said Huxley. So pleased was he with the wit of this remark that he repeated it: "Only to be rid of you." He reached below the counter, and the inner door—an unmarked black panel—slid aside. I pantomimed tipping a hat at Hux and headed into the station proper. I then walked down the corridor to McCrae's office; the door was open, so I rapped my knuckles against the steel jamb.

"Lomax!" he said, looking up. "Decided to turn yourself in?"

"Very funny, Mac. You and Hux should go on the road together."

He snorted. "What can I do for you, Alex?"

Mac was a skinny biological with shaggy orange eyebrows shielding his blue eyes. On the credenza behind his desk were holograms of his wife and his baby daughter; the girl had been born just a couple of months ago. "I'm looking for a guy named Joshua Wilkins."

Mac had a strong Scottish brogue—so strong, I figured it must be an affectation. "Ah, yes. Who's your client? The wife?"

I nodded.

"Quite the looker," he said.

"That she is. Anyway, you tried to find her husband, this Wilkins . . ."

"We looked around, yeah," said Mac. "He's a transfer, you knew that?"

I nodded.

"Well," Mac said, "she gave us the plans for his new face—precise measurements and all that. We've been feeding all the videos from public security cameras through facial-recognition software. So far, no luck."

I smiled. That's about as far as Mac's detective work normally went: things he could do without hauling his bony ass out from behind his desk. "How much of New Klondike do they cover now?" I asked.

"It's down to forty percent of the public areas."

People kept smashing, stealing, or jamming the cameras faster than Mac and his staff could replace them; this was a frontier town, after all, and there were lots of things going on folks didn't want observed. "You'll let me know if you find anything?"

Mac drew his shaggy eyebrows together. "Even Mars has to abide by Earth's privacy laws, Alex—or, at least, our parent corporation does. I can't divulge what the security cameras see."

I reached into my pocket, pulled out a fifty-solar coin, and flipped it. It went up rapidly but came down in what still seemed like slow motion to me, even after a decade on Mars; Mac didn't require a transfer's reflexes to catch it in mid-air. "Of course," he said, "I suppose we could make an exception . . ."

"Thanks. You're a credit to law-enforcement officials everywhere."

He smiled, then: "Say, what kind of heat you packing these days? You still carrying that old Smith & Wesson?"

"It's registered," I said, narrowing my eyes.

"Oh, I know, I know. But be careful, eh? The times, they are a-changin'. Bullets aren't much use against a transfer, and there are getting to be more of those each day, since the cost of the procedure is finally coming down."

"So I've heard. Do you happen to know the best place to plug a transfer, if you had to take one out?"

Mac shook his head. "It varies from model to model, and NewYou does its best to retrofit any physical vulnerabilities that are uncovered."

"So how do you guys handle them?"

"Until recently, as little as possible," said Mac. "Turning a blind eye, and all that."

"Saves getting up."

Mac didn't take offense. "Exactly. But let me show you something." We left his office, went farther down the corridor, and entered another room. He pointed to a device on the table. "Just arrived from Earth. The latest thing."

It was a wide, flat disk, maybe half a meter in diameter and five centimeters thick. There were a pair of U-shaped handgrips attached to the edge, opposite each other. "What is it?"

"A broadband disruptor," Mac said. He picked it up and held it in front of himself, like a gladiator's shield. "It discharges an oscillating multifrequency electromagnetic pulse. From a distance of four meters or less, it will completely fry the artificial brain of a transfer—killing it as effectively as a bullet kills a human."

"I don't plan on killing anyone," I said.

"That's what you said the last time."

Ouch. Still, maybe he had a point. "I don't suppose you have a spare I can borrow?"

Mac laughed. "Are you kidding? This is the only one we've got so far, and it's just a prototype."

"Well, then," I said, heading for the door, "I guess I'd better be careful."

THREE

My next stop was the NewYou building. I took Third Avenue, one of the radial streets of the city, out the five blocks to it. The NewYou building was two stories tall and was made, like most structures here, of red laser-fused Martian sand bricks. Flanking the main doors were a pair of wide alloquartz display windows, showing dusty artificial bodies dressed in fashions from about five mears ago; it was high time somebody updated things.

The lower floor was divided into a showroom and a workshop, separated by a door that was currently open. The workroom had spare components scattered about: here, a white-skinned artificial hand; there, a black lower leg; on shelves, synthetic eyes and spools of colored monofilament that I guessed were used to simulate hair. And there were all sorts of internal parts on the two worktables: motors and hydraulic pumps and joint hinges.

The adjacent showroom displayed complete artificial bodies. Across its width, I spotted Cassandra Wilkins, wearing a beige suit. She was talking with a man and a woman who were biological; potential customers, presumably. "Hello, Cassandra," I said, after I'd closed the distance between us.

"Mr. Lomax!" she gushed, excusing herself from the couple. "I'm so glad you're here—so very glad! What news do you have?"

"Not much. I've been to visit the cops, and I thought I should start my investigation here. After all, you and your husband own this franchise, right?"

Cassandra nodded enthusiastically. "I knew I was doing the right thing hiring you. I just knew it! Why, do you know that lazy detective McCrae never stopped by here—not even once!"

I smiled. "Mac's not the outdoorsy type. And, well, you get what you pay for."

"Isn't that the truth?" said Cassandra. "Isn't that just the God's honest truth!"

"You said your husband moved his mind recently?"

"Yes. All of that goes on upstairs, though. This is just sales and service down here."

"Do you have security-camera footage of Joshua actually transferring?"

"No. NewYou doesn't allow cameras up there; they don't like footage of the process getting out. Trade secrets, and all that."

"Ah, okay. Can you show me how it's done, though?"

She nodded again. "Of course. Anything you want to see, Mr. Lomax." What I wanted to see was under that beige suit—nothing beat the perfection of a high-end transfer's body—but I kept that thought to myself. Cassandra looked around the room, then motioned for another staff member to come over: a gorgeous little biological female wearing taste-ful makeup and jewelry. "I'm sorry," Cassandra said to the two customers she'd abandoned a few moments ago. "Miss Takahashi here will look after you." She then turned to me. "This way."

We went through a curtained doorway and up a set of stairs, coming to a landing in front of two doors. "Here's our scanning room," said Cassandra, indicating the left-hand one; both doors had little windows in them. She stood on tiptoe to look in the scanning-room window and nodded, apparently satisfied by what she saw, then opened the door.

Two people were inside: a balding man of about forty, who was seated, and a standing woman who looked twenty-five; the woman was a transfer herself, though, so there was no way of knowing her real age. "So sorry to interrupt," Cassandra said. She smiled at the man in the chair, while gesturing at me. "This is Alexander Lomax. He's providing some, ah, consulting services for us."

The man looked up at me, surprised, then said, "Klaus Hansen," by way of introduction.

"Would you mind ever so much if Mr. Lomax watched while the scan was being done?" asked Cassandra.

Hansen considered this for a moment, frowning his long, thin face. But then he nodded. "Sure. Why not?"

"Thanks," I said, stepping into the room. "I'll just stand over here." I moved to the far wall and leaned against it.

The chair Hansen was sitting in looked a lot like a barber's chair. The female transfer who wasn't Cassandra reached up above the chair and pulled down a translucent hemisphere that was attached by an articulated arm to the ceiling. She kept lowering it until all of Hansen's head was covered, and then she turned to a control console.

The hemisphere shimmered slightly, as though a film of oil was washing over its surface; the scanning field, I supposed.

Cassandra was standing next to me, arms crossed in front of her chest. "How long does the scanning take?" I asked.

"Not long," she replied. "It's a quantum-mechanical process, so the scanning is rapid. After that, we just need a couple of minutes to move the data into the artificial brain. And then . . ."

"And then?" I said.

She lifted her shoulders, as if the rest didn't need to be spelled out. "Why, and then Mr. Hansen will be able to live forever."

"Ah."

"Come along," said Cassandra. "Let's go see the other side." We left that room, closing its door behind us, and entered the one next door. This room was a mirror image of the previous one, which I guess was appropriate. Lying on a table-bed in the middle of the room was Hansen's new body, dressed in a fashionable blue suit; its eyes were closed. Also in the room was a male NewYou technician, who was biological.

I walked around, looking at the artificial body from all angles. The replacement Hansen still had a bald spot, although its diameter had been reduced by half. And, interestingly, Hansen had opted for a sort of permanent designer-stubble look; the biological him was clean-shaven at the moment.

Suddenly the simulacrum's eyes opened. "Wow," said a voice that was the same as the one I'd heard from the man next door. "That's incredible."

"How do you feel, Mr. Hansen?" asked the male technician.

"Fine. Just fine."

"Good," the technician said. "There'll be some settling-in adjustments, of course. Let's just check to make sure all your parts are working . . ."

"And there it is," Cassandra said to me. "Simple as that." She led me out of the room, back into the corridor, and closed the door behind us.

"Fascinating." I pointed at the left-hand door. "When do you take care of the original?"

"That's already been done. We do it in the chair."

I stared at the closed door and I like to think I suppressed my shudder enough so that Cassandra was unaware of it. "All right. I guess I've seen enough."

Cassandra looked disappointed. "Are you sure you don't want to look around some more?"

"Why? Is there anything else worth seeing?"

"Oh, I don't know," said Cassandra. "It's a big place. Everything on this floor, everything downstairs . . . everything in the basement."

I blinked. "You've got a basement?" Almost no Martian buildings had basements; the permafrost layer was very hard to dig through.

"Yes," she said. She paused, then looked away. "Of course, no one ever goes down there; it's just storage."

"I'll have a look," I said.

And that's where I found him.

He was lying behind some large storage crates, face down, a sticky pool of machine oil surrounding his head. Next to him was a stubby excimer-powered jackhammer, the kind many fossil hunters had for removing surface material. And next to the jackhammer was a piece of good old-fashioned paper. On it, in block letters, was written, "I'm so sorry, Cassie. It's just not the same."

It's hard to commit suicide, I guess, when you're a transfer. Slitting your wrists does nothing significant. Poison doesn't work and neither does drowning. But Joshua-never-anything-else-at-all-anymore Wilkins had apparently found a way. From the looks of it, he'd leaned back against the rough cement wall and, with his strong artificial arms, had held up the jackhammer, placing its bit against the center of his forehead. And then he'd pressed down on the jackhammer's twin triggers, letting the unit run until it had managed to pierce through his titanium skull and scramble the material of his artificial brain. When his brain died, his thumbs let up on the triggers, and he dropped the jackhammer, then tumbled over himself. His head had twisted sideways when it hit the concrete floor. Everything below his eyebrows was intact; it was clearly the same reptilian face Cassandra Wilkins had shown me.

I headed up the stairs and found Cassandra, who was chatting in her animated style with another customer.

"Cassandra," I said, pulling her aside. "Cassandra, I'm very sorry, but . . ."

She looked at me, her green eyes wide. "What?"

"I've found your husband. And he's dead."

She opened her pretty mouth, closed it, then opened it again. She looked like she might fall over, even with gyroscopes stabilizing her. "My . . . God," she said at last. "Are you . . . are you positive?"

"Sure looks like him."

"My God," she said again. "What . . . what happened?"

No nice way to say it. "Looks like he killed himself."

A couple of Cassandra's coworkers had come over, wondering what all the commotion was about. "What's wrong?" asked one of them—the same Miss Takahashi I'd seen earlier.

"Oh, Reiko," said Cassandra. "Joshua is dead!"

Customers were noticing what was going on, too. A burly flesh-and-blood man, with short black hair, a gold stud in one ear, and arms as thick around as most men's legs, came across the room; he clearly worked here. Reiko Takahashi had already drawn Cassandra into her arms—or vice versa; I'd been looking away when it had happened—and was stroking Cassandra's artificial hair. I let the burly man do what he could to calm the crowd, while I used my wrist phone to call Mac and inform him of Joshua Wilkins's suicide.

FOUR

Detective Dougal McCrae of New Klondike's Finest arrived about twenty minutes later, accompanied by two uniforms. "How's it look, Alex?" Mac asked.

"Not as messy as some of the biological suicides I've seen," I said. "But it's still not a pretty sight."

"Show me."

I led Mac downstairs. He read the note without picking it up.

The burly man soon came down, too, followed by Cassandra Wilkins, who was holding her artificial hand to her artificial mouth.

"Hello, again, Mrs. Wilkins," Mac said, moving to interpose himself between her and the prone form on the floor. "I'm terribly sorry, but I'll need you to make an official identification."

I lifted my eyebrows at the irony of requiring the next of kin to actually look at the body to be sure of who it was, but that's what we'd gone back to with transfers. Privacy laws prevented any sort of ID chip or tracking device being put into artificial bodies. In fact, that was one of the many incentives to transfer: you no longer left fingerprints or a trail of identifying DNA everywhere you went.

Cassandra nodded bravely; she was willing to accede to Mac's request. He stepped aside, a living curtain, revealing the synthetic body with the gaping head wound. She looked down at it. I'd expected her to quickly avert her eyes, but she didn't; she just kept staring.

Finally, Mac said, very gently, "Is that your husband, Mrs. Wilkins?"

She nodded slowly. Her voice was soft. "Yes. Oh, my poor, poor Joshua . . ."

Mac stepped over to talk to the two uniforms, and I joined them. "What do you do with a dead transfer?" I asked. "Seems pointless to call in the medical examiner."

By way of answer, Mac motioned to the burly man. The man touched his own chest and raised his eyebrows in the classic "Who, me?" expression. Mac nodded again. The man looked left and right, like he was crossing some imaginary road, and then came over. "Yeah?"

"You seem to be the senior employee here," said Mac. "Am I right?"

The man had a Hispanic accent. "Horatio Fernandez. Joshua was the boss, but I'm senior technician." Or maybe he said, "I'm *Señor* Technician."

"Good," said Mac. "You're probably better equipped than we are to figure out the exact cause of death."

Fernandez gestured theatrically at the synthetic corpse, as if it were—well, not *bleedingly* obvious but certainly apparent.

Mac shook his head. "It's just a bit too pat," he said, his voice lowered conspiratorially. "Implement at hand, suicide note." He lifted his shaggy orange eyebrows. "I just want to be sure."

Cassandra had drifted over without Mac noticing, although of course I had. She was listening in.

"Yeah," said Fernandez. "Sure. We can disassemble him, check for anything else that might be amiss."

"No," said Cassandra. "You can't."

"I'm afraid it's necessary," said Mac, looking at her. His Scottish brogue always put an edge on his words, but I knew he was trying to sound gentle.

"No," said Cassandra, her voice quavering. "I forbid it."

Mac's tone got a little firmer. "You can't. I'm required to order an autopsy in every suspicious case."

Cassandra opened her mouth to say something more, then apparently thought better of it. Horatio moved closer to her and put a hulking arm around her small shoulders. "Don't worry," he said. "We'll be gentle." And then his face brightened a bit. "In fact, we'll see what parts we can salvage—give them to somebody else; somebody who couldn't afford such good stuff if it were new." He smiled beatifically. "It's what Joshua would have wanted."

. . . .

The next day, I was sitting in my office, looking out the small window with its cracked pane. The dust storm had ended. Out on the surface, rocks were strewn everywhere, like toys on a kid's bedroom floor. My phone played "Luck Be a Lady," and I looked at it in anticipation, hoping for a new case; I could use the solars. But the ID said NKPD. I told the device to accept the call, and a little picture of Mac's face appeared on my wrist. "Hey, Alex," he said. "Come by the station, would you?"

"What's up?"

The micro-Mac frowned. "Nothing I want to say over open airwaves."

I nodded. Now that the Wilkins case was over, I didn't have anything better to do anyway. I'd only managed about seven billable hours, damn it all, and even that had taken some padding.

I walked into the center along Ninth Avenue, passing filthy prospectors, the aftermath of a fight in which some schmuck in a pool of blood was being tended to by your proverbial hooker-with-the-heart-of-gold, and a broken-down robot trying to make its way along with only three of its four legs working properly.

I entered the lobby of the police station, traded quips with the ineluctable Huxley, and was admitted to the back.

"Hey, Mac," I said. "What's up?"

"Morning, Alex," Mac said, rolling the *R* in "Morning."
"Come in; sit down." He spoke to his desk terminal and
turned its monitor around so I could see it. "Have a look at
this."

I glanced at the screen. "The report on Joshua Wilkins?"

Mac nodded. "Look at the section on the artificial brain."

I skimmed the text until I found that part. "Yeah?" I said,
still not getting it.

"Do you know what 'baseline synaptic web' means?"

"No, I don't. And you didn't either, smart-ass, until someone told you."

Mac smiled a little, conceding that. "Well, there were
lots of bits of the artificial brain left behind. And that big
guy at NewYou—Fernandez, remember?—he really got into
this forensic stuff and decided to run it through some kind
of instrument they've got there. And you know what he
found?"

"What?"

"The brain stuff—the raw material inside the artificial
skull—was pristine. It had never been imprinted."

"You mean no scanned mind had ever been transferred
into that brain?"

Mac folded his arms across his chest and leaned back in
his chair. "Bingo."

I frowned. "But that's not possible. I mean, if there was
no mind in that head, who wrote the suicide note?"

Mac lifted those shaggy eyebrows of his. "Who indeed?"
he said. "And what happened to Joshua Wilkins's scanned
consciousness?"

"Does anyone at NewYou but Fernandez know about
this?"

Mac shook his head. "No, and he's agreed to keep his
mouth shut while we continue to investigate. But I thought
I'd clue you in, since apparently the case you were on isn't
really closed—and, after all, if you don't make money now
and again, you can't afford to bribe me for favors."

I nodded. "That's what I like about you, Mac. Always
looking out for my best interests."

· · · · · · · · · · ·

Perhaps I should have gone straight to see Cassandra Wilkins and made sure we both agreed that I was back on the clock, but I had some questions I wanted answered first. And I knew just who to turn to. Juan Santos was the city's top computer expert. I'd met him during a previous case, and we'd recently struck up a small-f friendship—we both shared the same taste in Earth booze, and he wasn't above joining me at some of New Klondike's sleazier saloons to get it. I called him and we arranged to meet at The Bent Chisel, a wretched little bar off Fourth Avenue, in the sixth concentric ring of buildings. The bartender was a surly man named Buttrick, a biological who had more than his fair share of flesh, and blood as cold as ice. He wore a sleeveless gray shirt and had a three-day growth of salt-and-pepper beard. "Lomax," he said, acknowledging my entrance. "No broken furniture this time, right?"

I held up three fingers. "Scout's honor."

Buttrick held up one finger.

"Hey," I said. "Is that any way to treat one of your best customers?"

"My best customers," said Buttrick, polishing a glass with a ratty towel, "pay their tabs."

"Yeah," I said, stealing a page from Sergeant Huxley's *Guide to Witty Repartee.* "Well." I made my way to a booth at the back. Both waitresses here were topless. My favorite, a cute brunette named Diana, soon came over. "Hey, babe," I said.

She leaned in and gave me a peck on the cheek. "Hi, honey."

The low gravity on Mars was kind to figures and faces, but Diana was still starting to show her forty years. She had shoulder-length brown hair and brown eyes, and was quite pleasantly stacked, although like most long-term Mars residents, she'd lost a lot of the muscle mass she'd come here with. We slept together pretty often but were hardly exclusive.

Juan Santos came in, wearing a black T-shirt and black jeans. He was almost as tall as me, but nowhere near as broad-shouldered; in fact, he was pretty much your typical pencil-necked geek. And like many a pencil-necked geek, he kept setting his sights higher than he should. "Hi, Diana!" he said. "I, um, I brought you something."

Juan was carrying a package wrapped in loose plastic sheeting, which he handed to her.

"Thank you!" she said with enthusiasm before she'd even opened it; I didn't know a lot about Diana's past, but somewhere along the line, someone had taught her good manners. She removed the plastic sheeting, revealing a single, long-stemmed white rose.

Diana actually squealed. Flowers are rare on Mars; those few fields we had were mostly given over to growing either edible plants or genetically modified things that helped scrub the atmosphere. She rewarded Juan with a kiss right on the lips, and that seemed to please him greatly.

I ordered a Scotch on the rocks; they normally did that with carbon dioxide ice here. Juan asked for whiskey. I watched him watching Diana's swinging hips as she headed off to get our drinks. "Well, well, well," I said, as he finally slid into the booth opposite me. "I didn't know you had a thing for her."

He smiled sheepishly. "Who wouldn't?" I said nothing, which Juan took as an invitation to go on. "She hasn't said yes to a date yet, but she promised to let me read some of her poetry."

I kept my tone even. "Lucky you." It seemed kind not to mention that Diana and I were going out this weekend, so I didn't. But I did say, "So, how does a poet sneeze?"

"I don't know, how *does* a poet sneeze?"

"Haiku!"

"Don't quit your day job, Alex."

"Hey," I said, placing a hand over my heart, "you wound me. Down deep, I'm a stand-up comic."

"Well," said Juan, "I always say people should be true to their innermost selves, but . . ."

"Yeah? What's your innermost self?"

"Me?" Juan's eyebrows moved up. "I'm pure genius, right to the very core."

I snorted and Diana reappeared to give us our drinks. We thanked her, and she departed, Juan again watching her longingly as she did so.

When she'd disappeared, he turned back to look at me, and said, "What's up?" His face consisted of a wide forehead, long nose, and receding chin; it made him look like he was leaning forward even when he wasn't.

I took a swig of my drink. "What do you know about transferring?"

"Fascinating stuff," said Juan. "Thinking of doing it?"

"Maybe someday."

"You know, it's supposed to pay for itself now within three mears, because you no longer have to pay life-support tax after you've transferred."

I was in arrears on that, and didn't like to think about what would happen if I fell much further behind. "That'd be a plus," I said. "What about you? You going to do it?"

"Sure, someday—and I'll go the whole nine yards: enhanced senses, super strength, the works. Plus I want to live forever; who doesn't? 'Course, my dad won't like it."

"Your dad? What's he got against it?"

Juan snorted. "He's a minister."

"In whose government?"

"No, no. A *minister*. Clergy."

"I didn't know there were any of those left, even on Earth," I said.

"He *is* on Earth; back in Santiago. But, yeah, you're right. Poor old guy still believes in souls."

I raised my eyebrows. "Really?"

"Yup. And because he believes in souls, he has a hard time with this idea of transferring consciousness. He would say the new version isn't the same person."

I thought about what the supposed suicide note said. "Well, is it?"

Juan rolled his eyes. "You, too? Of course it is! Look, sure, people used to get all worked up about this when the process first appeared, decades ago, but now just about everyone is blasé about it. NewYou should take a lot of credit for that; they've done a great job of keeping the issue uncluttered—I'm sure they knew if they'd done otherwise, there'd have been all sorts of ethical debates, red tape, and laws constraining their business. But they've avoided most of that by providing one, and only one, service: moving—not copying, not duplicating, but simply moving—a person's mind to a more durable container. Makes the legal transfer of personhood and property a simple matter, ensures that no one gets more than one vote, and so on."

"And is that what they really do?" I asked. "Move your mind?"

"Well, that's what they *say* they do. 'Move' is a nice, safe, comforting word. But the mind is just software, and since the dawn of computing, software has been moved from one computing platform to another by copying it over, then immediately erasing the original."

"But the new brain is artificial, right? How come we can make super-smart transfers, but not super-smart robots or computers?"

Juan took a sip of his drink. "It's not a contradiction at all. No one ever figured out how to program anything equivalent to a human mind—they used to talk about the coming 'singularity,' when artificial intelligence would exceed human abilities, but that never happened. But when you're scanning and digitizing the entire structure of a brain in minute detail, you obviously get the intelligence as part of that scan, even if no one can point to where that intelligence is *in* the scan."

"Huh," I said, and took a sip of my own. "So, if you were to transfer, what would you have fixed in your new body?"

Juan spread his praying-mantis arms. "Hey, man, you don't tamper with perfection."

"Hah," I said. "Still, how much could you change things? I mean, say you're only 150 centimeters, and you want to play basketball. Could you opt to be two meters tall?"

"Sure, of course."

I frowned. "But wouldn't the copied mind have trouble with your new size?"

"Nah," said Juan. "See, when Howard Slapcoff first started copying consciousness, he let the old software from the old mind actually try to directly control the new body. It took months to learn how to walk again, and so on."

"Yeah, I read something about that, years ago."

Juan nodded. "Right. But now they don't let the copied mind do anything but give orders. The thoughts are intercepted by the new body's main computer. *That* unit runs the body. All the transferred mind has to do is *think* that it wants to pick up this glass, say." He acted out his example, and took a sip, then winced in response to the booze's kick. "The computer takes care of working out which pulleys to contract, how far to reach, and so on."

"So you could order up a body radically different from your original?"

"Absolutely." He looked at me through hooded eyes. "Which, in your case, is probably the route to go."

"Damn."

"Hey, don't take it seriously," he said, taking another sip and allowing himself another pleased wince.

"It's just that I was hoping it wasn't that way. See, this case I'm on: the guy I'm supposed to find owns the NewYou franchise here."

"Yeah?" said Juan.

"Yeah, and I think he deliberately transferred his scanned mind into some body other than the one that he'd ordered up for himself."

"Why would he do that?"

"He faked the death of the body that looked like him— and I think he'd planned to do that all along, because he never bothered to order up any improvements to his face. I think he wanted to get away, but make it look like he was dead, so no one would be looking for him anymore."

"And why would he do that?"

I frowned then drank some more. "I'm not sure."

"Maybe he wanted to escape his spouse."

"Maybe—but she's a hot little number."

"Hmm," said Juan. "Whose body do you think he took?"

"I don't know that, either. I was hoping the new body would have to be roughly similar to his old one; that would cut down on the possible suspects. But I guess that's not the case."

"It isn't, no."

I looked down at my drink. The dry-ice cubes were sublimating into white vapor that filled the top part of the glass.

"Something else is bothering you," said Juan. I lifted my head and saw him taking a swig of his drink. A little amber liquid spilled out of his mouth and formed a shiny bead on his recessed chin. "What is it?"

I shifted a bit. "I visited NewYou yesterday. You know what happens to your original body after they move your mind?"

"Sure," said Juan. "Like I said, there's no such thing as moving software. You copy it then delete the original. They euthanize the biological version once the transfer is completed."

I nodded. "And if the guy I'm looking for put his mind into the body intended for somebody else's mind, and that person's mind wasn't copied anywhere, then . . ." I took another swig of my drink. "Then it's murder, isn't it? Souls or no souls—it doesn't matter. If you wipe the one and only copy of someone's mind, you've murdered that person, right?"

"Oh, yes," said Juan. "Deader than Mars itself."

I glanced down at the swirling fog in my glass. "So I'm not just looking for a husband who's skipped out on his wife. I'm looking for a cold-blooded killer."

FIVE

I went by NewYou again. Cassandra wasn't in, but that didn't surprise me; she was a grieving widow now. But Horatio Fernandez—he of the massive arms—was on duty.

"I'd like a list of everyone who transferred the same day as Joshua Wilkins," I said.

He frowned. "That's confidential information."

There were several potential customers milling about. I raised my voice so they could hear. "Interesting suicide note, wasn't it?"

Fernandez grabbed my arm and led me quickly to the side of the room. "What the hell are you doing?" he whispered angrily.

"Just sharing the news," I said, still speaking loudly, although not quite loud enough now, I thought, for the customers to hear. "People thinking of uploading should know that it's not the same—at least, that's what Joshua Wilkins said in that note."

Fernandez knew when he was beaten. The claim in the putative suicide note was exactly the opposite of NewYou's corporate position: transferring was supposed to be flawless, conferring nothing but benefits. "All right, all right," he hissed. "I'll pull the list for you."

"Now that's service. They should name you employee of the month."

He led me into the back room and spoke to a little cubic computer. I happened to overhear the passphrase for accessing the customer database; it was just six words—hardly any security at all.

"Huh," said Fernandez. "It was a busy day—we go days on end without anyone transferring, but seven people moved their consciousnesses into artificial bodies that day, and— oh, yeah. We were having our twice-a-mear sale. No wonder." He held out a hand. "Give me your tab."

I handed him the small tablet computer and he copied the files on each of the seven to it.

"Thanks," I said, taking back the device and doing that tip-of-the-nonexistent-hat thing I do. Even when you've forced a man to do something, there's no harm in being polite.

. . . .

If I was right that Joshua Wilkins had appropriated the body of somebody else who had been scheduled to transfer the same day, it shouldn't be too hard to determine whose body he'd taken; all I had to do, I figured, was interview each of the seven.

My first stop, purely because it happened to be the nearest, was the home of a guy named Stuart Berling, a full-time fossil hunter. He must have had some recent success, if he could afford to transfer.

On the way to his place, I walked past several panhandlers, one of whom had a sign that said, "Will work for air." The cops didn't kick those who were in arrears in their life-support tax payments out of the dome—Slapcoff Industries still had a reputation to maintain on Earth—but if you rented or had a mortgage, you'd be evicted onto the street.

Berling's home was off Seventh Avenue, in the Fifth Circle. It was part of a row of crumbling townhouses, the kind we called redstones. I pushed his door buzzer and waited impatiently for a response. At last he appeared. If I wasn't so famous for my poker face, I'd have done a double take. The man who greeted me was a dead ringer for Krikor Ajemian, the holovid star—the same gaunt features and intense brown eyes, the same mane of dark hair, the same tightly trimmed beard and mustache. I guess not everyone wanted to keep even a semblance of their original appearance.

"Hello. My name is Alexander Lomax. Are you Stuart Berling?"

The artificial face in front of me surely was capable of smiling but chose not to. "Yes. What do you want?"

"I understand you only recently transferred your consciousness into this body."

A nod. "So?"

"So, I work for NewYou—the head office on Earth. I'm here to check up on the quality of the work done by our franchise here on Mars."

Normally, this was a good technique. If Berling was who he said he was, the question wouldn't faze him. Unfortunately, the usual technique of watching a suspect's expression for signs that he was lying didn't work with most transfers. I'd asked Juan Santos about that once. "It's not that transfer faces are less flexible," he'd said. "In fact, they can make them *more* flexible—let people do wild caricatures of smiles and frowns. But people don't want that, especially here on the frontier. See, there are two kinds of facial expressions: the autonomic ones that happen spontaneously and the forced ones. From a software point of view, they're very different; the mental commands sent to fake a smile and to make a spontaneous smile are utterly dissimilar. Most transfers here opt for their automatic expressions to be subdued—they value the privacy of their thoughts and don't want their faces advertising them; they consider it one of the pluses of having transferred. The transferee may be grinning from ear to ear on the inside, but on the outside, he just shows a simple smile."

Berling was staring at me with an expression that didn't tell me anything. But his voice was annoyed. "So?" he said again.

"So I'm wondering if you were satisfied by the work we did for you?"

"It cost a lot."

I smiled. "It's actually come down a great deal recently. May I come in?"

He considered this for a few moments then shrugged. "Sure, why not?" He stepped aside.

His living room was full of worktables covered with reddish rocks from outside the dome. A giant lens on an articulated arm was attached to one of the tables, and various mineralogist's tools were scattered about.

"Finding anything interesting?" I asked, gesturing at the rocks.

"If I was, I certainly wouldn't tell you," said Berling, looking at me sideways in the typical paranoid-prospector way.

"Right," I said. "Of course. So, *are* you satisfied with the NewYou process?"

"Sure, yeah. It's everything they said it would be. All the parts work."

"Thanks for your help," I said, pulling out my tab to make a few notes, and then frowning at its blank screen. "Oh, damn. The silly thing has a loose excimer pack. I've got to open it up and reseat it." I showed him the back of the unit's case. "Do you have a little screwdriver that will fit that?"

Everybody owned some screwdrivers, even though most people rarely needed them, and they were the sort of thing that had no standard storage location. Some people kept them in kitchen drawers, others kept them in tool chests, still others kept them under the sink. Only a person who had lived in this home for a while would know where they were.

Berling peered at the slot-headed screw, then nodded. "Sure. Hang on."

He made a beeline for the far side of the living room, going to a cabinet that had glass doors on its top half but solid metal ones on its bottom. He bent over, opened one of the metal doors, reached in, rummaged for a bit, and emerged with the appropriate screwdriver.

"Thanks," I said, opening the case in such a way that he couldn't see inside. I then surreptitiously removed the bit of plastic I'd used to insulate the excimer battery from the contact it was supposed to touch. Without looking up, I said, "Are you married, Mr. Berling?" Of course, I already knew the answer was yes; that fact was in his NewYou file.

He nodded.

"Is your wife home?"

His artificial eyelids closed a bit. "Why?"

I told him the honest truth since it fit well with my cover story: "I'd like to ask her whether she can perceive any differences between the new you and the old."

Again, I watched his expression, but it didn't change. "Sure, I guess that'd be okay." He turned and called over his shoulder, "Lacie!"

A few moments later, a homely flesh-and-blood woman of about sixty appeared. "This is Mr. Lomax from the head office of NewYou," said Berling, indicating me with a pointed finger. "He'd like to talk to you."

"About what?" asked Lacie. She had a deep, not-unpleasant voice.

"Might we speak in private?" I asked.

Berling's gaze shifted from Lacie to me, then back to Lacie. "Hrmpph," he said, but then a moment later added, "I guess that'd be all right." He turned around and walked away.

I looked at Lacie. "I'm just doing a routine follow-up," I said. "Making sure people are happy with the work we do. Have you noticed any changes in your husband since he transferred?"

"Not really."

"Oh? If there's anything at all . . ." I smiled reassuringly. "We want to make the process as perfect as possible. Has he said anything that's surprised you, say?"

Lacie crinkled her face even more than it normally was. "How do you mean?"

"I mean, has he used any expressions or turns of phrase you're not used to hearing from him?"

A shake of the head. "No."

"Sometimes the process plays tricks with memory. Has he failed to know something he should know?"

"Not that I've noticed."

"What about the reverse? Has he known anything that you wouldn't expect him to know?"

Lacie lifted her eyebrows. "No. He's just Stu."

I frowned. "No changes at all?"

"No, none . . . well, almost none."

I waited for her to go on, but she didn't, so I prodded her. "What is it? We really would like to know about any difference, any flaw in our transference process."

"Oh, it's not a flaw," said Lacie, not meeting my eyes.

"No? Then what?"

"It's just that . . ."

"Yes?"

"Well, just that he's a demon in the sack now. He stays hard forever."

I frowned, disappointed not to have found what I was looking for on the first try. But I decided to end the masquerade on a positive note. "We aim to please, ma'am. We aim to please."

SIX

I spent the next several hours tracking down and interviewing three other recent transfers; none of them seemed to be anyone other than who they claimed to be.

After that, the next name on my list was one Dr. Rory Pickover. His home was in a cubic apartment building located on the outer side of the First Circle, beneath the highest point of the dome; several windows were boarded up on its first and second floors, but he lived on the fourth, where all but one of the panes seemed to be intact. Someone was storing a broken set of springy Mars buggy wheels on one of the balconies. From another balcony, a crazy old coot was shouting obscenities at those making their way along the curving sidewalk. Most of the people were ignoring him, but two kids—a grimy boy and an even grimier girl, each about twelve but tall and spindly in the way kids born here tend to be—decided to start shouting back.

Pickover lived alone, so there was no spouse or child to question about any changes in him. That made me suspicious right off the bat: if one were going to choose an identity to appropriate, it ideally would be someone without close companions.

I buzzed him from the lobby. A drunk sleeping by the buzzboard was disturbed enough by the sound to roll onto his side but otherwise didn't interfere with me.

"Hello?" said a male voice higher pitched than my own.

"Mr. Pickover, my name is Alex Lomax. I'm from the NewYou head office on Earth. I'm wondering if I might ask you a few questions?"

He had a British accent. "Lomax, did you say? You're Alexander Lomax?"

"I am, yes. I'm wondering if we might speak for a few minutes?"

"Well, yes, but . . ."

"But what?"

"Not here," he said. "Let's go outside."

I was pissed, because that meant I couldn't try the screwdriver trick on him. But I said, "Fine. There's a café on the other side of the circle."

"No, no. *Outside.* Outside the dome."

That was easy for him; he was a transfer now. But it was a pain in the ass for me; I'd have to rent a surface suit.

"Seriously? I only want to ask to ask you a couple of questions."

"Yes, yes, but *I* want to talk to you and . . ." The voice grew soft. ". . . and it's a delicate matter, deserving of privacy."

The drunk near me rolled onto his other side and let out a wheezy snore.

"Oh, all right," I said.

"Good chap," replied Pickover. "I'm just in the middle of something up here. About an hour from now, say? Just outside the east airlock?"

"Can we make it the west one? I can swing by my office on the way, then." I didn't need anything from there—I was already packing heat—but if he had some sort of ambush planned, I figured he'd object to the change.

"That's fine, that's fine—all four airlocks are the same distance from here, after all! But now, I really must finish what I'm doing . . ."

. . . .

Of course I was suspicious about what Rory Pickover was up to and so I tipped Mac off before making my way to the western airlock. The sun was setting outside the dome by the time I got there to suit up. Surface suits came in three stretchy sizes; I put on one of largest, then slung the air tanks onto my back. I felt heavy in the suit, even though in it I still weighed only about half of what I had back on Earth.

Rory Pickover was a paleontologist—an actual scientist, not a treasure-seeking fossil hunter. His pre-transfer appearance had been almost stereotypically academic: a round, soft face, with a fringe of graying hair. His new body was lean and muscular, and he had a full head of dark brown hair, but the face was still recognizably his own. His suit had a loop on its waist holding a geologist's hammer with a wide, flat blade; I rather suspected it would nicely smash my fishbowl helmet. I surreptitiously transferred the Smith & Wesson from the holster I wore under my jacket to an exterior pocket on the rented surface suit, just in case I needed it while we were outside.

We signed the security logs and then let the technician cycle us through the airlock.

Overhead, the sky was growing dark. Nearby, there were two large craters and a cluster of smaller ones. There were few footprints in the rusty sand; the recent storm had obliterated the thousands that had doubtless been there earlier. We walked out about five hundred meters. I turned around briefly to look back at the transparent dome and the ramshackle buildings within.

"Sorry for dragging you out here, old boy," said Pickover. "I don't want any witnesses." There was a short-distance radio microphone inside that mechanical throat for speaking outside the dome, and I had a transceiver inside my fishbowl.

"Ah," I said, by way of reply.

"I know you aren't just in from Earth," said Pickover, continuing to walk. "And I know you don't work for NewYou."

We were casting long shadows. The sun, so much tinier than it appeared from Earth, was sitting on the horizon now.

The sky was already purpling, and Earth itself was visible, a bright blue-white evening star. It was much easier to see it out here than through the dome, and, as always, I thought for a moment of Wanda as I looked up at it. But then I lowered my gaze to Pickover. "Who do you think I am?"

His answer surprised me, although I didn't let it show. "You're the private-detective chap."

It didn't seem to make any sense to deny it. "Yeah. How'd you know?"

"I've been checking you out over the last few days," said Pickover. "I'd been thinking of, ah, engaging your services."

We continued to walk along, little clouds of dust rising each time our feet touched the ground. "What for?"

"You first, if you don't mind," Pickover replied. "Why did you really come to see me?"

He already knew who I was, and I had a very good idea who he was. I had my phone on the outside of my suit's left wrist, and it was connected to the headset in my helmet. "Call Dougal McCrae."

"What are you doing?" Pickover asked.

"Hey, Alex," said Mac from the little screen on my wrist; I heard his voice over the fishbowl's headset.

"Mac, listen, I'm about half a klick straight out from the west airlock. I'm going to need backup."

"Lomax, what *are* you doing?" asked Pickover.

"Kaur is already outside the dome," said Mac, looking offscreen. "She can be there in two minutes." He switched voice channels for a moment, presumably speaking to Sergeant Kaur. Then he turned back to me. "She's north of you; she's got you on her infrared scanner."

Pickover looked over his shoulder, and perhaps saw the incoming cop with his own infrared vision. But then he turned back to me and spread his arms in the darkness. "Lomax, for God's sake, what's going on?"

I shook my phone, breaking the connection with Mac, and pulled out my revolver. It really wouldn't be much use against an artificial body, but until quite recently Joshua Wilkins had been biological; I hoped he was still intimidated by guns. "That's quite a lovely wife you have."

Pickover's artificial face looked perplexed. "Wife?"

"That's right."

"I don't have a wife."

"Sure you do. You're Joshua Wilkins, and your wife's name is Cassandra."

"What? No, I'm Rory Pickover. You know that. You called me."

"Come off it, Wilkins. The jig is up. You transferred your consciousness into the body intended for the real Rory Pickover, and then you took off."

"I—oh. Oh, Christ."

"So, you see, I know. And—ah, here's Sergeant Kaur now. Too bad, Wilkins. You'll hang—or whatever the hell they do with transfers—for murdering Pickover."

"No." He said it softly.

"Yes," I replied. Kaur was a sleek form about a hundred meters behind Pickover. "Let's go."

"Where?"

"Back under the dome, to the police station. I'll have Cassandra meet us there, just to confirm your identity."

The sun had slipped below the horizon now. He spread his arms, a supplicant against the backdrop of the gathering night. "Okay, sure, if you like. Call up this Cassandra, by all means. Let her talk to me. She'll tell you after questioning me for two seconds that I'm not her husband. But—Christ, damn, Christ."

"What?"

"I want to find him, too."

"Who? Joshua Wilkins?"

He nodded, then, perhaps thinking I couldn't see his nod in the growing darkness, said, "Yes."

"Why?"

He tipped his head up as if thinking. I followed his gaze. Phobos was visible, a dark form overhead. At last, he spoke again. "Because *I'm* the reason he's disappeared."

"What? Why?"

"That's why I was thinking of hiring you myself. I didn't know where else to turn."

"Turn for what?"

Pickover looked at me. "I did go to NewYou, Mr. Lomax. I knew I was going to have an enormous amount of work to do out here on the surface now, and I wanted to be able to spend weeks—months!—in the field without worrying about running out of air or water or food."

I frowned. "But you've been here on Mars for six mears; I read that in your file. What's changed?"

"Everything, Mr. Lomax." He looked off in the distance. "Everything!" But he didn't elaborate on that. Instead, he said, "I certainly know this Wilkins chap you're looking for. I went to his shop and had him transfer my consciousness from my old biological body into this one. But he also kept a copy of my mind—I'm sure of that."

"That's . . ." I shook my head. "I've never heard of that being done."

"Nor had I," said Pickover. "I mean, I understood from their sales materials that your consciousness sort of, um, hops into the artificial body. Because of that, I didn't think duplicates were possible at the time I did it, or I never would have undergone the process."

Kaur was now about thirty meters away, and she had a big rifle aimed at Pickover's back. I held up a hand, palm out, to get the cop to stand her ground.

"Prove it to me," I said. "Prove to me you are who you say you are. Tell me something Joshua Wilkins couldn't know, but a paleontologist would."

"Oh, for Pete's—"

"Tell me!"

"Fine, fine. The most-recent fossils here on Mars date from what's called the Noachian efflorescence, a time of morphological diversification similar to Earth's Cambrian explosion. So far, twenty-seven distinct genera from then have been identified—well, it was originally twenty-nine but I successfully showed that both *Weinbaumia* and *Gallunia* are junior synonyms of *Bradburia.* Within *Bradburia* there are six distinct species, the most common of which is *B. breviceps,* known for its bifurcated pygidia and—"

"Okay!" I said. "Enough." I held up fingers to show Kaur which radio frequency I was using and watched her tap it into her wrist keypad. "Sorry, Sergeant," I said. "False alarm."

The woman nodded. "You owe me one, Lomax." She lowered her rifle and headed past us toward the airlock.

I didn't want Kaur listening in, so I changed frequencies again and indicated with hand signs to Pickover which one I'd selected. He didn't do anything obvious, but I soon heard his voice. "As I said, I think Wilkins made a copy of my mind."

It was certainly illegal to do that, probably unethical, and perhaps not even technically possible; I'd have to ask Juan. "Why do you think that?"

"It's the only explanation for how my computer accounts have become compromised. There's no way anyone but me can get in; I'm the only one who knows the passphrase. But someone *has* been inside, looking around; I use quantum encryption, so you can tell whenever someone has even *looked* at a file." He shook his head. "I don't know how he did it—there must be some technique I'm unaware of—but somehow Wilkins has been extracting information from a copy of my mind. That's the only way I can think of that anyone might have learned my passphrase."

"You think Wilkins did all that to access your bank accounts? Is there really enough money in them to make it worthwhile? It's gotten too dark to see your clothes but, if I recall correctly, they looked a bit . . . shabby."

"You're right. I'm just a poor scientist. But there's something I know that could make the wrong people rich beyond their wildest dreams."

"And what's that?" I said.

He stood there, trying to decide, I suppose, whether to trust me. I let him think about that, and at last Dr. Rory Pickover, who was now just a starless silhouette against a starry sky, said, in a soft, quiet voice, "I know where it is."

"Where what is?"

"The Alpha Deposit."

"My God. You'll be *rolling* in it."

Perhaps he shook his head; it was now too dark to tell. "No, sir," he replied in that cultured British voice. "No, I won't. I don't want to *sell* these fossils. I want to preserve them; I want to protect them from these plunderers, these . . . these *thieves*. I want to make sure they're collected properly, scientifically. I want them to end up in the best museums, where they can be studied. There's so much to be learned, so much to discover!"

"Does Joshua Wilkins now know where the Alpha Deposit is?"

"No—at least, not from accessing my computer files. I didn't record the location anywhere but up here." Presumably he was tapping the side of his head.

"But if Wilkins could extract your passphrase from a copy of your mind, why didn't he just directly extract the location of the Alpha from it?"

"The passphrase is straightforward—just a string of words—but the Alpha's location, well, it's not like it has an address, and even I don't know the longitude and latitude by heart. Rather, I know where it is by reference to certain geological features that would be meaningless to a nonexpert; it would take a lot more work to extract that, I'd warrant. And so he tried the easier method of spelunking in my computer files."

I shook my head. "This doesn't make any sense. I mean, how would Wilkins even know that you had discovered the Alpha Deposit?"

Suddenly Pickover's voice was very small. "I'd gone in to NewYou—you have to go there in advance of transferring, of course, so you can tell them what you want in a new body; it takes time to custom-build one to your specifications."

"Yes. So?"

"So I wanted a body ideally suited to paleontological work on the surface of Mars; I wanted some special modifications—the kinds of the things only the most successful prospectors could afford. Reinforced knees; extra arm strength for moving rocks; extended spectral response in the eyes so that fossils will stand out better; night vision so that I could continue digging after dark. But . . ."

I nodded. "But you didn't have enough money."

"That's right. I could barely afford to transfer at all, even into the cheapest off-the-shelf body, and so . . ."

He trailed off, too angry at himself, I guess, to give voice to what was in his mind. "And so you hinted that you were about to come into some wealth," I said, "and suggested that maybe he could give you what you needed now, and you'd make it up to him later."

Pickover sounded sad. "That's the trouble with being a scientist; sharing information is our natural mode."

"Did you tell him precisely what you'd found?"

"No. No, but he must have guessed. I'm a paleontologist, I've been studying Weingarten and O'Reilly for years—all of that is a matter of public record. He must have figured out that I knew where their prime fossil bed was. After all, where else would a bloke like me get money?" He paused. "I'm an idiot, aren't I?"

"Well, Mensa isn't going to be calling you anytime soon."

"Please don't rub it in, Mr. Lomax. I feel bad enough as it is."

I nodded. "But if he suspected you'd found the Alpha, maybe he just put a tracking chip in this new body of yours. Sure, that's against the law, but that would have been the simplest way for him to get at it."

Pickover rallied a bit, pleased, I guess, that he'd at least thought of this angle. "No, no, he didn't. A tracking chip has to transmit a signal to do any good; they're easy enough to locate, and I made sure he knew I knew that before I transferred. Nonetheless, I had myself checked over after the process was completed. I'm positive I'm clean."

"And so you think he's found another way," I said.

"Yes! And if he succeeds in locating the Alpha, all will be lost! The specimens will be sold off into private collections—trophies for billionaires' estates, hidden forever from science." He looked at me with imploring acrylic eyes and his voice cracked; I'd never heard a transfer's do that before. "All those wondrous fossils are in jeopardy! Will you help me, Mr. Lomax? Please say you'll help me!"

Two clients were, of course, always better than one—at least as far as the bank account was concerned. "All right," I said. "Let's talk about my fee."

SEVEN

After Rory Pickover and I went back into the dome, I called Juan, asking him to meet us at Pickover's little apartment at the center of town. Rory and I got there before him, and went on up; the drunk who'd been in the entryway earlier had gone.

Pickover's apartment—an interior unit, with no windows—consisted of three small rooms. While we waited for Juan, the good doctor—trusting soul that he was—showed me three fossils he'd recovered from the Alpha, and even to my untrained eye, they were stunning. The specimens—all invertebrate exoskeletons—had been removed from the matrix, cleaned, and painstakingly prepared.

The first was something about the size of my fist, with dozens of tendrils extending from it, some ending in three-fingered pincers, some in four-fingered ones, and the two largest in five-fingered ones.

The next was the length of my forearm. It was dumbbell-shaped, with numerous smaller hemispheres embedded in each of the globes. I couldn't make head or tail of it, but Pickover confidently assured me that globe on the left was the former and the one on the right the latter.

The final specimen he showed me was, he said, his pride

and joy—the only one of its kind so far discovered: it was a stony ribbon that, had it been stretched out, would have been maybe eighty centimeters long. But it wasn't stretched out; rather, it was joined together in a Möbius strip. Countless cilia ran along the edges of the ribbon—I was stunned to see that such fine detail had been preserved—and the strip was perforated at intervals by diamond-shaped openings with serrated edges.

I looked at Pickover, who was chuffed, to use the word he himself might have, to show off his specimens, and I half listened as he went on about their incredible scientific value. But all I could think about was how much money they must be worth—and the fact that there were countless more like them out there of this same quality.

When Juan finally buzzed from the lobby, Rory covered his specimens with cloth sheets. The elevator was out of order, but that was no problem in this gravity; Juan wasn't breathing hard when he reached the apartment door.

"Juan Santos," I said, as he came in, "this is Rory Pickover. Juan here is the best computer expert we've got in New Klondike. And Dr. Pickover is a paleontologist."

Juan dipped his broad forehead toward Pickover. "Good to meet you."

"Thank you," said Pickover. "Forgive the mess, Mr. Santos. I live alone. A lifelong bachelor gets into bad habits, I'm afraid." He'd already cleared debris off one chair for me; he now busied himself doing the same with another, this one right in front of his computer, a silver-and-blue cube about the size of a grapefruit.

"What's up, Alex?" asked Juan, indicating Pickover with a movement of his head. "New client?"

"Yeah. Dr. Pickover's computer files have been looked at by some unauthorized individual. We're wondering if you could tell us where the access attempt was made from."

"You'll owe me a nice round of drinks at The Bent Chisel," said Juan.

"No problem," I said. "I'll put it on my tab."

Juan smiled and stretched his arms out in front of him, fingers interlocked, and cracked his knuckles, like a safecracker preparing to get down to work. Then he took the now-clean seat in front of Pickover's computer cube, tilted the nearby monitor up a bit, pulled a keyboard into place, and began to type. "How do you lock your files?" he asked, without taking his eyes off the monitor.

"A verbal passphrase," said Pickover.

"Anybody besides you know it?"

"No."

"And it's not written down anywhere?"

"No, well . . . not as such."

Juan turned his head, looking up at Pickover. "What do you mean?"

"It's a line from a book. If I ever forget the exact wording, I can always look it up."

Juan shook his head in disgust. "You should always use random passphrases." He typed keys.

"Oh, I'm sure it's totally secure," said Pickover. "No one would guess—"

Juan interrupted. "—that your passphrase is 'Those privileged to be present—'"

I saw Pickover's artificial jaw drop. "My God. How did you know that?"

Juan pointed to some data on the screen. "It's the first thing that was inputted by the only outside access your system has had in weeks."

"I thought passphrases were hidden from view when entered," said Pickover.

"Sure they are," said Juan. "But the comm program has a buffer; it's in there. Look."

Juan shifted in the chair so that Pickover could see the screen clearly over his shoulder. "That's . . . well, that's very strange," Pickover said.

"What?"

"Well, sure, that's my passphrase, but it's not quite right."

I loomed in to have a peek at the screen, too. "How do you mean?"

"Well," said Pickover, "see, my passphrase is 'Those privileged to be present at a family festival of the Forsytes'— it's from the opening of *The Man of Property,* the first book of the Forsyte Saga by John Galsworthy. I love that phrase because of the alliteration—'privileged to be present,' 'family festival of the Forsytes.' Makes it easy to remember."

Juan shook his head in you-can't-teach-people-anything disgust. Pickover went on. "But, see, whoever it was typed even more."

I looked at the glowing string of letters. In full it said: *Those privileged to be present at a family festival of the Forsytes have seen them dine at half past eight, enjoying seven courses.*

"It's too much?" I asked.

"That's right," said Pickover, nodding. "My passphrase ends with the word 'Forsytes.'"

Juan was stroking his receding chin. "Doesn't matter," he said. "The files would unlock the moment the phrase was complete; the rest would just be discarded—systems that principally work with spoken commands don't require you to press the enter key."

"Yes, yes, yes," said Pickover. "But the rest of it isn't what Galsworthy wrote. It's not even close. *The Man of Property* is my favorite book; I know it well. The full opening line is 'Those privileged to be present at a family festival of the Forsytes have seen that charming and instructive sight—an upper middle-class family in full plumage.' Nothing about the time they ate, or how many courses they had."

Juan pointed at the text on screen as if it had to be the correct version. "Are you sure?"

"Of course!" replied Pickover. "Do a search and see for yourself."

I frowned. "No one but you knows your passphrase, right?"

Pickover nodded vigorously. "I live alone, and I don't have many friends; I'm a quiet sort. There's no one I've ever told, and no one who could have ever overheard me saying it, or seen me typing it in."

"Somebody found it out," said Juan.

Pickover looked at me, then down at Juan. "I think . . ." he said, beginning slowly, giving me a chance to stop him,

I guess, before he said too much. But I let him go on. "I think that the information was extracted from a scan of my mind made by NewYou."

Juan crossed his arms in front of his chest. "Impossible."

"What?" said Pickover, and "Why?" said I.

"Can't be done," said Juan. "We know how to copy the vast array of interconnections that make up a human mind, and we know how to reinstantiate those connections on an artificial substrate. But we don't know how to decode them; nobody does. There's simply no way to sift through a digital copy of a mind and extract specific data."

Damn! If Juan was right—and he always was in computing matters—then all this business with Pickover was a red herring. There probably was no bootleg scan of his mind; despite his protestations of being careful, someone likely had just overheard his passphrase and decided to go hunting through his files. While I was wasting time on this, Joshua Wilkins was doubtless slipping further out of my grasp.

Still, it was worth continuing this line of investigation for a few minutes more. "Any sign of where the access attempt was made?" I asked Juan.

He shook his head. "No. Whoever did it knew what they were doing; they covered their tracks well. The attempt came over an outside line—that's all I can tell for sure."

I nodded. "Okay. Thanks, Juan. Appreciate your help."

He got up. "My pleasure. Now, how 'bout that drink?"

I opened my mouth to say yes, but then it hit me—what Wilkins must be doing. "Umm, later, okay? I've got some more things to take care of here."

Juan frowned; he'd clearly hoped to collect his booze immediately. But I started maneuvering him toward the door. "Thanks for your help. I really appreciate it."

"Um, sure, Alex," he said. He was obviously aware he was being given the bum's rush, but he wasn't fighting it too much. "Anytime."

"Yes, thank you awfully, Mr. Santos," said Pickover.

"No problem. If—"

"See you later, Juan," I said, opening the door for him. "Thanks so much." I tipped my nonexistent hat at him.

Juan shrugged, clearly aware that something was up but not motivated sufficiently to find out what. He went through the door, and I hit the button that caused it to slide shut behind him. As soon as it was closed, I put an arm around Pickover's shoulders and propelled him back to the computer. I pointed at the line Juan had highlighted on the screen and read the ending of it aloud: "'. . . dine at half past eight, enjoying seven courses.'"

Pickover nodded. "Yes. So?"

"Numbers are often coded info," I said. "'Half past eight; seven courses.' What's that mean to you?"

"To me? Nothing. Back when I ate, I liked to do it much earlier than that, and I never had more than one course."

"But it could be a message."

"From whom?"

There was no easy way to tell him this. "From you to you."

He drew his artificial eyebrows together. "What?"

"Look," I said, motioning for him to sit down in front of the computer, "Juan is doubtless right. You can't sift a digital scan of a human mind for information."

"But that must be what Wilkins is doing."

I shook my head. "No. The only way to find out what's in a mind is to ask it interactively."

"But . . . but no one's asked me my passphrase."

"No one has asked *this* you. But Joshua Wilkins must have transferred the extra copy of your mind into a body, so that he could deal with it directly. And that extra copy must have revealed your passphrase to him."

"You mean . . . you mean there's another me? Another *conscious* me?"

"Looks that way."

"But . . . no, no. That's . . . why, that's *illegal*. Bootleg copies of human beings—my God, Lomax, it's obscene!"

"I'm going to go see if I can find him," I said.

"*It,*" said Pickover forcefully.

"What?"

"*It.* Not him. I'm the only 'him'—the only real Rory Pickover." He shuddered. "My God, Lomax, I feel so . . . so violated! A stolen, active copy of my mind! It's the ultimate invasion of privacy . . ."

"That may be," I said. "But the bootleg is trying to tell you something. He—*it*—gave Wilkins the passphrase and then tacked some extra words onto it, in order to get a message to you."

"But I don't recognize those extra words," said Pickover, sounding exasperated.

"Do they mean anything to you? Do they suggest anything?"

Pickover re-read the text on the screen. "I can't imagine what," he said, "unless . . . no, no, I'd never think up a code like that."

"You obviously just *did* think of it. What's the code?"

Pickover was quiet for a moment, as if deciding if the thought was worth giving voice. Then: "Well, New Klondike is circular in layout, right? And it consists of concentric rings of buildings. Half past eight—that would be between Eighth and Ninth Avenue, no? And seven courses—in the Seventh Circle out from the center? Maybe the damned bootleg is trying to draw our attention to a location, a specific place here in town."

"The Seventh Circle, off Eighth Avenue," I said. "That's a rough area. I go to a gym near there."

"The shipyard," said Pickover. "Isn't it there, too?"

"Yeah." Dry-dock work was so much easier in a shirtsleeve environment and, in the early days, repairing and servicing spaceships had been a major business under the dome. I started walking toward the door. "I'm going to investigate."

"I'll go with you," said Pickover.

I shook my head. He would doubtless be more hindrance than help. "It's too dangerous. I should go alone."

Pickover looked for a moment like he was going to protest, but then he nodded. "All right. But if you find another me . . ."

"Yes?" I said. "What would you like me to do?"

Pickover gazed at me with pleading eyes. "Erase it. Destroy it." He shuddered again. "I never want to see the damned thing."

EIGHT

I had to get some sleep—damn, but sometimes I do wish I were a transfer—so I took the hovertram out to my apartment. My place was on Fifth Avenue, which was a great address in New York but a lousy one in New Klondike, especially out near the rim; it was mostly home to people who had tried and failed at fossil hunting, hence its nickname "Sad Sacks Fifth Avenue."

I let myself have six hours—Mars hours, admittedly, which were slightly longer than Earth ones—then I headed out to the old shipyard. The sun was just coming up as I arrived there. The sky through the dome was pink in the east and purple in the west.

Some active maintenance and repair work was still done on spaceships here, but most of these hulks were no longer spaceworthy and had been abandoned. Any one of them would make a good hideout, I thought; spaceships were shielded against radiation, making it hard to scan through their hulls to see what was going on inside.

The shipyard was a large field holding vessels of various sizes and shapes. Most were streamlined—even Mars's tenuous atmosphere required that. Some were squatting on tail fins; some were lying on their bellies; some were supported by articulated legs. I tried every hatch I could see on these craft, but, so far, they all had their airlocks sealed tightly shut.

Finally, I came to a monstrous abandoned spaceliner—a great hull, some three hundred meters long, fifty meters wide, and a dozen meters high. The name *Skookum Jim* was still visible in chipped paint near the bow, which is the part I came across first, and the slogan "Mars or Bust!" had been splashed across the metal surface in a paint that had survived the elements better than the liner's name. I walked a little farther alongside the hull, looking for a hatch, until—

Yes! I finally understood what a fossil hunter felt when he at last turned up a perfectly preserved rhizomorph. There was an outer airlock door and it was open. The other door, inside, was open, too. I stepped through the chamber, entering the ship proper. There were stands for holding space suits but the suits themselves were long gone.

I walked to the far end of the room and found another door—one of those submarine-style ones with a locking wheel in the center. This one was closed; I figured it would probably have been sealed shut at some point, but I tried the wheel anyway, and damned if it didn't spin freely, disengaging the locking bolts. I pulled the door open, then took the flashlight off my belt and aimed it into the interior. It looked safe, so I stepped through. The door was on spring-loaded hinges; as soon as I let go of it, it closed behind me.

The air was dry and had a faint odor of decay to it. I headed down the corridor, the pool of illumination from my flashlight going in front of me, and—

A squealing noise. I swung around, and the beam from my flashlight caught the source before it scurried away: a large brown rat, its eyes two tiny red coals in the light. People had been trying to get rid of the rats—and cockroaches and silverfish and other vermin that had somehow made it here from Earth—for mears.

I turned back around and headed deeper into the ship. The floor wasn't quite level: it dipped a bit to—to starboard, they'd call it—and I also felt that I was gaining elevation as I walked along. The ship's floor had no carpeting; it was just bare, smooth metal. Oily water pooled along the starboard side; a pipe must have ruptured at some point. Another rat scurried by up ahead; I wondered what they ate here, aboard the dead hulk of the ship.

I thought I should check in with Pickover—let him know where I was. I activated my phone, but the display said it was unable to connect. Of course: the radiation shielding in the spaceship's hull kept signals from getting out.

It was growing awfully cold. I held my flashlight straight up in front of my face and saw that my breath was now coming out in visible clouds. I paused and listened. There was a steady dripping sound: condensation, or another leak. I continued along, sweeping the flashlight beam left and right in good detective fashion as I did so.

There were doors at intervals along the corridor—the automatic sliding kind you usually find aboard spaceships. Most ships used hibernation for bringing people to Mars, but this was an old-fashioned spaceliner with cabins; the passengers and crew would have been awake for the whole eight months or more of the journey out.

Most of the door panels had been pried open, and I shined my flashlight into each of the revealed rooms. Some were tiny passenger quarters, some were storage, one was a medical facility—all the equipment had been removed, but the examining beds betrayed the room's function. They were welded down firmly—not worth the effort for scavengers to salvage, I guess.

I checked yet another set of quarters, then came to a closed door, the first one I'd seen along this hallway.

I pushed the open button but nothing happened; the ship's electrical system was dead. There was an emergency handle recessed into the door's thickness. I could have used three hands just then: one to hold my flashlight, one to hold my revolver, and one to pull on the handle. I tucked the flashlight into my right armpit, held my gun with my right hand, and yanked on the recessed handle with my left.

The door hardly budged. I tried again, pulling harder—and almost popped my arm out of its socket. Could the door's tension control have been adjusted to require a transfer's strength to open it? Perhaps.

I tried another pull and, to my astonishment, light began to spill out from the room. I'd hoped to just whip the door open, taking advantage of the element of surprise, but the damned thing was only moving a small increment with each pull of the handle. If there was someone on the other side and he or she had a gun, it was no doubt now leveled directly at the door.

I stopped for a second, shoved the flashlight into my pocket, and—damn, I hated having to do this—holstered my revolver so that I could free up my other hand to help me pull the door open. With both hands now gripping the recessed handle, I tugged with all my strength, letting out a grunt as I did so. The light from within stung my eyes; they'd grown accustomed to the darkness. Another pull, and the door panel had now slid far enough into the wall for me to slip into the room by turning sideways. I took out my gun and let myself in.

A voice, harsh and mechanical, but no less pitiful for that: *"Please . . ."*

My eyes swung to the source of the sound. There was a worktable with a black top attached to the far wall. And strapped to that table—

Strapped to that table was a transfer's synthetic body. But this wasn't like the fancy, almost perfect simulacrum that my client Cassandra inhabited. This was a crude, simple humanoid form with a boxy torso and limbs made up of cylindrical metal segments. And the face—

The face was devoid of any sort of artificial skin. The eyes, blue in color and looking startlingly human, were wide, and the teeth looked like dentures loose in the head. The rest of the face was a mess of pulleys and fiber optics, of metal and plastic.

"Please . . ." said the voice again. I looked around the rest of the room. There was an excimer battery, about the size of a softball, with several cables snaking out of it, including some that led to portable lights. There was also a

closet with a simple door. I pulled it open—this one slid easily—to make sure no one else had hidden in there while I was coming in. An emaciated rat that had been trapped inside at some point scooted out of the closet and through the still-partially-open corridor door.

I turned my attention to the transfer. The body was clothed in simple black denim pants and a beige T-shirt.

"Are you okay?" I said, looking at the skinless face.

The metal skull moved slightly left and right. The plastic lids for the glass eyeballs retracted, making the non-face into a caricature of imploring. *"Please . . ."* he said for a third time.

I looked at the restraints holding the artificial body in place: thin nylon bands attached to the tabletop, pulled taut. I couldn't see any release mechanism. "Who are you?" I asked.

I was half prepared for his answer: "Rory Pickover." But it didn't sound anything like the Rory Pickover I'd met: the cultured British accent was absent, and this synthesized voice was much higher pitched.

Still, I shouldn't take this sad thing's statement at face value—especially since it had hardly any face. "Prove it," I said. "Prove you're Rory Pickover."

The glass eyes looked away. Perhaps the transfer was thinking of how to satisfy my demand—or perhaps he was just avoiding my eyes. "My citizenship number is AG-394-56-432."

I shook my head. "No good," I said. "It's got to be something *only* Rory Pickover would know."

The eyes looked back at me, the plastic lids lowered, perhaps in suspicion. "It doesn't matter who I am," he said. "Just get me out of here."

That sounded reasonable on the surface of it, but if this *was* another Rory Pickover . . .

"Not until you prove your identity to me," I said. "Tell me where the Alpha Deposit is."

"Damn you," said the transfer. "The other way didn't work, so now you're trying this." The mechanical head looked away. "But this won't work, either."

"Tell me where the Alpha Deposit is," I said, "and I'll free you."

"I'd rather die," he said. And then, a moment later, he added wistfully, "Except . . ."

I finished the thought for him. "Except you can't."

He looked away again. It was hard to feel for something that appeared so robotic; that's my excuse, and I'm sticking to it. "Tell me where O'Reilly and Weingarten were digging. Your secret is safe with me."

He said nothing, but my mind was racing and my heart was pounding—those fabulous specimens the other Rory had shown me, the thought of so many more of them out there to be collected, the incalculable wealth they represented. I was startled to discover that my gun was now aimed at the robotic head, and the words "Tell me!" hissed from my lips. "Tell me before—"

Off in the distance, out in the corridor: the squeal of a rat and—

Footfalls.

The transfer heard them, too. Its eyes darted left and right in what looked like panic.

"Please," he said, lowering his volume. As soon as he started speaking, I put a vertical index finger to my lips, indicating that he should be quiet, but he continued: "Please, for the love of God, get me out of here. I can't take any more."

I made a beeline for the closet, stepping in quickly and pulling that door most of the way shut behind me. I positioned myself so that I could see—and, if necessary, shoot—through the gap. The footfalls were growing louder. The closet smelled of rat. I waited.

I heard a voice, richer, more human, than the supposed Pickover's. "What the—?"

And I saw a person—a transfer—slipping sideways into the room, just as I had earlier. I couldn't yet see the face from this angle, but the body was female, and she was a brunette. I took in air, held it, and—

And she turned, showing her face now. My heart pounded. The delicate features. The wide-spaced green eyes.

Cassandra Wilkins.

My client.

She'd been carrying a flashlight, which she set now on another, smaller table. "Who's been here, Rory?" Her voice was cold.

"No one," he said.

"The door was open."

"You left it that way. I was surprised, but . . ." He stopped, perhaps realizing to say any more would be a giveaway that he was lying.

She tilted her head slightly. Even with a transfer's strength, that door must be hard to close. Hopefully, she'd find it plausible that she'd given the handle a final tug and had only assumed that the door had closed completely when she'd last left. Of course, I immediately saw the flaw with that story: you might miss the door not clicking into place, but you wouldn't fail to notice that light was still spilling out into the corridor. But most people don't consider things in such detail; I hoped she'd buy Pickover's suggestion.

And, after a moment's more reflection, she seemed to do just that, nodding her head, apparently to herself, then moving closer to the table onto which the synthetic body was strapped. "We don't have to do this again," said Cassandra. "If you just tell me . . ."

She let the words hang in the air for a moment, but Pickover made no response. Her shoulders moved up and down in a philosophical shrug. "It's your choice," she said. And then, to my astonishment, she hauled back her right arm and slapped Pickover hard across the robotic face, and—

And Pickover screamed.

It was a long, low, warbling sound, like sheet metal being warped, a haunted sound, an inhuman sound.

"Please . . ." he hissed again, the same plaintive word he'd said to me, the word I, too, had ignored.

Cassandra slapped him again, and again he screamed. Now, I've been slapped by lots of women over the years: it stings, but I've never screamed. And surely an artificial body was made of sterner stuff than me.

Cassandra went for a third slap. Pickover's screams echoed in the dead hulk of the ship.

"Tell me!" she demanded.

I couldn't see his face; her body was obscuring it. Maybe he shook his head. Maybe he just glared defiantly. But he said nothing.

She shrugged again; they'd obviously been down this road before. She moved to one side of the bed and stood by his right arm, which was pinned to his body by the nylon strap. "You really don't want me to do this," she said. "And I don't have to, if . . ." She let the uncompleted offer hang there for a few seconds, then: "Ah, well." She reached down with her beige, realistic-looking hand and wrapped three of her fingers around his right index finger. And then she started bending it backward.

I could see Pickover's face now. Pulleys along his jawline were working; he was struggling to keep his mouth shut. His glass eyes were rolling up, back into his head, and his left leg was shaking in spasms. It was a bizarre display, and I alternated moment by moment between feeling sympathy for the being lying there and feeling cool detachment because of the clearly artificial nature of the body.

Cassandra let go of Pickover's index finger, and for a second I thought she was showing some mercy. But then she grabbed it as well as the adjacent finger and began bending them both back. This time, despite his best efforts, guttural robotic sounds did escape from Pickover.

"Talk!" Cassandra said. *"Talk!"*

I'd recently learned—from Cassandra herself—that artificial bodies had to have pain sensors; otherwise, a robotic hand might end up resting on a heating element, or too much pressure might be put on a joint. But I hadn't expected such sensors to be so sensitive, and—

And then it hit me, just as another of Pickover's warbling screams was torn from him. Cassandra knew all about artificial bodies; she sold them, after all. If she wanted to adjust the mind-body interface of one so that pain would register particularly acutely, doubtless she could. I'd seen a lot of evil things in my time, but this was the worst. Scan a mind, put it in a body wired for hypersensitivity to pain, and torture it until it gave up its secrets. Then, of course, you just wipe the mind, and—

"You *will* crack eventually, you know," she said, almost conversationally, as she looked at Pickover's fleshless face. "Given that it's inevitable, you might as well just tell me what I want to know."

The elastic bands that served as some of Pickover's facial muscles contracted, his teeth parted, and his head moved forward slightly but rapidly. I thought for half a second that he was incongruously blowing her a kiss, but then I realized what he was really trying to do: spit at her. Of course, his dry mouth and plastic throat were incapable of generating moisture, but his mind—a human mind, a mind accustomed to a biological body—had summoned and focused all its hate into that most primal of gestures.

"Very well," said Cassandra. She gave his fingers one more nasty yank backward, holding them at an excruciating angle. Pickover alternated screams and whimpers. Finally, she let his fingers go. "Let's try something different," she said. She leaned over him. With her left hand, she pried his right eyelid open, and then she jabbed her right thumb into that eye. The glass sphere depressed into the metal skull, and Pickover screamed again. The artificial eye was presumably much tougher than a natural one, but, then again, the thumb pressing into it was also tougher. I felt my own eyes watering in a sympathetic response.

Pickover's artificial spine arched up slightly as he convulsed against the two restraining bands. From time to time, I got clear glimpses of Cassandra's face, and the perfectly symmetrical synthetic smile of glee on it was sickening.

At last, she stopped grinding her thumb into his eye. "Had enough?" she asked. "Because if you haven't . . ."

As I'd said, Pickover was still wearing clothing; it was equally gauche to walk the streets nude whether you were biological or artificial. But now Cassandra's hands moved to his waist. I watched as she undid his belt, unsnapped and unzipped his jeans, and then pulled the pants as far down his metallic thighs as they would go before she reached the restraining strap that held his legs to the table. Transfers had no need for underwear, and Pickover wasn't wearing any. His artificial penis and testicles now lay exposed. I felt my own scrotum tightening in dread.

And then Cassandra did the most astonishing thing. She'd had no compunctions about bending back his fingers with her bare hands. And she hadn't hesitated when it came to plunging her naked thumb into his eye. But now that she was going to hurt him down there, she seemed to want no direct contact. She started scanning around the room. For a second, she was looking directly at the closet door; I scrunched back against the far wall, hoping she wouldn't see me. My heart was pounding.

Finally, she found what she was searching for: a wrench, sitting on the floor. She picked it up, raised it above her head, and looked directly into Pickover's one good eye—the other had closed as soon as she'd removed her thumb and had never reopened as far as I could tell. "I'm going to smash your ball bearings into iron filings, unless . . ."

He closed his other eye now, the plastic lid scrunching.

"Count of three," she said. "One."

"I can't," he said in that low volume that served as his whisper. "You'd ruin the fossils, sell them off—"

"Two."

"Please! They belong to science! To all humanity!"

"Three!"

Her arm slammed down, a great arc slicing through the air, the silver wrench smashing into the plastic pouch that was Pickover's scrotum. He let out a scream greater than any I'd yet heard, so loud, indeed, that it hurt my ears despite the muffling of the partially closed closet door.

She hauled her arm up again, but waited for the scream to devolve into a series of whimpers. "One more chance," she said. "Count of three." His whole body was shaking. I felt nauseous.

"One."

He turned his head to the side, as if by looking away he could make the torture stop.

"Two."

A whimper escaped his artificial throat.

"Three!"

I found myself looking away, too, unable to watch as—

"All right!"

It was Pickover's voice, shrill and mechanical.

"All right!" he shouted again. I turned back to face the tableau: the human-looking woman with a wrench held up above her head and the terrified, mechanical-looking man strapped to the table. "All right," he repeated once more, softly now. "I'll tell you what you want to know."

NINE

Y ou'll tell me where the Alpha Deposit is?" asked Cassandra, lowering her arm.

"Yes," Pickover said. "Yes."

"Where?"

Pickover was quiet.

"Where?"

"God forgive me . . ." he said softly.

She began to raise her arm again. *"Where?"*

"Head 16.4 kilometers south-southwest of the Nili Patera caldera. There are three craters there, each just under a hundred meters wide, forming a perfect equilateral triangle; the Alpha starts just past the twin fossae about five hundred meters east of them."

Cassandra's phone was doubtless recording all this—as was my own. "I thought it was here in Isidis Planitia."

"It's not—it's in the adjacent planum; that's why no one else has found it yet."

"You better be telling the truth," she said.

"I am." His voice was tiny. "To my infinite shame, I am."

Cassandra nodded. "All right, then. It's time to shut you off for good."

"But I told you the truth! I told you everything you need to know."

"Exactly. And so you're of no further use to me." She took a multipronged tool off the small table, returned to Pickover, and opened a hatch in his side.

I stepped out the closet, my gun aimed directly at Cassandra's back. "Freeze," I said.

She spun around. "Lomax!"

"Mrs. Wilkins," I said, nodding. "I guess you don't need me to find your husband for you anymore, eh? Now that you've got the information he was after."

"What? No, no. I still want you to find Joshua. Of course I do!"

"So you can share the wealth with him?"

"Wealth?" She looked over at the hapless Pickover. "Oh. Well, yes, there's a lot of money at stake." She smiled. "So much so that I'd be happy to cut you in, Mr. Lomax—oh, you're a good man. I know you wouldn't hurt me!"

I shook my head. "You'd betray me the first chance you got."

"No, I wouldn't. I'll need protection; I understand that—what with all the money the fossils will bring. Having someone like you on my side only makes sense."

I looked over at Pickover and shook my head. "You tortured that man."

"That 'man,' as you call it, wouldn't have existed at all without me. And the real Pickover isn't inconvenienced in the slightest."

"But . . . *torture,*" I said. "It's inhuman."

She jerked a contemptuous thumb at Pickover. "He's not human. Just some software running on some hardware."

"That's what you are, too."

"That's *part* of what I am," Cassandra said. "But I'm also *authorized.* He's bootleg—and bootlegs have no rights."

"I'm not going to argue philosophy with you."

"Fine. But remember who works for who, Mr. Lomax. I'm the client—and I'm going to be on my way now."

I held my gun rock-steady. "No, you're not."

She looked at me. "An interesting situation," she said,

her tone even. "I'm unarmed, and you've got a gun. Normally, that would put you in charge, wouldn't it? But your gun probably won't stop me. Shoot me in the head, and the bullet will just bounce off my metal skull. Shoot me in the chest, and at worst you might damage some components that I'll eventually have to get replaced—which I can, and at a discount, to boot.

"Meanwhile," she continued, "I have the strength of ten men; I could literally pull your limbs from their sockets, or crush your head between my hands, squeezing it until it pops like a melon, and your brains, such as they are, squirt out. So, what's it going to be, Mr. Lomax? Are you going to let me walk out that door and be about my business? Or are you going to pull that trigger, and start something that's going to end with you dead?"

I was used to a gun in my hand giving me a sense of power, of security. But just then, the Smith & Wesson felt like a lead weight. She was right: shooting her with it was likely to be no more useful than just throwing it at her—and yet, if I could drop her with one shot, I'd do it. I'd killed before in self-defense, but . . .

But this wasn't self-defense. Not really. If I didn't start something, she was just going to walk out. Could I kill in cold . . . well, not cold *blood*. And she *was* right: she was a person, even if Pickover wasn't. She was the one and only legal instantiation of Cassandra Wilkins. The cops might be corrupt here, and they might be lazy, but even they wouldn't turn a blind eye on attempted murder under the dome.

"So," she said, at last, "what's it going to be?"

"You make a persuasive argument, Mrs. Wilkins," I said in the most reasonable tone I could muster under the circumstances. And then, without changing my facial expression in the slightest, I pulled the trigger.

I wondered if a transfer's time sense ever slows down, or if it is always perfectly quartz-crystal timed. Certainly, time seemed to attenuate for me then. I swear I could actually see the bullet as it followed its trajectory from my gun, covering the three meters between the barrel and—

And not, of course, Cassandra's torso.

Nor her head.

She was right; I probably couldn't harm her that way.

No, instead, I'd aimed past her, at the table on which the *faux* Pickover was lying on his back. Specifically, I'd aimed at the place where the thick nylon band that crossed over his torso, pinning his arms, was anchored on the right-hand side—the point where it made a taut diagonal line between where it was attached to the side of the table and the top of Pickover's arm.

The bullet sliced through the band, cutting it in two. The long portion, freed of tension, flew up and over his torso like a snake that had just had 40,000 volts pumped through it.

Cassandra's eyes went wide in astonishment that I'd missed her, and her head swung around. The report of the bullet was still ringing in my ears, but I swear I could also hear the *zzzzinnnng!* of the restraining band snapping free. To be hypersensitive to pain, I figured you'd have to have decent reaction times, and I hoped that Pickover had been smart enough to note in advance my slight deviation of aim before I fired.

And, indeed, no sooner were his arms free than he sat bolt upright—his legs were still restrained—and grabbed one of Cassandra's arms, pulling her toward him. I leapt in the meager Martian gravity. Most of Cassandra's body was made of lightweight composites and synthetic materials, but I was still good old flesh and blood: I outmassed her by at least thirty kilos. My impact propelled her backward, and she slammed against the table's side. Pickover shot out his other arm, grabbing Cassandra's second arm, pinning her backside against the edge of the table. I struggled to regain a sure footing, then brought my gun up to her right temple.

"All right, sweetheart," I said. "Do you really want to test how strong your artificial skull is?"

Cassandra's mouth was open; had she still been biological, she'd probably have been gasping for breath. But her heartless chest was perfectly still. "You can't just shoot me," she said.

"Why not? Pickover here will doubtless back me up when I say it was self-defense, won't you, Pickover?"

He nodded. "Absolutely."

"In fact," I said, "you, me, this Pickover, and the other Pickover are the only ones who know where the Alpha Deposit is. I think the three of us would be better off without you on the scene anymore."

"You won't get away with it," said Cassandra. "You can't."

"I've gotten away with plenty over the years," I said. "I don't see that coming to an end." I cocked the hammer, just for fun.

"Look," she said, "there's no need for this. We can all share in the wealth. There's plenty to go around."

"Except you don't have any rightful claim to it," said Pickover. "You stole this copy of my mind, and you committed torture. And you want to be rewarded for that?"

"Pickover's right," I said. "It's his treasure, not yours."

"It's *humanity's* treasure," corrected Pickover. "It belongs to all mankind."

"But I'm your client," Cassandra said to me.

"So's he. At least, the legal version of him is."

Cassandra sounded desperate. "But—but that's a conflict of interest!"

"So sue me."

She shook her head in disgust. "You're just in this for yourself!"

I shrugged amiably and then pressed the barrel even tighter against her artificial head. "Aren't we all?"

"Shoot her," said Pickover. I looked at him. He was still holding her upper arms, pressing them in close to her torso. If he'd been biological, the twisting of his torso to accommodate doing that probably would have been quite uncomfortable. Actually, now that I thought of it, given his heightened sensitivity to pain, even this artificial version was probably hurting from twisting that way. But apparently this was a pain he was happy to endure.

"Do you really want me to do that?" I said. "I mean, I can

understand, after what she did to you, but . . ." I didn't finish the thought; I just left it in the air for him to take or leave.

"She *tortured* me. She deserves to die."

I frowned, unable to dispute his logic—but, at the same time, wondering if Pickover knew that he was as much on trial here as she was.

"Can't say I blame you," I said again, and then added another "but," and once more left the thought incomplete.

At last Pickover nodded. "But maybe you're right. I can't offer her any compassion, but I don't need to see her dead."

A look of plastic relief rippled over Cassandra's face. I nodded, and said, "Good man."

"But, still," said Pickover, "I would like *some* revenge."

Cassandra's upper arms were still pinned by Pickover, but her lower arms were free, and they both moved. I looked down, just in time to see them jerking toward her groin, almost as if to protect . . .

I nodded in quiet satisfaction.

Cassandra had quickly moved her arms back to a neutral, hanging-down position—but it was too late. The damage had been done.

Pickover had seen it, too; his torso had been twisted just enough to allow him to do so.

"You . . ." he began slowly, clearly shocked. "You're . . ." He paused, and if he'd been free to do so, I have no doubt he would have staggered back half a pace. His voice was soft, stunned. "No woman . . ."

Cassandra hadn't wanted to touch Pickover's groin—even though it was artificial—with her bare hands. And when Pickover had suggested exacting revenge for what had been done to him, Cassandra's hands had moved instinctively to protect—

It all made sense: the way she plunked herself down in a chair, the fact that she couldn't bring herself to wear makeup or jewelry in her new body, a dozen other things.

Cassandra's hands had moved instinctively to protect *her own testicles.*

"You're not Cassandra Wilkins," I said.

"Of course I am," said the female voice.

"Not on the inside you're not. You're a man. Whatever mind has been transferred into that body is male."

Cassandra twisted violently. Goddamned Pickover, still stunned by the revelation, had obviously loosened his grip because she got free. I fired my gun and the bullet went straight into her chest; a streamer of machine oil, like from a punctured can, shot out, but there was no sign that the bullet had slowed her down.

"Don't let her get away!" shouted Pickover, in his high, mechanical voice. I swung my gun on him, and for a second I could see terror in his eyes, as if he thought I meant to off him for letting her twist away. But I aimed at the nylon strap restraining his legs and fired. This time, the bullet only partially severed the strap. I reached down and yanked at the remaining filaments, and so did Pickover. They finally broke, and this strap, like the first, snapped free. Pickover swung his legs off the table and immediately stood up. An artificial body has many advantages, among them not being dizzy after lying down for God-only-knew how many days.

In the handful of seconds it had taken to free Pickover, Cassandra had made it out the door that I'd pried partway open, and was now running down the corridor in the darkness. I could hear splashing sounds, meaning she'd veered far enough off the corridor's centerline to end up in the water pooling along the starboard side, and I heard her actually bump into the wall at one point, although she immediately continued on. She didn't have her flashlight, and the only illumination in the corridor would have been what was spilling out of the room I was now in—a fading glow to her rear as she ran along, whatever shadow she herself was casting adding to the difficulty of seeing ahead.

I squeezed out into the corridor. My flashlight was still in my pocket. I fished it out and aimed it just in front of me; Cassandra wouldn't benefit much from the light it was giving off. Pickover, who, I noted, had now done his pants back up, had made his way through the half open door and was now standing by my side. I started running, and he fell in next to me.

Our footfalls drowned out the sound of Cassandra's; I guessed she must be some thirty or forty meters ahead.

Although it was almost pitch-black, she presumably had the advantage of having come down this corridor several times before; I had never gone in this direction, and I doubted Pickover had, either.

A rat scampered out of our way, squealing as it did so. My breathing was already ragged, but I managed to say, "How well can you guys see in the dark?"

Pickover's voice, of course, showed no signs of exertion. "Only slightly better than biologicals can, unless you specifically get an infrared upgrade."

I nodded, although he'd have needed better vision than he'd just claimed in order to see it. My legs were a lot longer than Cassandra's, but I suspected she could pump them more rapidly. I swung the flashlight beam up, letting it lance out ahead of us for a moment. There she was, off in the distance. I dropped the beam back to the floor.

More splashing from up ahead; she'd veered off once more. I thought about firing a shot—more for the drama of it than any serious hope of bringing her down—when I suddenly became aware that Pickover was passing me. His robotic legs were as long as my natural ones, and he could piston them up and down at least as quickly as Cassandra could.

I tried to match his speed but wasn't able to. Even in Martian gravity, running fast is hard work. I swung my flashlight up again, but Pickover's body, now in front of me, was obscuring everything farther down the corridor; I had no idea how far ahead Cassandra was now—and the intervening form of Pickover prevented me from acting out my idle fantasy of squeezing off a shot.

Pickover continued to pull ahead. I was passing open door after open door, black mouths gaping at me in the darkness. I heard more rats, and Pickover's footfalls, and—

Suddenly something jumped on my back from behind me. A hard arm was around my neck, pressing sharply down on my Adam's apple. I tried to call out to Pickover but couldn't get enough breath out . . . or in. I craned my neck as much as I could, and shined the flashlight beam up on the ceiling, so that some light reflected down onto my back from above.

It was Cassandra! She'd ducked into one of the other rooms and lain in wait for me. Pickover was no detective; he had completely missed the signs of his quarry no longer being in front of him—and I'd had Pickover's body blocking my vision, plus the echoing bangs of his footfalls to obscure my hearing. I could see my own chilled breath but, of course, not hers.

I tried again to call out to Pickover, but all I managed was a hoarse croak, doubtless lost on him amongst the noise of his own running. I was already oxygen-deprived from exertion, and the constricting of my throat was making things worse; despite the darkness I was now seeing white flashes in front of my eyes, a sure sign of asphyxiation. I only had a few seconds to act.

And act I did. I crouched as low as I could, Cassandra still on my back, her head sticking up above mine, and I leapt with all the strength I could muster. Even weakened, I managed a powerful kick, and in this low Martian gravity, I shot up like a bullet. Cassandra's metal skull smashed into the roof of the corridor. There happened to be a lighting fixture directly above me, and I heard the sounds of shattering glass and plastic.

I was descending now in maddeningly slow motion, but as soon as I was down, Cassandra still clinging hard to me, I surged forward a couple of paces then leapt again. This time, there was nothing but unrelenting bulkhead above, and Cassandra's metal skull slammed hard into it.

Again the slow-motion fall. I felt something thick and wet oozing through my shirt. For a second, I'd thought Cassandra had stabbed me—but no, it was probably the machine oil leaking from the bullet hole I'd put in her earlier. By the time we had touched down again, Cassandra had loosened her grip on my neck as she tried to scramble off me. I spun around and fell forward, pushing her backward onto the corridor floor, me tumbling on top of her. Despite my best efforts, the flashlight was knocked from my grip by the impact, and it spun around, doing a few complete circles before it ended up with its beam facing away from us.

I still had my revolver in my other hand, though. I brought

it up and by touch found Cassandra's face, probing the barrel roughly over it. Once, in my early days, I'd rammed a gun barrel into a thug's mouth; this time, I had other ideas. I got the barrel positioned directly over her left eye and pressed down hard with it—a little poetic justice.

I said, "I bet if I shoot through your glass eye, aiming up a bit, I'll tear your artificial brain apart. You want to find out?"

She said nothing. I called back over my shoulder, *"Pickover!"* The name echoed down the corridor, but I had no idea whether he heard me. I turned my attention back to Cassandra—or whoever the hell this really was—and I cocked the hammer. "As far as I'm concerned, Cassandra Wilkins is my client—but you're not her. Who are you?"

"I *am* Cassandra Wilkins," said the voice.

"No, you're not. You're a man—or, at least, you've got a man's mind."

"I can *prove* I'm Cassandra Wilkins," said the supine form. "My name is Cassandra Pauline Wilkins; my birth name is Collier. I was born in Sioux City, Iowa. My citizenship number is—"

"Facts. Figures." I shook my head. "Anyone could find those things out."

"But I know stuff no one else could possibly know. I know the name of my childhood pets; I know what I did to get thrown out of school when I was fifteen; I know precisely where the original me had a tattoo; I . . ."

She went on, but I stopped listening.

Jesus Christ, it was almost the perfect crime. No one could really get away with stealing somebody else's identity—not for long. The lack of intimate knowledge of how the original spoke, of private things the original knew, would soon enough give you away, unless—

Unless you were the *spouse* of the person whose identity you'd appropriated.

"You're not Cassandra Wilkins," I said. "You're Joshua Wilkins. You took her body; you transferred into it, and she transferred—" I felt my stomach tighten; it really was a nearly perfect crime. "And she transferred *nowhere;* when the original was euthanized, she died. And that makes you guilty of murder."

"You can't prove that," said the female voice. "No biometrics, no DNA, no fingerprints. I'm whoever I say I am."

"You and Cassandra hatched this scheme together," I said. "You both figured Pickover had to know where the Alpha Deposit was. But then you decided that you didn't want to share the wealth with anyone—not even your wife. And so you got rid of her and made good your escape at the same time."

"That's crazy," the female voice replied. "I *hired* you. Why on—on *Mars*—would I do that, then?"

"You expected the police to come out to investigate your missing-person report; they were supposed to find the body in the basement of NewYou. But they didn't, and you knew suspicion would fall on you—the supposed spouse!—if you were the one who found it. So you hired me—the dutiful wife, worried about her poor, missing hubby! All you wanted was for me to find the body."

"Words," said the transfer. "Just words."

"Maybe so," I replied. "I don't have to satisfy anyone else. Just me. I will give you one chance, though. See, I want to get out of here alive—and I don't see any way to do that if I leave you alive, too. Do you? If you've got an answer, tell me. Otherwise, I've got no choice but to pull this trigger."

"I promise I'll let you go," said the synthesized voice.

I laughed, and the sound echoed in the corridor. "You promise? Well, I'm sure I can take that to the bank."

"No, seriously. I won't tell anyone. I—"

"Are you Joshua Wilkins?" I asked.

Silence.

"Are you?"

I felt the face moving up and down a bit, the barrel of my gun shifting slightly in the eye socket as it did so. "Yes."

"Well, rest in peace," I said, and then, with relish, added, *"Josh."*

I pulled the trigger.

TEN

The flash from the gun barrel briefly lit up the flawless female face, which was showing almost biological horror. The revolver snapped back in my hand, then everything was dark again. I had no idea how much damage the bullet would do to the brain. Of course, the artificial chest wasn't rising and falling, but it never had been. And there was nowhere to check for a pulse. I decided I'd better try another shot, just to be sure. I shifted slightly, thinking I'd put this one through the other eye, and—

And Joshua's arms burst up, pushing me off him. I felt myself go airborne and was aware of Joshua scrambling to his feet. He scooped up the flashlight, and as he swung it and himself around, it briefly illuminated his face. There was a deep pit where one eye used to be.

I started to bring the gun up and—

And Joshua thumbed off the flashlight. The only illumination was a tiny bit of light, far, far down the corridor, spilling out from the torture room; it wasn't enough to let me see Joshua clearly. But I squeezed the trigger, and heard a bullet ricochet—either off some part of Joshua's metal internal skeleton or off the corridor wall.

I was the kind of guy who always knew *exactly* how

many bullets he had left: two. I wasn't sure I wanted to fire them both off blindly, but—

I could hear Joshua moving closer. I fired again. This time, the feminine voice box made a sound between an *oomph* and the word "ouch," so I knew I'd hit him.

One bullet to go.

I started walking backward—which was no worse than walking forward; I was just as likely to trip either way in this near-total darkness. The body in the shape of Cassandra Wilkins was much smaller than mine—but also much stronger. It could probably grab me by the shoulders and pound my head up into the ceiling, just as I'd pounded hers—and I rather suspect mine wouldn't survive. And if I let it get hold of my arm, it could probably wrench the gun from me; multiple bullets hadn't been enough to stop the artificial body, but one was all it would take to ice me for good.

I decided it was better to have an empty gun than a gun that could potentially be turned on me. I held the weapon out in front, took my best guess, and squeezed the trigger one last time.

The revolver barked, and the flare from the muzzle lit the scene, stinging my eyes. The artificial form cried out— I'd hit a spot its sensors felt was worth protecting with a major pain response, I guess. But Joshua kept moving forward. Part of me thought about turning tail and running— I still had the longer legs, even if I couldn't move them as fast—but another part of me couldn't bring myself to do that. The gun was of no more use, so I threw it aside. It hit the corridor wall, making a banging sound, then fell to the deck plates, producing more clanging as it bounced against them.

Of course, as soon as I'd thrown the gun away, I realized I'd made a mistake. *I* knew how many bullets I'd shot, and how many the gun held, but Joshua probably didn't; even an empty gun could be a deterrent if the other person thought it was loaded.

We were facing each other—but that was all that was certain. Precisely how much distance there was between us I couldn't say. Although running produced loud, echoing footfalls, either of us could have moved a step or two forward or back—or left or right—without the other being aware of it. I was trying not to make any noise, and a transfer could stand perfectly still, and be absolutely quiet, for hours on end.

I'd only ever heard clocks ticking with each second in old movies, but I was certainly conscious of time passing in increments as we stood there, each waiting for the other to make a move. And I had no idea how badly I'd hurt him.

Light suddenly exploded in my face. He'd thumbed the flashlight back on, aiming it at what turned out to be a very good guess as to where my eyes were. I was temporarily blinded, but his one remaining mechanical eye responded more efficiently, I guess, because now that he knew exactly where I was, he leapt, propelling himself through the air and knocking me down.

This time, both hands closed around my neck. I still outmassed Joshua and managed to roll us over, so he was on his back, and I was on top. I arched my spine and slammed my knee into his balls, hoping he'd release me . . .

. . . except, of course, he didn't have any balls; he only thought he did. *Damn!*

The hands were still closing around my gullet; despite the chill air, I felt myself sweating. But with his hands occupied, mine were free: I pushed my right hand onto his chest—startled by the feeling of artificial breasts there—and probed around until I found the slick, wet hole my first bullet had made. I hooked my right thumb into that hole, pulled sideways, and brought in my left thumb, as well, squeezing it down into the opening, ripping it wider and wider. I thought if I could get at the internal components, I might be able to tear out something crucial. The artificial flesh was soft, and there was a layer of what felt like foam rubber beneath it—and beneath that, I could feel hard metal parts. I tried to get my whole hand in, tried to yank out whatever I could, but I was fading fast. My pulse was thundering so loudly in my ears I couldn't hear anything else, just a *thump-thump-thumping,* over and over again, the *thump-thump-thumping* of . . .

Of footfalls! Someone was running this way, and—

And the scene lit up as flashlights came to bear on us.

"There they are!" said a high, mechanical voice that I recognized as belonging to the bootleg Pickover. "There they are!"

"NKPD!" shouted another voice I also recognized—a deep, Scottish brogue. "Let Lomax go!"

Joshua looked up. "Back off!" he shouted, in that female voice. "If you don't, I'll finish him."

Through blurring vision, I saw Mac say, "If you kill him, you'll go down for murder. You don't want that."

Joshua relaxed his grip a bit—not enough to let me escape, but enough to keep me alive as a hostage, at least a little while longer. I sucked in cold air, but my lungs still felt like they were on fire. In the illumination from the flashlights I could see Cassandra Wilkins's face craning now to look at McCrae. As I'd said, most transfers didn't show as much emotion as biologicals did, but it was clear that Joshua was panicking.

I was still on top. I thought if I waited until Joshua was distracted, I could yank free of his grip without him snapping my neck. "Let go of him," Mac said firmly. It was hard to see him; he was the one holding the light source, after all, but I suddenly became aware that he was also holding a large disk. "Release his neck, or I'll deactivate you for sure."

Joshua practically had to roll his one good eye up into his head to see Mac, standing behind him. "You ever use one of those before?" he said. "No, I know you haven't. I work in the transference business, and I know that technology just came out. The disruption isn't instantaneous. Yes, you can kill me—but not before I kill Lomax."

"You're lying," said McCrae. He handed his flashlight to Pickover, and brought the disk up in front of him, holding it vertically by its two U-shaped handles. "I've read the specs."

"Are you willing to take that chance?" asked Joshua.

I could only arch my neck a bit; it was very hard for me to look up and see Mac, but he seemed to be frowning, and,

after a second, he turned partially away. Pickover was standing behind him, and—

And suddenly an electric whine split the air, and Joshua
was convulsing beneath me, and his hands were squeezing
my throat even more tightly than before. The whine—a high,
keening sound—must have been coming from the disruptor.
I still had my hands inside Joshua's chest and could feel his
whole interior vibrating as his body continued to rack. I
yanked my hands out and grabbed onto his arms, pulling
with all my might. His hands popped free from my throat,
and his whole female form was shaking rapidly. I rolled off
him; the artificial body kept convulsing as the keening continued. I gasped for breath, and all I could think about for
several moments was getting air into me.

After my head cleared a bit, I looked again at Joshua,
who was still convulsing, and then I looked up at Mac, who
was banging on the side of the disruptor disk. Now that he'd
activated it, he apparently had no idea how to deactivate it.
As I watched, he started to turn it over, presumably hoping
there was some control he'd missed on the side he couldn't
see—and I realized that if he completed his move the disk
would be aimed backward, in the direction of Pickover.
Pickover clearly saw this, too: he was throwing his robot-like
arms up, as if to shield his face—not that that could possibly
do any good.

I tried to shout "No!," but my voice was too raw and all
that came out was a hoarse exhalation of breath, the sound
of which was lost beneath the keening. In my peripheral
vision, I could see Joshua lying face down. His vicious
spasms stopped as the beam from the disruptor was no longer aimed at him.

But even though I didn't have any voice left, Pickover
did, and his shout of *"Don't!"* was loud enough to be heard
over the electric whine of the disruptor. Mac continued to
rotate the disk a few more degrees before he realized what
Pickover was referring to. He flipped the disk back around,
then continued turning it until the emitter surface was facing straight down. And then he dropped it, and it fell in

Martian slo-mo, at last clanking against the deck plates, a counterpoint to the now-muffled electric whine. I hauled myself to my feet and moved over to check on Joshua while Pickover and Mac hovered over the disk, presumably looking for the off switch.

There were probably more scientific ways to see if the transferee Joshua was dead, but this one felt right just then: I balanced on one foot, hauled back the other leg, and kicked the son of a bitch in the side of that gorgeous head. The impact was strong enough to spin the whole body through a quarter turn, but there was no reaction at all from Joshua.

Suddenly the keening died, and I heard a self-satisfied *"There!"* from Mac. I looked over at him, and he looked back at me, caught in the beam from the flashlight Pickover was holding. Mac's bushy orange eyebrows were raised, and there was a sheepish grin on his face. "Who'd have thought the off switch had to be pulled out instead of pushed in?"

I tried to speak and found I did have a little voice now. "Thanks for coming by, Mac. I know how you hate to leave the station."

Mac nodded in Pickover's direction. "Yeah, well, you can thank this guy for putting in the call," he said. He turned, and faced Pickover full-on. "Just who the hell are you, anyway?"

I saw Pickover's mouth begin to open in his mechanical head, and a thought rushed through my mind. This Pickover was bootleg. Both the other Pickover and Joshua Wilkins had been correct: such a being shouldn't exist and had no rights. Indeed, the legal Pickover would doubtless continue to demand that this version be destroyed; no one wanted an unauthorized copy of himself wandering around.

Mac was looking away from me and toward the duplicate of Pickover. And so I made a wide sweeping of my head, left to right, then back again. Pickover apparently saw it because he closed his mouth before sounds came out, and I spoke as loudly and clearly as I could in my current condition. "Let me do the introductions," I said, and I waited for Mac to turn back toward me.

When he had, I pointed at Mac. "Detective Dougal Mc-Crae," I said, then I took a deep breath, let it out slowly, and pointed at Pickover, "I'd like you to meet Joshua Wilkins."

Mac nodded, accepting this. "So you found your man? Congratulations, Alex." He then looked down at the motionless female body. "Too bad about your wife, Mr. Wilkins."

Pickover turned to face me, clearly seeking guidance. "It's so sad," I said quickly. "She was insane, Mac—had been threatening to kill her poor husband Joshua here for weeks. He decided to fake his own death to escape her, but she got wise to it somehow and hunted him down. I had no choice but to try to stop her."

As if on cue, Pickover walked over to the dead artificial body and crouched beside it. "My poor dear wife," he said, somehow managing to make his mechanical voice sound tender. He lifted his skinless face toward Mac. "This planet does that to people, you know. Makes them go crazy." He shook his head. "So many dreams dashed."

Mac looked at me, then at Pickover, then at the artificial body lying on the deck plating, then back at me. "All right, Alex," he said, nodding slowly. "Good work."

I tipped my nonexistent hat at him. "Glad to be of help."

. . . .

Three days later, I walked into the dark interior of The Bent Chisel, whistling.

Buttrick was behind the bar, as usual. "You again, Lomax?"

"The one and only," I replied cheerfully. Diana was standing in her topless splendor next to the bar, loading up her tray. "Hey, Diana," I said, "when you get off tonight, how 'bout you and me go out and paint the town . . ." I trailed off: the town was *already* red; the whole damned planet was.

Diana's face lit up, but Buttrick raised a beefy hand. "Not so fast, lover boy. If you've got the money to take her out, you've got the money to settle your tab."

I slapped two golden hundred-solar coins on the countertop. "That should cover it." Buttrick's eyes went as round as the coins, and he scooped them up immediately, as if he were afraid they'd disappear—which, in this joint, they probably would.

"I'll be in the booth in the back," I said to Diana. "I'm expecting Juan; when he arrives, could you bring him over?"

Diana smiled. "Sure thing, Alex. Meanwhile, what can I get you? Your usual poison?"

I shook my head. "Nah, none of that rotgut. Bring me the best Scotch you've got—and pour it over *water* ice."

Buttrick narrowed his eyes. "That'll cost extra."

"No problem," I said. "Start up a new tab for me."

A few minutes later, Diana came by the booth with my drink, accompanied by Juan Santos. He was looking at her with his usual puppy-dog-love eyes. "What can I get for you?" Diana asked him.

He hesitated—it was clear to me, at least, what he wanted—but then he tipped his massive forehead forward. "Gin neat."

She nodded and departed, and he watched her go. Then he slid down into the seat opposite me. "This better be on you, Alex. You still owe me for the help I gave you at Dr. Pickover's place."

"Indeed it is, my friend."

Juan rested his receding chin on his open palm. "You seem in a good mood."

"Oh, I am," I said. "I got paid."

The man the world now accepted as Joshua Wilkins had returned to NewYou, where he'd gotten his face finished and his artificial body upgraded. After that, he told people it was too painful to continue to work there, given what had happened with his wife. So he sold the NewYou franchise to his associate, Horatio Fernandez. The money from the sale gave him plenty to live on, especially now that he didn't need food and didn't have to pay the life-support tax anymore. He gave me all the fees his dear departed wife should have—plus a healthy bonus.

I'd asked him what he was going to do now. "Well," he said, "even if you're the only one who knows it, I'm still a paleontologist. I'm going to look for new fossil beds—I intend to spend months out on the surface. Who knows? Maybe there's another deposit out there even better than the Alpha."

And what about the other Pickover—the official one? It took some doing, but I managed to convince him that it had actually been the late Cassandra, not Joshua, who had stolen a copy of his mind, and that she was the one who had installed it in an artificial body. I told Dr. Pickover that when Joshua discovered what his wife had done, he destroyed the bootleg and dumped the ruined body that had housed it in the basement of the NewYou building.

Not too shabby, eh? Still, I'd wanted more. I'd rented a surface suit and a Mars buggy and headed out to 16.4 kilometers south-southwest of Nili Patera. I figured I'd pick myself up a lovely rhizomorph or a nifty pentapod, and never have to work again.

Well, I'd looked and looked and looked, but I guess the duplicate Pickover had lied about where the Alpha Deposit was; even under torture, he hadn't betrayed his beloved fossils. I'm sure Weingarten and O'Reilly's source is out there somewhere, though, and the legal Pickover is doubtless hard at work thinking of ways to protect it from looters. I wish him luck.

"How about a toast?" suggested Juan, once Diana had brought him his booze.

"I'm game," I said. "To what?"

Juan frowned, considering. Then his eyebrows climbed his broad forehead, and he replied, "To being true to your innermost self."

We clinked glasses. "I'll drink to that."

ELEVEN

TWO MONTHS LATER

I had my feet up on the desk when a camera window popped open on my monitor. The guy on my screen had obviously pushed the doorbell—that's what activated the camera—but had then turned around. New clients rarely showed up without booking an appointment first, so I reached for my trusty Smith & Wesson, swung my feet to the floor, and aimed the gun at the sliding door. "Intercom," I said into the air, then: "Yes? Who are you?"

The jamoke looked back at the camera—and I saw that half his face was dull metal with only traces of artificial pinkish beige skin still attached. But the voice! I recognized that cultured British accent at once. "Good afternoon, Mr. Lomax. I wonder if I might have a word?"

I placed the gun on the desk and said, "Open." The door slid aside, revealing the transfer in the—well, not the *flesh*. "Jesus, Rory," I said. "What happened to you?"

There was movement on the surface of the metal forehead—little motors that would have lifted eyebrows had they still been there, I supposed. "What? Oh. Yes. I need to get this fixed."

"Get into a bar fight?" I thought maybe the old broken-beer-bottle-in-the-kisser routine could slice through plastiskin.

"Me?" he replied, as if astonished by the notion. "No, of course not." He extended his right hand. "It's good to see you again, Alex." His handshake—controlled by the artificial body's computer—was perfect: just the right pressure and duration.

With the skin half blasted away, his face looked almost as robotic as that of the unauthorized copy of him I'd rescued from the *Skookum Jim*. I went back to my seat and motioned to the client chair. Pickover was carrying a boxy metal case with a thick handle attached to the lid. He placed it on my threadbare carpet then sat.

"What can I do for you?" I asked.

"I'm hoping to engage your services, old boy."

"You want me to get whoever did that to you?" I said, making a circular motion with my outstretched hand to indicate his damaged face. "A little revenge?"

"It's not that. Or, at least, it's not *precisely* that."

"What, then?"

Pickover rose and effortlessly picked up the metal case he'd just put down. "May I?" he said, gesturing with his free hand at my desk. I nodded, and he placed the box on the surface—and from the thud it made, the thing must have weighed fifty kilos. Memo to self: never arm-wrestle a transfer.

He unlatched the box, and I stood to survey its contents. The interior was lined with blue foam-rubber pyramids, and sitting inside was a hunk of gray rock, half a meter at its widest and shaped vaguely like Australia. Although it was mostly flat, there were five indentations in its surface. "What's that?" I asked.

"The counter slab to two-dash-thirteen-eighty-eight."

"Counter slab?"

"The negative to a positive; the other side. If you split rock that has a fossil within, there's the actual fossil—a shell, say—on one side, and there's a negative image, or mold, of the same thing on the other side. The part with the fossil is the slab; the other part is the counter slab. Collectors sometimes take the former and discard the latter, although a real paleontologist sees value in both."

"And two-dash-whatever?"

"The prefix two denotes O'Reilly and Weingarten's second expedition, and thirteen-eighty-eight is the catalog number of the type specimen of *Noachiana oreillii*—a kind of pentapod—that's now in the Royal Ontario Museum back on Earth. This is the other part of that piece of matrix; I know the slab like—well, like the back of the hand I originally had."

"Ah," I said.

"I knew I'd found a rich bed of fossils—but, of course, there might be several of those; there was no reason to think that what I'd discovered actually was Weingarten and O'Reilly's Alpha Deposit. Until I found this counter slab, that is—that's proof that I'm actually working the Alpha."

"Fair enough," I replied. "But what's that got to do with you getting your face blown off?"

Pickover reached into the box and lifted the counter slab about half a meter using both hands—I doubt it required the strength of both, but he was likely being careful with the specimen. He set it down and then removed a large square of bubble wrap. With it gone, I could see what was at the bottom of the box: a flat metal disk about forty centimeters in diameter and six centimeters thick. The device was broken open, its mechanical guts gummed up by Martian sand—but there was no mistaking what it was: a land mine.

"Holy crap," I said.

"Exactly," replied Pickover. "Someone booby-trapped the Alpha."

I gestured at Pickover's damaged face. "I take it there's more than one land mine, then?"

"Unfortunately, yes. One of those damn things went off near me. If I'd been right on top of it, it would have blown me to—and here's a word I've never had cause to use hitherto in my life—smithereens."

That's the difference between Pickover and me: I'd never once used "hitherto," but "smithereens" came up often in my line of work. He went on. "As is, it took out a wonderful specimen of *Shostakia* I'd been working on."

"What set the mine off?"

"I was jackhammering a few meters away to remove a piece of matrix, completely unaware of the mine buried under the sand. The vibrations from the hammer must have triggered it."

I frowned. The New Klondike Police Department wouldn't care about this. Keeping order—more or less—under the dome was all that mattered to them; what happened outside it interested Mac and his crew about as much as the opera did. Still, I said, "Have you spoken to the NKPD?"

If he'd had a nose left, Pickover might have wrinkled it in disgust. "I can't involve that lot. I'd have to show them where the Alpha is, and they're corrupt. And so I came to you."

Process of elimination; one way to get work. "Thanks. But what's the mystery, then? Surely it was Weingarten and O'Reilly who planted the land mines, no? After all, if they were leaving Mars for an extended period—"

"—they might want to protect their find," Pickover said, finishing for me. "That's what I thought at first—and certainly this thing has been in the ground for a long time." He'd already set the counter slab on my desktop, and he now reached into the metal box and pulled out the ruined land mine. "But I searched to see who had manufactured this device." He pointed to some incised markings on the disk's perimeter. "Of course, it wasn't *sold* as a land mine; those are illegal. It's described as a mining explosive that just happens to have a pressure-sensitive trigger switch; it could also be detonated by remote control, by a coded radio signal. Anyway, this was made by a company in Malaysia called Brisance Industries. The particular model is the Caldera-7, and the Caldera-7 was introduced eighteen months *after* O'Reilly and Weingarten were killed. No way it was part of the supplies brought along on any of their expeditions here."

"Then who booby-trapped the Alpha?"

"Ah! That's the question, isn't it? O'Reilly and Weingarten were killed at the end of their third voyage. They'd gone on their first voyage alone—just the two of them, two crazy adventurers thumbing their noses at all the moribund government space agencies by coming here on their own. It was on that first voyage that they'd stumbled on the Alpha. But working a dig is hard; it takes a lot of effort. And so on their second voyage, they brought an extra man with them, Willem Van Dyke. But once the second expedition got back to Earth, Weingarten and O'Reilly ripped Van Dyke off, giving him only a fraction of the proceeds from selling the fossils they'd collected."

"What about the third expedition?"

"The relationship with Willem Van Dyke was irreparably soured. Weingarten and O'Reilly didn't take anyone else along on the third."

"Ah," I said. "But obviously this Van Dyke knew where the Alpha was. You think he returned at some later point and placed land mines around the site?"

"He must have. After Weingarten and O'Reilly were killed, he was the only one left alive who knew the location of the Alpha. But the trail on him goes cold thirty-six years ago. He's had no public presence in all that time."

I went to fix myself a drink at the small wet bar on the wall opposite my tiny window. I didn't bother to offer Pickover one, although if I'd had an oil can, I might have told him to help himself to a squirt. "And so you want me to find Willem Van Dyke?"

"Exactly. Van Dyke may well know what happened to the specimens from the second expedition—which private collectors they were sold to. And when he later came back to Mars on his own, he might have worked the Alpha Deposit, at least some, and shipped more specimens back to collectors on Earth. I want to find those collectors and convince them to let me properly describe their specimens in the scientific literature. I'll never get the fossils *from* them; I understand that. They belong in public museums, but I know that's a lost cause. But perhaps I can at least do science on them, if I can find whoever the fossils were sold to. And the path to them begins with Willem Van Dyke."

"But you say he dropped out of sight thirty-six years ago? Hard to pick up the scent at this late date."

"True," said Pickover. "But the land mines provide a new clue, no?" He looked at me: two very human eyes set in that ravaged face. "Still, I guess it *is* what people in your profession call a cold case."

I thought about quipping, "They're all cold cases on Mars," but that wasn't up to my usual standard of repartee so I kept my yap shut. Still, it wasn't like I had any other work, and a cold case was win-win: if I didn't solve it, no one could blame me, and if I did, well, even better. "As you know, my fee is three hundred solars an hour, plus expenses." That was the same as I'd charged him the last time; it was a hundred more than what I'd quoted the transfer I'd thought was Cassandra Wilkins, but I have a soft spot for damsels in distress.

Pickover didn't look happy. Then again, with his current face, he probably *couldn't* look happy. "Deal," he said. "When can you begin?"

"Not so fast. There's one more thing."

"Yes?"

"I need to examine the evidence, as you paleontologists would say, *in situ.*"

"You want to see the Alpha Deposit?"

"Can't do the job otherwise."

Pickover looked at me the way Gollum would have if you'd asked to try on his ring. "But I have to protect those fossils."

"Don't you trust me?" I said, batting my baby blues.

"I was going to say—and you'll forgive me—'about as far as I can throw you,' but given how low Martian gravity is and how strong I am now, that's pretty darn far." He was quiet for a time, and I let him be so. "But, yes, I suppose I *do* trust you."

To which my inner voice said, "Idiot"—but my outer voice said, "Thanks."

"You do understand how precious the fossils out there are?" he asked. "To science, I mean?"

"Oh, yes," I replied. "They're invaluable." And I, at least, could still flash a killer smile. "To science, I mean."

TWELVE

After Dr. Pickover left my office, I settled in for some research. I started by confirming what he'd told me. He was right about the land-mine model, and that it had been made in Malaysia. I'd been to a lot of places on good old Mother Earth before I—*ahem*—had to leave, but that wasn't one of them.

I found a useful site that gave instructions for disarming Caldera-7 mines, and I took note of the procedure. In the exact center of each circular disk, there was a hole three centimeters in diameter. Pushing a probe into that would depress the disarm switch; pressure anywhere else on the surface would blow the mine up.

I had been hoping to somehow gain access to Brisance's customer database; I thought maybe Juan Santos could hack into it for me. One *could* access Earth computer networks from Mars, but the time lag varied from three minutes to twenty-two when we had line of sight to Earth, and was even longer at conjunction, when the signal had to be relayed behind the sun. Hacking that way would have driven Juan crazy, so he'd have probably farmed the work out to some Earthside black hat. But Brisance had gone out of business eleven years ago, and, given the kind of equipment it had made, I suspected all its customer records had been wiped back then.

And, anyway, they might not have sold direct to consumer. Indeed, the land mines might have been purchased here on Mars. Judging by the dilapidated condition of the mine Rory had brought to my office, it'd been in the ground a long time. So many Martian businesses had gone bankrupt, though, that I didn't hold out much hope for finding out who might have bought anything decades ago. But it was the best lead I had, and so I headed into the center of the dome and dropped in on New Klondike's Finest to see if they had any records of busting someone for selling land mines here.

Sergeant Huxley was behind his long red counter when I came in, and I did the tip-of-the-hat thing in his general direction. "Well, well, well, Hux, fancy meeting you here!"

"Ain't my lucky day," Hux said. "Seeing you."

"No sirree," I replied. "Your lucky day would be one on which flabby came back into style."

"And yours," said Hux, for once rising to the occasion, "would be one on which people decided that beady eyes look good on anything other than a weasel."

"Hey," I said, "my eyes are private. Says so right on my business card."

"You're a dick," Huxley said.

"In the nonvulgar sense. But you're one in the other sense."

I'd literally seen gears move in Pickover's head earlier today; here, I only got to figuratively watch them as Huxley tried to process this. Finally, he came back with, "Gumshoe."

"Flatfoot."

"Shamus."

"Pig."

"Gunsel."

I was surprised he knew that one—and I wondered if he knew both its meanings. If he did, my next jab would have to be even harsher. While I was phrasing my reply, Mac came in the front door of the station. I turned to him. "Why, Mac! You actually went outside?"

He smiled. "Well, no. I'm arriving at work for the first time today. My daughter had an appointment with the pediatrician."

"P.D. attrition?" I said, raising my eyebrows. "You mean the police department might actually lose old Huxley here at some point?" This one played better in my head than spoken aloud, and they both just looked at me. Crickets were one of the few Earth bugs that *hadn't* made it to Mars, which was probably the only reason I didn't hear any chirping just then. I cleared my throat. "Anyway, Mac, can I talk with you?"

"Surrrre," he said, his brogue rolling the *R*. He nodded at Hux, and the sergeant pushed the button that slid the black inner door open. Mac and I walked down the narrow corridor to his office, and we took chairs on opposite sides of his desk; the desktop looked like polished wood, but was fake, of course—either that, or Mac was even more corrupt than Pickover thought.

"What can I do for you, Alex?"

I fished out my tab and showed him a picture I'd taken of the Caldera-7 Pickover had brought in. "A client of mine came across one of these on the claim he was working. It's a land mine."

Mac squinted at the image. "Looks more like it *was* a land mine. How old is that thing?"

"Might date right back to near the beginning of the Great Martian Fossil Rush. Anybody ever sell devices like this here on Mars? It was officially marketed as a mining explosive."

"Well, not openly, that's for sure. But let me check." He spoke to his computer, asking it to display all records in the police database about land mines or mining explosives. "Bunch of accident reports involving explosives," he said, reading from his monitor, "but nothing of—no, wait a sec. This one's sorta interesting. Copy to wall." The wall opposite the door, which had been showing the green Scottish countryside, changed to a blowup of the report Mac had on his own monitor.

"Thirty years ago, just after the dome went up," said Mac. "Ship arrived here bringing a load of stampeders in hibernation, plus their supplies. Cargo was being offloaded, but one of the carrying cases had become damaged in transit—wasn't anchored properly in the hold, I guess. The worker who'd been unloading the ship could see inside, and recognized the objects within as land mines." Mac pointed at the wall, and a portion of an image expanded, showing a flat disk like the one Pickover had brought to my office, but in pristine condition. "Same kind of device, right?"

I nodded.

"It was in one of the last cases offloaded from the ship," Mac said. "All of the other cargo had been collected by that point. Could well have been more of the same kind of mines in other cases, but no way to tell—and no record of who collected them. And, of course, no one ever claimed the three mines that had been found."

I nodded. "What's the status of that ship?"

He made motions in the air, and the wall changed to show the answer. "The *B. Traven,*" he said. "Decommissioned in—no, check that. It's still in service, but under a new name, the *Kathryn Denning.* Owned and operated by InnerSystem Lines, a division of Slapcoff Interplanetary."

The ship's original name rang a faint bell, but I couldn't place it. "Can I get a list of who was on it when it arrived with the land mines?"

I expected Mac to want his palm greased, but he was in a generous mood; I guess his daughter's appointment had gone well. "Sure." He gestured at the wall some more, and a passenger manifest appeared.

I scanned the names, checking under V and D, and even W, for a Willem Van Dyke, but none was listed. Well, this clown hardly would have been the first person to come to Mars under an alias. "How many names are there?" I asked.

"One hundred and thirty-two," Mac's computer said helpfully; it always amused me that it had a brogue as thick as Mac's own.

"How many males?"

"Seventy-one."

"Can you download the full list into my tab—males and females?" I said to Mac.

He spoke a command to his computer, and it was done.

A gender change was possible, of course, but Rory himself would doubtless tell me that the simplest hypothesis was preferable, so I'd start by assuming there were only seventy-one suspects—if one could apply the word "only" to so many. I had my work cut out for me.

THIRTEEN

I'd returned to my office and was leaning back in my chair, feet once more up on my desk. Since I wasn't expecting anyone, I had my shoes and socks off, letting the dogs air out. I'd copied the seventy-one male names from the *B. Traven*'s passenger manifest onto my wall monitor, replacing my usual wallpaper, which looked like, well, wallpaper—alternating forest green and caramel stripes, like in the house Wanda and I had lived in all those years ago back in Detroit. It'd be too much to have a picture of her on display, but the pattern subtly reminded me of her, and I liked having it in my peripheral vision.

No distinction was made between biologicals and transfers on the passenger manifest, but the *B. Traven* had completed this voyage back when uploading into an artificial body cost, as the saying goes, the Earth. Anyone who could afford to transfer back then wouldn't have been rushing to Mars to try to make a fortune; he or she already *had* one. So it was a safe bet that all these men had been flesh and blood.

In the intervening years, thirty-two had gone back to Earth, and thirteen others had died; neither condition exonerated them from really being Willem Van Dyke, but it did make it hard to question them in the former case and impossible in the latter. And so I started with the twenty-six who were still here. One name immediately leapt out at me: Stuart Berling; I'd interviewed him during the Wilkins case. He was the full-time fossil hunter who had transferred the same day Joshua Wilkins supposedly had—the guy who'd opted to have his new face look like holovid star Krikor Ajemian. I'd told him I worked for NewYou's head office when I'd questioned him then; he'd been the first transfer to pass my patented where-do-you-keep-your-screwdrivers game—the Turning Test, if you will.

I decided to start by speaking to him, so I put my footwear back on. When I'd been a kid, I'd thought "gumshoe" referred to getting chewing gum stuck to the bottom of your shoe because you'd been skulking in unsavory neighborhoods; it actually refers to the soft-soled shoes favored by those in my line of work, because they make it easier to follow people without being heard. My pair was taupe, a color name I'd learned from the box the shoes had come in.

I opened my office door, hoofed it to the hovertram stop, rode over to Third Avenue and Seventh Circle, went over to Berling's redstone, pressed the illuminated door buzzer, and—

And *wow*.

"Why, it's—it's Mr. Lomax, isn't it?" said the voice from the perfect bee-stung lips on the flawless heart-shaped face.

I blinked. "Lacie, is—is that you?"

She smiled, showing teeth as white as the polar caps. "Guilty."

Berling's wife had been a plain Jane who'd looked every one of her sixty-odd years when I'd last seen her. But, well, if he was going to upload into a beefcake holo star's likeness, it did make sense that she'd opt for this. My fondness for old 2D movies made me think first of Vivien Leigh, but I'd be surprised if there were more than three people under the dome who knew who she had been. It came to me that Lacie's new face—and her supernova-hot body—had been patterned after that of Kayla Filina, who had starred as

Brigid O'Shaughnessy in last year's horrid remake of *The Maltese Falcon*.

"You look stunning," I said.

Lacie spun around, a perfect gyroscopically balanced pirouette. "Don't I, though?" she replied, flashing her pearly whites again. "Won't you come in?"

She stepped aside, I crossed into the townhouse, and the door slid shut behind me. "Is your husband home?" I asked. As before, the living room was filled with worktables covered with hunks of reddish rock.

"No. He's outside the dome, working his claim." She smiled broadly. "He won't be back for *hours.*"

"Ah. I was hoping to ask him some questions."

She was wearing a light blue dress that could have been painted on—and perhaps was. Its plunging neckline revealed the tops of two large perfect breasts. "What about me?" she said, placing exquisite hands on rounded hips. "You work for NewYou, right? Quality assurance? Well, I just transferred. Don't you have some questions for me?"

I had thought I'd have to come clean with Berling to get answers about his trip out from Earth on the *B. Traven* all those mears ago, but one doesn't blow a good cover unnecessarily. "I can see," I said, "that we did a magnificent job."

She tipped her head down, appraising her own body. "Oh, it looks great. Exactly what I was hoping for. But I do want to be sure that everything is functioning properly." She looked back up at me, aquamarine eyes beneath long dark lashes. "You know, while the work is still under warranty."

"Surely you and Mr. Berling have, um, tested things out."

"Yes, yes, of course—but he transferred first. I haven't yet had an opportunity to, ah, put this new body through its paces with a biological." She lifted her perfect eyebrows, and her forehead didn't crease at all as she did so. "It's like I'm a virgin again."

It's at moments like this that a man's morals are truly tested, and I asked myself the question that needed asking: could I actually bill Pickover for the time I spent making love with Lacie?

She took my hand, and I let her lead me to the bedroom. If you keep in good shape, sex on Mars is amazing, thanks to the low gravity. Zero-g, I'm told, is no fun: it's too easy to send your partner spinning across the room. But a third of a gee—well, that's just perfect. You can do acrobatics that put Earth-based porn stars to shame. And it's even better if, as Berling and his wife did, you have some handles mounted on the ceiling above the bed.

This wasn't my first time with a transfer, but Lacie was the best-looking one I'd ever been with, and she was a *very* generous lover. I'd heard it said that among biologicals, beautiful women got cheated on more often than plain ones, because the plain ones did all the things to keep their partners happy that the beauties wouldn't. Lacie still had the mind of someone who had had to work to interest men—and the body of someone who could have anyone she wanted. It was a very appealing combination.

When we were done—and it *was* a good thing that Berling was gone for hours—I had a sonic shower, and she buffed her plastic skin with a chamois.

I couldn't question her about Berling's arrival on Mars without telling her I wasn't with NewYou. I doubted she'd really be upset, but given that she might be able to pull my head off, I didn't want to risk it. Instead, I simply asked her to have him give me a call when he got home. But just as I was leaving, he called her. I stood out of view and listened. He'd had a good day out by the Reinhardt dunes, he said, and was heading to Ernie Gargalian's fossil dealership to sell his finds. I hadn't seen Gargantuan Gargalian for a few weeks, and so I made my way over there to intercept Berling; it was more seemly, I thought, to question him somewhere other than where I'd just banged his wife.

The sun was setting over Syrtis Major way, and the sky was growing dim. But Ye Olde Fossil Shoppe stayed open after dark every night: that's when the prospectors came back inside with their booty, and many wanted to sell immediately rather than storing fossils overnight in their homes and inviting thieves to come get them.

The walk over was pleasant—and not just because I was still grinning from my encounter with the now-lovely Lacie. Walking on Mars was virtually effortless, as long as you didn't have to wear a surface suit.

Ernie's shop was in the center of town near NKPD head-quarters, which said a lot about who was really in charge here. "Mr. Double-X!" he proclaimed with his usual precise enunciation as I entered. "To what do I owe the pleasure?"

Ernie Gargalian was sixty-five and hugely fat, with man boobs that were only perky thanks to Mars's low gravity. His thinning silver hair was slicked straight back from his forehead, and his pale face had been puffed out enough to fill in most of the wrinkles. His brown eyes were close to-gether and deeply set.

"Hey, Ernie," I said. "Has Stuart Berling been in yet?"

"Today? No. I haven't seen him all week."

"Well, he's on his way here. Mind if I wait?"

Gargantuan spread his giant arms, encompassing his showroom. "Fossils are fragile things, Alex. I don't want any rough stuff in the shop."

"Never fear, Ernie, never fear. Besides, Berling has transferred—and I'm not fool enough to get into a fistfight with someone who's presumably had mods for surface work."

"Oh, right," said Gargalian. "He's got that actor's face now, doesn't he? I don't hold with that." He made a circular motion in front of his own round visage. "If I were ever to transfer, I'd want to go on looking exactly as I always have. You aren't the same person if you change your appearance."

Ernie liked to call me "Mr. Double-X" because both my names ended in that letter, but he'd need an artificial body in Triple-X at least, and I doubted such things were stock items. But I didn't say that aloud; some jokes are best kept to yourself, I'd learned—after two broken noses.

A prospector came in, a woman in her thirties, biological, pulling a surface wagon with big springy wheels. Little wag-ons on Earth were traditionally red—I'd had one such my-self as a kid—but they tended to get lost outside here if they were painted that color. This one was fluorescent green, and it was overflowing with gray and pink hunks of rock, including one on top that I recognized, thanks to Pickover's little lesson, as a counter slab.

Our town's name harked back to the Great Klondike Gold Rush, but at the end of a good day those stampeders had carried their bounty of dust in small pokes. Fossil matrix was bulky; extracting and preparing the specimens was part of what Ernie and his staff did for their thirty-five percent of every transaction they brokered for prospectors with Earth-based collectors. It was much too expensive to ship rock to Earth that was going to be thrown away there. The tailings were discarded outside our dome; there was a small mountain of them to the east.

Ernie went to tend to the female prospector, and I looked around the shop. The fossils on display were worth millions, but they were being watched by ubiquitous cameras, and, besides, no one would try to steal from Gargantuan Gargalian, if they knew what was good for them. Ernie was one of the richest men on Mars, and he had on retainer lots of muscle to help guard that wealth. On Earth, a multimillionaire might own a mansion, a yacht, and a private jet. There was no point in owning a yacht on Mars, but Ernie certainly had the big house—I'd seen it from the outside, and the damn thing had turrets, for God's sake—and he had the airplane, too, with an impossibly wide wingspan; it was one of only four planes I knew of here on the Red Planet.

There was a chart on one of Ernie's walls: side-by-side geologic timelines for Earth and Mars. Both planets were 4.5 billion Earth years old, of course, but their stories had been very different. Earth's prehistory was broadly divided into Precambrian, Paleozoic, Mesozoic, and Cenozoic eras—and I knew a few were pushing for a new era, the Transzoic, to have begun the year Howard Slapcoff had perfected the uploading of consciousness. But on a meter-high chart, that slice wouldn't have been thick enough to see without one of the microscopes that dotted Ernie's shop.

Martian prehistory, meanwhile, was divided into the Noachian, Hesperian, and Amazonian eras, each named, the chart helpfully explained, for a locale on Mars where rocks characteristic of it were found (and yes, ironically for a time scale that stretched back billions of years, the place that gave us the term Noachian had been named by Schiaparelli in honor of Noah's flood).

Both worlds developed life as soon as they'd cooled enough to allow it—some four billion Earth years ago. But Earth life just twiddled its—well, its *nothings*—for the next three and a half billion years; it was mostly unicellular and microscopic until the dawn of the Paleozoic, 570 million years ago.

But Mars produced complex, macroscopic invertebrates with exoskeletons within only a hundred million years. All of the fossils collected here dated from the Noachian, which covered the first billion years. By the time multicellular creatures appeared on Earth, life on Mars had been extinct for hundreds of millions of years: two ships that didn't quite pass in the cosmic night . . .

Ernie and the woman were exchanging words. "Surely these are worth more than that!" she declared.

"My sincerest apologies, dear lady," he replied, "but *Longipes bedrossiani* is the most common of finds; they were everywhere. And see here? The glabella is missing. And on this one, there are only three intact limbs—not much of a pentapod!"

They went back and forth like that a while longer, but she eventually agreed to the price he was offering. He gave her a receipt, and she left, muttering to herself.

Since Berling hadn't yet shown up, I took the opportunity to ask Ernie a question. "So," I said, doing my best to sound nonchalant, "do you think anyone will ever rediscover the Alpha Deposit?"

Ernie's eyes, already mostly lost in his fleshy face, narrowed even further. "Why do you ask?"

"Just idle curiosity."

"You, Mr. Double-X, are curious about women. You are curious about liquor. You are curious about sports. You are *not* curious about fossils."

"But I *am* intrigued by money."

"True. And, to answer your question, I doubt it'll happen

anytime soon. In an unguarded moment many years ago, after perhaps one too many glasses of port, Denny O'Reilly said to me that the Alpha was only the size of a football field—an Earth one, that is."

"But why hasn't anyone else found it yet? I mean, it *has* been twenty mears."

"All we know is that it's somewhere here in Isidis Planitia—and Isidis Planitia is the flat bottom of the remains of a giant impact crater fifteen hundred kilometers in diameter. It's as big as Hudson Bay on Earth; you could fit over three hundred million football fields in it. Even with all the stampeders who've come here, there are still huge tracts of the plain that no one has ever set foot upon, my boy. Hell, no one's even found *Beagle 2,* and that presumably isn't even buried."

"Beagle 2?" I said.

"A British Mars probe. It was supposed to touch down on Isidis Planitia in 2003, but no signal was ever picked up from it."

"Is it worth something?"

"Sure, to a space buff, assuming it's not smashed to bits. I'd be glad to find a buyer for the wreckage, if someone brought it in."

"Maybe I should look for it. I was never any good at spotting fossils, but wreckage—that's something I understand."

"By Gad, you might make a decent sideline of it, at that," said Ernie. "There's even bigger salvage out there."

"Oh?"

"Tons of it. Denny and Simon landed on Mars in two-stage ships, like the old *Apollo* lunar modules, but much bigger. Each had a lower descent stage and an upper ascent stage. Unlike the old lunar modules, though, both stages were habitable. Anyway, the ascent stages are gone, of course—they all flew back to Earth. Two of them did indeed sell to collectors—the first crewed ships that had gone to Mars, after all! The third burned up on re-entry, as I'm sure you know."

"Yeah. What happened to the descent stages?"

"Two of three have been accounted for. You may have seen the original one. It's still out there on the planitia, where they first landed—although it's just a skeleton now; looters have taken all the good parts. The fact that it's here in Isidis is how we know the Alpha must be somewhere around here—Denny and Simon, of course, never said where it was. But it could be—and probably is—many hundreds of kilometers from that original landing site. They had Mars buggies on that mission that had a thousand-kilometer range."

"And the descent stage from the second expedition?" I asked.

"They crashed it in Aeolis Mensae."

"That's a long way from here."

"Exactly. See, Denny and Simon used *in situ* fuel production; they made their rocket propellant here from local material. Not only did they fill the ascent stage's fuel tanks here, but they reloaded the descent stage's tanks, at least in part, as well. After the ascent stage took off to bring them home—it had been perched atop the descent stage—they had the computer in the descent stage fire its engine and fly horizontally as far as the fuel would take it, just to disguise the location of where it had originally touched down. As I said, the first lander didn't necessarily touch down near where the Alpha was located. But the second lander had presumably been set down right by the Alpha, to serve as a base station while they mined it."

I nodded. "So they had to move it."

"Precisely."

"And the descent stage from the third mission?"

"God only knows what they did with it. But if it's intact, it would definitely be worth something."

Just then, Stuart Berling entered the shop. He had a memorable face now, but I guess I didn't, at least to him, because although his wife had recognized me at once, he didn't seem to know me at all. Oh, he looked at me suspiciously, but it seemed just typical prospector paranoia. The woman who'd been here earlier had glared at me the same way; no fossil hunter wanted another to know where his or her bounty had been found.

"Mr. Berling," I said, extending a hand that had recently been touching his wife's perfect new body. "What a pleasant surprise."

"Do I know you?"

"Alexander Lomax. I visited you at your home and asked you about your satisfaction with your transference."

Ernie was looking on in quiet amusement but said nothing.

"Oh," said Berling. "Right."

"I'd like to ask you some questions on another topic, if I may?"

"I told you I was happy with the work NewYou did. We really don't have anything else to discuss—and I've got business with Mr. Gargalian here."

"I'll gladly wait."

His brows drew together. "There's something fishy about you, Lomax."

This from a guy who was wearing somebody else's face. "Not at all," I said. "I'm just a contract researcher. I did some work for NewYou, and now I'm doing some for the New Klondike Historical Society." I didn't actually know if such a thing existed, but I figured it sounded plausible.

"About what?"

"I understand you came here early on, aboard a ship that was called the *B. Traven,* and—"

He lunged at me. I deked sideways, and he went sailing past, crashing into one of Ernie's worktables and tilting it backward a bit. A slab of rock slid toward the edge and started falling in Martian slo-mo. But Gargantuan Gargalian, moving with surprising speed for a man of his bulk, caught it before it hit the floor. "Stop it!" he demanded as he placed the fossil back on the table, which had now righted itself.

It wouldn't be much use, but I whipped out my gun anyway and pointed it at Berling—who, in turn, was pointing an artificial arm at me. "He started it!" Berling barked.

"What?" I said. "What did I do?"

Berling glared at me with the best approximation of rage his movie-star mask could muster. "How dare you bring that up? Damn you, how *dare* you?" His fists were balled, but they were rock-steady as he held them down by his hips; I guess transfers didn't quake when they were furious.

Even Ernie was on his side now. "You should know better than to mention the *Traven* to a survivor, Alex. I think you should leave."

I looked at them: the dashingly handsome transfer and the old fat biological. They both had expressions normally reserved for those who'd caught someone farting in an airlock. I holstered my gun and headed outside.

FOURTEEN

During the day, all sorts of people walked New Klondike's streets, although even more took hovertrams. But at night, decent folk mostly stayed indoors, especially as you got farther out toward the rim. Of course, I wasn't decent folk. There were hookers plying their trade and teenage hoods—the kids of failed stampeders who had nothing much to live for—hanging around, looking for anything to relieve their boredom, and if that happened to be rolling a drunk or breaking into a shop, so much the better.

Still, I didn't expect any trouble as I headed along Fourth Avenue toward my 11:00 p.m. date with Diana. After all, a good percentage of the lowlifes in town knew me on sight—and knew to avoid me. And even those who didn't know me could hardly assume I'd be an easy mark: I was muscular in the way most Martians weren't. But as I crossed the Third Circle, I was accosted by a tough-looking punk: biological, male, maybe eighteen years old, wearing a black T-shirt, with an animated tattoo of a snake with a rattling tail on his left cheek. "Gimme your money," he said.

"And if I don't?" I replied, my hand finding the Smith & Wesson.

"I cut you," he said, and a switchblade unfolded.

"Try it," I said, drawing the gun—for the second time in an hour; not a record, but close—"and I shoot you."

"Fine," said the punk. "Do me a favor." And he astonished me by spreading his arms and dropping the knife, which fell with typical Red Planet indolence to the fused regolith of the sidewalk.

"Okay," I said, keeping my gun trained on him, "I'll bite. How would that be doing you a favor?"

"I got nothing, man. Nothing."

"Been on Mars long?"

"Six weeks. Spent everything to get here."

"Where you from?"

"Chicago."

That was a place I *had* been to back on Earth; I could see why he'd wanted to get out. Keeping him covered, I bent over and picked up the knife. It was a beautiful piece, with a nicely carved wine-colored handle—I'd been admiring one like it a while ago in a shop Diana and I had visited over on Tenth. I retracted the blade and slipped it into my pocket.

"Man, that's mine," the punk said.

"Was yours," I corrected.

"But I need it. I need to get money. I gotta eat."

"Try your hand at fossil hunting. People get rich every day here."

"Tried. No luck."

I could sympathize with that. I reached into my other pocket, found a twenty-solar coin, and flipped it into the air. Anyone who had been on Mars long could have caught it as it fell, but he really was new here: he snatched at air way below the coin.

"Get yourself something to eat," I said and started walking.

"Hey, man," he said from behind me. "You're all right."

Without turning around, I gave him a hat tip and continued along my way.

· · · · · · · · · · ·

As I'd said, Diana and I weren't exclusive—and I was detective enough to pick up the signs that she'd been routinely seeing someone else for well over a month now, although I had no idea who. But that was fine.

My encounter with the punk had delayed me a bit, and by the time I got to The Bent Chisel, she'd already put her top on. "Hey," I said, leaning in to give her a quick kiss.

"Hey, Alex."

"All set to go?"

"Yup."

We walked back to her place, which was four blocks away. There was no sign of the kid who'd accosted me, so I didn't feel any need to mention it, but when we got into Diana's little apartment—it was even smaller than mine—and I'd pulled her into an embrace, she said, "Is that a gun in your pocket, or are you just happy to see me?"

I wondered if she knew she was paraphrasing Mae West. "Actually," I said, smiling, "it's a switchblade." I brought it out and told her the story of how I'd acquired it.

"Wow," she said. "It's nice."

"Yeah. My lucky day, I guess."

It was her turn to smile. "And now it's going to be your lucky night."

We headed into her little bedroom. My earlier encounter with Lacie had been athletic indeed, but Diana and I always had gentle, playful sex. She'd been here on Mars for a dozen years, and that had taken its toll; she had the typically weak musculature of the long-term inhabitants of this world. I couldn't go back to Earth for legal reasons; Diana was stuck here because she'd never be able to hack a full gee again. But, still, we made do; we always did. And I *was* happy to see her.

· · · · · · · · · · ·

Turned out there wasn't any New Klondike Historical Society, but I guess things like that are never created while the history is being made. In the morning I headed over to the shipyard. I started by checking in at the yard office, which was little more than a shack between two dead hulks. The yardmaster was Bertha, a husky old broad with a platinum blonde buzz cut.

"Hey, gorgeous," I said as I entered the shack. I wondered

briefly why whenever you said, "Hey, gorgeous," people thought you were being serious, but if you said, "Hey, genius," they thought you were being sarcastic.

"Hi, Alex. What's up."

"Just some research."

"No rough stuff, okay?"

"Why does everyone say that to me?"

"I've got two words for you: *Skookum* and *Jim.*"

"Okay; true enough. But it's a different ship I'm interested in this time."

She gestured at her computer screen. "Which one?"

"Something called the *B. Traven.*"

"Jesus," she said.

"What?"

"You don't know?"

"Know what?"

"The *Traven.*"

"What about it?"

"It was a death ship."

I looked at her funny. "What?"

"How'd you get to Mars?"

"Me? Low-end liner. I forget what it was called. *Saget, Saginaw*—something like that."

"*Sagan?*"

"That's it, yeah."

"Good ship. Made eight round trips to date."

"If you say so."

"And how long was the journey?"

"Christ, I don't remember."

"Right. You literally don't—because the *Sagan,* like most of the ships that come here, uses hibernation. They freeze you when you leave Earth and thaw you out when you arrive here. That kind of ship employs a Hohmann transfer orbit, which takes very little power but a whole lot of time to get here. Transit time if you leave at the optimum moment is 258 Earth days, but it all passed in a blink of an eye for you. The *Traven* was supposed to do the same thing—all of the passengers in deep sleep, with just a bowman to keep things running."

"Bowman?"

"That's what they call the person who stays awake during a voyage when everyone else is hibernating. After a guy named Bowman in some old movie, apparently."

"Ah, right," I said; I knew which one. "But something went wrong?"

"Crap, yeah. The bowman went crazy. He thawed out passengers one at a time and terrorized them—abused them sexually. By the time one of the people he'd awoken managed to get word out—a radio message to Lunaport—there was nothing anyone could do. Orbital mechanics make it really hard to intercept a ship that's several months into its interplanetary journey. The whole thing was quite a sensation at the time, but—how old are you?"

"Forty-one."

"You'd have been just a kid."

"The name of the ship didn't seem to ring a bell with Dougal McCrae at the NKPD, either." I said it to defend my ignorance; I probably *should* have known about this. But maybe we'd studied it in school on a Friday. Memo to all boards of education everywhere: never schedule crucial lessons for a Friday.

"Yeah, well, Mac's about your age," Bertha said, exonerating him, too.

"Anyway, that explains why a guy lunged at me when I brought it up. He'd been on that ship."

"Ah," said Bertha. "But what's your interest? I mean, if this is news to you, you can't be like the other person who was asking about it."

Needless to say, my ears perked up. "What other person?"

"A couple of weeks ago. The writer-in-residence."

I blinked. "We have a writer-in-residence?"

"Hey, there's more to New Klondike culture than The Bent Chisel and Diamond Tooth Gertie's."

"And Gully's Gym," I said. "Don't forget Gully's Gym."

Bertha made a harrumphing sound, then: "You know who Stavros Shopatsky is?"

"One of the first guys to make a fortune from fossils here. After Weingarten and O'Reilly, I mean."

"Exactly. He bought a ton of land under the dome from Howard Slapcoff. But he was also a writer—adventure novels; my dad used to read him. And so he donated one of the homes he built here to be a writer's retreat. Authors from Earth apply to get an all-expenses-paid round trip to Mars, so they can come and write whatever they want. They usually stay six months or so, then head back."

"Okay," I said.

"And the current writer is doing a book about the *B. Traven*."

"I understand it's still in service, but under a different name," I said.

"Really?" replied Bertha. "What name?"

"The *Kathryn Denning*."

"Oh, is that the *Traven*? Interesting. Yeah, she's still active." Bertha looked at a monitor. "In fact, she's on her way here. She's due to arrive on Friday."

"Can you let me know when she touches down? I'd like to give her a once-over."

"You didn't tell me why you were interested in this."

She said it in a way that conveyed if I expected her to help satisfy my curiosity, I had to satisfy hers. And so I did: "I'm tracking down what became of some cargo she brought here, back when she was called the *Traven*."

"It's been thirty years since she last sailed under that name. Surely you don't expect to find a clue aboard her at this late date?"

I smiled. "Can't hurt to have a look."

· · · · · · · · · · ·

My office was on the second of two floors. Instead of the rickety elevator, I always took the two half flights of stairs up. As I came out of the stairwell, I spotted a man at the end of the corridor. He could have been there to see anyone on this floor, but—

Jesus.

Well, not exactly. This guy was better-looking than Jesus. But he had the same longish hair, short beard, and lean face you saw in stained-glass windows.

It was Stuart Berling—unless the real Krikor Ajemian had come to Mars for some reason. I figured he was either here to beat the crap out of me for bringing up the *B. Traven,* or to beat the crap out of me for sleeping with his wife. Either way, discretion seemed the better part of valor, and I turned around and headed back to the stairwell. But— damn it!—he'd spotted me. I heard a shout of "Lomax!" coming from down the corridor.

I leapt, going down the whole flight at once. The thud of my landing echoed in the stairwell. I turned around and took the second set of stairs in a single go, too—but Berling could run like the wind, his transfer legs pumping up and down. Looking up the open stairwell from the ground floor, I saw him appear at the second-floor doorway. I hightailed it through the dingy lobby, almost colliding with an elderly woman who tossed a "Watch it, sonny!" at me.

The automatic door wasn't used to people approaching it at the speed I was managing, and it hadn't finished sliding out of the way by the time I reached it; my right shoulder smashed into it, hurting like a son of a bitch, but I made it out onto the street. I could head either left or right, chose left, and continued along.

Running on Mars isn't like doing it on Earth: if you've got decent legs, you propel yourself several meters with each stride, and you spend most of your time airborne. The street wasn't particularly crowded, and I did my best to bob and weave around people, but once you're aloft you can't easily change your course, and I finally did collide with someone. Fortunately, it was a transfer; the impact knocked him on his metal ass, but probably did him no harm—although he threw something a lot less polite than "Watch it, sonny!" after me as I scrambled to my feet. While getting up, I'd had an opportunity to look backward. Berling was still in hot pursuit.

I'd chosen left because it led to a hovertram stop. My lungs were bound to give out before Berling's excimer pack did; if I could hop a tram that pulled away before he could get on it, I'd be safe but—

—but there's never a hovertram handy when you need

one. The stop was up ahead, and no one was waiting at it, meaning I'd probably just missed the damn thing.

I continued along. There was a seedy tavern on my right called the Bar Soom—a name somebody must have thought clever at some point—and who should be coming out of it but that kid who'd tried to rob me last night. I was breathing too hard to make chitchat as I passed, but he clearly recognized me. He looked behind me, no doubt saw Berling coming after me like a bat out of Chicago, and—

And the kid must have tripped Berling as he passed, because I heard a big thud and the kind of swearing that could have made a sailor blush, if there had been any sailors on Mars.

I halted, turned around, and saw Berling trying to get up. "Damn it, Lomax!" he called, without a trace of breathing hard. "I just want to talk to you!"

Even though it seemed I now had an ally in this alley, I still didn't like my chances in a fight with a high-end transfer. Of course, maybe he'd spent all his money on that handsome face—I wondered if Krikor Ajemian got a royalty? But when in doubt it was safest to assume that a transfer had super strength, too. "About . . . what?" I called back, the two words separated by a gasp.

"The—that ship," he replied, apparently aborting giving voice to the cursed name.

I had my hands on my knees, still trying to catch my breath. Doesn't anyone phone for appointments anymore? "Okay," I managed. "All right." I walked back toward him, several people gawking at us. I nodded thanks at the punk as I approached. Berling's clothes were dusty—Martian red dust—from having skidded on the sidewalk when he'd been tripped, but otherwise he looked great, with not a hair out of place; I wondered how they did that. "What do you want to say?"

He turned his head as he looked left and right, noting the people around us, then moved his head side to side again, signaling "No." "Somewhere private," he said. And then, a little miffed: "I had been hoping for your office."

The number of my colleagues back on Earth who had

been shot dead in their own offices was pretty high. "No," I said. "The Bent Chisel—you know it?"

"That rat hole?" said Berling. He *did* know it. But he nodded. "All right."

I figured we both needed some time to cool off figuratively, and I needed to do so literally, too. "Twenty minutes," I said. "I'll meet you there."

He nodded, turned, and departed. I looked at the kid.

"What's your name?"

"Dirk," he said.

"Huh," I said. "Your name is Dirk, and you came at me with a knife."

"Yeah. So?"

I shook my head. "Forget it. You still need money?"

He nodded.

"I'm a private detective. I could use some backup for this meeting with Berling at The Bent Chisel in case things get ugly. Twenty solars for an hour's work, tops."

The snake's rattle shook on his face. "Okay," he said. "I'm in."

FIFTEEN

Buttrick looked up suspiciously as Dirk and I entered the bar. He opened his mouth, as if to issue an automatic complaint about me needing to pay off my tab, but closed it, presumably realizing I was uncharacteristically up-to-date.

"A pretty-boy transfer is gonna come in here in a few minutes," I said. "Long hair, short beard. Send him to the booth in the back, would you?"

"All right," Buttrick said as he polished a glass in classic bartender mode. "But no rough stuff."

I threw up my hands. "You wreck a joint one time . . . !"

Dirk and I headed to the back. I chose this booth because it was near the door to the kitchen, which had its own exit into an alleyway; it was always good to have an escape route in mind. This booth also had my favorite bit of graffiti carved into the tabletop: "Back in ten minutes—Godot."

Shortly after we sat—side by side, both of us facing the rest of the bar, Dirk on the inside of the booth and me on the outside—Diana appeared, and I got up and gave her a hug. She stretched up to kiss me on the cheek. "Hey, baby," I said.

Dirk, I noticed, was content to look at Diana's killer rack

while she and I spoke. "Hi, honey," she replied, smiling warmly at me; she had a great smile. I brushed some of her brown hair away from her brown eyes. "Good to see you."

"Good to see you, too," I replied, and I kissed her briefly on the mouth. Diana stole a look over her shoulder to see if Buttrick was watching. He was. She turned back to me, flashed her smile again, and said, "The usual?"

I nodded, and she tipped her head down to look at seated Dirk. "And for you, tiger?"

Dirk hesitated. I'd been there before: the moment when you're supposed to order something but can't really afford to.

"On me," I said, returning to the booth.

"Beer," he replied.

"Domestic or imported?"

"Domestic," I responded. No need to go crazy.

There were only three domestic choices, all synthetic. Diana rattled them off in what I realized was descending order of crappiness. Dirk hesitated again; he clearly hadn't been on Mars long enough to know the brands. "Bring him a Wilhelm," I said—which was a cute name for a beer, if you knew Mars history; Wilhelm Beer and his partner produced the first globe of the Red Planet back in 1830.

Diana headed off, hips swaying. I watched, and I imagined Dirk did, too. Blues was playing over the speakers—I think it was Muddy Waters. "When Berling gets here," I said to the kid, "watch him like a hawk. I don't know what his game is, but he's one angry man."

"Here he comes," Dirk replied.

It hadn't been twenty minutes, and that made me even more alert; Berling might have been getting here early to plan his own escape after an altercation. Buttrick pointed in our direction; Berling nodded and headed this way. He passed Diana, but he didn't spare her a glance; well, he *was* sleeping with Vivien Leigh. When he reached us, he sat down. I liked having the wide table between us; he couldn't grab my neck or punch me across it.

"Who's this?" he said, indicating Dirk with a movement of Krikor Ajemian's head.

"My assistant," I said, and before Berling could object to his presence, I pressed on. "You wanted to talk about—that ship."

He nodded. "You just startled me, is all, when you brought it up at Gargalian's." He looked past me, more or less at the door to the kitchen, which I knew had a round window in it. "You know, when I went to NewYou, I asked them if there was any way to edit out portions of my memories as they did the transfer, but they said that's not possible. I'd trade all my fossils to get rid of those memories, those flashbacks."

At that moment, Diana reappeared, depositing my gin and Dirk's beer. "And for you?" she said to Berling.

He looked at her with a blank expression. Alcohol was wasted on transfers, and most of them soon gave up paying for it; they could get a buzz or deaden their pain in other ways. Buttrick could rightly say, "We don't serve their kind in here"—but only because they almost never came in.

"Nothing," he said. Diana headed off. This time I didn't watch her depart; I didn't take my eyes off Berling.

"I didn't know the history of that ship when I brought it up," I said. "I'm sorry."

Berling scowled. "What happened aboard the *Traven*"—here in the darkened back corner, he was willing to utter part of the name—"was horrific."

I took a sip of my gin.

"You've got to understand," Berling continued. "We were young kids, most of us." He glanced at Dirk. "Kids like you. Some looking to make a fortune, some looking for adventure, some just looking to get away from Earth. We knew it'd be harsh, but we assumed it would be harsh *after* we got here." He shook his head. "You know why I'm still here? After all these mears? Because I'm terrified of spaceships—couldn't ever bring myself to fly on one again. Not after what happened on the *Traven*."

I tried to make light of it. "Turned out okay," I said. "You must have finally struck it big to buy new bodies for you and your wife."

"Yeah, I've had some luck at last. A couple of new species of rhizomorphs; previously unknown taxons always fetch top coin."

"Good for you. Never had much luck hunting fossils myself."

He placed his perfect hands on the scratched tabletop, palms down. "So, what exactly is it that you're investigating?"

"Some cargo that had been brought here aboard the *Traven* has turned up."

Berling narrowed his eyes. "Cargo?" But then he nodded. "You mean the land mines."

I kept an impassive expression. "What do you know about them?"

"I first heard about them after we landed—somebody discovered some in the cargo hold, or something like that, right?"

"Yes," I said.

"Christ, if I'd known about them while we were still in transit, I'd have set them off. Anything to put an end to it all."

I'd wondered if it had been Berling himself who had brought them on that voyage. After all, he clearly had access to high-quality fossils—which might mean the Alpha. But, judging by the deteriorated state of the unexploded mine Pickover had brought to my office, I'd assumed they'd been planted many years ago, and Berling had apparently only recently come into wealth. "Do you know who smuggled them aboard?" I asked.

"I didn't at the time. Like I said, I didn't even know they were there. But after we got to Mars, yeah, I figured it out. It was . . ." He trailed off.

"Yes?" I prodded, lifting my eyebrows.

Berling tilted his head. "How did you know my wife had transferred, too?"

Oh, crap. "I do quality-assurance follow-ups for New-You," I said. "You know that. She's on the list the franchise here gave me to interview next week."

"No, you don't," said Berling. "I was at NewYou a few

days ago, getting a couple of minor adjustments made. I asked the new owner there, Fernandez, about you. He said, sure, he *knows* you, but he doesn't employ you. Said when you'd talked to me before you were investigating the disappearance of the previous owner, Joshua Wilkins, who I guess had transferred the same day I had. But when you came to see me about that, Lacie hadn't transferred yet."

"I work for the head office on Earth," I said. "I stopped by your place, but you weren't home."

His eyes narrowed. "Lacie never mentioned that."

"Anyway," I said lightly, "you were saying the person who brought the explosives aboard the *Traven* was . . . ?"

But it was too late. Berling was on his feet. He didn't have enough to justify attacking me right there—but he certainly had his suspicions. "I knew I shouldn't trust you, Lomax," he said and stormed out.

I downed the rest of my gin. Dirk, wisely, didn't say a word.

SIXTEEN

I gave Dirk the twenty solars I'd promised him, and we exited The Bent Chisel and went our separate ways. I did not, however, give him back the switchblade I'd taken from him, even though I had it with me; it looked like it'd be a useful thing to carry, along with my phone, my tab, and my revolver.

I was sorry not to have gotten the information Berling had, but if this writer-in-residence fellow was doing a book about the *Traven,* he might know who had brought the land mines onboard. I decided to head out to see him; a little culture never hurt anyone. I took a hovertram since Shopatsky House, the writer's retreat, was way up by the north airlock station.

I'd expected the writer-in-residence to be a mousy academic, like Pickover. But when the green door slid open, it revealed a statuesque biological woman in her late twenties with flawless chestnut skin, sexy brown eyes behind long lashes, and a gorgeous mane of brown hair tumbling over her shoulders. The only thing remotely writerly about her appearance was that she wore honest-to-goodness eyeglasses, something I don't think I'd seen on anyone since leaving Earth.

"Hi," I said, smiling broadly. "I'm Alexander Lomax. I hear you're writing a book."

"I'm trying to," she said, without warmth. "I came here for peace and quiet." She crossed long arms in front of a lovely pair of breasts. "But people keep disturbing me."

"Sorry. I wanted to call ahead—but there's no listing for Shopatsky House in the directory."

"That's rather the point."

"You're writing about the *B. Traven,* right?"

She warmed a little at that. "Yes."

"I'm a private investigator. I'm looking into a matter that involves the *Traven.*"

"I really do jealously guard my time, Mr. Lomax. But as a writer, I often impose on others for help with my research—professors, doctors, scientists, what have you. And so, to keep the karmic balance, I'm always willing to help others who are looking for information, *if* they've done their homework." She peered at me over the top of her glasses; it was a look that was sexy when I'd seen it in old movies, and it was sexy here, too. "It's rude to just waste somebody's time asking them questions you could have answered on your own. So, let's see if *you've* done *your* homework. Why was that ship called the *B. Traven?*"

There's a pub trivia league that meets at The Bent Chisel. I used to make fun of its members—why bother to *remember* stuff, when your phone could *tell* you the answer to any question? But the name *did* faintly ring a bell, and—

And those who said I spent too much time watching old movies can suck it. "After B. Traven," I said, "who wrote the novel *The Treasure of the Sierra Madre,* the basis for the movie of the same name."

Luscious lips curved in a smile, and we both spontaneously said in unison, "'Badges? We don't need no stinkin' badges!'" She was grinning broadly now, and I added, "Of course, that's a misquote. What Gold Hat actually said was, 'Badges? We ain't got no badges. We don't need no badges! I don't have to show you any stinkin' badges!'"

She nodded. "Just like no one actually said, 'Play it again, Sam.'"

I did my best Bogey—an impression that hardly made an impression on anyone these days. "'Play it, Sam. You played it for her, you can play it for me. If she can stand it, I can.'"

"Mr. Lomax," she said, stepping aside and gesturing, "won't you come in?"

It was too early to say, "I think this is the beginning of a beautiful friendship," so I didn't—but I *thought* it.

Shopatsky House looked very comfortable. Most furniture on Mars was printed here, rather than shipped in from Earth, but a couple of these pieces looked like real wood—including the . . . the . . . I dug through my memory for the term; I'd only ever seen such things in movies before: the roll-top desk. Sitting on it was a red cube about ten centimeters on a side: a household computer. Damn things didn't have to be that big, but people tended to lose them if they were smaller.

There was also another piece of furniture I'd never seen in real life: a filing cabinet. If I had one, I'd keep bottles of booze in it; I didn't know anyone who had paper files.

I realized I'd lucked out with her little test. I'd seen that movie a hundred times, and back when it was made, it was normal for only a few names to appear on the credits, instead of every damn catering assistant and holography technician. The author's name had caught my eye because it had included just a single initial: "B. Traven." That film—about the quest for gold in Mexico—*did* have interesting resonances for the hunt for fossils on Mars.

But if this gorgeous writer's trivia question had been a more prosaic one—"What's my name?"—I would have failed. My detective skills quickly came to the rescue, though, because there was a third piece of furniture I'd never seen used for its intended purpose before: a bookcase. Every set of boxed-in shelves I'd ever encountered simply displayed curios, *objets d'art,* or—here on Mars—interesting rocks or fossils. But this one, made of reddish brown wood that had a warmth to it that none of the reddish things native to this planet had, was partially filled with real printed books—doubtless the single biggest repository of such things on all of Mars.

The first two shelves contained volumes by Stavros Shopatsky with lurid titles like *The Wanton Savior, The Shores of Death,* and *Pirates in the Wind.* The subsequent shelves had books grouped by authors—but not alphabetically. First Hayakawa, then Chavez, then Torkoff, then Cohen. "Are these the other writers who have been in residence here?" I asked.

"That's right," she said, nodding that lovely head of hers. "We're each supposed to bring at least five kilograms of our own books as part of our personal mass allowance. If our books are only in e-editions, we're to have leather-bound copies produced to bring with us."

My eyes tracked to the second shelf from the bottom, which was partially full. An odd little L-shaped thingy pressed against the last book to keep them all from toppling over. The name on the spines of the last three books was Lakshmi Chatterjee. I reached down and extracted the final volume; its title was *Lunaport: Valor and Independence.*

"And now you're writing about the *B. Traven?*"

"Exactly."

"I'm trying to find out who smuggled the explosives aboard the *Traven.*"

"Ah, yes," she said. "The land mines." She headed into the living room and motioned for me to sit down. I'd hoped she was going to take the green couch, meaning I could move in next to her, but she took the matching chair instead.

I leaned into the corner of the couch and swung my legs up, leaving my feet projecting off the cushions into the air. "How much longer will you be on Mars?" The question had nothing whatsoever to do with the investigation.

"Another seventy-one days."

I smiled. "Not that anyone's counting."

"The next writer is coming in then; I go back on the ship that's bringing him."

"You looking forward to going home?"

"Somewhat. I like it here."

"Where *is* home for you?"

She crossed her long legs. She was wearing tight-fitting pants that looked like black leather and a tight-fitting black top. "Delhi." She looked at a wall clock—an *analog* wall clock; it always took me forever to decode those. But the point was plain; I should move things along. "Do you know who brought the land mines aboard the *Traven?*"

"Sure. It was Willem Van Dyke—the same guy Weingarten and O'Reilly had taken along on their second voyage."

I shook my head. "I've seen the passenger manifest. He wasn't on the *Traven,* at least not under that name."

"He wasn't a passenger," Lakshmi said. "He was crew."

"You mean—you mean *he* was the monster? The one who thawed out passengers and terrorized them?"

"No, no. He was the backup bowman; the spare. He was supposed to be kept on ice the whole voyage, and only thawed out in an emergency."

"Ah," I said. "And do you know what became of him?"

"Of course. I'm covering that in my book."

I looked at her expectantly. "And?"

She tilted her head and brushed lustrous hair out of her eyes. "I'll send you an invitation to the book-launch party."

I smiled my most-charming smile. "Please, Lakshmi. I'd really like to know."

She considered for a moment, then: "I don't know how much you know about the history of human space flight."

"Some. What they taught in school." Except on Fridays.

"Well, did you know that some space scientists used to say it was *impossible* for humans to safely come to Mars, or live here?"

"When did they say that?"

"From the 1970s to, oh, say, 2030 or so."

"Why?"

"Radiation."

"Really?"

"Yup. Earth's magnetosphere and atmosphere protect people on Earth's surface from solar and cosmic radiation. And they argued that without those shields, you'd get too big a dose coming to Mars or staying on its surface."

I smiled. "Shall we turn off the lights and see if we glow?"

"Exactly. It was a risible contention. The scientists who were making it were either talking outside their field of expertise or were deliberately misleading people."

I lifted my eyebrows. "Why?"

"A turf war. Sure, here on Mars we get more radiation than people on Earth do—enough for each year living under the dome to increase by a whopping *one percent* your chance of getting cancer sometime in the next thirty years. The scientists saying cancer was a showstopper were all either in the business of unmanned probes or wanted to spend forever hanging in Low Earth Orbit." She paused. "You know anyone who smokes tobacco?"

"My grandmother used to."

"Yeah. Well, if she'd moved to Mars but left her cigarettes behind on Earth, she'd have *reduced* her chances of getting cancer."

"Okay," I said. "So?"

"So, getting cancer via space travel or while living on Mars is a vanishingly slim chance. But, then again, so is striking it rich finding fossils here. That happens, and so does the cancer thing—just very, very rarely. Well, Willem Van Dyke didn't discover fossil riches—Weingarten and O'Reilly did that, and they just brought him along for the ride. But he *did* win the other lottery, poor bastard: he's the one in a thousand who got cancer by traveling in space."

"And then what?" I asked.

"I'm still trying to find out. There are references thirty years ago to him having a terminal diagnosis, and I haven't turned up anything after that. Of course, he knew where the Alpha mother lode was, and even though Weingarten and O'Reilly ripped him off, he probably kept a few good fossils. I suspect he's long dead, but with the money those fossils would have fetched, he probably went out in style."

"Could he have transferred?"

"He might have possibly had enough money, yeah, but I doubt he'd have done that. This was decades ago, remember. Van Dyke was very religious. He believed he had an immortal soul and didn't believe that soul could be transferred into an artificial body. There were a lot of people like that back then. Even today, there are still some who want to overturn *Durksen v. Hawksworth* in the States."

I'd been all of twelve when that case had begun. A crazed gunman had shot President Vanessa Durksen. There had been no way to save her body, but Howard Slapcoff had successfully urged the president's chief of staff to have her mind transferred, and have the transfer serve out the rest of her term, instead of having the vice-president, who everyone agreed was a disaster, sworn in as her successor. Durksen had been well into her second term then, so there was no way she could stand for re-election, but a lot of pundits said the transfer could have won if she'd been eligible to run again. It had been a brilliant coup for Howard Slapcoff. Durksen had been scrutinized minutely by the whole planet—her every word, her every decision—to see if she'd changed in the slightest after transferring, and most people (except a few ideologues in the opposing party) agreed that she hadn't; mainstream acceptance of transfers really still being the same person began with that.

"Okay," I said. "Thanks. I appreciate the help."

She unfolded her long legs and rose. "Now, was there anything else? I really do have to get back to my book."

"No," I said. "But thank you." I tipped my nonexistent hat and, with considerable regret, left her and headed out into the dreary world under the dome.

· · · · · · · · · · ·

I spent the rest of the day searching for information about Willem Van Dyke. Although the Privacy Revolution of 2034 had made it a lot easier for people to not leave tracks wherever they went, most people still had pretty extensive online presences. But not Willem Van Dyke—or, at least not the Willem Van Dyke in question; it turned out to be an irritatingly common name. He really did seem to go off the grid thirty years ago, just as Rory Pickover and Lakshmi Chatterjee had said. I suppose he could have just headed out into the wilderness to die—but there was no death notice that I could find.

Once night fell, I went to see Rory Pickover at his apartment at the center of the dome. After he'd let me in, and we were seated in his yellow-walled living room, I dove into what I wanted. "You promised to take me to see the Alpha."

Pickover looked at me unblinkingly. I stared him down as long as I could, but his acrylic peepers weren't affected even by direct exposure to the desiccated Martian atmosphere, so he won. But I wasn't going to give up. "Seriously," I said. "I need to see it."

"It's nothing to look at," he replied.

Pickover himself was nothing to look at either, at the moment; most of the skin was still gone from his face. "I understand that. But I'm having no luck tracing Van Dyke—and there may be a clue to his whereabouts there."

"All right," Pickover said, surprising me; I'd expected the argument to last longer. "Let's go."

"Now?"

"Sure, now." He stood up. "It's dark out—that's my first line of defense in keeping you from recognizing landmarks. Second line of defense will be having you polarize your surface-suit helmet for the journey, meaning you'll barely be able to see out of it in the dark. Third line of defense will be my taking a circuitous route to get us there. Fourth line of defense is that by this late you must be tired, meaning you might even fall asleep on the journey—indeed, you'll want to, since it'll take hours, and we won't be able to accomplish much until dawn."

I'd kind of hoped to make it over to The Bent Chisel tonight to see Diana, but at least he was agreeing to take me. "All right," I said, getting up as well.

"Great. Bathroom's down there, old boy—better avail yourself before we head out, and . . ."

"What?"

"Oh, nothing. Haven't used it myself in months—not since I transferred. I hope I remembered to flush."

SEVENTEEN

Since the episode with Joshua Wilkins, I'd researched ways to kill a transfer, just to be on the safe side. Sadly, except for using a broadband disruptor, there didn't seem to be any reliable method. That made sense, of course: the bodies were designed to cheat death—they were highly durable, with vital components encased in protective armor. I'd tried to find a way, but it seemed kryptonite was hard to come by on Mars.

Even so, Pickover made me leave my gun in a locker at the western airlock station—I guess he was afraid I might try to do him in once he'd shown me where the riches were located. He didn't know I'd acquired a switchblade from Dirk, though, and he was too naïve to give me a pat-down before we headed out, so I kept that in my pocket.

My detective's brain was hard at work trying to figure out precisely where he was taking me. First clue: we'd exited through the western airlock, and this was the one bit of information that couldn't be misdirection for my sake, since it was where he'd parked his privately owned Mars buggy when he'd last returned from the Alpha.

Thank God Pickover had bought the buggy prior to transferring, because it was the expensive kind that had its own life-support system. If he'd been buying one today, he'd doubtless have opted for the cheaper—and more reliable—ones that simply provided transportation.

Pickover rented me a surface suit. He paid for it directly, since he would have ended up being expensed for it, anyway—but I didn't have to wear it for the long drive, although he did make me put the fishbowl over my head. On Earth, that would have been uncomfortable—normally, the suit's collar bore the weight of the helmet—but the thing wasn't heavy enough here to be bothersome. Pickover did make it opaque, though, before we started tooling along.

A planitia is a low plain, and just like their counterparts on Earth, they tended to be nothing but miles and miles of miles and miles. We chatted a bit at first, but having to listen to Rory's voice echo in the fishbowl was unpleasant, and after a time we both fell silent. I confess I wiled away the hours thinking about Diana, Lacie, and Lakshmi, separately and in various permutations.

I possibly did doze on the trip—tough guy like me doesn't often think about his childhood, but when my mom wanted me to sleep and I wouldn't, she used to take me for a drive. Pickover had also made me leave my tablet computer and phone behind; I had no tools that might help me calculate our location. But by the time we got to where we were going, the sun was rising in the east. I'd been hoping it would be coming up over jagged peaks or broken crater walls that I could match to topographical maps, but the illuminated part of the horizon—and, as I saw as the sun climbed higher, the horizon all the way around—was just more smooth ground, with one exception: to the west, there was the crumbling wall of a small crater.

I used the buggy's toilet then got into the rented surface suit—this one was kind of a drab olive green—and exited the vehicle. The buggy had springy wheels almost a meter across, and a boxy clear passenger cabin; the Martian atmosphere was tenuous enough that streamlining didn't matter for surface vehicles.

Pickover went to the buggy's trunk and pulled out a device that looked a bit like an upright vacuum cleaner with no bag attached.

"What's that?" I asked.

"A metal detector. I just got it yesterday."

"I'd have thought those would be useless on Mars," I said, "because of all the iron oxide in the soil."

"Oh, it's easy to tune metal detectors to ignore iron. But I did have a devil of a time finding one to rent. They're of no help in fossil hunting, of course, and the standard uses for such things—beachcombing, searching for archeological artifacts, and so on—simply don't apply here."

He handed it to me.

I raised my eyebrows. "You want me to do the mine-sweeping?"

"I can't," Rory said. "I tried—but the metal in my body interferes too much with the detector. You, on the other hand . . ."

The guy was more clever than I'd given him credit for. He hadn't brought me out here because I wanted to see the Alpha; he'd brought me out here because he needed the help of a biological.

He went back to the trunk and brought out another device: a tank of compressed gas with a flexible hose attached. "For blowing sand," Rory said, evidently anticipating my question.

"Okay," I said. "Show me where you found the first land mine."

"This way. Follow in my footsteps precisely. I've used this path numerous times; it's either free of land mines or they've all corroded like that one I brought to your office."

He led, dust rising from his footfalls. I still found it bizarre to see a person in street clothes walking unprotected on Mars. Pickover was wearing what I imagined paleontologists wore back on Earth: brown work boots, heavy khaki pants, and a flannel work shirt. He'd also put on a baseball cap with the logo of the Toronto Blue Jays; I guess transfers needed something to keep the sun out of their eyes, too.

We headed out about fifty meters—I counted the paces—and came to an area that had been marked off into a grid of meter-wide squares by monofilament. The strands were almost exactly the same color as the red dust, and I mentioned that they were hard to see. "Not in the infrared," Pickover replied. "I'm running a small current through them from that excimer pack, there. To me, they're bright white, but the average prospector won't notice them at all unless he trips over them."

He stepped over one of the strands, and I gingerly did the same. We did this five more times and then stopped. "We're still a ways from where the land mine went off," he said crouching, "but let me show you this. It's the spot where I found the counter slab for two-dash-thirteen-eighty-eight."

"The fossils are lying right out on the surface?"

"Occasionally," said Pickover, "but they're usually a short distance down—but only a short distance. See, on Earth, sedimentary rocks have been forming for billions of years. But on Mars, sedimentation came to an end over three and a half billion years ago, when the open bodies of water dried up. So, instead of ancient sediments being deeply buried, they're right on the surface—or just about. The water ice close to the surface here at the Alpha long ago either dissociated or sublimated, leaving eight or ten centimeters of loose, dry sand overtop of the ancient matrix. At the Alpha, that matrix is made out of areslithia—Mars stone. It's really just sand and silt fused with water ice; the ground here is as much as sixty percent water ice by weight. Do you see what that means, Alex?"

I didn't. "What?"

"Well, on Earth, most fossils are permineralized: the spaces in the original organic material have been filled in by minerals percolating through the ground; that new material replaces the original biological specimen, which ultimately disappears. But here at the Alpha, the fossils *are* the original material, simply embedded in the matrix. You can often get an Alpha fossil out of the matrix just by bringing the areslithia up to room temperature and letting the ice melt. That's why the fossils from here at the Alpha are so good—they're the actual ancient exoskeletons, unaltered, preserved in a dense slurry that's been frozen solid for over three billion years."

"Not completely, I bet. That land mine you brought in was corroded."

Pickover nodded. "Yes, true. Something—maybe a micrometeoroid impact a couple of decades ago—heated a patch of the soil enough that there was a small pocket of running groundwater, and that's what rusted out that mine. But most of the rest of this whole field"—he gestured expansively—"has been completely frozen since the Noachian."

"But that counter slab you brought to my office was solid, even at room temperature."

"Only because I'd infused it with a stabilizer, replacing the water content with thermoplastic."

"Ah."

He rose and continued walking. After about forty meters we came to a spot where there was a big divot out of the ground. "That's where the mine that blew up was," he said pointing. "And over there's where I recovered that one that was rusted through." He indicated a much smaller defect in the surface.

I began a slow minesweep of all 6,000 square meters of what Pickover had identified as the Alpha Deposit; he walked behind me.

While we walked along, I tried to commit landmarks to memory; this was my first time here at the Alpha, but I suspected it wouldn't be my last, and knowing the terrain is halfway to winning a battle. Going right back to the first *Viking* landers, people had been giving whimsical names to various Martian boulders. Off to my left was a big one that looked like the kind of car I'd seen in 1950s movies—it even had a couple of fin-like projections; I mentally dubbed it "Plymouth." And to my right was a head-shaped rock with craggy good looks; the old-movie buff in me felt "Hudson" was the perfect name for it.

It turned out the Alpha wasn't surrounded by land mines—which, after all, would have required a lot of them.

But there was an extant line of twelve, each about eight meters from the next, along the eastern perimeter of the Alpha; the one that had exploded and the one that had rusted out would have been two additional points along that line. I guess that meant New Klondike was indeed east of here, and Willem Van Dyke had assumed anyone out looking for the Alpha would come from that direction.

If this were an old battlefield, we'd just lob rocks at the remaining land mines and blow each of them up in turn. But that might damage precious fossils, and so instead we set about carefully clearing them. The mines were mostly buried under a couple of centimeters of dry sand. Rory used his blower at a shallow angle to remove the sand from on top of one of the mines, and sure enough, the deactivation hole was visible right in the middle of the disk. The hole was actually plugged with sand, which is something neither of us had anticipated but we both probably should have. But after a moment, a thought occurred to me. I had transferred the knife to the equipment pouch on my surface suit. I pulled it out.

"What's that?"

"A switchblade," I said.

He frowned, clearly unhappy that I'd brought a weapon along. But I handed it to him, and showed him the button that caused the blade to spring out. He had better balance than me, better reflexes, and had already proven he could survive a land-mine explosion. And so he stood over the mine, one leg on either side of it, and he bent over, positioned the closed switchblade above the deactivation hole, and pressed the button.

The blade shot out, nicely slicing through the sand, and its tip must indeed have hit the button down below because a little mechanical flag on the top of the mine, near the center, flipped over from red to green—just as the material I'd read said it would.

Rory couldn't let out a sigh of relief, but I could, and did. He then pried the mine up; it seemed stuck a bit in the permafrost beneath it, but it finally came free. We repeated the process eight meters farther along, deactivating and liberating another Caldera-7.

We could have continued on, deactivating all the other mines, but by this point I needed something to eat. And so we each picked up one of the deactivated mines and headed back toward the buggy; I'd bought some sandwiches from the little shop at the airlock station but needed to go inside the pressurized cabin so I could take off my fishbowl to eat them.

Before we did that, though, Pickover opened the buggy's trunk again, and we put the deactivated mines inside; on the way back home, we'd find someplace to dispose of them. There were brown fabric sacks in the trunk; part of a paleontologist's kit, I guessed. Pickover used some of them to make nests to carefully cushion the mines, just in case.

While he was doing that, I looked out at the area, which, to my eye, seemed no different from anywhere else on this part of Mars: endless orange plains under a yellow-brown sky, and—

Oh, Christ.

"Rory," I said, over my helmet radio, "do you have telescopic vision?"

He closed the trunk, straightened, and faced me. "Sort of. I've got a twenty-to-one zoom built-in. It helps when working on fossils. Why?"

I pointed toward the horizon. "Is that what I think it is?"

I watched as he turned his gaze. Nothing happened on his face, making me wonder what mental command he used to access the zoom function. "Who could that be?" he asked.

Damn. So it *was* another Mars buggy, sitting out on the planitia. We'd been tailed through the dark, all the way here from New Klondike. Normally, I'd have spotted a tail almost at once, but I'd had this stupid polarized fishbowl over my noggin for the whole ride out.

And Pickover had made me leave my gun behind.

EIGHTEEN

I think we should get out of here," I said into my headset microphone.

"We can't leave the Alpha exposed to looters," Pickover replied.

"Rory, we're defenseless."

"The fossils are defenseless."

"Damn it!" I intended the curse for him, but as I said it, the distant Mars buggy started moving in, kicking up a plume of dust as it did so, and Pickover took the words as a response to that.

"Yeah," he said. "They're barreling directly toward us."

The radio we were using was supposed to be encrypted, but whoever was coming at us now might have bribed the guy I rented my suit from to reveal the encryption code. The person or persons in that Mars buggy might well be listening in on everything I said to Pickover, and so now knew that they'd been spotted.

When two biologicals didn't want to use radio on the surface, they touched their helmets together and let the sound pass between them. Pickover wasn't wearing a helmet. I wondered if he'd opted for super hearing as well as super vision—although I couldn't imagine what use the former would be for a fossil hunter. I turned off my radio and shouted, "They might be listening in on our communications."

The Martian atmosphere was only about one percent as thick as Earth's; it conducted sound, but not very well. Pickover was looking at me but it was clear that he hadn't heard what I'd said. I walked over to him and motioned for him to stand still. I then leaned my helmet against his artificial head.

"I say!" he exclaimed as I did so.

I spoke only slightly louder than normal. "They may have been listening to our radio. Turn yours off." I pulled my head away, and he nodded but didn't do anything else, again making me wonder how that worked for a transfer—what did he do inside his mind that deactivated the transmitter? But although I could make noise—my helmet was pressurized—his jaw was flapping in the tenuous Martian air and wasn't making any sound I could hear. I was good at reading lips—a marketable skill for a detective—but the restrained movements of his were different enough from those of a biological that I wasn't able to make out what he was saying.

I touched my helmet to his forehead—the only time in recent memory that I'd done something similar was head-butting a drunk at The Bent Chisel. "I can't hear you," I said loudly. "Let's separate. They can only come after one of us in that vehicle. You stay here. I'll see if I can draw them away from the Alpha, okay?"

He nodded his head; it slid against the helmet. It was fortunate that his hair was synthetic; the last thing I needed was a smear of oil obscuring my vision through the fishbowl. Having finished quarterbacking our next play, I snapped, "Break!" and started running in a direction perpendicular to the incoming buggy.

I could run like the wind inside the dome—but the surface suit and air tanks added fifty kilos to my normal ninety, and the layer of dust on the plain made it hard to get good footing. Still, I put everything I had into it, hoping the intruder would go after me: it was the nature of all predators, human or otherwise, to chase after someone who was trying to escape. Looking to my right, it did seem the buggy—still some distance off—was veering toward me.

Of course, I had no idea what I'd do if whoever it was *did* intercept me. Even if they didn't have a gun, anything that would smash my helmet would do to finish me off out here.

My heart was pounding, and I was sweating inside the suit—which was not a good thing: I was fogging up the fishbowl. The suit did have dehumidifier controls, but I'd have to stop running to fiddle with them, and I didn't want to do that. And since the fog was on the inside of the helmet, I couldn't wipe it away with my hands, either, and—

And *damn!* The surface of Mars was littered with rocks, and my boot caught on one, and I went flying. At least I came back down in slo-mo; I had plenty of time to brace myself for the impact. I looked toward the buggy and could make it out in more detail now. It was yellow—not an uncommon color for such things—and it had a pressurized habitat, meaning whoever was chasing me was more likely biological than not.

I scrambled to my feet and started running again. There was no doubt now that the buggy was coming at me, rather than Pickover. I'd expected it to rush right up to me, but it skidded to a stop about seventy meters away, spinning through a half turn. Ah, it had come to the periphery of the Alpha, and the driver had slammed on the brakes; either they knew about the land mines, or they didn't want to risk damaging any exposed fossils by driving over them.

The buggy's boxy habitat swung backward on hinges, and I saw the white cloud of condensation that occurs when breathable air is vented into the Martian atmosphere. Coming through the cloud were two figures in surface suits. The helmets were polarized, so I couldn't see who was inside, but the person on my left, wearing a red suit, was a curvy female, and the one on my right, in a blue suit, had the bulk of a man. The woman was carrying what might have been a pump-action shotgun, although where someone would get such a thing on Mars, I had no idea; it's not like they were needed to kill varmints here.

They started running toward me, and I now weaved left and right as I ran. I wasn't sure what I was running *for*—there was no shelter, although I thought hills were starting to peek over the horizon, which suggested we might be near Syrtis Major.

I looked to my left, trying to spot Pickover, but couldn't make him out. I looked back to my right and saw the woman in red fire the shotgun. There was almost no report from the blast in this thin air, but I saw the lick of flame. She didn't come anywhere near to hitting me—suggesting she wasn't experienced with a gun.

When they weren't weighed down by surface suits, you could see at a glance if a runner was new to Mars or not; it took a while to get the hang of sailing so far with each stride. But I couldn't tell about this woman. The man, though, was an old hand; he was close enough now that I could make out details of the suit he was wearing. It had an old-fashioned helmet that was glass only at the front. No one rented suits like that anymore, so this guy probably owned his—and had for at least ten mears.

Another blast from the shotgun. If they hit me in the suit, it probably wouldn't kill me; the pressure-webbing in the fabric would double nicely as a reasonably bulletproof lining. But although the helmet was impact resistant, it wasn't shatterproof; alloquartz did a great job of screening out UV, and wouldn't break if you dropped it—especially in Mars's gravity—but the warranties specifically disclaimed micrometeorite damage, and I imagined lead shot coming in at high speed was a good approximation of such impacts.

I decided to reactivate my radio. I did that by hitting a control in the suit collar with my chin; it was just to the left of the tube that snaked around from behind, bringing air into the fishbowl. "Pickover," I said, "remember, they may be listening in. Don't tell me where you are—but I'm heading west, and they've opened fire on me."

The cultured English accent: "Roger."

Another male voice on the same circuit, half out of breath from running. "Professor Pickover, is that you?"

Pickover, surprised: "Yes. Who is this?"

"Professor, my name's Darren Cheung. I'm with the United States Geological Survey. We thought you were someone looting the fossil beds."

"It's a trick, Pickover!" I shouted.

But the little paleontologist wasn't as naïve as I feared. "The girls can flirt and other queer things can do," he said. If it was a code for me, I didn't know it. He added, "What's that mean?"

"Professor," said the same male voice, "we're wasting time."

Pickover's voice was harsh. "Get him, Alex."

I appreciated his faith in me, but I didn't have any idea just then *how* to get him—or the woman who was also closing rapidly. There was another blast—visual, not aural—from the shotgun, and this time I was hit in the shoulder. The impact knocked me sideways, and I sent up a dust cloud when I fell. Beneath the dust, there were loose rocks. I grabbed one about the size of a grapefruit, scrambled to my feet, and continued running. My shoulder hurt, but the suit seemed intact, and—

And, no, damn it, there was a chip out of my helmet. It hadn't broken all the way through, but the structure had doubtless weakened; another hit, and I'd be sucking in nothing but thin carbon dioxide.

The man was slightly outpacing the woman, and that was working to my advantage—she seemed reluctant to shoot again with him in front of her; perhaps she was worried about going wide enough of her mark to hit him instead of me.

I had no such compunctions. The man was now close enough that I could throw my rock at him. All that bench-pressing at Gully's paid off, and I had plenty of experience throwing things under Martian gravity—as Buttrick at The Bent Chisel could testify. I hit the man right in the faceplate, and it cracked in a spider-web pattern that probably obscured his vision but I didn't think was going to result in him gasping for breath, unfortunately.

Still, it slowed him down enough that the woman was now in front again, and she brought the shotgun up to her red-suited shoulder. She was clearly about to fire when Pick-over's voice burst into my helmet, and hers, too, presumably. "Look out, Alex!"

I swung my head to the right and saw our Mars buggy rushing toward us, a great cloud going up behind it. As I leapt to one side, I was touched that Pickover was willing to drive over his precious fossil beds to rescue me. He slammed the brakes in a way that would have made a screeching sound in a real atmosphere, and popped the clear habitat roof open. I leapt in, and he put his metal to the pedal. I thought he was going to take us through a wide one-eighty, but instead he aimed directly for the woman in red. I struggled to pull the lid down over the habitat as he continued to roar toward her, clearly aiming to mow her down. But she was aiming, too—right at us.

That the woman was reasonably new to Mars was now obvious. The best way to stop a car on Earth was to shoot out the pneumatic tires, but we favored springy wiry things. The angle between the spokes changed constantly under computer control, and each spoke led not to a continuous rim but to a separate pad. A camera up front watched for obstacles, and the spokes configured themselves to make it possible to go over most rocks without even touching them. Trying to shoot such wheels out was useless, but she none-theless fired at our left front tire—and it didn't slow us down at all.

The man in the blue suit started running back toward their yellow Mars buggy. He wasn't going as fast as he'd been before; I suspect he'd slowed down not so much out of fatigue—having a guy hurtling toward you in a motorized vehicle tended to get the old adrenaline going—but be-cause he was having trouble seeing through the cracks in his faceplate.

Pickover had to make a choice: go after the woman with the gun or after the apparently unarmed man who had a chance of getting back to his buggy. I could think of argu-ments for either selection, and didn't gainsay the one Rory made: he decided to pursue the woman, who was running like the wind.

There was no way she could outrace us on a flat surface, but even a planitia has some craters on it, like God had peppered it with his own shotgun. She was heading straight for the one I'd noticed before; it was maybe thirty meters across. The crater wall rose in front of us. To get up it, she had to drop the shotgun, and it skittered with Martian indolence down the crater face. She scrambled up, gloves clawing for purchase. Damn, but I wished I had my gun! It would have been easy to take her out while her back was to us. Our springy wheels did their best, but when the slope exceeded forty-five degrees, they weren't able to get enough traction, and we started backsliding.

I unlatched the habitat lid, and it fell open, letting me hop out. The buggy managed to reverse its slide and climb back up a bit farther after the weight of me and my surface suit was no longer in it. But soon the slope proved too much again, and Pickover abandoned the buggy, too; the vehicle came to rest half-on and half-off the sloping, crumbling crater wall. I flipped open the trunk, exposing the land mines. The activation knob was on the underside of the mine, dead center, behind a little spring-loaded safety door. I reactivated both mines, and saw that the flags on their upper surfaces turned red. I then picked up one of the mines, supporting it underhanded by its rim.

The man had succeeded in his retreat; I could see him in the distance clambering into their buggy. I'd thought he was going to hightail it away from here, but he came charging toward us again. I chinned my radio: "One warning only: get out of the buggy!"

It was possible that the damage to his helmet had wrecked his microphone in addition to impairing his vision. Or maybe he just didn't feel inclined to take orders from me. Either way, he kept racing my way at a clip I couldn't outrun. I took a bead on the approaching vehicle, and flung the land mine the way you'd toss a discus. It spun through the air and—

Ka-blam!

—hit the flat front of the buggy's habitat, exploding on impact. The canopy was reduced to crystalline shards that went flying. I saw the man in the blue suit throw up his arms, trying to cover his face—

His *exposed* face: the glass visor of his helmet was gone. He gasped for breath—and I imagine he felt the linings of his lungs seizing up in the wicked cold of an equatorial Martian day.

His vehicle was still moving, though—the habitat was wrecked, but the chassis was intact and those big wheels kept on rolling, propelling it at high speed along the wall of the crater and—God damn it!—straight toward me and our Mars buggy.

I ran as fast as I could, but the incoming vehicle plowed into our buggy, and the other land mine I'd activated in preparation for throwing it went off, and I watched as the axles snapped on the incoming yellow buggy and our buggy burst into flames that almost immediately were snuffed out by the carbon dioxide atmosphere.

We were all marooned in the middle of nowhere.

NINETEEN

I rushed over to the man in the blue surface suit. He'd tumbled out of the wreckage and was still desperately trying to cover his face. I looked around for anything that could help him do that: tarpaulin, plastic sheeting, even paper. But there was nothing.

I doubted he could still hear me, given that the air was out of his helmet, but I said, "Hold on!" anyway. I used my gloved hands in addition to his own to try to make a new front for his helmet. For a moment, I thought it was working, but even though clouds of air were still coming out of the tubes attached to his tank, his fingers went slack and his arms dropped down, and there were now huge gaps that I couldn't cover.

And so at last I got a good look at his face. His nose had bled—low air pressure or the impact—but the blood had now frozen onto his face, a narrow face that was Asian, perhaps sixty years old, with thick gray hair. I didn't recognize him. His mouth worked for a few moments—gasping for air, or hurtling invective at me, I couldn't say which. And then it just stopped moving, about half open. I took no pleasure in watching this man expire, even though he'd tried to kill me—but I didn't waste any tears over it, either.

I'd lost track of Pickover during all this, and, swinging my head in the fishbowl, I saw no sign of him—which meant he must be inside the crater, along with the lady in red. I looked around for the discarded shotgun and found it. Damn thing had gone barrel-down into the dust and probably had a bunch of it in the bore now. Still, I grabbed it and scrambled up the crater's rim, which was about three meters high, and peered over the edge.

I'd expected to see Pickover having captured her at this point. After all, she was now unarmed and he was much more nimble as a transfer than she—whoever she was—could possibly be in a surface suit. But Pickover was—well, I couldn't exactly say he was a lover not a fighter . . . but he definitely wasn't a fighter. Although it was true she no longer had a gun, she did apparently have a lasso: a loop of what, judging by its dark color, were fibers made of carbon nanotubes, meaning it would be almost impossible to break even with a transfer's strength. And she'd managed to get it around his ankles and had pulled it tight. While I watched, she gave the lasso a yank, pulling Pickover's legs out from under him. He tumbled backward—a body slam, not a slo-mo fall—landing flat on his back and sending up a cloud of dust.

As it happened, Pickover was facing my way; she had her back to me. I could make it two for two, pumping shot into her from behind, but her suit might protect her. And, besides, I had questions I wanted to ask. I hauled myself up over the crater rim and clambered down the crumbly incline. The two of them were just shy of the crater's central bulge.

Pickover tried to get to his feet. The woman yanked the lasso again, and he tumbled backward once more. I think she'd have preferred to hog-tie him, but she didn't have enough rope for that—I imagine she'd improvised the lasso out of line she'd brought along to help with climbing; she must have thought the Alpha might have been deep in some crevasse, and—

Yes, that was it. She didn't have another real gun, true—but she had a piton gun attached to her suit's belt, and she bent over now and positioned it against the center of Pickover's artificial chest. She presumably hoped that firing a metal spike into his innards would damage *something* that would incapacitate him. She pulled the trigger.

Pickover screamed and his torso convulsed. It was like watching a biological getting defibrillated, but the intent was the opposite. I had made it down to the reasonably flat bottom of the crater. There was hoarfrost along this part of the wall, since it hadn't yet been touched by the rising sun.

The woman, who was straddling Pickover, moved the piton gun farther down his chest and fired again. Once more, Rory convulsed from the impact. I brought the shotgun to my shoulder and Pickover seemed to be tucking his knees up toward his torso, maybe to protect his nuts and bolt.

I fired, the recoil pushing me backward a bit—and Pickover got his knees through the woman's spread legs and kicked her in the chest with his bound feet. She went flying up a good two meters, and the bulk of my shot flew through the gap that had appeared between her and Pickover before she came down again.

Rory rolled onto his side so she wouldn't fall on top of him, and I hurried in. She hit the ground before I'd closed all the distance and was in a push-up posture, trying to get to her feet, by the time I got there. I grabbed her shoulder and flipped her onto her back, then loomed over her with the shotgun aimed right at her helmet.

"Can you hear me?" I said into my suit radio.

I gave her time to weigh whether she wanted to reply—and, after a moment, she did, although the connection was staticky and hard to make out. "Yes."

"I want to see your face. There are two ways that can happen. One is I blast open your helmet. The other is you depolarize it. Your choice."

She just lay there. Maybe she was hoping blue boy would come to her rescue, jumping me from behind. I wanted to see her face when I broke the news—not out of any sick desire to watch her feel hurt, but because her reaction would be a useful clue to the nature of their relationship.

"Five seconds, lady," I said. "One. Two. Three."

She moved her right hand to the bank of buttons on her

left forearm, and the bowl went from reflecting a distorted image of me to being transparent.

And that face I did know, a gorgeous symphony in chocolate shades: brown skin, brown hair, brown eyes. Lakshmi Chatterjee, New Klondike's writer-in-residence.

"Sweetheart," I said, "I thought we had something special."

"We still could," she replied. She indicated Pickover, who was lying on his side. "With him out of the picture, you, me, and Darren split it three ways."

"Just two ways, honey. Darren is dead."

Her brown eyes went wide, but she didn't seem too broken up by it, and, after a moment, she said, "Even better."

I looked over at Pickover, and, yeah, I thought about it for half a second. Now, you could say that all things being equal, it made more sense to share the wealth with Rory, who'd never tried to kill me, than with Lakshmi, who'd happily shoot pitons into my chest, too, if given the chance. But old Dr. Pickover wasn't going to let these fossils be sold, so there was no sharing to do with him.

Still, I *liked* the guy.

"No dice," I said. I reached down and wrenched the piton gun from her and sent it flying—it was easy enough to toss it clear over the crater's rim. "Roll over," I said. "Face down."

Lakshmi hesitated, so I pushed the shotgun muzzle right up against her fishbowl. She nodded within and turned onto her stomach. "Don't move," I said.

I went over to Pickover. If he'd been knifed, the standard advice would be to leave the blades in, lest removing them exposed gaping wounds through which he'd bleed to death. But I thought in this case the metal spikes might be causing electrical shorts inside him, and so I grabbed them—my suit's gloves insulating me—and pulled them free. One came out clean; the other was covered with black machine oil. I tossed them aside.

"You okay?" I asked.

He looked no worse for wear—although the workings of his face were still exposed. "I think so."

I glanced at his bound ankles. "You still have my switch-blade?" He'd kept it after using it to disarm the two mines.

"In the pouch," he said.

I opened his equipment pouch and took out the knife. I tried to cut through the material, but my guess had been right: it was carbon nanofiber; the knife didn't even make a mark on it. Still, that didn't mean we were out of luck. I went over and kicked Lakshmi none too gently in the thigh. "Up," I said.

She got to her feet.

"You made the lasso," I said, pointing. "Untie it."

She hesitated for a moment then bent over to do so. It took a particularly good figure to look attractive through a surface suit, but, admiring her from behind, it was clear that that was precisely what she had.

"Come on!" I said. "Hurry up!"

"I can't," she said after trying for a bit. She held up her hands. "The gloves are too thick."

"Take them off, then."

"It's fifty below zero!"

I considered. "All right. Rory, can you manage it?"

He sat up. A jet of oil squirted from one of the holes in his chest, but he didn't seem to notice. His fingers were unencumbered, and I imagined he'd opted for a super-high degree of dexterity, since part of his job was preparing minute fossils. I kept the shotgun trained on Lakshmi, while he struggled to loosen the loop—and, at last, he succeeded.

He surprised me by holding out a hand so I could help him get up—but that might just have been the natural thought of the middle-aged mind within the transfer body; I was counting on him not actually being severely injured. I put my gloved hand in his naked one and pulled him to his feet. He nodded his thanks and stepped out of the lasso. I bent over, picked it up, and slipped it over Lakshmi's head and shoulders, pulled it down past her breasts, then cinched it tight, binding her arms below the elbow to her waist—which, again, emphasized her remarkable figure.

I took the other end of the cord, holding it like a leash. I gave her a little shove, and she started walking in front of us. Pickover fell in next to me. I had to let go of the cord to let her, and then me, scramble up the inner crater wall and down the outer one. We'd come out about thirty degrees around the rim from where I'd gone in, and—

"Oh, yeah," I said. "I probably should have mentioned that."

Pickover's artificial jaw had dropped to half-mast. Lakshmi stopped dead in her tracks. "How are we going to get home?" she exclaimed, looking at the two wrecked buggies.

"That's a very good question," I replied. Mars had no telephone system outside the dome, no global positioning system, and no string of communications satellites—it was the frontier. And the planet's weak and wonky ionosphere was no use for bouncing signals, so radio worked only more or less over line of sight—meaning there was no way to call all the way back to New Klondike for help. "Given how long it took to get here," I continued, "and even allowing for Rory possibly not having taken the most direct route out, I'd guess it'd take days to walk home." In this gravity, even in the suit, I could easily manage it—and I suspected Lakshmi was in good enough shape to do it, as well. Except for one thing: I looked at the air gauge built into my suit's inner left sleeve. "I've got five hours left."

Lakshmi was still bound with the lasso. I rotated her arm in a way that probably wasn't pleasant and read her gauge. "And she's got three." I didn't add, but I certainly thought, *Which means if I take her tanks, I've got a total of eight.* I looked at Pickover. "We should head out."

"You're not abandoning me here!" Lakshmi exclaimed.

I turned to her. "Why not? You were prepared to kill me, and you just tried to kill Dr. Pickover."

"Not kill him, just disable him—with damage that would be easy to repair."

"Well, tell you what, sweetheart: you can start walking; you, at least, should more or less know the way."

"I'm new to Mars; you know that. Darren was navigating. I honestly don't have a clue which way to go."

"If you ask him nicely, Rory might point you in the right direction."

He was looking down at his chest, probing the holes in it with his fingers, and—

And, no, actually, he was probing the holes she'd made in his work shirt. I hadn't paid much attention to it until now, but it was a somewhat tattered flannel number sporting a light and dark gray plaid and pockets over both breasts. Above his left breast was a logo showing what I was pleased with myself for recognizing as a trilobite, and beneath that, some words that were too small for me to read.

"This was my lucky shirt," he said. "Got it when I was doing fieldwork at the Burgess Shale; I brought it all the way from Earth." He looked at her. "And you wrecked it."

The upper hole was merely a rip; the lower one was now badly stained by oil.

Lakshmi took on a desperate tone. "Please, tell me which way to head."

"It doesn't make any difference," I said. "You won't get anywhere near the dome before your air runs out. At least if you stay here, we'll know where your body is, and can come back and give you a decent burial."

"You bastard," said Lakshmi.

"I'm just telling you the truth."

Rory looked around, getting his bearings. "That way," he said, pointing in a direction somewhat more northerly than what I would have guessed but not so much so that I doubted his word. "Walk that way."

"Thank you," she said to Rory. Then, to me: "You're going to die, too, Lomax. Yes, you've got more air than I do—but it's still nowhere near enough."

I smiled. "It wouldn't be if I were going to walk it. But I'm not."

"You expect a rescue?" She looked relieved. "Then I'm waiting right here with you."

"Oh, no. I'm heading out, too. But Rory's going to carry me."

"I am?" said Pickover.

"You are. Bend over a bit."

He did so, putting his hands on his knees. I climbed onto his back piggyback style. It was easy for him to take the weight—the combination of low gravity and a transfer's strength. "And you're going to run," I said. I thought about digging in my heels as if they were spurs and yelling, "Giddyap," but I didn't think the paleontologist would appreciate that. So instead I simply said, "Let's go."

Lakshmi looked furious, but Pickover did indeed start running, leaving her behind. It took Pickover a hundred meters to find the right gait with me on his back, but he finally did. The horizon went up and down as he ran along, his powerful legs sailing from one footfall to the next. Holding on to him wasn't difficult. The miles and miles of miles and miles shifted one by one from being in front of us to behind us, and soon enough Lakshmi's cursing faded away as we moved out of radio range.

TWENTY

D r. Pickover and I reached the vicinity of New Klondike by mid afternoon. To his credit, Rory had taken a straight path all the way back, with no attempt to disguise the route. Polarizing the fishbowl at night had rendered me almost blind, but here in broad daylight it just made looking out at the world comfortable—so I now had a rough idea of where the Alpha Deposit was.

"Almost there," said Pickover, via radio. It was astonishing listening to someone who had been running at high speed for hours but wasn't out of breath. I looked at my air gauge; I still had twenty-odd minutes left. I'd never thought of the dome as pretty before, but it sure looked that way as it came into view, glistening in the sunshine.

"Okay," I said to Pickover. "No point in making a spectacle of ourselves. Let's walk the rest of the way."

The scientist stopped and bent his knees, lowering himself a bit. I hopped off his back. It felt good to not be bouncing up and down anymore.

"We have to go back for her," Pickover said, as I fell in beside him. "Get more bottled air, get another buggy. Go rescue her."

I reached over and held his forearm with my suit glove. "Rory, she's dead by now. She has to be."

"But if—"

"If what? She had less air than me, and I'm almost empty. Even if she did manage to conserve her oxygen, there's no way she could still be alive by the time we got back out there."

"Yes, but . . ."

"But what? She tried to kill both of us."

"I know. I just don't want it on my conscience, I guess."

"I had mine removed years ago," I said. "Makes things easier."

We walked on in silence. The dome in front of us was an impressive feat. Building it would have been impossible even forty years ago, but nanoassemblers had constructed the whole thing molecule by molecule, extracting the source silicon dioxide from the Martian soil, modifying it into ultraviolet-opaque alloquartz, and laying it down in the pattern Howard Slapcoff's engineers had programmed. Its rim was anchored into the permafrost, and its great weight was borne by curving struts and the central support column, all made of carbon nanotubes.

We went through the airlock, and I returned the surface suit. The person who had rented us the suit wasn't on duty anymore—which was a good thing, since I would have felt obliged to clock him for having revealed the radio-encryption key to Lakshmi. Adding insult to injury, Pickover lost his damage deposit because of the chip out of my helmet.

I collected my little tablet computer, phone, shoulder holster, and gun from the locker, put the tab in my right hip pocket, slipped the phone around my left wrist, placed the pistol in the holster, and draped the holster over my shoulder. My clothes were clean, but Pickover was covered with dust, and he'd gotten a fair bit of it in the exposed workings of his face. I used the john while he went through the cleaning chamber, where air jets blasted dust off him, and vacuum hoses sucked up the stuff that wouldn't blow away.

When Pickover was done, we headed out onto Ninth Avenue. "What now?" he asked.

I gave him an appraising look. "You've been missing most of your face for God knows how long, and you've got two holes in your chest. I'm thinking it's time you visited NewYou."

He shuddered. "I get so angry when I think about what they did. A bootleg copy of me!"

"I know. But the people who did that are gone, and so is the bootleg—and you *do* need to get fixed up, and they're the only game in town."

"All right," he said. "But will you come with me?"

"You're the client; I charge by the hour. You really want to pay someone to hold your hand?"

"Please, Alex."

I'd been hoping to go home, have a shower, change, and then maybe go see Diana. But I said, "Okay."

"Thank you."

I made Pickover wait for me while we stopped at a shop so I could buy a sandwich; the ones I'd bought before had gone up with the buggy. Meat was synthesized directly—no need for messy, smelly animals—and the place we went into printed a passable roast beef on an algae bun. I ate it as we walked along. We had to cross right through the center of town, since NewYou was on Third and about halfway out to the other side of the dome. Before we went in, I think Pickover would have liked to have taken a deep breath to steel himself—so to speak—but he couldn't.

We were greeted inside by Horatio Fernandez, he of the massive arms. "My God," he said, looking at Pickover, "what happened to you?"

I spoke before Pickover could answer. "Little accident with some climbing gear."

"And your face?" asked Fernandez.

"Cut myself shaving," Pickover replied.

"Jesus," said Horatio. "Let's get you into the workshop."

Pickover looked at me. "I'll wait," I said. "Don't worry."

Fernandez called out, "Reiko!" A woman came through a doorway to mind the store. Fernandez headed into the back, and Pickover followed.

I remembered Reiko Takahashi from the Wilkins case,

and so I went over to say hello. She was petite, about twenty-eight, and very pretty for a biological.

"Hello, Mr. Lomax," she said, smiling perfect teeth.

I was pleased she remembered my name. "Alex," I said.

"Alex, yes. Hi."

"Hi."

She moved closer and looked around, making sure we were alone, I guess. "Are you working on another case?"

"My friend needed some maintenance, and I'm keeping him company."

"Ah."

Reiko had long black hair that went halfway down her back. Three streaks of orange went through it, one behind each ear, and the third exactly down the center. She had brown eyes, and eye shadow that matched the streaks, and was wearing a dark gray pantsuit over a silky blouse that was also the same shade of orange. "What brought you to Mars?" I asked, making conversation.

She smiled mischievously. "A spaceship."

"Ha ha. Seriously, though?"

She looked at me for a moment, as if trying to decide whether she wanted to confide something. But then she simply said, "Something to do."

I turned on the patented Lomax charm. "Well, I'm glad you came." I gestured at the front window. "This planet is so dreary; we can use all the beauty we can get."

She dipped her head a little, pleased. Then she looked up at me without straightening her neck back out. "I'm glad you dropped in," she said.

"Thank you." I dialed it up a notch. "I'm certainly glad I did, too."

Her voice grew tentative. "I'd been thinking of coming to see you, actually."

"Oh?"

"Uh-huh."

"Why didn't you?"

"I'm . . . forgive me, but I just wasn't sure you were the right man."

I put a finger under her chin and lifted her lovely face. "Of course I am. Why don't we go somewhere and talk?"

She looked around. "No, this will do. We're alone."

"We are indeed," I said.

"You see, there's a matter I need help in investigating."

Oh. "And what might that be?"

She looked at me for several seconds, sizing me up. "Okay," she said. "But you have to promise not to tell anyone."

"Tell anyone what?"

It was amazing how many people would ask you to pledge silence then go on even when you hadn't. I was feeling pleased about that insight when she started speaking, but by the time she'd finished, I'd found myself taking a step backward.

"It's just this," she said. "Denny O'Reilly was my grandfather."

TWENTY-ONE

I'm sure my poker face cracked; that was *quite* a claim. "Really?" I said.

She nodded. "My mother was his daughter; his only child. And I'm his only grandchild."

I'd seen photos of Denny O'Reilly. He'd been a white guy, and Miss Takahashi had exquisite Asian features. She'd obviously previously encountered surprised expressions like the one I must have been wearing. "My grandmother was from Kyoto," she said. "And my mother married a man from Tokyo. Despite that, I was hoping I'd still have a little bit of the luck o' the Irish in my genes. I thought I could retrace my grandfather's steps and find the Alpha."

"But you didn't."

"I didn't."

"And now you work here?" I raised my eyebrows. "Forgive me, but, well, if you're Denny O'Reilly's granddaughter, shouldn't you be, you know, rolling in it?"

"My grandmother was his mistress, not his wife."

"He didn't leave anything to your grandmother?"

"He didn't leave anything to *anyone*. He died intestate. And in the jurisdiction he lived in, that meant it all went to his actual wife. She had no children—and, for that matter, neither did Simon Weingarten. I'm the only surviving heir of either of them—except the courts did me out of my due."

"Ah. And when you failed to find riches here, you had to get a job."

"Exactly." She gestured at one of the floor models. "Have you ever thought about transferring, Mr. Lomax? A man in your line of work, it might come in handy."

"You on commission, Reiko?"

She smiled. "Sorry."

"So, what exactly were you hoping I could help you with?"

"Well, like I said, I wasn't sure if I needed a detective, or what. But someone broke into my apartment last week."

"What did they take?"

"Nothing. But the place was ransacked. I called the police, and they took my report over the phone, but that's all."

"Do you know what the thief was looking for?"

She said, "No," but I could tell she was lying.

There was still no one else in the shop. It was my turn to decide if I wanted to confide in her. "You asked if I had a case. I'm actually investigating an old one: the fate of Willem Van Dyke."

Her eyes opened wider.

"I see you know the name," I said.

"Oh, yes. He came to Mars on the second expedition with my grandfather and Simon. Horrible man; tried to sell all the fossils out from under them."

"That's what your grandfather said?"

"Yes. Why do you care what happened to Van Dyke?"

"I have a client who doesn't like loose ends."

"Was that him? Your client? Going into the back?"

I nodded.

"He looked in bad shape."

"He'll be okay."

"What's his name?"

"Rory Pickover."

That was Mr. Pickover? Wow."

"Yeah. His face needs a little work."

"I'll say. Why's he interested in this?"

"You know he's a scientist, right? He wants to find any fossils from the Alpha that might have gone into private collections, and he figures Van Dyke might be the key to that."

"Ah," said Reiko. "Well, maybe I can help, too. The diary mentions some names."

"Whose diary?"

"My grandfather's."

"He kept a diary of the second expedition?"

"Yes, I believe so. And of the first, as well. I've never seen those, but . . ."

"But what? What diary are you referring to?"

"There was one of the third mission."

"Really?" I said. "But wouldn't that have been lost when their ship burned up on re-entry?"

"No. My grandfather beamed it home to my grandmother just before he and Simon left Mars. Of course, they were going to spend the months of the return voyage in hibernation, and only thaw out to handle re-entering Earth's atmosphere. But he broadcast the diary just before he left Mars—in terms of his conscious time, that was less than a day before he died."

"And you have copies of this diary?"

"Well, *a* copy, yes. A bound printout of it."

I felt my eyebrows go up. "On paper?"

"Uh-huh. My grandmother never wanted it to get out; parts of the diary are very personal, and you know how things take on a life of their own once they get online. But she wanted me to know where I'd come from, and who my grandfather had been. So about a year ago, just before she died, she had a bound printout of it made, then erased the files. I have the one and only copy."

"And it's here on Mars?"

She didn't answer.

"Is it?" I said.

Another hesitation, then a small nod.

"That's what the thief was looking for," I said. There was no point in raising my tone to make it a question; it was obviously true.

She nodded again meekly.

"Does the diary reveal the location of the Alpha?"

"No. If it did, I wouldn't be working here. But, as I said, he mentions some collectors he'd done business with in the past."

"Who else knows about—"

Just then, the front door slid open, and an elderly man shuffled in. "Excuse me," Reiko said, and she went over to speak to him. From what I overheard, he was a prospector trying to decide between spending the money he'd made from his finds either on transferring or on passage back home.

I pulled out my tab and looked at the encyclopedia entry on Denny O'Reilly, particularly the stuff on his personal life. There was no mention of a mistress, although he had indeed been married at the time he'd died, and that woman, who had been dead herself for a dozen years, had inherited his estate; she'd doubtless had the money to transfer at some point, but had been killed unexpectedly in a plane crash.

The elderly customer was looking at a sample body in the window display. The man happened to be black and the body was white, but its build was similar to his own.

Since she was still busy, and since Rory would probably be a while longer, I stepped outside onto the street and used my wrist phone to call Dougal McCrae.

"Hello, Alex," he said from the tiny screen.

"Hey, Mac. Did you guys investigate an incident at the home of a Reiko Takahashi recently?"

He looked away from the camera. "Two secs." Then his freckled face turned back to me. "Yeah, a B&E. Kaur handled it. Strange; nothing taken."

"What can you tell me about Miss Takahashi?"

He looked off camera again. "No wants, no warrants. Life-support tax paid in full. Came here three months ago. Works at NewYou—you've met her, remember?"

I nodded. "Thanks, Mac. Talk to you later."

"One thing while I've got you, Alex."

"Sure."

"We've had a couple of missing-persons reports."

"Oh?"

"Yes. A woman named Lakshmi Chatterjee and a man named Darren Cheung. Logged out of the dome, but apparently never returned. They rented a Mars buggy, and she rented a surface suit; the rental firm wants them back."

"I can imagine so."

"Same log shows that you and Dr. Pickover went out shortly before them."

"I brought my suit back."

"With a cracked helmet."

"Shoddy workmanship," I said.

Mac looked at me dubiously.

"Anyway," I said, "I'll let you know if I see them."

"You do that, Alex."

I nodded, shook the phone off, and started to head back inside. I was startled by the door sliding open before I'd reached it—it was the old man, coming out. "What did you decide?" I asked amiably.

He narrowed his eyes, as if wondering what business it was of mine. But he answered nonetheless. "I'm going home."

He didn't look like he was in good enough shape to hack the gravity on the mother world. "Really?" I said.

"Yup. Going back to Lunaport. No damn fossils anywhere there; I've had my fill of dead things."

I nodded; he'd do fine there. *"Bon voyage,"* I said. I'd once made the effort here on Mars to see Luna without a telescope; it's about as bright as Mercury is as seen from Earth's surface, which is to say not very bright at all. I squeezed past the old codger and went inside.

"Sorry you didn't make a sale," I said to Reiko, jerking my thumb toward the front door.

"So am I," she replied. "Sure I can't interest you?"

I looked at her pretty face and thought that she interested me just fine. But what I said was, "About your grandfather's diary . . ."

"Yes?"

"The thief didn't find it. I trust you've got it somewhere safe."

"Oh, yes."

"Here at NewYou?"

"No."

"Then where?"

She compressed her lips, and the color went out of them.

"Reiko, if you want me to investigate this, you have to trust me."

She considered. "There's a writer here, doing an authorized biography of my grandfather. She's got it."

I seriously doubted we had more than one writer, but I asked anyway. "Who?"

"Her name's Lakshmi Chatterjee. She's staying at Shopatsky House."

"I thought she was doing a book about the *B. Traven*," I said.

"What's that?" asked Reiko.

It occurred to me that being a writer—or even just claiming to be one—was a great cover. You could tell people you were doing a book on just about anything, and they'd take you into their confidence. Still, if Lakshmi had the diary already, she obviously wasn't the one who'd searched Reiko's place. "Who else besides Lakshmi knows about the diary?"

"No one. At least, no one here on Mars. Lakshmi promised to keep it a secret."

At that moment, Pickover came out of the back room. His face had been repaired, and although there were still two rips in his favorite shirt, I had no doubt that whatever damage there'd been underneath had also been fixed. He was followed by Horatio Fernandez. The two of them went over to the cash station to settle up.

"Okay," I said to Reiko. "I'll see if I can figure out who broke into your place, and, if I do, I'll lean on them a bit—make sure they leave you alone in the future."

"Thank you, Mr. Lomax."

"Alex. Call me Alex."

She smiled, showing the perfect teeth again. "Thank you, Alex."

Pickover was finished. I said goodbye to Reiko, and he

and I headed outside. As soon as the door slid shut behind me, I turned to him. "You okay?"

"Good as new," he said.

"Did he put a tracking chip in, do you think?"

"I watched him like a hawk—easy to do when someone is working on your face. I don't think so. But I'll get myself checked, as before."

"Good, okay. Don't forget." I paused, then: "Here's a shocker for you. Miss Takahashi is Denny O'Reilly's granddaughter."

"Oh, really?"

"No," I said, unable to resist. "O'Reilly." I waited for him to laugh—but I guess he was only laughing on the inside. "Anyway," I said. "Yes, she is. Her grandmother was Denny's mistress. That mechanical ticker of yours ready for another shock? There's a diary of Weingarten and O'Reilly's last voyage. Denny transmitted it to Miss Takahashi's grandmother before they left Mars."

Rory's plastic face lit up almost—almost literally. "Oh, my God! If he recorded any paleontological details—I have to see it! There's no known record of what they'd found on the third expedition. Who knows what treasures the Alpha yielded that were lost when their ship burned up?"

"Don't sweat it," I said. "I'll get it for you. It's at Shopatsky House, and, as we both know, the position of writer-in-residence is now vacant. I'll go retrieve it."

"And what about me?" asked Pickover.

I smiled my most reassuring smile. "Go home and clean some fossils. I'm going to swing by my office, then head out to get the diary. This shouldn't take long."

TWENTY-TWO

There was a sign outside Shopatsky House that I hadn't seen the last time, because I'd approached it then from the opposite direction. It was a white rectangle with dark green lettering, and it talked about who Stavros Shopatsky had been and explained that although some might view this site as a tourist attraction—as if Mars got many tourists—it was actually a private home with a hardworking author within, and people should be quiet and respect the writer's privacy.

But the sign, like so much in New Klondike, had been vandalized. Someone had carved "Books Suck" into it. Everybody's a critic.

Most homes had their front doors well secured—and some other potential entrance that was easy to break in through. I went around back. The grounds were covered with ferns that did well in the dim sunlight we got here.

It used to be people left a spare key under a rock—and Mars had *plenty* of rocks. But unless you were a transfer, you probably used a biometric lock these days, and few people stored a spare finger somewhere in their backyard. I did a cursory search anyway but didn't find anything. Still, there was a big window in the back—writers, I hear, like to stare out into space, which must be good work if you can get it. The window was probably alloquartz or shatterproof glass, but the molding around the window might, I thought, be made of less-stern stuff, and indeed that turned out to be the case.

Fortunately, Shopatsky House was on the outer rim, with a backyard that no one could see unless they happened to be right on the other side of the dome, looking in. I used the switchblade I'd gotten from Dirk to cut through the molding on all four sides of the window. Pressing in at the bottom made the heavy pane angle out at the top, and I managed to get it to fall toward me. I jockeyed it the half meter down to the ground.

There was no way short of wearing a full surface suit to avoid leaving DNA and other identifying things behind, and so I didn't even bother to try to cover my tracks. After all, I'd been in the house earlier with Lakshmi's permission; if Mac's people ever did investigate this break-in, that fact would exonerate me.

I looked around the small home and quickly found the writing station. Lakshmi apparently wrote with a keyboard; there was one sitting on a little table next to a recliner chair, opposite a monitor wall. I understood that those who were serious about words and how punctuation was wielded preferred keyboards to voice-recognition.

I looked everywhere in this room that might conceal a paper diary, but it clearly wasn't here. I moved into the living room, which had the roll-top desk, and started looking through its cubbyholes and drawers but, again, *bupkes*.

I went to the wall that had the bookcase leaning against it, and looked at each of the spines in turn. As I'd noted before, they weren't alphabetical but chronological, with Lakshmi's own books at the end. There were about eighty books in all, and—yes, yes, there it was: a short hardcover volume, with no printing on the spine, inserted at the far right of the second shelf from the top.

The thick front cover was blank, too, but the title page said, "Journal of Denny T. O'Reilly." The pages were filled with text in a nice font—a proper little book.

I heard a sound, wheeled around, and saw the front door

sliding open. There was no way for me to make it out the same way I'd come in without crossing the line of sight of whoever was arriving. I ducked farther into the room with the bookcase, then peered around the jamb of that room's open doorway to see who was entering.

My heart jumped. It was as if I were seeing a ghost.

A beautiful, brown-haired, brown-eyed, brown-skinned ghost.

It was Lakshmi Chatterjee, back from the dead.

I moved deeper into the room. The entryway wasn't carpeted, and I could hear what sounded like hard-soled shoes being dropped. I didn't hear anything else for a bit, which might have meant she was just standing there, but more likely meant she was now walking barefoot. I didn't know how she'd been rescued, but she was probably sweaty and tired; if she was like me, she'd head for the shower—and I wasn't sure where that was in this house. If it was off the other room, no problem—I could make good my escape while she was in there. But if it was off this room—and there *was* another closed door opposite the one I'd just come through—well, then, I was in trouble.

She took a right, not a left, and I let out my held breath—but she was going first to the kitchen, not the bathroom, damn it. Still, if she buried her head in the refrigerator, I might be able to sneak past her. I heard sounds that I couldn't quite identify, and then some sort of machine started up. I ducked back out of view and waited. It took her a few moments to emerge from the kitchen, and when she did so, she was magnificently, totally, wonderfully nude. The washing machine must have been in, or just off of, the kitchen; I recognized now the sound of electrostatic spin cleansing.

She turned left, facing me in all her curvy perfection, and her mouth dropped open in absolute shock.

"Hello, Lakshmi," I said, stepping toward her, my gun in my hand.

"What are you doing here?" she demanded.

"I might ask you the same thing. How'd you get home?"

"None of your damn business." She noticed that I was holding the diary. "Put that back."

"Not a chance."

"You walk out of here with it, and I'm calling the police."

"Let's call them right now. Tell them what you tried to do to Dr. Pickover and me."

"Let's do that," she said, hands now on her lovely hips. "Tell the whole solar system where the Alpha Deposit is."

I considered my options. I could just shoot her—but the body would eventually be discovered, and Mac would have no trouble tracing the bullet to my gun. I could simply run for it—she doubtless had no idea yet that I'd removed the back window, and so would be surprised when I headed that way instead of toward the front door. Or I could stay here and see what developed; it is, after all, not my norm to run out on a beautiful naked woman.

I decided, somewhat reluctantly, to simply leave. I walked slightly toward her, pointing the gun at her, then headed for the little office, now backing away from her. I made it most of the way to the hole where the window had been, reholstered the gun so one of my hands would be free to climb out, turned around, and—

Pow!

She'd grabbed something heavy—I didn't know what— and thrown it at me. On Earth, she'd have needed a baseball pitcher's arm to hurl whatever it was so far, but here it was easy. She might have been a lousy aim with a shotgun, but she hit me right between the shoulders. The impact sent me tumbling over her windowsill, and I went headfirst into her backyard—my noggin, sadly, not hitting soft ferns but rather the large sheet of alloquartz I'd removed earlier. It took me a second to regain my senses. I was scrambling to my feet when I heard Lakshmi shout, "Freeze!"

I didn't exactly do that. Instead, I rolled onto my butt and sat looking up at her as she leaned out the window, perfect breasts hanging down.

"Or what?" I said. There was no way she had a concealed weapon.

"Or you die."

"How?"

"The self-destruct device in that book you're holding."

"Oh, come on!"

She shrugged as if it were of no real concern to her. "Look inside the back cover."

I did so and, lo and behold, stuck there was a piece of plastic about the size of an old-fashioned business card and several millimeters thick—the kind of explosive someone had cleverly nicknamed "cardite." Such things had transceiver chips inside them and could indeed be detonated by remote control. I tried to rip the back cover off the book, but the hardcover binding was too tough.

"You don't have the remote," I said, looking back at Lakshmi.

"Wanna bet?"

"Reiko Takahashi has it."

"No, she doesn't. It's geared to my computer."

"You're bluffing."

"Try me. It'll blow the book to bits—and take off your arm, at least, it if doesn't outright kill you."

"Let's call Miss Takahashi and find out," I said, lifting my left arm to bring my wrist phone closer to my face.

"You seem to think you're in the driver's seat here, Mr. Lomax. You're not." She spoke over her shoulder: "Persis?"

It was hard to make out from here, but her computer—that red cube I'd seen before sitting on the roll-top desk—replied in a female voice: "Yes, Lakshmi?"

"In thirty seconds from my mark, detonate the explosive in the book—and please do a countdown."

"Mars seconds or Earth seconds?" asked Persis. Since the Martian sol was 1.03 times the length of an Earth day, Martian seconds were 1.03 times as long as Earth ones.

"Oh, for Pete's sake!" declared Lakshmi. "Mars seconds!"

Nothing happened for a moment, and then Lakshmi realized she had to say, "Mark." She did so, and I heard Persis counting down.

Thirty. Twenty-nine. Twenty-eight.

"Toss the book aside, Lomax."

I drew my gun. "Abort the countdown, Lakshmi."

I was hoping she wouldn't think of the obvious. But she did; she crouched down beneath the windowsill, out of my line of fire.

"Twenty-two. Twenty-one. Twenty."

But since she was crouching, she wasn't looking. I scrambled forward, just below the sill, surged to my feet standing on the alloquartz pane, grabbed Lakshmi by her wrists, hauled her out through the window, rolled back on my spine, and flipped her past me onto the bed of ferns.

"Seventeen. Sixteen. Fifteen."

I tossed the book aside; unlike cordite, cardite wasn't finicky about such things.

"I don't think either of us wants that destroyed," I said, jerking my head toward it as I pulled my gun again and aimed it at Lakshmi, who was now appealingly spread-eagled with her tushy facing up.

"Persis," she said, "abort!"

There was only one problem. Persis apparently couldn't hear Lakshmi now. *"Eleven. Ten."*

"Oh, crap," I said.

"Eight. Seven."

Lakshmi rolled onto her back and leapt to her feet, jumping a good meter off the ground as she did so. "Abort!"

"Five."

"Abort!" she shouted as gravity slowly pulled her down.

"Four."

"Abort!" she shouted again.

"Three."

"Abort!" she shouted once more as she lunged toward the window. I was back on my feet and danced out of the way to let her do so.

"Two."

"Abort!"

"Aborted," said Persis calmly.

Before Lakshmi could make it in through the window, I jumped over and grabbed her wrists. We struggled for a bit, but although she was strong—recent arrivals from Earth tended to be, by the standards of most Martians—I was stronger. When it ceased to be fun, I pushed her toward the dome, and said, "Keep walking." I made sure she went three times as far as I'd thrown her—well out of Persis's earshot, or whatever you called it when a computer was listening. "Stand there," I said. "Don't do anything. Just stand there."

She did so, although now that she'd lost the upper hand, she seemed moved to modesty. She used one arm held horizontally to cover the nicest parts of her breasts and another held vertically with fingers splayed to partially conceal what I'd already seen plenty of down there.

I fetched the book from where I'd tossed it, then pulled out the switchblade and started carving through the thick back cover, separating it from the spine. When the back cover was free, I flung it as far as I could—which meant it went sailing clear out of sight.

"And now," I said, still keeping the gun trained on her, "I'm going to leave, taking this book with me."

"You won't be able to make sense of it," she said. "It's a personal diary, full of Denny's own private shorthand. Why do you think they needed a historian to write the authorized story?"

"Well, if it turns out that I require your help, I know where to find you. And don't plan on any more trips out to the Alpha. Not only is it fortified, but I killed your buddy Darren Cheung, and I'll kill you, too, if need be, to protect it. You might be able to count on police protection here under the dome—although you'd be a fool to stake your life on that—but you go out on the planitia again, and you're *mine,* understand?"

She was staring at the ground, but at last she nodded. I used the barrel of my pistol to lift her chin up and said into her dark eyes, "Here's looking at you, kid." And then I headed on my way.

TWENTY-THREE

I decided it was prudent to not go where it would be *too* easy for Mac to find me, just in case Lakshmi did call in the break-and-enter. He wouldn't look for long, but he'd certainly try my office and apartment, so I went by Gully's Gym, had a sonic cleaning there, and changed into the blue track pants and black muscle shirt I kept in my locker. I checked the mirror to make sure I was kempt and sheveled, then headed over to Pickover's place.

When I got there he was doing precisely what I'd suggested he do: cleaning a fossil. "Goodness!" he said, looking at me. "What happened to you?"

"What?"

He pointed at my forehead. "That's a hell of a goose egg."

I probed the area he'd indicated. "Oh. Yeah. I took a fall."

He might not have been a detective, but he *was* a scientist. "Falling in this gravity doesn't cause injuries like that."

"True. I went flying onto a piece of alloquartz."

"My God."

"Anyway," I said, "the good news for that conscience of yours is that Lakshmi Chatterjee is alive."

"And kicking, apparently," he replied—but he did look relieved. "How'd she get back here?"

"I have no idea. But I got the diary from her."

He held out his hand, and I gave it to him. "Sorry about the back cover," I added.

Pickover flipped it open to the first page and began reading. After a few moments, he looked up. "That's O'Reilly's voice, all right—his tone."

"I'm going to have to work my way through it," I said.

"I want to read it, too," Pickover replied. We considered for a moment. I couldn't recall the last time the fact that I wanted to read something prevented somebody else from simultaneously reading it, too. I suppose *somewhere* in New Klondike there might be a paper scanner, but I had no idea where.

"All right," I said. "It'll probably make more sense to you than me, anyway—you go first. Just, for God's sake, keep your door locked, and don't let Lakshmi Chatterjee anywhere near it."

"She drove stakes into my heart like I was a vampire," Pickover said. "She's the last person I'd allow in here."

"Good. Start reading. How long do you think it'll take you?"

He riffled the pages, gauging the density of content. "Two or three hours, I suppose."

"Did you get yourself checked for tracking chips?"

"Yes. I'm clean. I'm sure Fernandez wanted to put one in, but I didn't give him an opportunity."

"Okay. I'll be back."

"Where are you going?"

"To get some dinner. You may not have to eat, Rory, but I do."

....

And I did precisely that, going over to The Bent Chisel. Buttrick was his usual nasty self. I headed back and waited for Diana to come and offer me service. Truth to tell, what I wanted wasn't on the menu, but she wasn't off for several more hours, so that would have to wait. I ordered a drink, plus steak and green beans; the former would be vat-grown, the latter, synthesized.

Diana returned with my Scotch on the rocks, and I made short work of it. There weren't many other customers this time of day, so she motioned for me to scooch over a bit, and she placed her shapely bottom next to mine. "Whose husband whacked you on the forehead this time?"

"It wasn't like that," I said.

"Riiiiight," she replied and she squeezed my thigh.

"Seriously," I said. "Hey, you're a cultured gal. Do you know anything about the writer-in-residence here?"

"Lakshmi Chatterjee? Sure."

"Is she any good?" It was the first time in my life, I think, I'd asked that about a woman and didn't mean for the words "in the sack" to be understood.

"She's great. I read her book about Lunaport when I heard she was coming here. She's like the Shelby Foote of that war."

"Ah," I said. I'd never heard of him, but I imagine with a name like that he got beat up a lot as a kid. "Seems like a sweet deal, getting an all-expenses-paid trip to Mars."

"Well, she has to work for it," Diana said.

"Oh, yeah. She's writing a book on the *B. Traven*." Or maybe she's doing an authorized biography of Denny O'Reilly. Or something.

"Not just that," said Diana. "She has to meet with beginning writers in the community and critique their manuscripts."

"Really?"

"Yeah. That's how these things go: most of the time is the writer's own, but some of it has to be spent working with newbies."

"How does that work?"

"You make an appointment, send in a manuscript in advance, and she meets with you for an hour to go over it."

"At Shopatsky House?"

"I guess."

"You write poetry," I said.

She winced. "I write bad poetry."

There are some things even I couldn't dispute with a

straight face, so I let that pass and simply said, "You could make an appointment to see her."

"Oh, God, no. I couldn't show my poetry to her. She's *excellent.*"

"That's what she's there for. To help beginners."

"I can't, Alex."

"Please, baby. I need you to get into that house."

"Why don't you go yourself?"

"I've been there." I pointed to my forehead. "That's where I got the goose egg."

Diana was suddenly huffy. She started to get up.

"It's not like that, babe," I said. I lowered my voice—not because anyone could listen in on us in the back, but so Diana, in her topless splendor, would have to lean in to hear me. "I, ah, let myself into her place. She had a, um, document that I needed to access."

"Let yourself in?" Diana said coldly. "So her locks were programmed to recognize you?"

"No, sweetheart—honest. I removed the back window and snuck in. We fought, but I got away with the document. But prior to that, she attacked me and Pickover out on the surface—tried to kill us both."

Diana frowned. "Pickover is a transfer."

"Didn't stop her from shooting spikes into his chest—or coming at me with a shotgun."

"God!" A beat. "But what's this all about?"

"She thinks we know where the Alpha Deposit is."

"And do you?"

This time, my poker face didn't fail me. "Of course not."

"But she tried to kill you."

"Uh-huh."

"And you want to send me off to be alone with her?"

"Well, um, she doesn't have anything against *you.*"

"Why do you need to get me into her house?"

"So you can plant a bug there, so I can listen in on her conversations. She's got at least one more accomplice—someone helped her out today, I don't know who, but I need to find out."

"Why? What difference does that make?"

The difference was that at least one more person apparently knew the location of the Alpha Deposit—the person who had come to Lakshmi's rescue there. Also, a bug in Lakshmi's place might let me know if she was ignoring my warning and planning another trip to the Alpha. But I simply said, "Please, baby. I need you to do this."

Diana sat back down but a little farther on the bench from me than before.

"Well?" I said, after she'd been quiet for a bit.

"Okay," she replied. "But you've got to take me out."

"I'd be happy—"

"To Bleaney's."

I frowned. Bleaney's was the pricey nightclub where prospectors who had struck it rich went to celebrate. "Deal," I said, leaning over and kissing her on the cheek.

I'd just put it on the expense claim I was going to give Pickover.

....

After leaving Diana at The Bent Chisel, I actually went most of the way back to Shopatsky House, since the Windermere Clinic was near there. Old Doc Windermere—a walrusy-looking biological with a handlebar mustache—would dig out a bullet or patch up a knife wound without feeling a need to involve those pesky folks at the NKPD; taking care of the bruise on my forehead was nothing by comparison, but I figured I might as well give him this bit of business, too. Gloria, his receptionist/nurse—a breathy little pink-haired bundle of energy—was always glad to see me, and, frankly, I rather liked seeing her, too. I think the doc watered his anesthetic down the same way Buttrick watered down his booze, but a gander at Gloria was usually enough to take the pain away, at least for a few minutes.

It was a slow night for fights, I guess; I didn't have to wait to get in. Doc Windermere played a couple of healing beams over my forehead, and, as I could see in the cracked mirror opposite me, the swelling went down, and the purple color faded away.

I thanked the doc, paid Gloria in cash, and then headed

over to Pickover's place, figuring he should be finished reading Denny's journal by now.

"Well?" I said after he let me into his apartment. "Anything exciting in the diary?"

"Yes, indeed," he replied, taking a seat; I did the same. "Weingarten and O'Reilly contacted several people back on Earth, trying to arrange the sale of fossils in advance; the diary includes descriptions of some of the fossils—and it's got the name of the collector they'd previously sold the decapod to!"

"The what?"

"The decapod! There's only one known specimen—they brought it back on their second mission." He held the diary up triumphantly. "My guess is that they were ancestral to the pentapods that came to dominate later—and now I know whose collection it's in! I tell you, Alex, we may not even need to track down Willem Van Dyke!"

That sounded like my fees were about to dry up, so I quickly protested. "There are still some leads for him I'd like to follow up on."

Rory was in an expansive mood. "Oh, of course, my boy, of course! Your field and mine, we both say the same thing: leave no stone unturned!"

"Good," I said. "Now what?"

"Now, we should head out to the Alpha again. We can't leave those wrecked buggies there; someone's bound to spot them sooner or later. And we need to finish clearing out the land mines. Are you up for another road trip, old boy?"

Driving to the Alpha took a lot of hours, and that meant a lot of solars for me. "Why not?" I said. "But we'll need another buggy to get there."

"Do we rent or borrow one?"

"Borrow," I said. "I don't know how Lakshmi and that Darren Cheung fellow managed to tail us in the dark the last time, but they might have put a tracking device in your buggy."

"That's illegal," Rory said. I made no reply, and finally he nodded. "Okay," he said. "So who do you know who has a clean buggy we could borrow?"

There were only two reasons to own a buggy: you spent a lot of time prospecting far from the dome, or you liked to race. Isidis Planitia is a plain, after all—it was great for racing. And my buddy Juan Santos liked machines of all types, not just computers. I called him. "Juan," I said to the little version of his face that appeared on my left wrist, "can I borrow your buggy?"

"Wow, Alex," he replied. "We must have a bad connection. It sounded like you said, 'Can I borrow your buggy?'"

"I know I dented it last time, but—"

"Dented? You call that a dent?"

"I had it fixed."

"We should have *you* fixed—make sure those defective genes of yours don't get passed on."

"How 'bout if you loan it to me, but I don't do the driving?"

"Who's going to drive it?"

"Dr. Pickover."

"That little mouse?"

"Standing right here," said Rory.

"Oh!" said Juan. "Um, sorry. I mean—um, yeah, sure, I guess you guys can borrow my buggy. But, God's sake, be careful this time, would you?"

· · · · · · · · · · ·

Juan's buggy was white with jade green pinstriping. As I'd promised, Rory Pickover did the driving as we made the trip out to the Alpha Deposit again in the dark. This time he didn't ask me to polarize my helmet, and he let me bring my gun, tab, and phone along. There are only so many times you can have a man save your life before you have to start trusting him, and I guess Rory finally trusted me. It was nice that at least one of us had faith in my good intentions.

I watched through the canopy as first Venus and then Earth set. The sky was breathtaking. Even on the highest mountaintop on Earth, the atmosphere is still much denser than it is here on Mars, and Mars's two tiny captured-asteroid moons never reflected much light. On a clear night like tonight, the Milky Way was dazzling as it arched overhead.

"There's one other thing," Rory said, "that the diary revealed."

I looked at him, a dark form illuminated only by the stars and the blue dashboard indicators. "Oh?"

"Yes. O'Reilly said he'd left a large paper map of the Alpha in the lander's descent stage—with the precise locations of where they'd found the fossils they'd excavated marked on it. That sort of information is crucial scientifically."

"Why'd they leave the map behind, then?" I asked.

"They were planning to return. The diary said they were going to pick up excavating where they'd left off." He looked briefly at me. "I've got to have that map, Alex."

"I'm sure," I said. "But Ernie Gargalian told me nobody knows what became of the third lander."

Rory's voice was soft. "I do."

"Really?"

"Yes. I didn't want to tell you back at New Klondike. You never know who's listening, or where there's a microphone. But, yes, I'm pretty sure of where it is."

We hit a bump that was enough to lift me from my seat a bit. I cinched the shoulder belt tighter. "How'd you find it?"

"Satellite photos."

I frowned. "Lots of people must have looked for it that way."

"Yes, I'm sure they did. But they didn't know what to look for or where to start. I knew it had to be near the Alpha Deposit—and I had the advantage of knowing where that was."

"Ernie thinks they might have moved it," I said.

"Like the second lander? No. If they *had* crashed it somewhere else, somebody would have found the wreckage."

"Then what?"

"They buried it, right where they'd touched down."

"The Martian permafrost is rock-hard," I said. "It'd take forever to dig a hole big enough for a spaceship."

Pickover took on the lilting tone I imagined he normally reserved for talking to students. "And why do we call it permafrost, Alex?"

"Because it's permanently frozen."

"*What's* permanently frozen?"

"The soil."

"You can't freeze something that's already a solid."

"Oh, right, okay. Well, the water in the soil, then."

"Exactly. Isidis Planitia is a giant, shallow impact basin. Billions of years ago, it was filled with water. That water didn't disappear; most of it is now locked into the soil. As I told you, core samples show the ground around the Alpha is as much as sixty percent water."

"So they melted it?

"I think so, yes. Weingarten and O'Reilly had to have had a plan to hide their descent stage. I think they had the on-board computer fire its big landing engine until the frozen water melted, turning the soil into mud. The down blast would have blown the mud aside, creating a pit. The descent stage would have settled down into that, and, after the engine was cut, the mud would have flowed back in, burying it."

"Neat. But what would that look like from orbit?"

"Well, any surface rocks would have sunk into the mud. So, what you'd see is a circular area free of such things, maybe forty or fifty meters across. To the untrained eye, it'd look pretty much like a crater. Even at a one-meter orbital survey, it would be hard to tell from one; you'd have to look at multiple lighting angles to notice that it was a circle that didn't have any concavity."

"And you've found such a thing?"

"Yes."

"Because you had the Alpha as a starting point," I said. But then I shook my head. "No, no—it's the other way around, isn't it? You found this circular thingamajig first— and *that* led you to the Alpha."

"You *are* a good detective, Alex. That's right. I knew there was no way to just stumble upon the Alpha, not in all the vastness of Isidis Planitia. And I knew that the prospectors here mostly lacked the geological training to interpret orbital-survey images. I'd suspected they'd buried the de-scent stage—the one they took on the third mission would have made a great part of a permanent habitat. And so I started looking at satellite photos. There aren't that many that have been made in the last forty years; most of the Mars photo-survey maps are much older than that, and nobody has bothered to update them, because, after all, Mars is a dead world. But there *was* a Croatian satellite survey about fifteen years ago, and I accessed those images. Took me months of poring over photographs, but I finally found it."

"Nice work," I said.

"Beats hiking around endlessly, looking for the Alpha."

"Did you ever meet Dougal McCrae?" I asked. The bootleg Pickover had, of course, but I didn't recall this one ever having the pleasure.

"No."

"You'd like him. Chief detective at the NKPD. He doesn't like to have to get up from his desk to investigate, either."

"I've logged over five thousand field hours on Earth and Mars," Pickover said, sounding slightly miffed with me.

"Sorry." I turned to look through the canopy at the darkness. On long car trips, I sometimes felt a duty to help keep the driver alert. But Pickover was in no danger of falling asleep, although I supposed he might get bored with no one to talk to. "Do you mind if I nod off?"

"It's fine," he replied. "I'm listening to music."

· · · · · · · · · · ·

When I woke, the sun was coming up and we were pulling in near where we'd been before: the ruins of Lakshmi's and Pickover's buggies were about thirty meters to our right. I got into the surface suit I'd rented—it was brown this time— and Pickover swung the blockish canopy back. We headed outside.

"First things first," Rory said. "Let's see if we can find that map." He paused. "How meta! Looking for a map without out a map!"

"Where do we start?" I asked.

Pickover pointed past the crater he'd tussled with Lakshmi in. "About five hundred meters that way. I don't want to drive in again—tire tracks take too long to disappear."

We started walking. It felt good to stretch my legs. "Oh,

say," I said, "there's something I've been meaning to ask you about. You said something odd to that guy, Darren Cheung—something about flirty girls?"

Rory rattled it off: "'The girls can flirt and other queer things can do.'"

"Yeah. What's that mean?"

"It's an old mnemonic for the Mohs scale of mineral hardness. If he'd really been with the US Geological Survey, he'd have known it."

We continued on. Soon enough, Pickover gestured at the terrain in front of us. *"Voilà!"*

I didn't see what he was referring to. "Yes?"

He sounded disappointed in me. "Right there—see? A circle, forty meters in diameter?"

I tried to make it out, and—

Ah. It was almost exactly the same ruddy color as the surrounding terrain and it was covered with dust—but nothing else; it lacked the usual litter of small rocks, and had no little craters marring its surface.

I said, "How do we get at the descent stage?"

"Well, it can't be very far down; the permafrost gives way to bedrock at a depth not much greater than the height of the descent stage, and its engine couldn't blast through that. Its top is probably just below the surface."

"Okay," I said.

"There were two hatches in the descent stage," Rory said. "One was on the outside of the hull for getting out onto the surface, and the other was on top, for connecting to the ascent stage. The upper access hatch should be right in the center of the circle." He'd brought along his geological equipment, including a big pickax. "The descent stage is circular in cross-section, and about ten meters wide." After taking a bead on a couple of distinctive rocks outside the circle, he assuredly made his way to its exact center.

I followed behind him. If I understood what Pickover had said, this whole round area had briefly been a massive quagmire of soil and water twenty mears ago. The footing didn't seem any different from the rest of the plain.

He swung his pickax. The point only went in maybe ten

centimeters before it clanged against something metallic. Pickover dropped to his robotic knees and started digging into the permafrost with his bare hands. I wasn't strong enough to be of any use, so I simply watched, gloved hands on my surface suit's hips.

It took him a few minutes to expose a circular metal hatch about eighty centimeters wide. It was slightly convex and had a wheel set into its center. Pickover gestured at it. "Be my guest, Alex." I gripped the wheel with both of my gloved hands and tried to turn it, but it wouldn't budge; it was either locked from the other side, or the works were gummed up with Martian dust.

Pickover loomed in and grabbed the wheel with his naked fingers. It was odd watching a man exert himself without, you know, visibly exerting himself. He didn't grunt or screw up his face; he just calmly did what I'd been incapable of doing: turning the wheel. He spun it through 180 degrees, then pulled on it to swing the hatch open.

It was dark inside, but a ladder with rungs that curved to match the circumference of the opening descended into the ship. He scrambled down into the blackness. I was startled a moment later when light started coming up at me. I hadn't seen him take a flashlight with him, and—

No. It wasn't portable lighting; it was the spacecraft's internal system. Well, excimer batteries *did* hold charges for a long time . . .

I looked around for something to keep the hatch from closing. There wasn't anything suitable at hand but, then again, the Martian zephyrs couldn't possibly blow it shut. I made my way down the ladder.

The interior of the descent stage was maybe five meters tall, with that height divided into two levels. The ladder continued all the way down to the bottom, which is where Pickover was, so I got off on the upper floor and started looking around. This floor was a disk divided into six pie-shaped wedges.

The first wedge contained cupboards and lockers filled with mining equipment and medical supplies. I checked for the map, but it wasn't there.

The second wedge—moving to the right—was a small galley, but the cupboards here were bare; well, running out of chow was one of the reasons their expedition would have come to an end.

Wedge three was a sleeping compartment with a wide foam mattress on the floor. I looked around, but, again, no map.

Wedge four was a toilet of a kind I had no idea how to use.

Wedge five was a little work area, with tools for cleaning fossils, much like the stuff I'd seen at Ernie's shop or in Rory's apartment.

I'd thought wedge six might be the other stateroom, but I guess that was down below; it was a storage room. A white space suit, streaked with Martian dust, was slumped way over on a chair. I tried to pick it up to get at the cabinets behind it, and—

Oh, my God! "Rory!" I shouted. "Up here!"

I felt the deck plates vibrate as he scrambled up the ladder from below. He was soon standing behind me, looking over my shoulder.

"It's not empty," I said, pointing at the space suit. "There's a body inside."

The suit was an old-fashioned one, with a gold-mirror-finish helmet visor that had been flipped down. There was no nameplate on the suit, nor any national flag or logo. "It must be Willem Van Dyke," I said. "He'd have known they were planning to bury the third lander, maybe. When he came here to plant the land mines, he must have taken refuge down here—maybe there was a dust storm, or something?"

Rory loomed in and looked for the release that would let him flip up the visor to expose—what? Rotted flesh? A skull? I didn't know what to expect after all these years. He found the release, and—

Rory gasped and staggered backward. I peered at the face—which seemed to be remarkably intact. The eyes were closed, and the chestnut hair was disheveled—but it was all still attached to the head. True, the skin was an ashen shade, but I'd seen people who were alive with worse complexions.

"My . . . God," said Rory. He was now holding on to a ledge jutting from the wall. "My God."

"What?" I said.

Rory's mechanical eyes were wide. "That's not Willem Van Dyke."

"Then who is it?"

Rory shook his head slightly, as if he himself couldn't believe what he was saying. "It's Denny O'Reilly."

I looked back at the corpse. "But—but he died on re-entering Earth's atmosphere . . ."

Rory's voice became a little sharp. "That's O'Reilly, I tell you."

"You mean . . . he was marooned here?"

"Apparently."

"By Simon Weingarten?"

"It sure looks that way." Rory pointed at a thick cable going from a red connector on the front of the suit to a similar connector on one of the straight walls. "He was plugged into the ship's life-support system."

"Surely they weren't on bottled air all the time they were on Mars," I said. "Shouldn't he have been able to recycle it, or manufacture more?"

"Yes," said Pickover. "For a time. The equipment was rated for months of use, but it would have given out at some point." He shook his head. "Poor blighter."

I don't think I'd ever actually heard anyone say that before, but it certainly applied here. It must have been terrible for O'Reilly: abandoned alone for weeks, or maybe even months, on Mars, and then finally asphyxiating.

Suddenly there was a great clang audible even via the thin Martian air as—

Jesus!

—as the hatch overhead came crashing shut.

I looked up and saw the wheeled locking mechanism on this side of the hatch rotating. We were being sealed inside the same metal coffin Denny O'Reilly had been left in all those years ago.

TWENTY-FOUR

I scrambled for the ladder—as much as one could scramble in a surface suit—but Dr. Pickover, unencumbered by such a thing, beat me to it. Probably just as well; he *was* stronger than me.

Pickover struggled to keep the locking wheel from being turned any further, but, damn it, whoever was on the other side managed a massive jerk of the wheel, knocking Rory off the ladder. He was now dangling from the wheel by both arms, with a two-story drop below. The twisting of the wheel had put the ladder behind him, and he seemed to be having trouble re-engaging with it. The wheel jerked once more, and—

Holy crap!

—Pickover was dislodged or let go, but either way, he came falling down the shaft in Martian slow motion.

I thought about reaching out to grab him, but there didn't seem to be much point; it'd probably just bring me tumbling down on top of him. He hit the floor, bending at the knees as he did so, but he still collapsed into a heap.

"Rory!" I called, and I slid down the ladder. When I reached the bottom—my first time on the lower level—I helped him to his feet.

Newcomers to Mars often did themselves injuries because they felt superhuman but were still flesh and blood. But Pickover *was* superhuman. Still, it was a nasty height to fall from, even here. Pickover's plastic face winced in pain as he rolled up his pant leg to expose his right ankle. Biological injuries were easy to spot: blood, bruising, swelling. There was no sign of any of that as Pickover probed the ankle with his fingers. "It's bent," he said, at last. "I can barely flex it."

I thought of Juan's Mars buggy up on the surface. Even if we could get out of here, if whoever had sealed us in had stolen or wrecked the buggy, there was no way Pickover could run me all the way back to New Klondike this time. I looked at my wrist air gauge; Rory could stay in here indefinitely, but I couldn't. We'd been sealed in by somebody stronger than Pickover, meaning it was either a transfer or a biological who'd had something to help him turn the wheel. Even if we could undo the seal, anyone on the outside with a gun could easily pick me off as I tried to haul myself up out of the hatch.

"Is it Lakshmi again?" asked Pickover, as he rolled his pant leg down. "Or do you suppose someone else followed us this time?"

I'd been alert while we were leaving the dome, and hadn't had my visor polarized on this trip. "No one could have," I said. "I'm sure of that."

He looked up at the hatch. "Could they have tracked Juan's buggy?"

"I don't see how. He said he'd swept it for bugs before we picked it up. And it's a lot harder to track vehicles here than people think; there's no GPS equivalent, and . . ."

"Yes?"

I blew out air—a luxury I might not have much longer. "And I'm an idiot," I said. I reached into my equipment pouch and pulled out the switchblade I'd gotten from Dirk. I pushed the button that caused the blade to spring out. Rory looked alarmed as I turned the knife around so that the blade was aiming toward my chest.

"Hang on, old boy!" Pickover said. "We're not done for yet."

But I was just maneuvering the knife to hand it to him. "You've got super strength," I said. "Can you break the haft open?"

He took the knife from me, looked at it for a moment, and indicated that he was going to snap the wine-colored handle by flexing it with his hands, as if to give me a chance to stop him. But I nodded for him to go ahead, and he did so.

The handle broke in two, and Rory split the pieces open. There was the channel for the blade, the spring mechanism—and the tracking device. I reached over, prized the little chip out, let it drop in slow motion to the deck, and ground the heel of my boot into it until it was crushed. Dirk, or whoever had hired him, had known it would be impossible to plant a tracking device on me—but having one in a knife I'd be bound to seize was another matter.

"Lakshmi Chatterjee must have hired the punk I got the knife from," I said. "That's how she managed to follow us out here in the dark, but . . ." I frowned.

"What?" said Pickover.

"Well, I—hmmm. How'd she know that *I* would be heading out to the Alpha? Did you tell anyone you were hiring me, Rory?"

"No, of course not."

"Still, you could have been seen coming to my office. Back when half your face was missing, you'd have been quite conspicuous."

"I—I hadn't thought about that," Rory said. "I'm not used to being clandestine."

"Well, what's done is done," I said.

Pickover was trying hard to be unflappable, but, despite his reserved face, his voice had become higher, and he was darting his eyes about nervously. "So, what now?" he asked. "We seem to be prisoners."

I looked around the lower level. It had a smaller interior diameter than the upper one, implying there was a donut of equipment or tanks surrounding us. "What about blowing the hatch?" I said. "Aren't spaceship hatches supposed to have explosive bolts?"

"I'll check," said Pickover. He headed up the ladder, hauling himself up with his arms and letting the foot with the damaged ankle dangle freely. Once he was at the top of the shaft, he looked around. "I don't see any controls for that," he called down. He tried the wheel again, but it didn't budge.

I moved off the ship's centerline into one of the four compartments on the lower floor, found a bucket seat, and dropped myself into it. I looked down at the deck plating, pissed at myself for having been so easily duped with the switchblade. Pickover was banging around up at the top of the shaft, trying various things to get the wheel moving again.

After a time, I looked up. The chair I was in was facing the curving bulkhead in front of me, but it was on a swivel base, and I slowly rotated it toward the central shaft; my instincts wouldn't let me keep my back to people, even though there was no one here but dead-as-a-doornail Denny and stainless-steel Rory. I looked more or less in the middle distance, at where the ladder began, but after a time my attention fell on the opposite bulkhead—which had a red door with a locking wheel in its center. Of course: the other exit—the one that would have led outside had the lander been sitting on the surface. But, damn it all, it *wasn't* sitting on the surface. It was buried in the Martian permafrost.

What goes down must come up.

"Rory!" I said into my fishbowl's headset.

"Yes?"

"Come down here."

It didn't take him long. "What?" he said, when he was standing between me and the red door.

"This is the descent stage, right?"

"Yes."

"So beneath our feet," I said, tapping the hull plating with my boot, "there are fuel tanks."

"They're actually in a torus around this level."

"Ah, okay. But below us, there's the descent engine, right? A big engine cone; a big landing rocket?"

"Yes."

"So, assuming there's any fuel left, what happens if we fire that engine?"

Pickover looked at me like I was insane. I get that a lot. "The engine cone is probably totally plugged with soil," he said.

"Would we blow up, then?"

He frowned in a subdued transfer way. "I . . . I don't know."

"Well, let's find out. There's got to be a control center."

"It's here," said Pickover, pointing to his right. I came over to the room he was standing next to. It had a curving control console, following the contour of the outer bulkhead. There was a bucket seat in front of it identical to the one I'd just vacated. I looked at Pickover.

"I don't know how to fly a spaceship," he said.

"Neither do I. And I bet Weingarten and O'Reilly didn't really, either. But the ship should know." I waved my arm vaguely at the ceiling lights. "The electrical system is working; maybe the ship's computer is, too." I lowered myself into the seat, and Pickover took up a position behind me. I scanned the instruments, but Pickover spotted what I was looking for first and reached over my shoulder to press a switch.

There was a big square red light on the console that flashed in what looked like a random pattern—but I knew it wasn't; it was one of those lights that robots in old sci-fi flicks used to have that flashed in time with spoken words, once per syllable. Such lights didn't really serve any purpose on robots, but they *were* handy to indicate that a computer was talking in a spaceship cabin that might or might not be pressurized. There wasn't much air in the lander, and all of it was unbreathable, but it was sufficient to convey faint sound. I cranked up the volume on my suit's external microphones. "Repeat," I said.

"I said, can I be of assistance?" replied a male voice; in the thin air, I couldn't say much more about it than that, although I thought it sounded rather smug.

"Yes, please," I said. "Can you open the hatch?"

"No," the computer replied. "Both egress portals are manually operated."

"Can you blow the top hatch?"

"That functionality is not available."

"All right," I said, crossing my arms in front of my chest. "We'd like to take off."

"Ten. Nine. Eight."

"Wait!" I said, and "Hold!" shouted Pickover.

"Holding," said the voice.

"Just like that?" I said. "We can just take off? You know we're buried in Martian permafrost."

"Of course. I engineered the burial."

"Um, is it safe to take off?" asked Pickover.

"Well, safe-ish," said the computer.

"What kind of answer is that?" I asked.

"An approximate one," replied the prim voice.

"I'll say," I said. And then it occurred to me to ask another question. "Do you know how long you've been turned off?"

"Thirty-six years."

"Right," I said. "Do you know why Simon Weingarten marooned Denny O'Reilly here?"

"Yes."

"Spill it."

"Voiceprint authorization required."

"Whose?"

"Mr. Weingarten's or Mr. O'Reilly's."

"They're both dead," I said.

"I have no information about that."

"I can show you O'Reilly's body. It's upstairs."

"Be that as it may," said the computer.

I frowned. "What other information has been locked?"

"All navigational and cartographic records."

I nodded. If the lander ever was moved, no one but Simon or Denny could ask the computer how to get back to the Alpha. "All right," I said. "We need to get out of here. That door"—I pointed to the other side of the ship—"is it an airlock?" I couldn't see the computer's camera, but I was sure it had one, and so it should have known what I was indicating.

"Yes."

"The outer door is sealed?"

"Yes."

"Does it swing in or out?"

"Out."

I motioned to Pickover. He walked over and worked the wheel that opened the inner door, which swung in toward him. There was a chamber with curving walls between the inside and outside hulls of the ship, big enough for one person. "Is there a safety interlock that will prevent us from opening the outer door while the inner one is open?" I asked.

"Yes," said the computer.

"Can it be defeated?" I assumed there must be a way to turn it off, since it'd be a pain in the ass to have to cycle through the airlock during testing back on Earth.

"Yes."

"Do so."

"Done."

"Okay. I propose that you fire the engine to lift the ship up out of the ground so that the airlock is just above the surface. Can do?"

"Can do," said the computer.

"All right," I said. "Rory, are you ready?"

"As ready as I'll ever be."

I got out of the chair and moved over to stand behind him. "Nothing personal," I said, "but if whoever is outside opens fire, you've got a better chance of surviving than I do."

The paleontologist nodded.

"Computer," I said.

"My name is Mudge," the machine replied.

I heard Pickover snort; the name must have meant something to him. "Fine, Mudge," I said. "We're ready."

"Ten," said Mudge, and he continued in the predictable sequence.

There was a wheel set into the outer door, which was also red. Pickover moved over and grabbed it with both hands, ready to start rotating it as soon as it was above the ground. I grabbed onto a handle conveniently set into the wall of the airlock, in case it turned out to be a rough ride.

"Two," said Mudge. "One. Zero."

The whole ship began to shake, and I heard the roar of

the engine beneath my feet and felt it transmitted through the deck plates and the soles of my boots. We did not explode, for which I was grateful. But we didn't seem to be going anywhere, either.

"Mudge?" I called.

The computer divined my question. "The permafrost is melting beneath us and, by conduction, at our sides, as well. Give it a moment."

I did just that, and soon did feel us jerking upward. I tried to imagine what the scene looked like outside: perhaps like a cork working its way slowly out of a wine bottle.

There was a rectangle in front of Pickover, above the wheel, that I'd stupidly taken as decorative, but it was a window in the outer airlock door. Light was now streaming in from the top of it, and the strip of illumination was growing thicker centimeter by centimeter as the ship rose out of its muddy tomb. I couldn't make out any details through the window, though: it was streaked with reddish brown muck.

If whoever had locked us in had been standing guard, I hoped—old softy that I am—that he or she realized what was going on, since I imagined the superheated rocket exhaust would spray out in all directions once the cylindrical hull was fully above ground.

Soon the entire height of the window was admitting light. Our ascent was still slow, though. Pickover was craning to look out the port, presumably to see when the bottom of the door was above ground—

—which must have been *now,* because he gave a final twist to the locking wheel and hauled back and kicked the door outward with the leg that had the uninjured ankle.

Suddenly we popped higher into the air—free now from the sucking wet melted permafrost. Pickover threw himself out the airlock with a cry of *"Geronimo!"*

I scrambled to follow suit, but by the time I got to the precipice, we were already dozens of meters above the ground; even in Martian gravity, the jump would surely break my legs and probably my neck, too.

"Abort!" I yelled over my shoulder. "Mudge, lower us back down!"

The vibration of the hull plating changed at once, presumably as the computer throttled back the engine. We hung in the air for a moment, like a cartoon character after going off a cliff, and then started to descend.

Pickover had ended up spread-eagled in the mud, but was now getting to his feet and trying to run, despite his bad ankle. The cylindrical habitat had reduced its altitude by half. Pickover was having a terrible time gaining traction in the mud; I didn't want to singe him. "Cut the engine!" I called to Mudge. The hull suddenly stopped vibrating, and we began dropping like a rock. I was afraid the ship would fall right back down into the hole it had previously occupied, especially since it was probably widened now by the rocket exhaust. When I figured my chances were at least halfway decent for surviving, I leapt out of the airlock, trying for as much horizontal distance as I could manage.

When I landed, my legs went like driven piles into the muck. No sooner had they done so than a shock wave went through the melted permafrost as the massive lander impacted the surface behind me. I twisted my neck to see. The lander had hit half-on and half-off the hole, and now was teetering toward me; it looked like it was going to topple over any second. I tried to pull myself up and out of the mess, but it was going to take some doing—and the chances of the ship falling precisely so that I ended up poking safely through the open airlock doors instead of being crushed seemed slim. It was too bad we hadn't brought along the lasso that Lakshmi had used on Pickover earlier; he could have employed it to haul me out of the quagmire.

That is, if he himself could get solid footing. Behind me, the tottering ship was making a groaning sound, conveyed through the attenuated atmosphere and picked up by my still-open external helmet microphones.

I was pushing myself up out of the mess as fast as I could, but a surface suit really wasn't designed for those sorts of gymnastics. For his part, Pickover was staggering away from me like Karloff fleeing the villagers, the mud still sucking at his every step.

Suddenly—it was always suddenly, wasn't it?—a shot rang out, audible because my external mikes were still cranked way up. The bullet whizzed past me and impacted the mud. I swung my head within the fishbowl, trying to make out the assailant. There: about ten o'clock, and maybe thirty meters away—a figure, probably a man, in an Earth-sky-blue surface suit, holding a rifle aimed at me.

TWENTY-FIVE

Pickover finally reached solid ground, it seemed, but as soon as he did, he threw himself down, presumably to make a harder target for whoever was shooting at us. As proof that he was back on *marsa firma,* the belly flop sent up not a splash of mud but a cloud of dust.

I pulled myself a little farther out of the muck, removed the Smith & Wesson from my shoulder holster, then took a bead on Mr. Blue Sky. There was no way to call "Freeze!" to him, so I just squeezed the trigger, setting off the oxygenated gunpowder, and watched with satisfaction as he slumped over.

But speaking of freezing, I think the mud was starting to do that again. I didn't want to end up as one of Pickover's fossils, and so, with a final Herculean effort—as in the Greek hero, not the Agatha Christie detective—I hauled myself out of the thickening sludge.

And just in time, too! With a dinosaurian groan, the ship came tumbling down. I spun around in time to see it hit, and it splashed me from helmet to boot with filth. I used my gloved hands to wipe the front of my fishbowl clean, although it was still streaked with mud, and looked at the fallen lander. The sealed circular hatchway stared out at me like a cyclopean eye.

There was no way anyone could enter through the airlock again; it was face down and buried. I hadn't seen it happen, but I suspected that the outward-opening door had been slammed shut when the curving hull had hit the muck. If we were going to get back inside, we'd have to find a way to unseal the top hatch. But that was a problem for later; for now, I made my way over to Pickover. "It's safe to get up," I said once I'd reached him. His bum ankle was making it hard for him to do so, so I gave him a hand. While walking over, I'd scanned around for anyone else—but Mr. Blue Sky seemed to be alone. We headed over to see him.

"You okay?" I said to Pickover, as we closed the distance.

"Yeah, but that jump didn't do my ankle any favors; it's worse than before."

The sun was high, and there were a few thin clouds overhead. We got those naturally sometimes, although I wondered if they were actually our rocket exhaust or water vapor from the melted permafrost. Phobos is hard to see during the day, and catching sight of Deimos is a good sign that you don't need your eyes fixed; I managed the former, but not the latter, although who knew if the little terror was up, anyway.

I still had my gun out. Blue Sky looked like he was slumped over unconscious, but he could just be playing possum, waiting until we were near enough that he couldn't miss. But as we got closer, he really did seem out of it, and when I knelt next to him, I could see why. "Ooops," I said.

Pickover sounded aghast. "You just killed a man, and the best you can manage is 'Ooops'?"

"Well, he *did* try to kill us," I said. My bullet had gone a little higher than I'd intended and had shattered his helmet, exposing him to the subzero cold and the razor-thin atmosphere. It was an odd sight: the youthful face was clearly dead, the eyes were locked open and staring straight ahead, and a trickle of blood, already frozen, extended down from a corner of his mouth. But the snake tattoo on his left cheek was still animated, the rattle on the tail moving back and forth. It was Dirk.

"I know him," I said.

"Oh?"

"Yeah. Dumb punk, recently arrived from Earth." I shrugged a little.

"Ah," said Rory, I guess because he needed to say something. But, then, after a moment, he went on. "Hello, what's this?"

Lying on the ground nearby was an excimer-powered jackhammer, like the one Joshua Wilkins had used to fake the suicide in the basement of NewYou.

"He must have used it to push the locking wheel against your strength, Rory."

"Ah, right. But what should we do with this poor devil? We can't just leave him here."

"No," I said softly. "We can't."

For once, Rory was being more mercenary than me. "It's the color of his surface suit," he said. "Anyone coming this way is bound to spot him. We don't want people stopping near the Alpha for any reason."

I pointed back the way we'd come. "But even if we bury him, that giant lander lying on its side is bound to attract some attention."

"Then we've got to move it."

"How? Juan's buggy can't haul that."

"There's no reason to assume the ship is no longer flight-worthy," Pickover said. "Let's get Mudge to fly it back to New Klondike."

Normally, I'd have had Pickover carry the corpse, since it would have been no hardship for him, but he was still limping. I put Dirk in a fireman's carry, and we took him back toward the pit left by the lander. We could have used the jackhammer to dig a grave through the permafrost, but the pit, and the area for a bunch of meters around it, was still mushy enough to make it possible, though difficult, to inter him by hand, so we did that instead. When it was done, I stood over the spot for a few minutes, trying to think of something appropriate to say. But, for once, I was at a loss for words.

I assume it was Dirk who had rescued Lakshmi when we'd abandoned her here. She hadn't seemed like she expected the cavalry to come charging over the hill—so my guess was that while she and Darren Cheung had followed us, via the tracking chip in the switchblade, he had tailed them, hoping for his own crack at Alpha riches. And, to his credit, when he came upon Darren dead and Lakshmi getting that way, he'd rescued her rather than left her to die. Maybe there was *some* honor among thieves after all.

It wouldn't do to leave Dirk's buggy here. I knew from the old movies I liked that the terms "manual" and "automatic" used to refer to types of automobile transmissions, but the switch on the buggy's dashboard labeled with those two words simply selected whether the vehicle drove itself or not. I had Rory help me rotate the buggy so that it was facing northeast—vaguely toward Elysium—and then set it on its way; the buggy's excimer battery showed a three-quarters charge still, so the damn thing should go thousands of klicks before running out of power.

We then turned our attention back to the lander—and discovered we had another difficulty. If there was a way to talk to Mudge from the outside, we had no idea what it was. I doubted there was an external microphone; that sort of thing got burned off on entering an atmosphere, even one as thin as Mars's.

Still, Pickover could probably manage a decent volume, so I suggested he shout. He called Mudge's name a few times, but there was no response—although, even if the computer heard, it was also unlikely that there was a loudspeaker on the outside of the ship.

The cylindrical hull was partially buried in the mud, and the mud was congealing fast. The engine cone and a portion of the lower hull—but not enough to reveal the airlock door—was overhanging the original hole in the ground. The top hatch, now facing outward, was a couple of meters up; somewhat more than half of the ship's diameter was still above the surface. We moved close, and I boosted Pickover onto my shoulders so he could look at the locking wheel. He was having a hard time perching himself on me since he couldn't really flex his right ankle.

"It's been jammed with a crowbar," he said—or transmitted; I picked it up over my suit radio rather than the external mike. I felt Pickover's weight shifting on my shoulders as he struggled with the crowbar, but at last he got it free. He tossed it aside, then struggled a bit more and soon had the hatch open. "Mudge!" he called out.

My suit mike picked up the faint voice. "Can I be of assistance?"

"Can you get this ship airborne from its current posture?" Pickover asked.

"Most likely," Mudge replied.

"How much fuel do you have in reserve?"

"The sensor isn't designed to operate on its side," said Mudge, "but I estimate that the tank is about one-fifth full. Not nearly enough to make orbit, let alone escape velocity, I'm afraid."

"Can you fly to New Klondike?"

"Where is New Klondike?"

Right. The damn computer had spent the last four decades asleep.

"About 300 kilometers east of here," said Pickover.

"I would require a navigator," replied Mudge, "but the ship is capable of covering that distance."

"You fly it back, Rory," I said, craning my neck upward. "I'll get Juan's buggy and use it to tow the two wrecked ones away."

"Sounds like a plan," said Pickover, and he scrambled up into the access hatch; I was glad to have his weight off my shoulders. "Okay," he said. "I'm inside and—Jesus!"

"What?"

"Scared me half to death!"

"What?" I said again.

"Old Denny's corpse got dislodged when the lander toppled. I backed down the access tube right onto it."

"Yuck," I said, because he expected me to say something.

I headed back toward Juan's buggy, following the footprints Pickover and I had left earlier. The buggy was intact, thank God. I'd faced murderous transfers before—but I didn't want to face an angry Juan Santos ever again. I didn't pressurize the cabin, though. "Rory?" I said into my headset.

"Here, Alex."

"Buggy's in good shape. You can take off whenever you're ready. I want to watch the launch, though. Give me a couple of minutes to get in position."

"Copy," said Pickover, in good astronaut fashion. I tooled around the rim of the crater and headed toward the dark bulk of Syrtis Major Planum. We weren't far north of the equator, and the sun was now nearly overhead. I did an S-shaped maneuver in the buggy and stopped short before I got to the part of the surface that had been melted; I didn't know how the springy tires would do on a kind of muck they'd never been designed for. I could now see the descent stage from a three-quarters view, favoring the top. "Okay," I said into the radio.

"Roger," replied Pickover, clearly still enjoying the notion of piloting a spaceship. But then he had to turn the reins over to the real pilot. "Mudge? We're all set."

I couldn't hear Mudge's reply, but after a moment, Pickover said, "Oh, right. Go ahead."

I saw a small hatch open on the side of the ship, and a thruster quad emerged—a cluster of four attitude-control jets. Another cluster emerged ninety degrees farther around the ship's circumference; I imagined there were two more at the other cardinal points.

On the quad close to me, the jet that was pointing down came to life, and the corresponding one on the other visible unit, near the top, did so, too. The cylindrical stage vibrated for a bit, and then, slowly at first and then more rapidly, it started to roll. I didn't want to think about Pickover—let alone the corpse—being rotated around like they were on the spin cycle.

The upper level of the descent stage was still partially hanging out over the pit, but by pumping the attitude-control jets off and on, and supplementing the rotational force with a little backward *oomph* from the jets that were facing forward, Mudge managed to at last dislodge the ship and half push and half roll it completely onto muddy ground, so that no part of it was jutting over the pit. After a few more adjustments, the ACS quads stopped firing. I heard Pickover talking again to Mudge. "Yes, I'm holding on. Whenever you're ready."

Apparently Mudge was raring to go, because as soon as Pickover said that, the big engine cone at the rear ignited, shooting out a plume of flame. The massive cylinder pushed forward, sliding at least twice the ship's length along the ground, digging a furrow as it did so, before it started to angle up toward the butterscotch sky. I watched it lift higher and higher and then streak toward the eastern horizon.

Once it was gone from view, I spun the Mars buggy around and headed back to that small crater with the two other wrecked buggies. And, of course, Dirk's excimer jackhammer was waiting for me there. I had no idea *which* fossils were the most valuable, but I wandered around and used the hammer to remove four choice-looking slabs, which I put in the trunk of Juan's buggy, along with the jackhammer. If I understood what Pickover had said correctly, it was best to keep the slabs frozen; I'd drop them off at a secret locale of my own on the way back.

Before removing each slab, I'd used my tab to take photographs of the specimens in the ground, and wider shots that established their precise locations and orientations; I'd placed my phone in the shots, so that dimensions could be worked out, too.

I couldn't literally cover our tracks—or the buggy's—but the ever-shifting Martian dust would do that soon enough. Still, I did make an effort to hide the wounds I'd just made in the soil.

Juan's buggy, like most models, had a trailer hitch, and I hooked up a line so that I could drag both wrecks, one behind the other. I wouldn't take them back to New Klondike because people would ask awkward questions about how they'd come to be destroyed, and because hauling that much weight all the way would make the journey take forever. But I did drag them thirty kilometers—not back east, in the direction we'd come, but south. They'd doubtless be stumbled upon at some point, but they would be nowhere near the Alpha.

I then finally got to give Juan's buggy a workout. This part of Isidis Planitia wasn't quite as good as the Bonneville Salt Flats, but it still let me pull some great skids, and I spun the buggy through a couple of three-sixties, just for fun. And then, at last, I headed home. I had no really good map of how to get there—and I wouldn't have been able to retrace the course to return here—but I knew the dome was to the east, and so I just started driving that way, confident I'd eventually pick up the New Klondike homing beacon. And, indeed, after about ninety minutes, I did.

The sun had reached the western horizon behind me by the time I was approaching New Klondike. When I was back in phone range, I checked in with Pickover; he was safe in his apartment and happier than I'd ever heard him. He'd found the map aboard the descent stage—it had been rolled up for storage, he said, but was as big as a kitchen tabletop, a fact he knew because he now had it covering his own and was poring over it excitedly.

As I got closer to the dome, I saw that Mudge and Pickover had put the descent stage down vertically on one of the circular fused-regolith landing pads; it was resting on articulated tripodal legs that must have been previously stored within the hull. The pads were numbered with giant yellow painted numerals at three places on their rims; this one was number seven.

There'd be some paperwork to take care of before the descent stage could be brought inside to the shipyard. I drove on to the garage building near the south airlock and returned Juan's buggy, pleased to see that although it was mud-splashed, it was otherwise no worse for wear.

I then entered the dome, returned my rented surface suit—getting the damage deposit back this time—and headed to my little windowless apartment. On the way, I listened to the voice mail that had accumulated while I was out, including a message from Diana that said Lakshmi

Chatterjee had had a cancellation and could see her to talk about her poetry tomorrow at 2:00 p.m. It was less necessary now, I suspected, to bug Shopatsky House; Dirk had almost certainly been her accomplice. But it was still probably worth finding out if Lakshmi had revealed the location of the Alpha to anyone else or was planning another trip out to it.

Despite all I'd been through today, I was totally clean—the surface suit had kept all the dust and mud out. But I definitely needed a shower. Once I got home, I stripped and headed into the stall, opting to treat myself to a water rinse. (The irony was that it was water showers that were noisy; sonic showers were ultrasonic and didn't interfere with your hearing—not a lot of people sang while taking sonic showers.)

But while other sounds were being drowned out by the jets of H_2O, someone must have jimmied the lock on my apartment door. Or maybe they'd broken in earlier, and had simply been hiding until now. Either way, when I turned off the nozzles, what I heard was not the *drip-drip-drip* that I really needed to get fixed, but rather a low, unpleasant voice that said, "Freeze."

TWENTY-SIX

The door to my shower stall was alloquartz—not bulletproof, but, as they used to say about watches that you
could get wet, bullet-*resistant*.

I turned slowly in the little stall so that I was facing the
intruder, and so he might feel a little intimidated. The air
was steamy, and there was the transparent door between us,
with beads of water on it, but I'd lay money that the mug
facing me was a transfer. Unfortunately, my money was in
my wallet, in the other room, along with my pants.

The guy was big, the kind of bruiser that people would
have called "Moose" on a planet that had any. He was aiming a gun at me—and, indignity of indignities, I soon recognized that it was my own.

"What can I do for you?" I said, as amiably as I could
manage. He hadn't told me to stick my hands up, so I hadn't.

"You have something I want." His voice was slow, thick.

I looked down. "That's what all the boys say."

"Stow it," said the man. "I'm talking about the diary. We
can do this one of two ways. You tell me where it is, I get
it, I leave, and you go towel off and put baby powder on your
butt. Or you make me rip this joint apart looking for it, and
I leave powder burns right above that six-pack of yours."

"You make a tempting case for the former option," I said.

It clearly took him a moment to digest this, but then he nodded. "Good."

"It's in a safe in my living room. The safe opens to simultaneous scanning of my fingerprint and me uttering a passphrase—a combination lock, if you will."

He jerked the Smith & Wesson to indicate I should step out. If he'd been standing closer, I might have been able to slam the alloquartz door into his arm—my bathroom wasn't much bigger than a closet—but that wasn't going to work. As I opened the door, he moved out into the living room. I dripped my way across to join him.

"Where's the safe?" he asked.

"In the wall. Behind the couch."

The couch was a threadbare affair upon which I'd pursued many a threadbare affair. It was heavy—it pulled out into a bed, for those occasional times I had an overnight guest who wasn't going to share mine—but not so heavy that I couldn't easily move it in Martian gravity. Still, I indicated for Moose to take an end, in hopes that his doing so would destabilize the situation enough that I could recapture my gun. But he *was* a transfer: he bent and put his left hand under the bottom of the couch and swung it away from the wall all by himself, without once taking the gun off me.

The safe couldn't be installed flush with the wall, of course; that would have made it protrude into my neighbor's apartment, and Crazy Gustav and I made a point of staying out of each other's way. Instead, it jutted from the wall at floor level. It was about forty centimeters tall and wide, and half that deep. Moose looked disappointed: he'd probably been hoping for a standalone unit he could just grab and run off with, but the safe's back was clearly fused to the wall. "Open it," he said in the same cow's-moo voice he'd used before.

I crouched next to it, making it look like a random choice that I happened to be between the safe and him. I placed my thumb on the little scanning plate, which of course not only read the pattern of ridges but also checked the temperature and looked for a pulse. I then uttered my favorite quote: "'Experience has taught me never to trust a policeman. Just when you think one's all right, he turns legit.'"

The lock moved aside with a *chunk*, I grabbed the pistol from within—one should always have a spare of anything vital to one's profession—rolled onto my side, swung the gun around, and aimed it at Moose.

The big transfer stared at me. "What are you going to do?" he said. "Shoot me? It'll just bounce off." He lifted his gun higher, as if taking a bead. "I, on the other hand—"

"—still don't have what you came for." I jerked my head toward the safe. He could see it had a few things in it—I kept some mementos of Earth in there—but the diary was conspicuously absent. I was still more or less supine, and he was towering over me from the other side of the couch. I shifted my aim from his chest to the ceiling-mounted lighting unit and squeezed off a shot. The room was plunged into darkness. I was hoping he didn't have the infrared-vision upgrade, whereas I knew the layout of my apartment intimately. I sprang to my feet and worked my way along the wall my place shared with Crazy Gustav's unit to the wall that separated this room from my bedroom.

My neighbors might call the police at the sound of a gunshot, and the police might come if they were called—but I was surely on my own for at least the next few minutes. I was betting Moose didn't have much experience with a revolver. Still, if he did get hold of me, he doubtless had strength enough to snap my neck.

Being naked, my footfalls weren't making any noise on the carpetless floor, whereas Moose's clodhoppers were coming down with thuds. If I could get to the bathroom, I could lock the door behind me and hole up in the alloquartz shower stall until help arrived—an ignominious way to survive, but what the heck.

But before I'd gotten that far, the damn main door to my apartment swung open, emitting light from the corridor. Of course: Moose had broken the lock on it when he'd let himself in. Silhouetted on the threshold was Dr. Rory Pickover.

Moose swung around and fired—I guess he *did* know how to use the gun after all. Pickover was propelled backward by the impact and stumbled into the opposite corridor wall. He winced in pain as he looked down at his torso, then looked up with his plastic features drawn together. His voice was full of barely controlled rage. "I am getting really tired," he hissed, "of people shooting bits of metal into my chest." He crouched low then leapt, all his transfer's strength against Mars's feeble gravity. It was impressive—you fall in slow-mo on Mars, but you leap even faster than you can on Earth—and he slammed into Moose's chest, knocking him backward onto the couch.

I had never seen a transfer hit another transfer before, and, to be honest, Pickover fought like a girl: like a super-strong, excimer-powered girl. He smashed Moose in the face, and the sound was like two metal buckets crashing together. Moose was now seated on the couch, and I got my arm around his neck from behind. I couldn't cut off his air supply, but I could flip him over the back of the couch, and I did so. Pickover, meanwhile, grabbed the bottom of the couch in the little gap between it and the floor caused by the stubby couch legs, and he flipped the thing right over, and then he pushed it like a snowplow blade against the wall, trapping Moose in the triangular space.

I'd danced out of the way just in time and got to my feet, aiming the gun at the opening nearest Moose's head, in case he tried to come out. Pickover sat on the couch, and after a moment I clambered on it, too—which was quite uncomfortable for me, since my butt had to rest on the right angle between the couch's back and the unupholstered bottom.

Our combined weight was more than Moose could push off him, at least starting in a cramped space where he couldn't get any leverage. As we sat there—me naked, Pickover with a smoking bullet hole in his chest (and another favorite shirt ruined, I imagined), furniture upturned—Crazy Gustav happened to appear in the corridor, heading to his apartment. His sandy hair, as always, was askew, and he looked at me from his pinched, stubbly face. "Hey, Lomax," he said, "you really know how to class up a joint."

I crossed my legs demurely. "Thanks." I thought about asking him to call the cops, but Crazy Gustav had no fondness for them, and we seemed to have the situation under control. So instead, I just tipped my nonexistent hat at him, and Gustav went into his apartment, shaking his head.

TWENTY-SEVEN

I wanted to go get some clothes, but my weight was part of what was keeping Moose trapped. "Okay, big fellow," I called out. "Let's start with the basics. Who are you?"

"Nobody," he rumbled from beneath us, his voice muffled.

"Captain Nemo was nobody," I said. "Everybody else is somebody."

"Not me."

"What's your name?"

"Don't have one."

"Come on. People have to call you *something*."

"Trace."

A cool name for a copy, I thought. "I take it you're hired muscle, Trace. But hired by who?" If he corrected me to "Hired by whom?" I'd fire a shot through the couch at him.

"Actual."

"Who's that?"

"That's all I ever call him. Actual."

"He a good boss?"

"You kidding?"

"No. If he sucks, maybe you want to change allegiance. Is he a good boss?"

"He's skytop."

I knew a lot of old-fashioned slang—old movies did that to you—but I hadn't heard that one for a while; Trace might as well have called him "groovy."

"And where is this . . . this skytop gentleman? Down on Earth?"

"No."

"Here on Mars?"

"No."

"Where then?"

"Figure it out."

I took a breath. "Fine, be that way—but don't say I didn't give you a chance. Anyway, the professor and I can't very well sit here all day. So, first things first: toss the gun out from under there."

Trace didn't do anything.

"Well?" I said.

"I'm thinking."

His transfer brain operated at the speed of light, instead of the pokey chemical-signaling rates used by biologicals, but stupid had its own velocity, and I waited while he weighed his options.

And, at last, he reached a conclusion. The Smith & Wesson went skittering out from underneath and came to rest beneath my framed *Casablanca* movie poster. I couldn't go retrieve the gun just now, but at least we were making progress.

But then I heard that annoying *ping* that I could only hear when the front door to my place was open: the elevator had arrived. There were the sounds of people moving along the corridor, and then Detective Dougal McCrae and Sergeant Huxley were standing there in the open doorway, looking at us. Mac was in plain clothes and had his piece out, and Hux, in his dark blue uniform, was carrying that garbage-can-lid thing that I knew was the broadband disruptor. "We had a report of two gunshots," Mac said, rolling the *R* in "report." "And I recognized the address."

It didn't seem the time to point out that all gunshots make a report—well, unless a silencer is used.

Mac went on. "We sometimes let one go. But two?"

"Thanks for dropping by," I said. "There's a transfer behind the couch. A thug. He broke in here."

"While you boys were having some fun," said Huxley.

"While I was in the shower, you cretinous pinhead."

Mac raised his voice. "This is the New Klondike Police. Come out with your hands up. And I should warn you, we have a broadband disruptor. Don't make us use it."

Trace had two options, neither of which was particularly dignified. He could crawl out head first on my right, or he could worm his way out feet first on my left. I could tell that he'd opted for the former by the way the couch was now shaking beneath us.

When he was no longer behind the couch, he rose and held up his hands; the galoot was big enough that his fingertips were touching my ceiling.

"If you gentlemen will excuse me," I said, and I headed to the bedroom, pausing along the way to pick up my S&W. I quickly threw on some clothes—by this point, the dry air we had under the dome had sucked up all the moisture, and I was no longer wet. I put on black jeans and a T-shirt that was so dark blue you'd have thought it was also black if you didn't have the jeans to compare it to.

I thought about taking a moment to comb my hair; in my business, it didn't hurt to have a slightly wild-and-crazy look, but right now I was downright Gustavian. But no sooner had I picked up the comb than I heard an all-too-familiar electronic whine. I ran out of the room and saw, in the stark light spilling in from the corridor, Trace standing spread-eagled with all his limbs vibrating and a look of agony on his face.

"Jesus!" I shouted. "Rory, get out! Get out right away!"

The paleontologist looked puzzled but he knew by now to heed my advice. He dashed out into the corridor. Huxley was holding the disruptor in both hands, with the disk aimed squarely—or roundly—at Trace.

Mac could have intervened but he didn't; he simply kept his own gun trained on the transfer. After about ten more seconds, Huxley pulled out the control that deactivated the disruptor, and Trace collapsed like a skyscraper undergoing controlled demolition.

"Why'd you do that?" I demanded.

Huxley sounded defensive. "He came at us," he said. "He came right at us."

"Aye," said Mac. "He did. I'd warned him we had a disruptor, Alex—you heard me. But . . ." He lifted his hands philosophically.

Normally, one of us might have rushed in to look at a downed man to see if he was still alive, but I doubted any of us knew how to tell with a transfer. Huxley put down the disruptor, leaning it against the wall that had the poster for *Key Largo*. I called out, "Rory! It's safe to come back!"

Dr. Pickover appeared in the doorway a moment later. "Is he—" But even the transfer hesitated over whether "dead" was the right word.

I prodded Trace with my foot—I hadn't had time yet to put on shoes or socks. He didn't move. "I think so."

"All right," said Mac. He lifted his left arm and pointed at his wrist phone to let me know we were now on the record. "We had reports of two weapons discharges. Who shot first?"

"I did."

"Then you'll have to—"

I cut Mac off and pointed up. "I did—but I shot out the light, see? I agree hitting the switch would have been more genteel, but there's actually no regulation against shooting inanimate objects. I thought my chances were better in the dark."

Huxley appeared dubious—but then, he appeared dubious when he looked at a waffle iron, as if he suspected there must be some trick involved in getting bumps to make dents. But it was Mac's opinion that counted, and Mac nodded. "All right," he said slowly, looking at the downed transfer. "What was he doing here?"

"He broke in. Looking for money, I guess. I happened to be in the shower and startled him when I came out."

"Okay," said Mac. "And the second shot?"

"Dr. Pickover here showed up, and this goon fired at him."

Mac looked thoughtfully at the massive heap on the floor.

"Never quite sure what to do with a dead transfer, but if we keep frying them at this rate, my coroner is going to need to find another job."

"Take him to NewYou," I suggested. "See if they can ID him."

Mac nodded. He began to look around my apartment. "Sorry," I said, interposing myself between him and the wall unit he'd been about to examine. "Not without a warrant."

"It's a crime scene, Alex."

"Only because Huxley fried the guy. You can't manufacture crimes just so you can nose around a man's home."

"Guns were fired."

"True. But I haven't filed a complaint, and neither has Dr. Pickover."

Mac scratched his left ear. "All right," he said. "You'll at least let me take some pictures of the body before we move it?"

I gestured toward it. "Be my guest." While he was doing that, I spoke to my phone, asking it to find an electrician who could come in and fix my ceiling light. By the time I was done with that, Mac was ready to go. He had taken Trace's arms, and Huxley had his legs, and they'd balanced the disruptor on Trace's belly, and were carrying him out my door into the corridor. "Mind if I tag along?" I asked.

"About as much as you minded me searching your apartment," Mac said.

Touché, I thought.

But Pickover spoke up. "We're heading to NewYou, anyway, Detective. I've got a damaged ankle, not to mention *this.*" He indicated the bullet hole. "And Mr. Lomax is being paid to be my bodyguard."

"I can see he's doing a wonderful job," said Huxley, pointing at Pickover's chest.

But Mac knew when he was beaten. "All right," he said. "Let's all go there."

TWENTY-EIGHT

Mac and Huxley had come to my apartment in a police car, but it was much smaller than a prowl car would have been on Earth, and, try as the four of us might, we couldn't get Trace stuffed into the back seat. My neighborhood was rough, but we had to go through classier parts of town to get to NewYou, and so just lashing him to the roof wasn't going to do. Mac finally gave up and called for the paddy wagon. I had no fondness for that particular vehicle—twice people had thrown up on me inside it—so Pickover and I headed out on our own while Hux and Mac waited. Normally, I'd have hoofed it, but Pickover's ankle was still a problem; we hopped on the hovertram.

They say you can judge a city by the quality of its public transportation. New Klondike's trams were covered with graffiti and filled with garbage; things were nasty around the edges in a frontier town, and, frankly, I liked it that way. It took us about ten minutes, with all the stops, to get as close to NewYou as the tram would take us.

We hadn't been able to talk about anything of substance on the tram—too many people listening—but now that we were out on the street, I said, "Any idea who the big guy was working for? Who 'Actual' might be?"

Pickover frowned, then: "The big bloke referred to him as 'he,' so it's presumably not Lakshmi." We were very near the center of the dome now. Overhead, all the supporting struts came together in a starburst pattern around the central column.

"Yeah, I don't think it's Lakshmi, either—but not because of that. Lakshmi knows where the Alpha is, and presumably Trace was after the diary because he *doesn't* know where the Alpha is and thinks it might tell him."

"Who else knows about the diary?" Pickover asked.

We continued along. "I only told you, but God knows how many people Miss Takahashi told." There was a pebble in front of me. I kicked it, and it skittered ahead for most of a block.

We beat Mac and company to NewYou. When we entered, Reiko Takahashi was on duty. I would normally look at her with honest admiration; she was, as I have perhaps mentioned once or twice, quite lovely. But I found myself averting my eyes. She'd long known that her grandfather was dead; I didn't have to be the bearer of *that* bit of news. But that her grandfather's body was here, on Mars, would come as a shock. Pickover limped up to the counter Reiko was standing behind, and they spoke for a few moments. She said Mr. Fernandez was in the workroom and could doubtless make him right as rain; I frowned, trying to remember the last time I'd seen rain. Reiko pointed to the door to the back. Pickover looked over at me, I gave him a thumbs-up, and he disappeared.

Reiko crossed the floor. Her long hair was gathered into a ponytail today, so the orange stripes were only partially visible. "Hello, Alex," she said, smiling. Her demeanor gave no hint that she'd heard anything from Lakshmi about my having made off with the diary.

"Hi, Reiko. I like your hair like that."

She tipped her head demurely. "Thanks." She indicated the doorway Pickover had gone through. "Does everyone who spends time with you end up in that sort of shape?"

"Actually, he got off lucky. The NKPD will be here shortly with—ah, here they are now."

The front door slid open, and Mac and Hux came in. They'd gotten a stretcher somewhere along the way, and Trace's giant body was on it, covered from head to toe by a thin gray sheet.

Miss Takahashi's perfectly manicured fingers went to her mouth. "Oh, God!" she said, moving over to stand next to Mac. "What happened?"

"This gentleman," Mac said, "attacked us, and we had to, um, deactivate him."

Reiko's eyebrows drew together. "Let me get Mr. Fernandez." She hustled into the back, her high heels clicking. Moments later, she reappeared, followed by her boss.

"Detective McCrae?" Fernandez said. "What's up?"

Mac repeated what he'd said to Reiko, and then he pulled back one end of the sheet, revealing Trace's face. A transfer's skin color didn't change after death, and the eyes didn't necessarily close; Trace's green eyes were wide-open, although whatever the disruptor had done to his circuitry had caused one pupil to contract to little more than a pinpoint while the other was so dilated it looked like he'd just come from an eye exam. Of course, he was absolutely still, but he looked like he could leap back into action at any moment. At least with a human stiff, you knew they were out of the game for good.

"How'd this happen?" Fernandez asked. He looked ashen—worse than the dead guy; maybe he was worried about a liability suit if one of his uploads had failed.

"We used a broadband disruptor on him," Mac said.

Fernandez nodded. "Right, right. I'd heard that you guys had a prototype unit."

"Anyway, do you recognize him?"

"Sure," said Fernandez. "That's Dazzling Don Hutchison."

I'd heard the name before, so I had another look. "It is?"

"Well, it's not really him," Fernandez said. "But that's his face. Licensed and everything. The estate gets a royalty each time we use it. Don't get much call for it, though—nobody remembers him anymore."

"Who the hell is Dazzling Don Hutchison?" asked Mac.

I opened my mouth to reply, but so did Hux—and he had

so little in life, I decided to let him beat me to it. "He was a football player," he said. "With the Memphis Blues."

"And he's dead?"

"Twenty years, at least," said Hux.

"But this isn't him uploaded?" said Mac to Fernandez. "This is someone else who bought his face?"

"I'd assume so."

"Can you identify who this is—was?"

"People who choose to use something other than their own face usually want to guard their anonymity."

"Sure," said Mac. "But you must have some way to tell who's who, so you can see if they're still under warranty or whatever. A serial number or something."

Fernandez went into his back room and returned a moment later holding a small scanning device. He aimed it at the body. "No transponder, meaning he opted for an anonymizer package. I'll have to open him up to have a look."

"Do that, please," said Mac.

"I've already got Mr. Pickover opened up. Let me finish his repairs then I'll take care of this."

"How long for an ID?" asked Mac.

"I'll need another hour on Pickover."

"All right," said Mac. He turned to me. "A drink, Alex?"

"Another time."

Mac looked at Miss Takahashi then back at me and gave me a knowing wink. "Right, then. Come along, Sergeant Huxley." The two of them left the shop, and Fernandez went into the back room, closing the door behind him. Nobody had bothered to cover up Trace again, so I did—leaving just me and Reiko alone in the showroom, the two of us biologicals surrounded by unoccupied transfer floor models of various body types and colorations.

"Disconcerting," she said, "seeing a dead transfer like that."

"Yes." I took a breath, then: "Reiko, I have something to tell you that—"

The alloquartz outer door slid open, and a filthy, ancient prospector came in. "You got a washroom?"

Most retail staff had a pat answer along the lines of,

"Sorry, it's for customer use only." Apparently, NewYou had a canned response, too. "Sir," Reiko said, flashing her brilliant smile, "we can set you up so that you never have to use a washroom again! Come on in and let me show you the very best that modern science has to offer!"

The old fossil hunter looked like he was going to call Reiko an unkind name but then he caught sight of me and thought better of it. He turned around and beetled outside.

"You were about to say, Alex?"

"You might want to have a seat."

Her expression suggested she thought this was unnecessary—and, indeed, it probably was; even if you fainted on Mars, you likely wouldn't break anything. But she went to the stool behind the cash desk, sat, and looked at me expectantly. "Well?"

"First, your grandfather is dead. Unequivocally so. I don't want to say anything that gets false hopes up, so let's be clear about that up front."

She nodded.

"But," I continued, "he did *not* die re-entering Earth's atmosphere all those years ago. He died here, on Mars. I know, because Dr. Pickover and I have recovered his body."

"My . . . God." Her eyes were wide. "Are you sure? I mean, I don't doubt you've found *someone's* body, but—"

"I'm sure. Or, more to the point, Dr. Pickover is sure; he's the one who identified the corpse."

"My God. Where . . . where is the body now?"

"In the descent stage."

"Pardon?"

"We found the descent stage that was left here on Mars at the end of their third mission."

"Take me to it. I'll rent a surface suit."

"No need—or, at least, there won't be any need shortly. We've moved the descent stage here, to New Klondike. It's outside the dome now, but I'm going to get it hauled into the shipyard. You can come down once that's done and have a look."

She seemed dumbfounded and more than a little shaken; perhaps she was now glad she'd taken my advice to sit down.

"I don't get it," she said, delicate hands folded in her small lap. "Why was he still on Mars?"

"It looks like he was marooned here."

"By who? By—by Simon Weingarten?"

"Pretty much the only suspect."

"Wow," said Reiko. "Wow."

I wanted to go take care of getting the lander brought inside. "I've got an errand to run. I should be back in time to hear whatever identification details Mr. Fernandez can give us."

Reiko nodded, and I went out through the alloquartz sliding door. Just past it, there was a big wet spot on the wall; perhaps Reiko should have let the old prospector use the john after all.

I headed to the shipyard in the Seventh Circle between Eighth and Ninth Avenues, and made my way to Bertha's shack. She was hunched over like an albino gorilla, looking at work orders. "Hey, dollface," I said.

"Oh, Alex, I was just about to text you. The *Kathryn Denning* has touched down outside the dome. They're offloading its cargo now."

"Thanks," I said. I reached into my pocket and pulled out a fifty-solar coin. "You'll let me know when I can get aboard to poke around?"

She took the money and nodded her jowly head.

"Great," I said. "Until then, I've got a ship I want hauled inside."

She looked at me blankly. "You have a ship?"

"Uh-huh."

"Where'd you get a ship?"

"Found it abandoned. Salvaged it."

"It'll cost to have a tractor bring it in, and you'll have to pay rent on a berth for as long as it's here."

"I have an alternative proposal," I said.

She narrowed her pig-like eyes. "Yeah?"

"Yeah. You haul it in for free, and you let me keep it here for free."

"Funny," she said. "I don't smell booze on your breath."

"Hear me out. You do that, and we'll charge people to

tour the ship—say, twenty solars a head, which we'll split fifty-fifty."

"Ain't no one gonna pay to see some dead hulk," Bertha said. She gestured out the shack's tiny window. "We're knee-deep in them here."

"They'll pay to see this one. It's Weingarten and O'Reilly's lander from their final expedition."

"Holy crap," she said. "Really?"

"Uh-huh."

"Fifty-fifty, huh?"

"Right down the middle—with one condition. I get two days of exclusive access before we open it to the public."

"What for?"

"I'm looking for clues."

"I've always said you were clueless, Alex."

I thought about asking her if she knew Sergeant Huxley; it seemed like a match made in heaven. But I simply smiled and said, "Do we have a deal?"

"Deal."

"How soon can you have it hauled inside?"

"Portia—the gal who operates the tractor—is out getting a bite to eat. But I'll get her to do it when she comes back."

"Great, thanks. The ship's on pad seven. You'll make sure no one comes near it?"

"Yes, of course." She gestured at the shipyard. "Keeping away looters is half my job; I'm good at it."

"I know. Thanks."

"Fifty-fifty, remember," Bertha said, holding up her left arm and tapping the face of her wrist phone with a sausage-like finger to let me know that it had recorded the arrangement.

I feigned a hurt tone. "After all we've been through, you don't trust me?"

"Would you?" she asked simply.

"I see your point."

TWENTY-NINE

I'd have enjoyed watching the descent stage being hauled inside by the tractor—I don't care how big a boy gets, he still loves watching large machines at work. But I'd seen the process before. The giant south airlock was over 300 meters wide and fifty deep. If a ship could fit in—the *Skookum Jim* barely would have squeezed in sideways—it could be brought inside the dome; if it didn't, there was no other way to get it in. The whole process of filling or draining the lock took about an hour.

I headed back to NewYou, grabbing some synthetic sushi on the way. I got there just as Pickover was coming out of the workroom. His shirt still had a rip in it, but I presumed his chest was repaired, and he was no longer limping. I let him settle up with Fernandez—at this rate, Rory was going to have to sell a pentapod or two to stay afloat. And then I turned to Fernandez. "Can we take a crack at Dazzling Don now?"

"Absolutely," he replied.

Just then, Mac came through the front door. Mercifully, Huxley was no longer with him; Mac himself was carrying the disruptor disk under one arm—maybe he was afraid that Trace wasn't really dead.

"Okay," Fernandez said generally to the room. "Come along."

I'd assumed Pickover was going to join us, but he waved me off and went to have a word with Miss Takahashi. Maybe he wanted to try his luck—or maybe, as someone who had bought and paid for immortality, the notion of attending the autopsy of a transfer was too unsettling. In any event, only Mac and I followed Fernandez into the workroom. Given his massive arms, I had no doubt Horatio had been able to carry Trace here on his own. In fact, I suspected he'd done it as soon as we'd left; having a fried transfer in the middle of his showroom probably wasn't good for business.

Dead humans always looked smaller than they had in life, but for whatever reason that effect didn't apply to transfers. Doubtless Fernandez was used to dressing and undressing transfers—people might be born naked, but no one wanted to pop into a new body that wasn't wearing clothes. He undid the buttons on Trace's shirt, exposing a chest that was surprisingly doughy. I found myself thinking the guy should have worked out—but then realized how ridiculous that was.

Fernandez got a small cutting laser and aimed it at the top of the chest, just below the Adam's apple. With practiced efficiency, he played the beam downward. I'd once seen a biological autopsy and had been impressed by all the blood that had spilled out when the chest was opened, but there was none of that here, although the melting plastiskin gave off an odor like burnt almonds.

Fernandez put on blue latex gloves, and as he pulled the chest flaps apart, I could see why: the melted skin was tacky, and some of it stuck to the gloves.

Beneath the skin was a layer of foam rubber, and beneath that was a skeleton that had the purplish pink sheen of highly polished alloy. There was nothing corresponding to organs inside the chest. Indeed, a lot of it seemed to be empty space.

Fernandez got a tool—like pliers, but with oddly shaped jaws—and he attached it to one of a pair of cylinders positioned more or less where the lungs should have been. The tool seemed to unlock something; there was a loud click, and the cylinder came free. Fernandez pulled the cylinder out and placed it on the table next to the body. The cylinder was covered with lubricant, which he wiped off with a green cloth, and then he got a large magnifying glass with a light attached and looked at the metal casing. "This is a ballast unit," he said. "Gives heft to the torso. We don't advertise the fact, but they've got serial numbers on them."

He said the word "Keely," then spoke a string of numbers into the air.

His computer responded in a pleasant female voice. "Transfer completed—" and it named a date two years ago.

"Where was the transfer done?" Fernandez asked.

"The body was assembled here," said Keely, "at this NewYou franchise."

"That was before I started working here," Fernandez said to me. He spoke to Keely again. "And what's this person's name?"

"Unknown," said Keely.

Fernandez frowned. "There has to be a record of the transference," he said—but whether he was telling me, or reminding his computer, I didn't know. He tried rephrasing his question. "Who came in for a transfer that day?"

"Nobody."

I frowned, thinking of what Trace had said: "I'm nobody."

"There had to be a source mind copied into this body," Fernandez said into the air. "Whose mind was scanned that day?"

"No one's."

"Then how was the transfer made?"

"I don't know," said Keely.

"You're sure it was done here?" Mac asked.

"That ballast unit was taken from our stock," the computer replied.

"Curiouser and curiouser," I said, looking at Fernandez. "You said the face was off-the-rack, so to speak. What about the rest of the body? Did it have any special modifications?"

The female voice answered. "Option package five selected: superior strength. No other modifications to standard body."

"He said he was hired muscle," I said. "I guess he was. But who hired him?"

"Who indeed?" asked Mac. He looked at Fernandez. "What *do* you do with a dead transfer? A funeral for a transfer seems like an oxymoron."

"Yeah," said Fernandez. "Transfers do get destroyed every once in a while, of course, but not often; I don't think we've had more than a couple of cases here on Mars." He paused. "Well, with no record of who transferred into this body, there's no way to contact next of kin. I guess I'll just strip him down for spare parts." He looked at the body stretched out before him. "Although I gotta say, I rarely need any so big."

....

When Mac and I went back through the sliding door into the showroom, I was surprised that not only was Pickover gone, but so was Reiko Takahashi.

Fernandez, who came out a moment later, was angry; he didn't like that his shop had been left unattended. Then again, it wasn't as if anyone was going to steal a transfer body; there was nothing you could do with one until it had had a consciousness moved into it, and that was hardly a do-it-yourself affair.

I asked my phone to get hold of Pickover. He didn't answer, which could mean he was in trouble, or it could mean he was indeed getting it on with Miss Takahashi; even I had eventually learned that you don't answer your phone when you're in bed with a lady.

Reiko had been anxious to see her grandfather's body, but I doubted Pickover would go to the descent stage without me, and only teenagers went to the shipyard to make out. I looked around the showroom for any sign of a struggle; there couldn't have been a loud one or we'd have heard it in the next room. But there was no indication of anything amiss—excepting for the missing miss.

I looked at Fernandez, who was using his own phone, presumably to call Reiko. "No answer?" I said.

"No." He shook the phone off. "She wouldn't just disappear. She's not like that."

"Alex," said Detective McCrae. "What's going on?"

I took a deep breath; I needed to give him something so he wouldn't shut me down. "Reiko Takahashi is Denny O'Reilly's granddaughter."

Fernandez's eyeballs looked like they were going to pop out. I went on. "Denny O'Reilly didn't die when his ship burned up on re-entry. Rather, he was marooned here by Simon Weingarten. Reiko had a hard copy of a diary written by her grandfather, which he transmitted back to Earth before he was marooned, but she loaned it to Lakshmi Chatterjee, who is the writer-in-residence here in town."

Mac sounded incredulous. "We have a writer-in-residence?"

"That's what I said! They have to advertise these things better."

"So, this Lakshmi person has the diary?" asked Mac.

"No. Not anymore. It's somewhere safe—but that big bruiser, Trace, thought I had it; that's why he broke into my apartment." I turned to Fernandez. "I was told during the Wilkins case that there were no security cameras upstairs."

"That's true," he said.

"But do you have them down on this floor?"

"Yes, of course."

"Can we see a playback?"

"This way." He led us through the sliding door again; beyond the workshop there was a small office. He turned on a wall monitor and spoke to Keely. "Camera two playback, quad speed, starting thirty minutes ago."

The camera was obviously mounted above the cash desk and showed the transparent door that led outside. The door slid open and—well, the expression "I thought I saw a ghost" perhaps didn't apply when a transfer was involved, but there, in the doorway, illuminated rather dramatically from behind, was Trace—or rather an exact duplicate. There wasn't just one Moose; there were Meese.

"Well," said Fernandez, "it *is* an off-the-shelf face. Keely, normal speed."

I'd been so intent on the mug's mug I hadn't initially noticed that he was packing heat. But Miss Takahashi clearly did, for she froze in the video. Moose the Second rapidly closed the distance between him and her and signaled for her to be quiet.

Pickover had initially been oblivious, but he soon spotted the man and then the gun. The big transfer couldn't do much to Pickover, but he could kill Reiko, and Pickover clearly realized that. He looked back at the door to the room we'd been standing in, as if wondering whether to call for help, but after a second he decided against it. The camera had recorded audio, too, but none of them said a word. Pickover was flexing his legs ever so slightly; now that his ankle was fixed, I think he was trying to decide if he could leap across the room and tackle the other transfer.

But just then the door slid open again, and a *third* transfer with Dazzling Don Hutchison's face came in. That was enough to make Pickover think better of trying to be a hero; either one of the giants could rip his metal skull off his titanium spine. It was galling that all of this had been going on just meters away from me. The transfer who had entered first gestured with his gun, and Reiko headed out the door, followed by Pickover.

Mac was already on his phone, calling the police station to see if the strange party—two giant twins, a transferee paleontologist, and a hot little biological—had been seen by any of the public security cameras, but, of course, most of those had long ago been smashed.

"Who'd want to kidnap Professor Pickover?" Fernandez asked.

"Maybe they wanted Miss Takahashi instead," Mac said.

"Why would anyone kidnap her?" asked Fernandez.

"Ransom?" I suggested. "If they knew she's Denny O'Reilly's granddaughter, they might have figured there was money to be had." I turned to Fernandez. "Did you know?"

He crossed his massive arms in front of his chest. "Are you accusing me?"

"No. No. I'm just asking. You looked surprised when I mentioned it."

"I *was* surprised. I mean, she's Japanese; he was Irish. I'd never even suspected."

"Right," I said. "I doubt anyone did. But she told me." I

walked closer to the wall. "And she told me when I was standing right about there." I pointed to a spot in the image, which now showed the empty showroom. "Which means a record of her telling me *was* made, by the same security camera that made this picture. You could have reviewed it and found out."

"I had no reason to go over the security recordings," Fernandez said.

"Does anybody else have access to them?" asked Mac. "Any of the other employees able to call them up?"

"Well, the Wilkinses could, of course—the previous owners. But Cassandra's dead, and Joshua has gone off to be a fossil hunter."

"Anyone else?" asked Mac.

"Reiko has access, too, but she'd hardly be spying on herself. None of the other employees can unlock the security footage, though, and I swear I didn't know who Reiko's grandfather was."

Mac pulled out a handheld sensing device and headed into the showroom. Transfers didn't leave behind DNA, but they might still shed cloth fibers or have unusual dirt in their footprints that could be useful. While he busied himself with that, I gestured toward the staircase. "Horatio," I said, "there's something I want to see up in the scanning room."

Fernandez shrugged. "Okay." I let him lead the way to the second-floor landing. He went into the left-hand room, and I followed him, closed the door behind me, pulled out my gun, and, as he turned around to face me, I aimed it at the middle of his chest.

THIRTY

"All right," I said to Horatio Fernandez. "Spill it. Where is Rory Pickover?"

His eyes were wide, but he was showing commendable composure for a guy with a gun trained on him. He spread those massive arms. "I have no idea."

"You know what he does for a living, right?"

"Sure. He's a paleontologist."

"And you know he recently came into some wealth."

"I don't know anything about that."

"Little academic suddenly had the money to transfer."

"Well, yeah, I guess."

"And you just opened up his chest to do repairs."

"Uh-huh."

"And while you had him open, you put in a tracking chip."

"That's illegal."

"Yes, it is. But you did it."

"Why would I?"

"You figure he's found the Alpha Deposit, or some other major cache of fossils, and you want to know where it is. Rory had himself scanned for tracking chips after he initially transferred, but he'd all but told Joshua Wilkins that he was going to do that, and so Wilkins hadn't put one in. And he could clearly see what was in your hands as you worked on his face before, so you couldn't put one in when you were doing those repairs—but he had himself checked, just to be sure. But this time you were working in his torso, and he hasn't had a chance to be scanned since leaving here, which means the chip you just put in is active. So where is he?"

"I tell you, I did no such thing."

"You may, or may not, give a damn about Dr. Pickover. But Reiko was your coworker, and maybe your friend. Tell me where they are."

"Mr. Lomax, honestly, I swear to you—"

"This argument ends now. There's no security camera up here, is there? That's what you said. So, I'll tell the NKPD that you went nuts and came at me, and I had to shoot you in self-defense. It'll get sticky for a while, sure, but I'll get off—and you'll be dead. Unless you tell me right now where Dr. Pickover is."

I let him think for a few moments, then cocked the hammer. "Well?"

He blew out air then spoke over his shoulder. "Keely? Locate Rory Pickover."

A portion of the wall nearest us changed to a map of New Klondike, with the radial avenues in red and the circular roads in blue. It took a few moments, but soon a set of crosshairs appeared over the map, with a glowing white point at their center. Rory—and presumably Reiko and the two meese—were located on Sixth Avenue and heading south. "Zoom in," Horatio said to Keely, and the view expanded to show just the single block of Sixth Avenue between the Fourth and Fifth Circles. The dot was moving quickly; they must have been on a hovertram.

"Do you have a portable tracking device?" I asked.

Horatio went to a cupboard and got a small disk-shaped dingus. He made a few adjustments on it and handed it to me. One of its faces was a viewscreen showing a miniature version of what was on the wall. "All right," I said. "You stay up here for five minutes, do you hear me? Start counting Marenerises, and don't stop until you've hit three hundred." I backed away, opened the door while keeping my gun on him, closed it behind me, and headed downstairs.

Mac was bent over, running his scanner along the floor.

"Pickover has a tracking chip in him." I held up the device that Fernandez had given me.

Mac straightened. "Is that a fact?" he said, in a tone that conveyed he knew there was a story to tell.

"Aye," I said, imitating his brogue. "'Tis."

Mac had left the disruptor disk leaning against the cash counter. He retrieved it, and he and I headed out of the shop.

The little one-seater police car Mac had returned here in didn't have a place for me, but it did have a rear bumper and a couple of handholds on the back that could be used to transport a standing person. I positioned myself there, Mac placed the disruptor in the little gap behind the seat, he got in, and we took off down the street, Mac navigating using the device I'd gotten from Fernandez.

From my perch at the back, I couldn't see the tracking device, and I pretty much had to concentrate on holding on for dear life as Mac sent us careening along. But from what I'd seen on the display before I'd given Mac the tracking device, Rory, and likely Reiko and the meese, were heading toward the south airlock—or some point between it and here. The three transfers could just walk right out onto the Martian surface, but Reiko would have to be stuffed into a suit, and that would take time; if they'd actually wanted Rory instead of Reiko, I suspected they'd dump her before reaching the airlock.

Mac could call ahead to the airlock station and ask the guards there to try to detain the meese, but there wasn't a lot biologicals could do against two giant transfers programmed for super strength, and Mac's principal job was protecting Howard Slapcoff's investment; the last thing old Slappy would want is the airlock station being wrecked.

Pedestrians were gawking at us, and at one point when we had to pause to avoid hitting a recycling truck, I gave them a jaunty wave.

The road we were on took us by the shipyard. It was possible that that had been the meese's destination, but Mac was giving no sign of slowing down. I looked over at the sea of dead hulks—shattered dreams, broken lives, abandoned hopes. I just barely made out the descent stage we'd recovered off in the distance.

Mac hit the siren just then, and it startled me enough that I almost lost my grip. But as soon as the vehicle in front of us got out of the way, he shut it off. The dome was never far overhead anywhere in New Klondike, but it had now dipped quite a bit lower; we were at the outer ring where only one- and two-story buildings were possible.

Mac brought us to an abrupt stop. I hopped off the bumper and came around to the side of the car. The gullwing door rose, and Mac clambered out. He retrieved the disruptor, and we headed over to the complex of airlocks.

"They're stationary," Mac said, holding up the tracking dingus so I could see its circular display. "Outside—about half a klick southeast of here. I tried calling for backup, but the other three cops who are on duty today are dealing with a small riot over by the east airlock—somebody accused somebody else of claim-jumping, and it's gotten out of hand."

I nodded and started making my way to the suit-rental counter when Mac motioned me through a door labeled "Official Use Only." Inside was a change room for the police, with four suits hanging from racks. Two were navy blue and bore the initials NKPD across the back and had the police crest on each shoulder; the other two were nondescript plainclothes affairs. We suited up. Mac opted for one of the blue suits, and I took one of the plain ones, in a drab gray.

We went through a personnel airlock and came out on the Martian sands. The sky was dark, and the stars were out in all their glory. Off in the distance was a spaceship, lying on its side. In the dim light, it was hard to make out its contours, but it was a small vessel—a hibernation ship, not a luxury liner with cabins like the *Skookum Jim,* and—

Of course. It was the *Kathryn Denning,* formerly the *B. Traven,* the infamous death ship, recently returned to the Red Planet.

And, judging by the display on the tracking device Mac was holding, the meese had taken Rory Pickover right to it.

THIRTY-ONE

If a ship needed dry-dock repairs it was hauled inside, but most vessels that came to Mars were never brought into the dome—rather, they were prepped for turnaround out on the planitia. Mac and I started walking the 500 meters to the *Kathryn Denning*. Bertha had said earlier that the ship's cargo—which presumably consisted mostly of people in hibernation units—was being offloaded. It looked like that had been completed; we could see the wheel ruts made by the vehicles that had been involved.

Also visible in the dust were footprints. There were two sets of large running shoes and a smaller set of work shoes, but no space-suit boots. The meese had indeed disposed of Reiko at some point; I hoped she was okay.

From the look of the tracks, Rory had been walking in front, with a moose behind and to either side of him. I doubted he'd been leading the way, though; rather, they'd been propelling him along, and—

"See that?" I said over the suit radio.

"Aye," replied Mac.

The tracks told the story. Rory had tried to run: you could see the place where he'd leapt up, and where he'd impacted ten meters farther ahead. The meese had leapt as well, and there were clear signs that they'd all ended up tussling on the ground. And then for the rest of the way, there were only the two large sets of tracks, but one had adopted a shorter gait; I assumed a moose had picked up and carried Rory—who might well have been screaming and kicking—from that point on.

The spaceship was a stubby spindle, with its front and rear points lifted above the ground. Cargo hatches—some open, some closed—were visible, and there was a ramp coming down from what looked to be an airlock door. We walked closer, and I shined my suit's chest light up at the hull, which was a yellowish beige.

Along the bow, in script letters, were the words *Kathryn Denning*. My light was hitting the hull obliquely, revealing just beneath and behind that name some slightly raised lettering that had been painted over; under normal full-on lighting conditions I doubt it would be visible at all, and if I hadn't already known it said *B. Traven*, I probably couldn't have made it out.

A spaceship was a good place for a hostage-taking: it was designed to survive micrometeoroid impacts, which meant it could take a hail of bullets, too. It also had its own life-support system—and it could take off if need be.

Mac walked up the ramp, which was pretty steep, and he tried the door. It was locked. Mac told his phone to get him the New Klondike office of InnerSystem Lines; this close to the dome, his phone worked fine, and I could hear his conversation over our shared radio link.

The phone rang four times, and I thought perhaps everyone had gone home for the day. But then a woman's voice said, "InnerSystem. How can I help you?"

"I'm Detective Dougal McCrae of the New Klondike Police Department, and this is an emergency. I'm standing outside the *Kathryn Denning,* and need access to the interior."

"Just a second," said the woman, then: "I'm told I need an authorization code word from you."

"The code word is 'jasper,'" said Mac.

"Yes, right, okay," said the woman. "Well, to get in, you just need to punch in the master skeleton-key combination code on the keypad next to the airlock; it'll open any door on the ship, including the airlock one. Let me know when you're in position, and I'll recite it to you."

The keypad was behind a hatch helpfully labeled "Keypad" in English; there was also some Chinese, which doubtless said the same thing. Mac opened the little hatch and said, "Go."

"Five zero four," said the woman, then, "three two nine, three one seven, five one zero."

Mac pressed keys and the door slid about fifteen centimeters to the left; presumably it had been spring-loaded but held in place by the lock. The slight displacement revealed a recessed handle. Mac put his gloved fingers into it and pulled the outer door the rest of the way, revealing a chamber no bigger than an old-fashioned phone booth—something I'd seen in plenty of movies but never in real life.

Mac was still carrying the disruptor as he entered the tiny chamber. I pushed myself inside. It belatedly occurred to me that the surface suit Mac was wearing was probably bulletproof. I wondered if the plain one I'd chosen was similarly equipped.

Mac turned around and pulled the outer door shut. He then pressed the one large button on the airlock's left wall; it was labeled "Cycle" in English, and again presumably the same thing in Chinese. I couldn't hear air being pumped into the chamber, but I felt the growing pressure of it on my suit. When the pressure reached that of the ship's interior, a green light went on above the inner door, and, for good measure, it popped aside fifteen centimeters, revealing a recessed handle just like the one on the outer door.

Mac shimmied around—it really *was* meant to be a one-person airlock—and pulled on the handle, sliding the door all the way aside.

He still had the tracking device, but it was hard for him to operate it and hold the disruptor, so he handed the tracker to me. I tried to use finger gestures on the display to zoom in, but it wasn't responding to the touch of my glove. Since we were now at normal air pressure, I pulled off my right glove and tried again. The dot indicated that Rory was about thirty meters toward the stern, and I gestured to Mac that we should start walking in that direction.

The interior of the ship was well lit—in fact, *too* well lit. We tended to keep things a bit dimmer on Mars, since we only got about one-quarter of the sunlight Earth did. I found myself squinting. But I also peered around, trying to picture the horrors that had occurred aboard this ship all those years ago, and my mind started playing tricks. I was still breathing the same bottled air I had been out on the surface, but it now had an iron tang to it, as though it smelled of blood.

I assumed the meese hadn't counted on being tracked here and so wouldn't be expecting us. Still, the broadband disruptor wasn't easily aimed. If they'd kept Reiko rather than Rory, Mac could have fired the disruptor blindly into a room. But we couldn't risk taking out Rory, too.

Mac and I walked stealthily down the corridor, me in true gumshoe fashion and him in flatfoot mode. We soon heard voices up ahead and made an effort to be even quieter. The voices were muffled not because they were coming from behind a closed door—they weren't—but rather because Mac and I were still wearing our fishbowls. I undogged the fasteners, lifted mine off, and tucked it under my arm.

In reality, the air inside the ship *did* smell different: it was musty and stale. Without the helmet, I could hear the voices more clearly. It must have been the two meese: they had the same thick-and-slow speech Trace had had. They occasionally interrupted each other, which was strange and hard to parse: two identical voices overlapping.

Rory, if he was still with them, wasn't saying anything. I consulted the scanner and tried to judge the location the voices were coming from. It looked like the meese and Rory were now in separate rooms: the two thugs sounded like they were ahead but to the left and Rory was showing as ahead and to the right. I indicated that Mac should head off to immobilize the meese, and that I'd rescue Dr. Pickover; my phone had recorded the lock-override code that had been dictated to Mac and could play it back to me if I needed it for another door.

Sure enough, the little corridor we were in had come to

its end, and there were two doors in front of us. The one on the left had its door open, and I could actually see the broad back of one of the meese through it; he was wearing the same clothes as before. The door on the right was closed. It had a sign on it, and although I couldn't make out the writing the symbol above it was clear: a caduceus; this was the sickbay.

I put my glove back on and looked at Mac. This was almost too easy. If Rory was safe behind the closed door on the right, Mac could take out the meese on the left, then we could spring the professor and be on our way. Except for one thing: Mac probably thought the kidnappers deserved due process, blah, blah, blah. Fine; he could use the disruptor to hold them at bay until the cavalry finally finished with the riot and showed up.

We didn't have a lot of time to think. The meese hadn't yet detected us, but if either of them happened to look out the open door of the room they were in, they'd see us. And so, while we still had the element of surprise, Mac shifted the disruptor so that he was holding it like a shield, and he surged forward, shouting through his surface suit's speaker, "NKPD! Freeze!"

THIRTY-TWO

The visible moose turned to face us, looking startled. I ran toward the door on the right and hit the keypad, and pounded out the skeleton-key numbers as fast as my phone read them back to me. I had my gun out, just in case Rory wasn't alone, and—

And he wasn't. The paleontologist was lying on his back on the one and only examination bed in the sickbay. He'd been strapped down, doubtless with the aid of the meese, and his work shirt removed—small consolation, I'm sure, that this time he wasn't going to lose another favorite garment. Looming over him was a scrawny, pale man with shoe-polish-brown hair in his mid-thirties—younger than me, but a toothpick; there was no question which of us would win in a fight. Still, the man was holding a cutting laser, which he'd been in the middle of using to make a vertical incision in Rory's chest, not unlike the one I'd seen Horatio Fernandez carve in Trace's corpse. A deepscan was displayed on the wall; it took me a second to realize that it was showing the interior of Rory's torso.

I gestured with my gun at the pale man. "Drop the laser and put your hands up."

"Alex!" said Rory, lifting his head to look at me.

"Hands up!" I said again to the scrawny man, who had ignored me. Meanwhile, next door, Mac shouted, "I said, freeze!" I was torn; if he needed backup, I should perhaps go help him. But a moment later, I heard Mac say, "That's better. This is a broadband disruptor. It's already taken down one of you today. Don't make me use it again. Keep your hands above your heads."

I cocked my pistol and aimed it at the thin man's face. "Make like your goons," I said. "Reach for the sky."

The man set down the laser and did so. His arms were skeletal.

"Who are you?" I demanded.

"Take a hike," he replied in a reedy, weak voice.

I turned my phone, attached to the suit's left wrist, so that it could see his face. "Identify this person."

"Error twenty-three," replied the device, which I had programmed to use Peter Lorre's voice. "No probable match."

I shook the damn thing off and looked back out into the corridor. Mac was now marching the meese toward the airlock. I turned back to the emaciated man. "What the hell are you doing opening up Dr. Pickover?"

Rory answered that: "I told the goons the diary is sealed inside my torso."

I made an impressed face. "And is it?"

"Yes. I had Fernandez put it in there for safekeeping." I looked at the deepscan. There was indeed the ghostly outline of an object the right size next to one of the ballast cylinders. "The goons threatened to kill Reiko if I didn't give them the diary. I *had* to tell them where it was."

There were two chairs in the room, padded enough to be comfortable even under Earth gravity. I set my fishbowl on one of them, then pointed to the other one; the scrawny man sat on it and lowered his hands. I moved back to Pickover. The restraints were built into the medical bed, but although a patient couldn't undo them once strapped in, the release mechanisms were plainly labeled. I lifted the latch for each of the four restraints, and Rory sat up, the incision on his chest opening a bit as he did so. A biological would be rubbing his wrists and ankles now to restore circulation, but Rory just sat there, looking daggers at his captor.

"Let me have the diary," I said.

Rory hesitated for a moment then did what the skinny man had been about to do before I'd interrupted him: he stuck a hand through the plastiskin and foam rubber just below his metal sternum, rummaged around, and pulled out the diary—still missing its back cover, but sealed now in a plastic bag. He handed it to me.

The bag was slick with clear lubricant. I didn't want the damn thing slipping around, so I removed the little bound volume from the bag and shoved it into my surface suit's hip pocket.

"What's become of Miss Takahashi?" I asked.

Rory's face lit up. "She escaped, Alex—with my help; I created a diversion. Those big blokes wanted to get rid of her; they want to get rid of everyone they think knows where the Alpha is, and they figured she must know, because she's read the diary." Rory was now putting his work shirt back on. "I kept telling them the diary doesn't disclose the location, and Reiko told them the same thing, but they didn't believe us."

I spoke to my phone while keeping my gun aimed at Rory's captor. "Call Reiko Takahashi."

"Shunted to voice mail," said Peter Lorre.

"Call Horatio Fernandez at NewYou."

Three rings, then: "Hello, Alex."

"Horatio, has Miss Takahashi returned?"

"No."

"She escaped"—I looked at Rory—"how long ago?"

"Forty minutes, I'd say."

"She escaped forty minutes ago. And I'm with Dr. Pickover."

"I'll let you know when she arrives here."

I shook the phone off. "Who are you?" I said again to the seated man.

"Get stuffed."

"My phone would know you if you were a longtime Mars resident—so you aren't. I'll assume you came here on this ship, and you're too chicken to go out into the dome. That's probably wise: New Klondike is a rough place, and it wouldn't be long before someone there decided to snap you in two." I took a step closer. "I might even decide to do it myself, and—"

I hadn't paid any attention to his clothing until now, but the shirt he was wearing was burnt orange with a circular patch over the left breast, a patch bearing the "ISL" logo of InnerSystem Lines; it was a uniform top. "Christ, you're part of the *crew.*" I spoke to my phone again. "How many crew on the *Kathryn Denning?*"

"Two," wheezed Peter Lorre. "A primary bowman and a backup bowman. The former normally travels awake, while the latter makes the voyage in hibernation and is only thawed out in emergencies."

"So which are you?" I demanded.

"Go climb a tree," said the man.

"There aren't any for a hundred million kilometers," I replied. I looked at the phone again. "Get the names of the two bowmen from the InnerSystem office here."

"A moment." Then: "The primary bowman is Beverly Kowalchuk. The backup is Jeffrey Albertson."

"So you're Albertson," I said. I gestured with my gun for him to get to his feet.

He hesitated for a moment then did get up. It was the exact opposite of the effect one normally observed with someone newly arrived from Earth. Usually, the freshly thawed stand with way too much energy and actually lift themselves off the ground a bit; I'm tall enough that I'd bumped my head on ceilings a few times shortly after my own arrival here. But Albertson got slowly to his feet, wincing as he did so; if he was weak here, movement back on the mother world must have been excruciating for him.

"Those thugs of yours," I said. "One of them has already been fried—by the broadband disruptor you just heard that police officer talking about. We haven't identified him yet, but we will—same with whoever it is inside the other two."

The thin man shrugged. "Uno and Dos are the only names they've got."

Pickover brightened. "Oh, I get it! Alex, the third one

wasn't called Trace; rather it was *Tres*—Spanish for three; sounds the same, but spelt different. *Uno, Dos, Tres."*

"Huh," I said. "How high do the numbers go, Jeff?"

"Jump off a cliff."

"So what the hell's the matter with you, anyway?" I asked, not expecting an answer.

Rory was now standing beside me. "My grandfather looked the same way," he said. "It takes a lot out of you."

"What does?"

"Well, I suppose it could be anything, but . . ."

I waved the gun. "On the examining bed."

Albertson glared at me, but then did as I'd commanded. He simply sat on the bed's edge, but it was enough. The ship's computer obviously recognized him, even if my phone hadn't, and his medical records came up on a monitor in the room. I scanned them quickly. "'Stage-four lymphatic cancer.' And *those* numbers *don't* go any higher." I looked at him. "Tough luck. I wouldn't want to die in jail."

Albertson crossed his arms defiantly in front of his chest. I idly wondered if I could bring myself to rough up somebody in such bad shape, and—

"Oh, my," said Pickover. He'd been looking at Albertson's medical record in more detail; I imagine the scientific gobbledygook meant more to him than it would have to me. "Alex, look at this."

He was pointing at some text on the screen. I squinted to make it out, and—

And I guess this wasn't Albertson after all. Not only was the date of birth given, but the computer had also helpfully calculated his age and placed it in brackets after the date: "78 years."

I turned back to him, and—

And—

God.

And he was the *backup* bowman. He—Christ, yes. I'd never heard of anything like this, but . . .

He *looked* like he was in his thirties. Biologically, he probably *was* in his thirties.

"You've been doing this forever," I said. "For decades.

You keep making trips back and forth between Earth and Mars—spending eight months or more each way in hibernation. I didn't know it was possible to do that many stints in deep freeze, but—"

Cancer.

A man who'd been diagnosed with terminal cancer decades ago.

"You're Albertson, all right," I said. "But that's not the name you were born with—was it, Willem?"

"Why don't you—"

"Take a long walk off a short pier? The nearest one of those is back with the trees."

Rory was staring at the man now, his eyes wide. "My . . . God," he said. "Willem Van Dyke—I never thought I'd see you in the flesh, but . . ." He shook his head. "The disease has taken a lot out of you, but, yes, I can see it now. Well, well, well. There are a million things I'd like to ask you about the second expedition, but . . ." He drew his artificial eyebrows together, and his voice turned angry. "Christ, you almost killed me!"

Van Dyke slid off the examining bed. "I did no such thing. That incision in your torso can be sealed easily enough. And besides, you can't be killed."

"Not here," said Rory. "Not now. *Before.* You're the one who brought the land mines along on the *B. Traven.* You're the one who booby-trapped the Alpha. Damn it, you blew half my face off! You could have killed me!"

"You can't be killed," Van Dyke said. "You're not alive."

Rory spluttered in a mechanical way. I looked at Van Dyke. "Those mines were passive protection," I said, "and you planted them long ago. But when you learned that Denny O'Reilly's granddaughter was coming to Mars, you decided you had to take active steps, right?"

Van Dyke said nothing. I let out a theatrical sigh. "You're not getting how this works, Billy-boy. I ask you questions, you answer—or you die. It's really not a difficult concept."

Van Dyke was looking not at me but at the wall where a freeze-frame of the deepscan of Rory was still being displayed. I suppose it galled Van Dyke that Rory could have comfortably taken the scanner's radiation forever, when it was radiation exposure that had given Van Dyke cancer. But he said nothing.

"All right," I said. "I'll tell you. You knew Denny O'Reilly had a mistress whose last name was Takahashi, of course. And you work for InnerSystem Lines—you get to see the passenger manifests for all their ships; you check them each time you return to Earth. When you saw there was a Reiko Takahashi booked to come to Mars, you got curious. It didn't take much digging to find out who she was. And, well, a collector of one sort knows collectors of other sorts: she'd doubtless made inquiries about selling the only extant copy of her father's diary—and you figured it might note the location of the Alpha. Couldn't have something like that kicking around. And so you sent in the clones."

"They're not clones," Van Dyke snapped.

"Work with me," I replied. "You've spent most of the last thirty-plus years on ice. Physically, you're—what?—thirty? Thirty-two?"

Van Dyke glared at me defiantly for a moment, and I raised the gun higher. "Thirty-eight," he said at last. And then, acknowledging that he didn't even look that old despite the ravages of cancer, he added, "I stay out of the sun."

"I guess it's a good deal for InnerSystem Lines," said Rory. "Your training stays fresh. From your point of view, it's been only a couple of years since you first started your job. You just thaw out for a few days or weeks between each journey, while this ship is prepared for its next voyage."

"I usually don't even bother coming out of deep freeze here on Mars," Van Dyke said. "When I do come back to living here, I'm going to come back in style."

"You're going to transfer," I said.

Van Dyke snorted.

"What?" I said.

"Like I would ever do *that.*"

"But that's the cure for cancer. Hell, that's the cure for *everything.*"

"No," said Van Dyke. "It isn't—but there *will* be a cure for cancer."

"That's what they've been saying *forever*," said Pickover. "But it seems like it's always twenty years in the future."

"They *are* making progress," Van Dyke said. "I check every time I come out of hibernation. I'm guessing it's just ten years off now . . ."

"And if you can stay on ice for most of that time," I said, "you can get the cure." I shook my head. "But why not just transfer? I know it was hellishly expensive back when you were first diagnosed, but—"

"That's not the reason."

I frowned and it came to me. "Lakshmi—the writer-in-residence here—told me that you're devoutly religious. Is that why you haven't transferred?"

"Transferring," he said. "Such crap. It's *not* the same person."

Rory tilted his head to look at the man who'd been slicing him open. "People feel differently about it now."

"God doesn't," said Van Dyke.

Rory couldn't dispute that and so he fell silent.

"And what are you going to do when they find a cure?" I asked. "When you're well again?"

"Go fly a kite."

"Okay. I'll tell you. Weingarten and O'Reilly promised you a share of the proceeds from the Alpha. And you want what you think is coming to you. When you're well, you're going to work that claim."

"And you're out to stop anyone who might exploit it first," said Rory.

"Hence hiring the thugs with Dazzling Don Hutchison's face," I added. But then I found myself taking a step backward. "No," I said. "No, wait a minute. You didn't hire those guys." The word "skytop" was echoing in my head—the decades-old slang Tres had used. "Christ, you *are* those other guys. You're—my God—you're all three of them. You *have* transferred. That's why Tres called you 'Actual'—you're the actual Willem Van Dyke, and they're copies."

Van Dyke looked like he was going to deny it. But someone who had gone to such extraordinary lengths to stay alive doubtless had a certain appreciation for what my Smith & Wesson could do to him. "I've made proxies, that's all," he said, in his thin, disease-ravaged voice. "I'm the real me; I'm the one with the soul. Those are just knockoffs. I made a deal with the guy who runs NewYou here to produce them in secret."

"Horatio Fernandez?" Rory asked.

"No, no. His name is—"

"Joshua Wilkins," I supplied.

"That's him. Nasty man, but he could be bought. I had him create the three Dazzling Dons a couple of years ago."

"It's illegal to make multiple versions of the same person," Rory said. "It's *obscene* to do so."

"They were disposable—and they aren't people."

"What do they think about that?" I asked.

"Same thing I do, of course."

"Why three guys who look the same?"

Van Dyke lifted his eyebrows as if it were obvious. "To remind them that they *aren't* real people. They're ersatz; interchangeable; disposable."

I nodded. "And I bet they were supposed to be each other's alibis—one would be seen in public while the others did whatever needed to be done to protect the Alpha; they were never meant to all be seen in the same place at the same time. But then one of them was shut down, and so you figured a bigger force was needed next time."

And that explained why Tres had rushed Huxley, even though Mac had told him they had a broadband disruptor. Tres was probably as ignorant of what one could do as Willem Van Dyke had been; they all had minds three decades out-of-date.

"Okay," I said. "Let's go."

"Where?"

"Prison, ultimately, I imagine."

"I'm not going to jail," Van Dyke said.

"No? You roughed me up, shot Dr. Pickover, and then kidnapped him and Miss Takahashi with the intention of murdering them."

"I did no such thing. Uno, Dos, and Tres did all that, not me. And Tres is deactivated, and Uno and Dos are already in police custody."

"You masterminded it all."

"You'd have a hard time proving that."

I stole a line from Mudge the computer. "Be that as it may."

"Regardless," said Rory, "you booby-trapped the Alpha."

"Even if I did—and I admit nothing—that's outside the police's jurisdiction."

I gestured with the gun. "Walk." I picked up my helmet and got him out into the brightly lit corridor, followed by me and then Rory. I continued to speak: "If I were you, I'd do a deal with the police. You said it yourself: you've only got a couple of years left. Don't waste them in court. Cop a plea, pay a fine, forget about the Alpha, and get back to being on ice—and, who knows, maybe someday they *will* find a cure for cancer."

The corridor switched from carpeted to uncarpeted as we approached the airlock, and our six footfalls were now making a fair bit of racket.

The airlock door was closed. I wondered how Mac had managed to get through; there's no way he could have crammed himself and the two meese in all at once. It was a puzzle in logic—the kind Juan Santos enjoyed.

There were also three of us, but there was no reason we had to all go through at once. It was a toss of a coin whether Rory should exit first, or Van Dyke and I should. Of course, Van Dyke needed to get into a surface suit to do so, but there was a surface suit hanging by the door, and—

Ah, and it had the name Jeff Albertson on it. Well, he *was* part of the crew.

The light above the inner airlock door suddenly changed from green to red: someone was coming through from the other side. I supposed Mac could be returning, after having handed over the meese to other cops. Or it could be Bertha or someone else from the shipyard, or Beverly Kowalchuk or one of the local InnerSystem staff. Without knowing who it was, it seemed premature to get Van Dyke into a surface suit; maybe there was a moose out there named Cuatro, and having Van Dyke suited up would be playing right into his giant hands. "Don't bother changing," I said. "Not yet."

I held my gun in front of me with both hands and aimed it at the airlock door. It wasn't long before the light above it changed back to green, the door popped open that fifteen centimeters to reveal the recessed handle, someone pulled the door aside the rest of the way, and—

And a transfer with holovid star Krikor Ajemian's face was standing there in front of us.

THIRTY-THREE

B erling?" I said, looking at the transfer framed in the airlock doorway. "Stuart Berling?"

He scowled. "Lomax? What the hell are you doing here?" But then his gaze shifted to Willem Van Dyke, and his brown eyes went wide. "My God," he said shaking his handsome head. "My God, it's true. You haven't aged a day."

"Do I know you?" Van Dyke replied. He gave no hint that he recognized the famous face in front of him, and, indeed, if he'd spent most of the last three decades on ice, he probably didn't.

"I'm Stu Berling," the transfer said.

Van Dyke spread his arms slightly. "Should I know you?"

"I was on the—on this damned ship."

"When?"

"Thirty years ago. The last time it sailed under the name—" He swallowed, then managed to get it out: *"B. Traven."*

"Oh," said Van Dyke, softly.

"I'd had questions about that for decades," said Berling. "But now I've got money—and money buys answers. A guy at InnerSystem's office here in New Klondike told me you were aboard. I couldn't believe it—couldn't believe you were still part of the crew after all these years."

"I don't know who you are," said Van Dyke.

"I'm the one who woke you. During the flight. All those years ago."

"No, you're not."

Berling seemed pissed that this was being disputed. "I am, damn you."

"I don't know what that geeky kid—he was just eighteen or nineteen—grew up to look like, but you're not him. You're a damn transfer, a *nothing.*"

Berling's tone was venomous. "I'm more of a man than you ever were. It was four days before I was able to get past that madman, get to your hibernation chamber, wake you up. And you didn't do a thing to stop him."

"There was nothing I could do," said Van Dyke. "He had guns; I was unarmed."

"You were the backup bowman," snapped Berling. "You were the only other crew member. You should have stopped him."

"I tried," said Van Dyke. "That kid saw me try."

"You had smuggled land mines aboard," said Berling.

"The official report said it was Hogart Pierce, the primary bowman, who had done that."

"Pierce was dead," said Berling. He gestured behind himself. "They shot him as he came out that airlock here on Mars. When they found the land mines, they said he'd been smuggling them for some client here. But it wasn't him; it was you."

Van Dyke looked like he was going to utter a reflexive denial, so before he could, I asked Berling, "How'd you figure it out?"

"Like I said, money unlocks things. I started digging into this." He pointed at the scrawny man, but looked at me. "Van Dyke had come to Mars once before that hellish journey, did you know that?"

"On Weingarten and O'Reilly's second expedition," I said.

Berling nodded. "And why didn't he come back on the third?"

"He'd had a falling-out with Weingarten and O'Reilly," I said, "over how to split profits, and—ah. As you greased enough palms to dig into Van Dyke's past, you discovered— what? That he was a munitions expert? Former bomb-disposal guy?"

"Black-market arms dealer," said Berling.

Van Dyke sneered, apparently offended by the term. "My expertise was in putting high-powered buyers in touch with those who had things of great value to sell. That's why Simon and Denny brought me aboard . . . literally."

"But then they double-crossed you," I said. "Or you double-crossed them."

Van Dyke said nothing.

"And, my God," I said, taking a half step backward. "You—God, yes, of course! You sabotaged their ascent stage on the third expedition. You couldn't have used the same model of land mine to do it—those were introduced after that ship left Earth. But an earlier model would have worked just as well—or some other explosive you had access to, as an arms dealer. You killed Simon Weingarten."

"And Denny O'Reilly," said Berling.

"No," I said, "but only because Weingarten marooned O'Reilly here." Berling looked surprised at this bit of news, but before he could speak, I went on. "So you're a murderer," I said to Van Dyke. "No wonder you're in no hurry to meet your maker."

"You could have halted the insanity," Berling said, also to Van Dyke. Pickover, wisely, was staying out of all this.

"No, I *couldn't!*" Van Dyke shouted at him. "The land mines were locked in a cargo hold; there was no way to get at them during the flight."

"You could have detonated them by remote control," said Berling.

"That would have blown up the ship!"

"It would have stopped him."

"It would have killed us all."

"It would have stopped *him.*" Berling was reaching his boiling point; he looked like he was going to explode.

"Stuart . . ." I said gently.

He wheeled on me. "That madman abused us. He tortured us. And Van Dyke could have stopped it. He could have stopped him. Instead it went on for another two months. Two months before we reached Mars, two months of horrific abuse."

"I'm sorry," Van Dyke said.

"Sorry!" shouted Berling. "That's not enough. I can't go home. I can't go back to Earth. I'm rich now—but there's nothing to spend it on here. I could never lock myself aboard another spaceship for months. And it's your fault." He didn't take a deep breath; he couldn't. But he did stop and look around—and then he shuddered. "Right over there—right down that hallway? See? That's where he first . . . where he first . . ."

"Stuart," I said again, as gently as I could. "It was thirty years ago."

"It's *not* thirty years for me! I relive it over and over again."

"I am sorry," Van Dyke said again. "There really was nothing I could do, and—"

Berling moved with a transfer's speed, and with the same violent temper I'd experienced from him at Ye Olde Fossil Shoppe. He leapt forward, landing less than half a meter from Van Dyke, and he rammed Van Dyke back against the wall—hard.

Maybe a healthy man could have taken it. And, of course, if this Van Dyke had been one of his transfer copies, he'd have survived it easily. But he wasn't—and he didn't. Berling's open palm crushed Van Dyke's chest. Berling took a step back, a look of horror on his face—as dramatic as a transfer's expression could get. "Oh, God . . ." he said.

Van Dyke crumpled to the floor. I rushed in and felt for a pulse. "His heart's stopped."

"Oh, God . . ." Berling said again, very softly.

I stretched Van Dyke out on his back and placed hands over his sternum to start chest compressions, but—

But his sternum was caved in and it felt as though the heart beneath it had been crushed. There was nothing to lose by this point, and so I did the compressions, but I could feel bone breaking further and an appalling squishiness beneath it all.

"Oh, God . . ." Berling said for a third time. "I didn't mean—I didn't want . . ." His jaw dropped. "I—I just wanted to *talk* to him."

"You killed that man," said Rory, speaking at last, his voice faint.

"I—I'm sorry. I—"

Rory did a series of body and facial movements that I guess were akin to taking a deep breath; he was clearly composing himself, and thinking about what to say. "All right, okay, I understand that you were a victim of abuse, but . . . but *he* wasn't the abuser, and . . ." He paused and shook his mechanical head slightly. "I'm sorry, you poor blighter, but you must know that even the NKPD won't be able to turn a blind eye to your killing him. InnerSystem is a division of Slapcoff Interplanetary; they'll demand to know what happened to their crew member, and the police will have to investigate."

Berling spun on his heel. I'd seen biologicals take hostages before: they often put an arm around someone's neck from behind—but even a broken neck could be repaired on a transfer. Instead, Berling had reached around from behind to clasp Pickover's forehead. His other arm had grabbed one of Rory's own just below the elbow. He propelled the paleontologist into the airlock.

"Don't take him," I said. "Take me. I'm the better hostage— you can easily overpower me."

"No dice," said Berling. "The police have that disruptor thing. They won't dare use it on me so long as I'm next to this guy."

"Alex . . ." said Rory, pleadingly.

Berling squeezed, and I saw indentations, like the beginning of finger holes for a bowling ball, appear in Rory's forehead. "Shut up!" snapped Berling. Rory did so. Berling released his grip on Rory's arm just long enough to pull the inner airlock door closed. There were a couple of minutes until the cycling process would finish, so I went down on one knee next to Van Dyke to see if there was anything at all that could be done, but he was gone.

I put on my fishbowl. The light above the airlock door turned green: Berling and Pickover had exited and were presumably now making their way down the ramp to the ground. Neither of them needed to eat or drink, and they could go months without charging up; my guess was that Berling would drag Rory out into the Martian desert. Of course, Rory still had a tracking chip in him, unbeknownst to Berling. But it would be better to stop them on the open planitia, rather than let them get somewhere that could be defended.

I cycled through the airlock as quickly as I could, and—

And whatever combinations of people Mac had chosen to get him and the meese out of the *Kathryn Denning* hadn't worked as intended. Berling and Rory were halfway down the ramp that led from the airlock to the ground, Berling still holding Rory's arm and clutching his skull. One of the meese was sprawled face down about twenty meters to the right—Mac had apparently used the disruptor on him—and the other moose and Mac were facing off against each other about forty meters farther along.

THIRTY-FOUR

Merely resisting arrest wasn't cause to use deadly force, and Mac, who ultimately worked for Howard Slapcoff, would be the last guy in the solar system to say a transfer was entitled to less than a biological was; the first moose must have actively attacked him.

Right now, Mac's back was to me. He had the disruptor disk aimed at the second moose, and they seemed to be at an impasse: the moose was refusing to move, and Mac's only recourse would be to kill him if he didn't.

Mac and I were still on the same radio frequency, and so I spoke to him. Rory should be tuned in as well, but his captor, Stuart Berling, wouldn't be able to hear. "Mac, it's Alex. I'm in the open airlock of the *Kathryn Denning* behind you. A transfer named Stuart Berling came storming in, and he's killed Albertson and taken Dr. Pickover captive; they're on the ramp in front of me."

There was silence long enough that I thought Mac's radio must be on the fritz. But then Mac's brogue came through, punctuated by some static; I wondered if the fact that he'd recently fired the disruptor had anything to do with that. "Aye, Alex, I saw the transfer coming toward the ship. I tried to stop him, but had my hands full with the two goons."

"Only one goon left," I said.

"You noticed that," said Mac. He and the moose were now slowly circling each other; I think Mac had started the movement so that he could change his perspective and get a glimpse of me. The transfer he was holding at bay would have already seen me and Berling and Pickover. "One of the goons took the opportunity to run back toward the ship," Mac said. "He went after the incoming transfer—Berling, did you say his name was? The goon wouldn't halt, and I had to fry him."

"Yeah. He must have figured that Berling was coming after Albertson—which he was."

Mac and the moose had rotated 180 degrees; Mac was now looking right at me. Berling and his captive Pickover were standing motionless halfway down the ramp.

"Mac," I said, speaking again after a pause, "are you in radio communication with the transfer thug?"

"Aye, I can be."

"What frequency?"

"Thirty-seven."

"Switching," I said, touching controls on my wrist. Then: "Okay, big fella. This is Alex Lomax. Which one are you? Uno or Dos?"

There was a pause while he thought—presumably not about what the answer was, but rather about whether to answer at all. But at last, he did. "Uno."

"Okay, Uno, I want you to consider something. Sorry to be the bearer of bad news, but the guy you call Actual—the actual Willem Van Dyke—is dead."

"You'll pay for that!"

"Hang tight. *I* didn't do it. But he is gone; sorry about that. And you know Tres got wasted at my apartment, and Dos is lying in a heap over there." I pointed. "No Actual. No other duplicates. Just you. That means *you* are Willem Van Dyke. Under *Durksen v. Hawksworth,* under the laws of just about every country: the biological original is gone and one transfer exists. You are Willem Van Dyke now. Sure, maybe Detective McCrae can pin a few petty things on you, and maybe he can't—he'd have to prove that you personally, not

Dos or Tres, were responsible, and that'd take some doing. But even if he can, you're potentially immortal now; don't squander that. We can all walk away from this."

Uno had his back to me now, but he stopped and turned around; Mac could have zapped him with the disruptor, but I guess Uno trusted him not to by this point. He was clearly looking over at me—which meant he was looking in the general direction of Berling and Rory, too.

I thought that if Uno could be won over, he might help in saving Rory; there wasn't much I could do, armed with a gun, against a strong transfer. And as long as Rory and Berling were locked together there was nothing Mac could do with the disruptor. But Rory was strong, too—and if Uno and Rory both went against Berling, Berling might go down.

I couldn't see Uno's expression from this distance—although I suspected he could see mine, and so I tried a kindly smile. It seemed to work. He nodded—I could make out that much—and slowly lifted his arms into the classic "I surrender" pose.

"Very good," I said. Below me on the ramp, Berling was craning his neck to look back my way while still holding Rory as a shield in front of him. I doubted I could as easily talk him into letting his hostage go, but I held up fingers to indicate a new radio frequency—two and five—in hopes that Berling might want to parley for Rory's release.

Berling tilted his head, presumably doing something internally that switched radio frequencies. "Okay, Lomax," he said. "Talk."

"We all want to walk away from this, Stuart," I said. "Think about what's on the line. You've uploaded—you can live forever. You've found great fossils, and you'll find even more—you're rich." I paused, wondering if bringing Lacie into it was wise or not, but decided I needed every bit of persuasion I could muster. "And you've got an amazingly beautiful wife waiting for you. You don't need to throw all that away."

I wanted some feedback—some evidence that this was making sense to him—but he said nothing and so, after a time, I went on. "And you *don't* have to throw it away," I said.

"If Uno, over there, accepts the role of the real Willem Van Dyke, then Van Dyke isn't dead, see? No homicide. No need for you to take a hostage. No need for *any* of this. All you—"

Motion caught my eye. Uno—in the body of Dazzling Don Hutchison—still had his hands held up, but he must have just crouched low, and then snapped those powerful legs straight, because he was flying up, up, up into the dark sky. He kept his right arm bent, but then stuck his left arm straight out from the shoulder; he looked, for all the world, as he flew higher and higher, like he was going to throw a Hail Mary pass. But he wasn't holding anything in either hand, and—ah—he was actually twisting around his vertical axis as he went up, and now was starting the slow descent. I'm sure he wanted to come down faster, but—

Yes, he'd angled backward a bit. He was going to come down right on top of Mac. Mac was fumbling to get the disruptor disk aimed up over his head, but soon abandoned that notion and simply scrambled to get out of the way. Even under Martian gravity, having 150 kilos of mass conk you on the head could do a lot of damage.

As Uno came down onto the planitia, he flexed his knees, and they bore the brunt of the impact. Still, a cloud of dust went up, and for a moment I wasn't sure what was happening. But soon Uno came barreling out of the cloud, heading straight toward Mac, who was hunched over and scuttling away. And then this Dazzling Don did what the real Dazzling Don had done countless times—he tackled the other player, driving Mac face first into the dirt. Mac landed on the disruptor; Uno pushed himself up off Mac, then grabbed Mac's shoulders and tossed him aside. He seized the disruptor disk and started running toward me.

No, *not* toward me. Toward Rory Pickover and Stuart Berling. "You killed Actual!" Uno said, no sign of exertion in his mechanical voice—just raw fury. I realized that he, too, must have selected frequency twenty-five; even from forty meters away he could make out the finger signs I'd presented to Berling.

He was closing the distance fast. "Uno, don't!" I yelled. "Don't!"

Uno slowed a bit, but only to get a good look at the disruptor and find its controls. And although I knew from experience that turning it off was harder than it should be, turning it on had never been a problem . . .

There were now only about fifteen meters between Uno and the Berling/Pickover pair, still on the ramp. It was my turn to jump. The airlock was higher up than I'd have liked, but I stepped onto the ramp, then leapt off. "Berling!" I shouted, as soon as I'd landed on the planitia. "Let Pickover go. Get back into the airlock! You'll be safe inside."

Berling didn't move.

"For God's sake!" I called. "Lock yourself back inside the ship!"

He stood there. Of course he couldn't do that; he could never lock himself in that death ship again.

Uno had come to a stop now. He held the disruptor in front of him, one hand in each of the grips on the opposite sides of the disk.

"Uno, for God's sake, let Dr. Pickover go! You don't want to do this!"

But he did. He must have pressed the twin triggers, because suddenly both Berling and Rory went stiff and then their bodies started spasming and—

And—Christ!—Berling was still gripping Rory's forehead, and his hand was clenching.

The high-pitched whine of the disruptor was barely audible in this thin air, but its effects were obvious. Both transfers looked like they were receiving massive electrical shocks.

"Stop!" I shouted, and "Stop!" shouted Mac.

But Uno kept holding down the triggers, and the two transfers kept vibrating, and—

And I saw Rory's head being deformed—as if the broadband frequencies coursing through his system weren't doing enough damage.

"For God's sake!" I yelled.

Uno didn't seem to know how to turn off the device, but he did twist his giant body, aiming the disk away from Berling and Rory. They both stopped jerking. Berling toppled sideways and fell off the ramp, his limbs stiff. He landed with a small thud and a big puff of dust next to me. Rory fell forward and skidded down the ramp, his partially crushed head leading the way.

"You didn't have to do that!" I said. "You didn't have to take out Dr. Pickover!"

Uno's voice had an infinite calmness. "That wasn't Dr. Pickover," he replied. "That was nobody." And then he stretched out his arms and began to slowly flip the disk end over end, and, as it was facing up, he said, "And I'm nobody, too—and with Actual gone, I have no reason to be." The disk continued to flip around, and the emitter side ended up facing toward Dazzling Don Hutchison's face. The giant body started to convulse as Uno's fists clenched shut on the twin triggers. He kept spasming for about twenty seconds as Mac and I rushed toward him from opposite directions. And then he toppled backward, still convulsing as he went down in slo-mo, until he was lying on his back, the disk held up over him.

Mac loomed in and pulled out the off switch, and suddenly everything was very, very still.

THIRTY-FIVE

I walked slowly over to where Mac was standing, and we stood wordlessly for a time: two weary biologicals in surface suits amid four dead transfers lying there on the Martian sands in nothing but street clothes.

Finally, backup arrived in the form of Huxley, Kaur, and another cop, rumbling out onto the surface in a pressurized van. Mac conferred with them, and the three newcomers set about photographing the bodies and taking various scanner readings and measurements. While they were busy with that, I took Mac up into the *Kathryn Denning* and showed him the corpse of Willem Van Dyke.

There wasn't much to say, and so Mac and I barely spoke. I left him inside the ship, taking readings with his scanner, and I trudged slowly down the ramp. All of this action had taken place by the south airlock. I had plenty of bottled oxygen, and so I decided to walk around the dome to the west airlock—just to clear my head a bit, and to avoid human company.

It was a little over three kilometers to that airlock, and I shuffled along, raising dust clouds as I did so, like Pig-Pen in the old *Peanuts* animated cartoons. After about a kilometer, I decided to try calling Reiko Takahashi again, and I was relieved when her lovely face popped up on my wrist.

"You're okay?" I asked into my fishbowl's headset.

Her orange-striped hair was mussed. "Exhausted," she said. "My God, it was terrifying."

"But you're okay now?"

She nodded. "How's Mr. Pickover? Have you found him yet?"

She'd had enough of an upset for one day; I'd tell her later that Rory was dead. "He's with Detective McCrae right now."

"Oh, good."

"Rory said he created a diversion so you could get away."

"He did indeed, the sweet old fellow. He started singing 'God Save the King' at the top of his lungs—or, well, at top volume anyway. Those two giant jerks were mortified, and I managed to run off." She paused. "If you see him, won't you thank him for me?"

"Of course."

"Thanks," she said. "Look, I'm still pretty shook up. I'm going to take something and go to bed."

"I don't blame you. But can you let Fernandez know you're okay? He's been worried, too."

"I'll call him now," she said, and she shook off from her end.

I continued walking slowly. My shadow, falling to my right, walked along with me. The silence was deafening.

I had genuinely liked Rory Pickover, strange little man though he had been. He'd had something I'd seen all too rarely on Mars: selfless devotion to a cause rather than to personal gain.

The dome was on my right. I was walking about thirty meters away from it; I had no particular desire to make eye contact with anyone within. Earth was hanging above the horizon, brilliant and blue. My phone could have told me which hemisphere was facing me right now, but I didn't ask. I liked to think it was the side with Wanda on it. And although I couldn't tell what phase it was in, I wanted it to be a crescent Earth, with the part Wanda was on in night-time, too. I wanted her to be looking up, looking across all those millions of kilometers, at the red planet in her sky. I wanted her to be thinking of me.

I continued slowly along. For the first time ever, in all the mears I'd lived here, I felt heavy.

When a man's client is killed, he's supposed to do something about it. It doesn't make any difference what you thought of him. He was your client and you're supposed to do something about it. And it happens I'm in the detective business. Well, when someone who's hired you gets killed, it's bad business to let the killer get away with it, bad all around, bad for every detective everywhere.

Of course, the killer *hadn't* gotten away with it. Uno was dead. Still, Pickover had come to me for protection, and I'd failed him.

I'd never get paid for the work I'd done on this case, but that didn't matter. And there was no one to bill for any further work. But Rory had wanted to track down the fossils Weingarten and O'Reilly—and no doubt Van Dyke—had sold on Earth, not for gain, not for profit, not to line his own pockets, but so they could be described for science, for posterity, for all time, for all humanity.

And there were surely other paleontologists who could do that work, if I could locate those fossils. Maybe there'd even be a previously unknown genus amongst the specimens. And maybe whoever described that new form in the scientific literature might be persuaded to name it *Pickoveria*.

I arrived at the western airlock and left the police-department surface suit there. My office was near here, and I walked over to it. I went up to the second floor and made my way down the corridor. Once inside my office, I used the sink at the wet bar to wash my face and hands, and then I collapsed into my chair.

I sat for a few moments, thinking, then called Juan Santos on my desktop monitor. Juan's wide forehead and receding chin appeared on the screen. "You put a lot of kilometers on my buggy," he said.

I tried to rally some of my usual spirit. "A shakedown. Good for it. Keep it running smoothly."

"You could have at least filled the gas tank."

"It doesn't *have* a gas tank."

"That's beside the point."

"Hey," I said, "at least I brought it back in perfect condition."

"You mean I just haven't found the damage yet. Not surprising, considering how much mud it was covered in."

"You wound me, Juan."

"Not yet. But if I can find a baseball bat . . ."

This could go on for hours—but I wasn't in the mood. "Look," I said, "I've become acquainted with a computer that's almost forty years old. Problem is, files on it are locked to someone long dead. Can you help me out?"

"Do you know the make or model?"

"No, but it was installed in a Mars lander."

"That long ago?"

He was going to find out soon enough, anyway: "It was installed in Weingarten and O'Reilly's third lander."

"And you've found the computer?"

"More than that."

"You've found the *ship?*"

"Uh-huh. The descent stage."

"Where is it?"

"I had it brought to the shipyard. I was hoping you could meet me there."

"All right."

"In about half an hour?"

"Um, yeah. Yeah, okay."

"Thanks," I said and broke the connection. I got a spare gun from the office safe and brought it and my usual piece with me as I headed over to the hovertram stop. I had a sinking feeling that we hadn't seen the last of the day's excitement, and if Juan was going to be my backup, I wanted him armed.

A tram pulled up, and I hopped on. I changed trams at the transfer point outside the Amsterdam, a classy gym that appealed to nicer people than those I liked to hang out with, and took another tram to the stop closest to the shipyard. I got off and hustled over to the yardmaster's shack, but Bertha wasn't there. Still, it was easy enough to spot the descent stage, sitting vertically on its stubby trio of legs, with the airlock on the side and the access hatch on top, and the whole thing streaked with mud. I headed over to it.

One of the landing legs was aligned with the airlock door, and had ladder rungs built into it. I climbed up and cycled through the airlock.

"Welcome back," Mudge said, as soon as I was in. "Can I be of assistance?"

"You defeated the overrides before so that both the inner and outer airlock doors could be kept open simultaneously," I said. "Do that again, please."

"Done."

I heard a faint calling of my first name. I headed back into the airlock chamber and saw Juan Santos wandering among the hulks. "Over here!" I shouted through the open door and waved.

He caught sight of me, jogged over with the typical Martian lope, and climbed the ladder. I made room for him, and he stepped inside, put his hands on his hips, and looked around the circular chamber. "Like a page out of history," he said.

"Or a cage with a mystery."

"You should leave the poetry to the lovely Diana," Juan said. His face took on a wistful look as he contemplated his favorite waitress, but after a moment, he narrowed his eyes. "The computer is still active?"

"I am," said Mudge. "Can I be of assistance?"

Juan stretched his arms out, fingers interlocked, until his knuckles cracked. "Okay," he said into the air. "Now listen carefully. Everything I say is a lie." He paused, then: "I am lying."

"Puh-leeze," said Mudge.

Juan looked at me and shrugged good-naturedly. "It was worth a try. Is there a terminal I can use?"

"In there," I said, pointing to one of the four rooms on the lower level. Juan entered, and I slipped off my phone and placed it on a piece of equipment, with the lens facing him, just to keep an eye on him. The whole point of coming back here was to get the secret Mudge must now know—the precise map of how to get between the Alpha and New Klondike, and, therefore, the reverse—and I'd be damned if I let Juan extract that info for his own uses. Of course, there was no reason to think he suspected Mudge, or I, knew where the Alpha was; the wreck of Weingarten and O'Reilly's second lander had been salvaged from Aeolis Mensae, and he probably assumed this one had been recovered from somewhere equally far from the mother lode.

I climbed up the interior ladder; I wanted to give O'Reilly's space suit a more thorough examination for signs of foul play. But it wasn't in the room we'd left it in. Well, the ship had come crawling out of the mud, fallen over, rolled around, flown halfway across Isidis Planitia, gone from vertical to horizontal to vertical again, and been hauled by a tractor. Being tossed around like a rag doll wasn't quite the fate one of the richest men in the solar system had anticipated, I'm sure.

"Mudge," I said into the air, "what happened to Denny O'Reilly's body?"

"A combination of eating too much and not exercising enough."

"I mean, where is it now?"

"In the room on your right."

I entered that wedge-shaped compartment, and—

And that was odd. Yes, O'Reilly's suited body was in here, sprawled on the floor, but the cupboard doors were hanging open. I was sure they'd been closed when I left the ship. I suppose they could have been knocked open during the flight, but—

I entered the next room. Its cupboards were open, too. As were the ones in the next chamber, and the next one. There could be no doubt: someone had searched the ship.

"Alex?" called Juan from below.

I hustled down the ladder, entered the chamber he was in, and stood behind him. "Yes?"

He swiveled in his chair to face me. "I've unlocked the computer."

"That fast?"

"Sure. Like you said, it's a forty-year-old machine. Most

security systems get hacked within *weeks* of being released. Ask it whatever you want."

I'd wait until I was alone to get the instructions to return to the Alpha. "Mudge," I said, "the ship has been searched since I left it. Did someone beside Dr. Pickover enter?"

"Who is Dr. Pickover?" asked the computer.

"Rory. The person who flew here with you earlier."

"Yes. After this ship was hauled through the airlock by a tractor, someone came aboard."

"Who?"

"I don't know."

"Biological or transfer?"

"I don't know what you mean." Damn. No, he wouldn't. Transferring had been something for only the insanely rich that long ago.

"Male or female?"

"Female."

"Age?"

"Perhaps twenty-eight or twenty-nine."

"Skin color?"

"Brown."

"Eye color?"

"Brown."

"Hair color?"

"Brown."

"Straight or curly?"

"Straight."

I thought about asking if she was hot, but I doubted Mudge would have an opinion. Of course, there were hundreds of women on Mars who fit that description, but I'd lay money he was describing Lakshmi Chatterjee.

"The woman was alone?" I asked

"Yes," said Mudge.

"Did you overhear her speak to anyone—on her phone, maybe?"

"Yes."

"Who was she talking to?"

"I don't know, and I could not make out the voice."

"What did she say?"

"She said, 'Hello.' There was a pause, then she said, 'Absolutely.' Another pause, then—"

"Did she say anything *important?*"

"I don't know what qualifies."

"List all the proper nouns she used in her phone conversation."

"In the order she first used them: Shopatsky House, Darren Cheung, Persis, Isidis Planitia, Dirk, Lomax, Mars—"

"Stop. What did she say about Lomax?"

"'If we can't take Lomax out, then we need an insurance policy.'"

"Continue the conversation from that point on."

"There was another pause, then: 'No, Dirk saw them together at The Bent Chisel; they're clearly an item, and she's coming to see me in a couple of hours; she's tailor-made for the part.' Another pause, then—"

"Stop." I looked at my wrist phone; it was 2:08 p.m., and Diana's appointment had been slated to start at 2:00. My heart started pounding. "Juan, we've got to go. Diana's in trouble."

THIRTY-SIX

Juan Santos looked up at me, piecing it together. "Diana?" he said. *"My* Diana?"

"Yes, yes," I replied. "She's at Shopatsky House right now." I headed through the descent stage's open airlock door and scrambled down the exterior ladder; Juan followed. As soon as we were both out on the shipyard grounds, I swore. "It'll take forever to get to Shopatsky House from here by tram."

"We won't take a tram," Juan said. "We'll take my Mars buggy."

"It'll take even longer to go get that."

"It would if the buggy was still outside. But it's not. I had it brought in for a thorough cleaning after I got it back from you—I've never seen mud on a buggy before." It was impossible to wash a car outside the dome; the atmosphere was too thin for sonic cleaning, the low air pressure caused water to boil away, and the ubiquitous dust dirtied things up again immediately anyway. "The sonic car wash is just inside the south airlock," continued Juan. It meant running in precisely the opposite direction from where we wanted to go, but he was right: using his buggy would get us to the writing retreat much faster than the tram would. I thought bout calling the NKPD, but I didn't want a repeat of the asco that had occurred at the *Kathryn Denning*.

We ran to where the buggy was parked; it was indeed ow clean, its white body glistening and not a speck of dirt bscuring its jade pinstripes. Juan was about to get into the river's seat, but I said, "Let me." He frowned, but went round to the other side. He knew I'd been to Shopatsky louse before.

I put the pedal to the metal. The lack of streamlining on Mars buggies was no impediment out on the surface, but in ere I could feel the drag on the cubic habitat cover. Still, ve were making great progress, and were soon on the heels f the very hovertram we'd have otherwise taken. I swerved round it. If the tram had had a driver, said driver might ave given me the finger, but the computer that ran the thing eemed to take my maneuver with equanimity.

As I cut in front of the tram, a pedestrian was crossing ae street ahead of us. It was hard to tell at the speed we vere going, but he looked biological—meaning I might kill im if I hit him, instead of just knocking him flying. I lapped the flat of my hand against the center of the steering vheel, and—

Holy crap!

The sound almost burst my eardrums. Apparently a horn esigned to be used in a thin atmosphere shouldn't be used 1 a thick one. The guy in front of me leapt a good meter nd a half straight up.

"Sorry!" Juan shouted at the guy. *"Sorry!"*

We continued on, the dome getting higher and higher bove our heads as we made it closer to the center.

"Stop! Police!"

It was a cop in a blue uniform. I ignored him; the worst hing he could do is give chase on foot.

But in the next block, another cop caught sight of us. Why s there never a police officer around when you want one, nd they're everywhere when you don't? This guy was more mbitious than the first cop. He stepped into the middle of he street and stood, legs spread, in our way. He had a gun, nd he held it in both outstretched hands aimed right at us.

I hit the horn again, spun the buggy in a one-eighty, then took a right-hand turn onto the Third Circle. The cop didn't fire—probably didn't want to deal with the paperwork that followed a weapons discharge—and if he shouted anything after us, my ears were still reverberating too much from the horn blast for me to make it out.

This close to the center, the curvature of the concentric roadways was obvious, and I had to bank the buggy so much that the left-hand wheels actually lifted from the ground. More people were crossing the street in front of us, and I careened right then left then right again to miss them—one by just centimeters.

This route took us by NewYou. I tried to look in the showroom window as we raced past, but there was too much glare. After hurtling along a quarter of the arcing road, we took off down Third Avenue, heading out toward the dome's edge again. Suddenly a dog—one of the handful on the planet, an honest-to-goodness Mars rover—was chasing us. We bipeds could manage a good clip in this gravity, and quadrupeds could move like the wind. This one—a lab, it looked like—was running at a speed a cheetah on Earth would have envied, and—

"Son of a bitch!" I yelled—rather aptly, I thought. The damn thing had leapt onto the buggy's short hood, making it hard to see what was up ahead.

"Slow down!" Juan shouted.

I stole a glance at him. He looked terrified—but whether over what I was doing to his buggy or what was about to happen to us, I couldn't say. The dog was yelping something fierce, but seemed to be enjoying the ride. I craned my neck trying to see around his bulk. We hit something small in the road—rubble or rubbish of some sort—and the car bounced and Juan let out a yelp of his own.

This wasn't the street I wanted to be on, so I made a hard left at the next intersection, but there was a hovertram dead ahead. I slammed on the brakes. The buggy started spinning. The dog decided this was a good time to get off, and he did so. I was pressed over into Juan's side in a way that pushed the boundaries of a good bromance. When the car

topped spinning, we were facing in precisely the wrong
direction. I did a quick U-turn, then headed on toward Shopatsky House, out at the rim. We were on the correct radial
artery now—and it looked like smooth sailing for most of
the rest of the way. Ah, the open road! All this rig needed
was stereo speakers blaring out classic 2040s rock 'n' roll.

I ran the buggy right up onto Shopatsky House's fern-
covered lawn and popped the canopy. Juan and I jumped
out, and we bounded over to the building, sailing three meters with each stride. I left the buggy running, just in case
we needed a fast getaway.

I thought about kicking the front door in, but that's actually hard to do, and my ankle couldn't be fixed as easily as
Pickover's had been. And, anyway, I didn't have to do it. If
Lakshmi had been as busy with underhanded stuff as things
seemed to indicate, she wouldn't have had time to replace
the back window I'd so carefully removed earlier.

I gave Juan the spare gun I'd brought for him, and we ran
around to the rear, me taking out my own gun as I did so.
Juan probably wasn't the best choice for backup—he was a
thin guy with typically underdeveloped Martian musculature—
but he was better than nothing. I motioned for him to stay out
of sight; I wanted Lakshmi to think I'd come alone.

There weren't any winds or precipitation under our dome;
the main reason for fixing the window would have been to
keep nasty folk out, but with the window hidden back here,
facing toward the dome's edge, no one probably even knew
that it was gone. I crouched low and made my way over. I'd
hoped to overhear something that would give away the situation within—either "actually, for your rhyming scheme,
you need a word with emphasis on the penultimate syllable"
or "and so, before you die, it's only fitting that you know
exactly how I plan to take over this entire planet." But instead I heard precisely nothing, and so I rose up enough to
peek into the hole where the window had been.

The room had been straightened a bit since my struggle
with Lakshmi—but only a bit. I clambered over the sill and
entered the house, holstering and then unholstering my gun
as I did so. I walked out of that room into the living room,

and there was Diana. She was seated at one end of the cushioned green couch and had a serene look on her round face. Her makeup was tasteful, her brown hair was up, her brown eyes were open, and, all in all, she looked perfectly fine—except for the bullet hole in the middle of her forehead.

THIRTY-SEVEN

My heart was jackhammering, and my eyes were stinging. I took a step toward Diana's body, but then Lakshmi's voice said, "Freeze."

I froze as much as I could, but I was quaking with fury.

"Drop your gun," Lakshmi said.

I had no proof that Lakshmi herself was holding a gun, but the hole in Diana was pretty good evidence that someone around here was packing. I let my Smith & Wesson go, and it fell gently to the floor.

"God damn it," I hissed. "You didn't have to kill her."

"She was dead when I got here," Lakshmi said.

"Oh, come on!"

"She was dead when I got here," Lakshmi repeated. "I'm not going down for this."

"How'd she get in, if you weren't here?" I demanded.

"Same way you did, I suppose. Through the rear window."

"I'm not buying that," I said. "And neither will the NKPD."

"Persis?" Lakshmi said into the air.

But there was no response from the Shopatsky House computer. I heard Lakshmi moving around behind me. I imagine she'd ducked her head into the room with the roll-top desk. "Someone took Persis," she said.

"How convenient," I replied. "No record of what went down. But you won't get away with it."

"I didn't shoot her," Lakshmi said again. "She was already dead when I arrived."

"Bull!" I said. "She had an appointment to see you!"

"And I was running late for it. She let herself in—through the hole where my window used to be, which she could only have known about because you must have told her. And someone else must have been in here, having gained access the same way—someone who'd come to rob me, I suppose—someone looking for the O'Reilly diary, perhaps. Whoever it was clearly was startled by Diana and let her have it."

"It's a neat story, sister. But it doesn't hold water."

"*Mister* Lomax," she said sharply. "I'm a professional writer. My plots most certainly *do* hold water."

"May I turn around?" I asked.

"All right."

I did so. She was dressed in red slacks and a tight-fitting silver top that showed a little cleavage. And she did indeed have a gun—a Morrell .28 revolver that seemed larger than it really was because her hands were dainty. Or maybe all guns look bigger when they're aimed at you.

"I should put a bullet through you right now," she said. "You've already broken into my place once before, and now you're here again."

"I'd advise against it," said Juan calmly from behind her. "In fact, if I may be so bold, I suggest that you drop the gun." I doubt Juan had heard any of our previous conversation from outside. His tone, although excited, didn't contain the rage that I knew would be in it if he were aware of what had happened to Diana.

Lakshmi had nerves of steel, I'll give her that. "I don't know who you are," she said, still facing me, "but you can't shoot me fast enough to prevent me from firing at Lomax first."

Juan was new to this sort of thing. Of course, he should have shot her without announcing his presence—what I get

for bringing an amateur along. And I doubted he had it in him
to fire at Lakshmi—under normal circumstances, that is.

"Nobody needs to die here," I said. You get good at calculating other people's lines of sight in my game. We were
all pretty much in a row: Juan in the room with the missing
window, Lakshmi in the open doorway to that room, me
facing them both, and behind me, not yet really visible to
Juan, Diana's dead body, seated on the couch.

I went on: "I mean, nobody *else* has to die here." I was
speaking to Lakshmi but looking beyond her at Juan. "Diana
was a good woman, Lakshmi. You had no right to kill her."

That did it. Juan's normally calm face twisted in rage.
Just as he pulled the trigger, I dove for the floor—there was
a good chance that the bullet would go right through Lakshmi, after all, and it could have gone on to take me out, as
well. The moment she was hit, Lakshmi squeezed her own
trigger, but I was already out of her line of fire, and the
projectile sailed past where I'd been and lodged in the green
couch next to Diana. Juan's bullet didn't make it all the way
through Lakshmi's body—which was a good thing; poor
Juan wasn't made of particularly stern stuff, and he'd have
been tortured if one of his slugs had gone into Diana even
though she was already dead.

Lakshmi, though, was still alive. Juan's aim was lousy;
he'd merely hit the writer in the shoulder. Still, she was
discombobulated enough that I was able to spring up from
the floor, retrieve my gun, and then wrest hers from her. I
then knocked her down and stood over her, my pistol aimed
right between her breasts.

Juan rushed over to Diana, in some desperate hope that
she was only injured and not dead. I heard him making small
sounds.

Lakshmi looked like she was falling into shock from the
gunshot wound. If I was going to get any additional information out of her, it would have to come soon. "Stick with me,
sweetheart."

But she didn't. Her eyes fluttered up into her skull.

I didn't want to plug Lakshmi if it wasn't necessary, not
because she didn't deserve it but because it would result in

too much of a hassle with the cops—not to mention the administrators of the writer-in-residence program. She could have been faking being in shock, but the ever-widening pool of blood behind her suggested she wasn't. I shoved Lakshmi's little gun into my waistband, then looked for something to tie her up with. I supposed I could use my belt, but I'd spent enough of this case running around naked; I didn't want to end up in a big chase with my jeans around my ankles.

Juan was still on bended knee in front of Diana, as if he couldn't believe she were dead. "Cover Lakshmi," I said to him. He seemed a bit shocky himself, but he nodded, rose, and lifted his weapon. I saw he wasn't really pointing it at Lakshmi, but about a half meter from her; amateurs like Juan always found it hard to pull the trigger again after they'd seen up close the sort of damage a bullet could do.

I stepped into the other room and found a white terry-cloth bathrobe hanging in the closet. I pulled the sash out of the loops, brought it to the living room, and used it to bind Lakshmi's wrists. The cloth soaked up blood from the surrounding puddle, the red stark against the white fabric.

Then, as it often does, fate took a hand. The doorbell sounded. A portion of the living-room wall changed to the view from the front-door camera. Standing on the stoop was none other than Sergeant Huxley of New Klondike's Finest.

THIRTY-EIGHT

I motioned for Juan to follow me, and we hustled into the back room of Shopatsky House. The doorbell sounded again as we climbed through the missing window. My first thought had been that the cops had pieced together Lakshmi's involvement in all this, but then it occurred to me that Huxley was perhaps simply following up on the buggy joyride; Juan's vehicle was still sitting on the fern-covered lawn.

I didn't have time for the cops right now. Yes, Lakshmi needed medical attention, but even Hux would have the good sense to walk around the house when no one answered, and he'd doubtless find the hole where the window had been and go in to investigate.

Juan and I made our way along the edge of the dome, the alloquartz cool to the touch. I knew the clear wall next to me was curved, but from here it seemed completely flat. Juan kept saying, in a shaky voice, "My poor Diana."

We had gone a hundred meters or so counterclockwise along the edge of the dome. Outside, on our right, we could see rocks casting shadows beneath the yellow-brown sky. In the distance, a couple of Mars buggies were going along at low speed.

To our left now was a warehouse, with cracked walls and a couple of boarded-up windows. Rent tended to be cheap out on the rim, despite it being the only place where you could get uninterrupted views of the vast Martian plain—people preferred to live near the center, if they could afford it, so that they could see something human instead of the vast unchanging monotony of the world that had crushed their dreams. "Let's go," I said, gesturing for Juan to pick up the pace. We headed down one wall of the warehouse and exited out onto the radial street.

A horn sounded—not as loud as the one on Juan's buggy, but still jarring; we'd come out onto the road in front of a tram. "Come on!" I said.

We ran the short distance to the tram stop, passing a few other people as we did so: a dour middle-aged male prospector dragging a wagon that had nothing in it but mining tools; a teenage girl who glared belligerently at me, but then thought better of starting anything; and a thirty-something woman who was dressed like a banker or a lawyer—encounters with either of which usually spelled trouble for me.

We got on the tram. There were five other biologicals onboard and one transfer. The biologicals were staring at little screens; the transfer was looking off into space—or, more precisely, I suspect, was watching a movie or something that only she could see. It was generally better not to sit on the filthy tram seats. Juan knew that, but he was so shaken he plunked himself down. We were soon passing the Windermere Medical Clinic.

I managed to get Juan, who was still mostly out of it, to change trams at the appropriate point, and when that tram reached the stop closest to the shipyard, I tapped him on the shoulder. He got up, and we headed over. But Juan was still shaky, and he looked nauseous. "Take a few minutes," I said. "There's a kybo over there." I pointed to the outhouse past Bertha's shack. "Join me when you're ready."

He nodded and headed over to the small structure. I hustled over to the descent stage and clambered back aboard the cylindrical vessel.

"Can I be of assistance?" Mudge asked as soon as I was inside.

"Yes," I said, to Mudge, "you can be of assistance."

The computer sounded awfully pleased. "What can I do for you?"

"Has anybody entered since I last left?"

"No."

"Good. First things first, then: you flew here from the Alpha Deposit."

"Yes."

"So you must know the way back."

"Of course."

"Display written instructions for returning there, please."

"That information is locked."

"I'm sure it *was* locked. And I'm sure it isn't anymore."

"Well, well, well," said Mudge. "I'm surprised."

There were four monitors in a row along the curving outer wall. The far left one lit up with black text on a pale green background. If Mudge hadn't been so old, there'd probably have been a way to transmit the instructions to my tablet computer, but I didn't have time to fool around figuring out how. Instead, I just pulled out the tab and took a picture of the text, checked to make sure the photo was legible, then slipped the device back in my pocket.

"Okay," I said. "Now, erase that information—permanently."

"Are you sure you want me to do that?"

"Yes. Wipe it. Use the strongest possible erasure method."

"Done."

I blew out air. "Good. Now to the matter I asked you about before. Denny O'Reilly was marooned here on Mars. Correct?"

"Yes," said Mudge.

"Simon Weingarten took off without him. Correct?"

"Yes."

"On purpose?"

"Yes, that's right."

"How long did O'Reilly survive after being marooned?"

"He turned me off to conserve power for the life-support systems after seven days. I don't know how much longer he lived after that."

"Why did Weingarten abandon O'Reilly?"

I was leaning back against one of the walls of the wedge-shaped room. I'd expected the answer to be the prosaic one: "He wanted all the money for himself." But what Mudge said surprised me. "The love affair between Simon and Denny had taken a turn for the worse."

"Love affair?" I repeated.

"Yes."

I was down on the lower floor; I stepped into the central shaft and did a quick three-sixty: there was indeed no second bedroom down here.

"What went wrong?" I asked.

"Denny had promised to leave his wife when they returned to Earth, but Simon had discovered that Denny was involved with another woman on Earth, and that he had a young son by her and intended to take up with her upon his return."

"And who was the other woman?" I asked.

"Katsuko Takahashi."

I nodded. Reiko's grandmother. "Why didn't O'Reilly blow the whistle on Weingarten?" I asked. "All he had to do was radio Earth and blab that he'd been left behind."

"Sending a radio signal to Earth is a tricky matter," said Mudge, "and, as onboard computer, I was in charge of such things. Before he left, Simon programmed me to not allow Denny to send any such messages."

"Are you aware that this ship's ascent stage was destroyed re-entering Earth's atmosphere?"

"No," said Mudge. "But that explains why I have been unable to contact Currie."

"Who?"

"My counterpart; the computer aboard the ascent stage."

"Simon Weingarten perished on re-entry, too," I said.

"Noted," said the computer dispassionately.

A thought occurred to me. "Mudge, did you arrange the transmitting of Denny O'Reilly's diary back to Earth?"

"Yes."

"When?"

"Three hours before Simon departed in the ascent stage."

"So, Denny didn't know he was going to be marooned at that point?"

"I assume not."

"Then why did he send the diary?"

"Space voyages are risky. There was always a chance the return trip might fail. And, of course, Denny believed that he and Simon were going to spend that voyage in hibernation. He was afraid he was about to go to sleep and never wake up."

"Who did you send the diary to?"

"Katsuko Takahashi. It was encrypted; she alone had the decryption key."

"Did you—" I stopped and turned around. Juan was coming through the airlock. A little color had returned to his face. He nodded at me but didn't say anything. I turned back to face Mudge's console. "Did O'Reilly send copies to anyone else?"

"No."

"Not to his wife?"

"No."

"Did you keep a copy of the diary?"

"No. Denny ordered it wiped after it was sent. He was cognizant that someday this descent stage might be found."

I looked at Juan. "Could you recover it?"

"How did you delete the file, Mudge?" Juan asked.

"Blastron protocol 2.2b," the computer replied.

Juan shook his head. "It's gone for good."

Which meant that I had the one and only copy in my pocket. It belonged, of course, to Reiko Takahashi, who was still my client. I'd return it to her—after making a copy for myself, of course.

My phone played "Luck Be a Lady" from *Guys and Dolls*. The little screen showed Dougal McCrae's face, the signal presumably making it in through the open airlock door. I was surprised it had taken this long for that shoe to drop. Huxley must have reported the shooting of Lakshmi

Chatterjee, not to mention the discovery of Diana's body, some time ago. I accepted the call. "Hello, Mac."

"Ah, Alex," said the freckled face. "Just thought I'd touch base. Make sure you're doing okay."

I tried not to look or sound puzzled. "Well as can be expected."

"Dr. Pickover's body is at the station now, along with those of the other three transfers." He paused. "I'm so sorry it turned out this way, Alex."

"Me, too." I peered at him, waiting for him to go on, but he didn't. "Um, Mac, did—has Sergeant Huxley called anything in?"

"Since when?"

"Last hour or so?"

"No. After he'd finished out by the *Kathryn Denning,* he went home. His shift was over."

"Ah," I said. "Um, he's not a wannabe writer or poet, is he?"

Mac laughed. "Huxley? God, no. I don't think he even *reads,* let alone writes."

"Okay," I said.

But Mac's eyes had narrowed. "What's up?"

"Nothing. Thanks for the call." I shook off.

The Windermere Medical Clinic was indeed near Shopatsky House; it seemed like a good bet, so I had my phone call it. Hot little pink-haired Gloria answered. "Hey, babe," I said, "just calling to check up on Lakshmi Chatterjee. That was a nasty gunshot wound to the shoulder. She still there?"

Pay dirt. "Oh, hi, sexy," she replied in that breathy voice of hers. "Didn't know she was a friend of yours. Might have sterilized the scalpel if we'd known that."

"How's she doing?"

"We got her all cleaned up and sent her on her way."

"She was a bit shocky earlier."

"Oh, we took care of that, of course. She's fine now."

"Thanks. Is the man who brought her in still there, by any chance?"

"No. No, he left even before she did. Said he had some business to take care of."

"Thanks, angel." I shook my wrist again, and the screen went dark.

"Alex?" said Juan, looking at me. Of course, he'd over-heard the conversations.

"It looks like Lakshmi has a friend on the police force," I said. "And I'd bet money that the business he had to take care of was . . ." I trailed off, not wanting to upset Juan.

"Yes?" he said. "What?"

"Well, it wouldn't be the first time the NKPD had lost a body," I said gently. "I bet Huxley went back to dispose of Diana's."

THIRTY-NINE

Doubtless Huxley would have the body moved before I could make it back to Shopatsky House. And I was so tired, if I did run into him there, even he might get the jump on me. Yes, I wanted revenge—but I wouldn't get it if I didn't get some sleep.

But sleep didn't come easily, not in a bed I'd shared with Diana. I took some melatonin, which usually puts me out, but it didn't work. Instead, I mostly lay on my back, staring up at the ceiling, which had a slowly rotating fan hanging from it.

My gut was churning, and my head was whirling—it was an odd sensation; I think perhaps it was what they call feeling guilty. If I hadn't sent Diana to see Lakshmi, she'd still be alive, still waiting tables, still writing poetry, still laughing and smiling and thinking about a better tomorrow.

Even if Huxley was on the take, even if Diana's body was now disposed of, I'd find some way to make Lakshmi Chatterjee pay—or, on the slim chance that she'd been telling the truth (I suppose there was a first time for everything), I'd make whoever *had* done it pay.

I got up in the morning, showered, and was eating synthesized bacon and eggs when my phone started playing its ringtone. I looked at my wrist; the ID said "NewYou." I accepted the call, and Horatio Fernandez's face appeared. "Alex, I'm worried. Reiko was supposed to be here almost half an hour ago, so I headed over to her place, just to see if she was okay. She's not there."

"She took something to help her sleep last night. Maybe she's just out like a light."

"No, no. She's *gone*. The door had been broken open, and the place was empty."

"Damn!" I'd assumed she was safe, what with Willem Van Dyke and all three meese dead. But—

Christ. Lakshmi Chatterjee. I'd warned that bitch not to go back to the Alpha—but maybe she thought if she had my client as a hostage, she'd be able to get away with it. One good day raiding the beds there would make her insanely rich, after all; I wouldn't be surprised if she was planning to head back on the *Kathryn Denning* with a steamer trunk full of fossil loot as soon as that ship was ready to go.

"Okay," I said. "I'll see if I can find her." I said goodbye, then called Mac, who had just gotten into the police station.

"Morning, Alex."

"Mac, Reiko Takahashi is missing again. Her place was broken into. I suspect she's been taken outside the dome. Can you check for me?" There were only four airlock stations; Lakshmi had to have taken her through one of them. I could have hoofed it to each one, but that would have taken all morning, and the security guards didn't have to take my bribes, but they *did* have to answer Mac's questions.

"I'll get Huxley to check," Mac said.

"No!" I said. Then, more calmly, "No. I'd take it as a personal favor, Mac, if you could make the inquiries yourself."

"What's going on, Alex?"

"Oh, you know me and Huxley."

Mac frowned dubiously.

"Please, Mac. I'll owe you one."

While I waited for Mac to call back, I got ready to go out the door. I was just doing up my shoelaces when my phone rang again.

"She went out of the north airlock," Mac said. "And she

wasn't alone. She was with that writer-in-residence woman, Ms. Chatterjee."

"Ah. Did they rent a Mars buggy, by any chance?"

"No," said Mac. I was relieved; that meant they couldn't have gone far, and—

"No," Mac said again. "They drove up to the airlock in one, and they took it outside."

Oh, crap. "What color was it?"

"The buggy? Jesus, Alex, I didn't ask. What difference does that make?"

"None. When did they leave?"

"They logged out of the dome at 5:57 a.m."

I looked at my wall clock; four hours ago. And if they were outside the dome, they weren't the NKPD's concern.

"Thanks, Mac. I'll be in touch." I shook the phone off. Shopatsky House was near the north airlock, and I'd bet solars to soy nuts that the Mars buggy Lakshmi had taken Reiko outside in was white with jade green pinstripes—the one I had conveniently left running on the front lawn of the writing retreat.

If it had only been Lakshmi heading to the Alpha, I'd have been half tempted to just let her drive right on out there. The deposit was still guarded by a row of land mines, and I'd shed no tears if she was blown sky-high. But Reiko was my client, and I couldn't take having another one of those die on my watch.

I made another phone call. Juan Santos looked like he'd gotten even less sleep than I had. "Hey," I said, "you're a hacker. You must have a way to shut off your Mars buggy by remote control, no?"

He yawned, then, "Sorry. Yeah. I was thinking about that. You left it running at Shopatsky House, right? I figured I should go collect it this morning. The excimer battery should last for weeks, but—"

"Lakshmi has taken it outside the dome."

"Hell, Alex. I can't afford to lose that vehicle."

"I know, I know. I'll get it back for you. What's the re-mote shutoff code?"

He told me, and my phone recorded it. "But if you're

using your phone to send it, you'll have to be within a hundred meters or so for it to be picked up," he added.

"Right, okay. And the code to turn it back on?"

He told me that, too.

"Thanks."

"Alex, I need—"

But I shook the phone off, grabbed my gun, and ran out my apartment door.

．．．．．．．．．．．

It would eat up half a day getting to the Alpha by Mars buggy; that would never do. And although O'Reilly and Weingarten's descent stage could fly there quickly, assuming it had enough fuel left, I'd have to get the damn thing hauled onto the planitia first, and that would take forever. And so I went to see the one person I knew who had every luxury item, including an airplane: Ernie Gargalian of Ye Olde Fossil Shoppe.

"Mr. Double-X!" Gargantuan exclaimed as I came into the empty store.

"Hey, Ernie."

"I hear you've had some adventures of late, my boy."

"Oh?"

"They say you've recovered Simon and Denny's third lander."

"Who would 'they' be?"

"I keep my ear to the ground, my boy."

I suspected if Ernie ever actually adopted that posture, he wouldn't be able to get back up. "Well, yeah," I said. "There might be a market for it."

"For the ship?"

"There's a collector for everything," he said. "Would you like me to see what I can arrange?"

"I guess, sure. So, listen, can I borrow your airplane?"

Ernie had a hearty laugh, I'll give him that. "By Gad, my dear boy! You do have gumption."

"You can't spell gumption without P-I." Actually, maybe you could—but you'd have to do it phonetically.

"And just where might you take my plane, Alex?"

"To the Alpha Deposit."

Ernie's demeanor changed instantly. "You know where it is?"

"Yes."

"Very well. When do we leave?"

I'd expected this to be the price I'd have to pay. Rory wouldn't have liked it—but Rory was dead. Reiko, on the other hand, was probably still alive, but quite likely wouldn't be for much longer. "Right now," I said.

Just then a customer tried to enter. "No, no," said Ernie, hurrying to the door. "We're closed."

The customer—a woman in her forties—pointed at the laser-etched sign. "But the sign says . . ."

"A typo!" declared Ernie. "I'll get it fixed."

Crossing the room had been enough to set Ernie to huffing and puffing; there was no way he could walk all the way out to the edge of the dome; his plane, I knew, was parked outside the north airlock, coincidentally the same one Lakshmi and Reiko had exited through. But a man of Gargalian's stature—literal and figurative—did not trifle with public transit. He went into his back room and emerged floating on a hoverchair—and I saw that he'd also fetched a rifle.

It was a tight fit to get the hoverchair out through the shop's doorway, but he did it. I followed, and he spoke a command that locked up his store.

The chair zipped along so quickly that I was huffing and puffing myself by the time we got to the north exit. Ernie had a surface suit stored there that looked like the bag Phobos had come in. It was a struggle for him to get into it—it was a struggle for him to do pretty much anything—but he eventually managed it.

I had to rent a suit yet again. This time, it was the shade of green people used to associate with money. Ernie's was deep purple; he resembled an enormous eggplant in it.

Ernie's plane was one of three currently parked here. It was dark gray and had a gigantic wingspan—close to forty meters, I'd say. The front part of the cockpit looked like it had originally been designed to hold two side-by-side seats but had been modified for a single double-wide chair. I was relegated to the back; the habitat was teardrop-shaped, tapering toward the rear, so there'd only ever been one chair there. Once we were inside, Ernie set about powering up the plane.

Not only did you need big wings to fly on Mars, you needed a long runway to take off. The one here was a solid kilometer of Isidis Planitia that had been cleared of rocks. We made it almost to the end before I felt us rising.

I'd flown in small planes on Earth but never before on Mars, and I'd been in hibernation when I'd come here, so this was my first aerial view of New Klondike and environs. I craned my neck to see the city as we sped away from it: a large, shallow dome, glistening in the sun—looking for all the world like God had dropped a contact lens. Then there was nothing but Martian landscape stretching to the horizon below and the yellow-brown sky above. I pulled my tab out of my suit's equipment pouch and dictated the directions I'd gotten from Mudge to the back of Ernie's great loaf of a head.

The plane moved quickly but silently. I kept looking down, hoping to spot the white Mars buggy. Of course, it was always possible that Lakshmi had headed somewhere else, in which case I'd kick myself for letting Ernie know where the Alpha was, and—

—and there it was, up ahead, tooling along. We were arriving just in the nick of time; they were now just a few kilometers shy of the Alpha Deposit.

Airplanes on Mars need clear open stretches to touch down, just as they did to take off, and although Isidis Planitia was a plain, it wasn't a plain plain, and landing our plane was going to be a pain. Ernie was circling, looking for a place to set down. Not much sound carried in the thin Martian air, but our giant wingspan would make us impossible to miss if Lakshmi or Reiko happened to look up.

Ernie swore in Armenian, and his massive head swung left and right as he continued to search. Finally, he muttered, "Here goes nothing!" and we started to descend.

The patch of ground he'd picked didn't have any boulders,

at least, but there were still plenty of rocks up to and including basketball size. The plane had the same sort of adaptive wheels that buggies had, although larger in diameter. Still, when we hit, we bounced several times as the wheels encountered rocks they couldn't negotiate. My breakfast gave an encore performance at the back of my throat.

We skidded a considerable distance, with Gargantuan yelling *"Yeehaw!"* When we at last came to a stop, Ernie and I dogged down our helmets, and he made the canopy swing open. He needed both hands to climb down, and so he dropped his rifle overboard, then used the rungs built into the side of the plane to lower his bulk to the surface. Once he was down, he bent over—with great difficulty—and picked his rifle back up.

I followed him down, then looked out at the wide expanse of Martian terrain in front of me. Ennio Morricone's "The Ecstasy of Gold" was running through my head. It was, after all, greed that had driven the Great Martian Fossil Rush, the Great Klondike Gold Rush, and the Great California Gold Rush, and Morricone's haunting theme captured that madness well.

Juan's Mars buggy was on the horizon, coming toward us; the plane had landed in a kilometer-wide strip between it and the eastern edge of the Alpha—the edge that was salted with land mines.

I walked out past the wing tip and told my phone to transmit the OFF code Juan had given me.

The white buggy continued to barrel in. At this distance, I couldn't see if it had green pinstriping; I suppose it was always possible that this was a different Mars buggy.

I told the phone to transmit again . . . and again . . . and again.

The damn thing was still closing, and Lakshmi must have had the accelerator right down to the floor. She was veering to the south a bit, clearly intending to go around our airplane. I had the phone send the OFF sequence once more, wondering if somehow Juan had made a mistake when he gave it to me; he had looked like he'd just woken up, after all, and—

—and, at last, the buggy was slowing. It skittered to a stop about seventy meters ahead of me. I could see movement within the canopy; of course, when the power went off, the life-support shut off, too. I imagine Lakshmi and Reiko were hustling to get their surface-suit helmets on. I had briefed Ernie on the way here, so he understood what was going down. He had his rifle butt against his shoulder and the barrel aimed at the buggy.

I'd put my holster on the outside of my suit. I pulled out my gun and ran toward the stalled vehicle—and the sight of me charging in with weapon drawn had the effect I wanted. Lakshmi popped the canopy on Juan's car—it opened mechanically rather than electrically, for safety reasons—and she and Reiko scrambled out.

My legs were longer than theirs, and I soon overtook them. We stood facing each other with just five meters of rusty, dusty plain between us. Reiko was in a suit of a darker green than my own and Lakshmi again had on a red one. All of us still had our fishbowls polarized, meaning the women might not have yet identified me; I, of course, could tell which of them was which by their heights.

Behind me, as a glance over my shoulder confirmed, Gargantuan Gargalian was waddling in, and he was now raising his rifle. It looked like Lakshmi Chatterjee's stint as Shopatsky House writer-in-residence was about to end with a bang.

FORTY

I looked down at my wrist controls to see what frequency
my radio was using, then held up my left hand with three
fingers raised, then changed it to four fingers.

Lakshmi dipped her opaque helmet slightly in a nod.
Both she and Reiko touched their own wrist controls, presumably punching in frequency thirty-four. But neither of
them said anything, instead waiting for me to speak. And
so I did: "All right. The jig is up. Let her go."

I glanced over my shoulder again, just to get a sense of
where Ernie now was, and—

Oh. He'd never met either of them, and their helmets were
polarized. He'd had to choose which woman to take a bead
on, and he'd mistakenly chosen Reiko. I opened my mouth
to say something, but stopped when a pair of hands reached
for the butterscotch sky. One of the raised hands, I saw now,
was holding a tiny pistol. But the person raising her hands
in surrender wasn't Lakshmi Chatterjee—it was Reiko
Takahashi.

Lakshmi reacted instantly, her right arm lashing out to
seize the gun, which she promptly pressed into Reiko's side.
In the second it took for that to happen, it hit me: it hadn't
been Lakshmi who had kidnapped Reiko; it had been Reiko

who had kidnapped Lakshmi, so that she could force Lakshmi to show her where the Alpha was. Reiko must have broken her own door lock before going to get Lakshmi—preparing an alibi for when she returned home alone; no one would blame her if she'd had to off her captor to get away.

"Back off, Lomax," Lakshmi said, "or the little bitch gets it." She must have recognized my voice, since all four of us still had polarized fishbowls—which was half the reason I hadn't figured out the dynamic between Lakshmi and Reiko; I hadn't been able to see their expressions.

I kept my gun aimed at Lakshmi. "You won't shoot me. I'm the only one who knows the code to turn your buggy back on."

"If I shoot you," Lakshmi said, "a seat opens up on that airplane—so I don't need the code."

I chinned the control that depolarized my helmet; the sun was high enough now that it wouldn't be in my eyes facing this way. Lakshmi must have decided it was indeed better that we see each other, because her fishbowl grew transparent, too.

Ernie was on the same radio frequency as me, of course. He spoke for the first time. "My dear lady," he said, "we're all after the same thing. But the Alpha Deposit has wealth galore, enough to satiate the desires of each of us. There's no call for anything disagreeable to happen here."

"Who are you?" Lakshmi said.

"Ernest Gargalian," he replied, with a portly, courtly bow. "Proprietor of Ye Olde Fossil Shoppe." He depolarized his own helmet, revealing his round face and slicked-back hair.

Judging by her expression, Lakshmi recognized neither his name nor that of his establishment, which was too bad because no one who did know Ernie would ever threaten him. His operatives would avenge his death—and some of them were transfers. "Just so you know," I said to Lakshmi, "if this godforsaken planet has a Mister Big, he's it."

Reiko must have chinned her polarization control, too, because her helmet also grew clear. Her voice was filled with wonder. "You're Ernie Gargalian?"

"At your service."

"I—I didn't know you were on Mars. I didn't know you were even still alive."

Ernie scowled. "Yes?"

"You . . . you knew my grandfather," said Reiko.

"Ah, yes, indeed," replied Ernie. "Alex here told me that you're Denny's granddaughter. I was just a pup when I first met him and Simon at the Tucson Gem and Mineral Show. I was one of the first dealers to do business with them."

"What . . . what was he like?"

"An astute businessperson. As it appears, if I may be so bold, you yourself are. Why did you kidnap the lovely lady here?"

"She double-crossed me," Reiko replied. "She told me she was going to write a book about my grandfather. I gave her access to my grandfather's diary. I'd hoped she'd find a clue in there that would help us locate the Alpha Deposit, but when she did—"

"She didn't figure out where the Alpha was from the diary," I said. "Did you, Lakshmi? You had that punk, that kid—Dirk—you had him plant a tracking chip on me. And then you followed me here."

Lakshmi nodded. "That's right. The diary was useless. I found the Alpha without it." She looked at Reiko. "So why should I cut you in?"

"Because it's *mine,*" Reiko said. "My grandfather found it, so it belongs to me."

Reiko still had her hands in the air. Lakshmi still had a gun pressed into her side. Ernie still had his rifle aimed at the two women. Ennio Morricone was still playing in my head.

There was movement in the distance. It might have been a dust devil; they were common on Mars. I wasn't sure, though, and I knew better than to give away that I'd noticed anything. I kept my eyeline toward Lakshmi. Whatever I'd seen was still far away, so I sought to stall: "All right, then; okay. We have a little misunderstanding here, that's all. But there's no reason we can't all just walk away from this."

Lakshmi shook her head, brown hair brushing first one then the other side of her fishbowl. "Reiko told me on the way here that you've recovered her grandfather's body, isn't that right?"

I nodded.

"That's the way that *had* to go down," Lakshmi continued. "Even back then, when only three people knew where the Alpha was. First Denny O'Reilly and Simon Weingarten decided to cut Willem Van Dyke out of the picture. Then Weingarten decided to get rid of O'Reilly. It's the *only* way something like this can go down—with one person taking everything. That's human nature."

"My dear woman," said Ernie, "there are riches enough over yonder"—I don't think I'd ever heard anyone say "yonder" before in real life, but something about being out here, at the edge of the frontier, seemed to lend itself to using that word—"to satisfy even my appetite, and yours as well. We can all profit here. You'll need a sales agent, after all."

I didn't often wish I was a transfer, but I did just then, if only for the telescopic eyes. The thing—whatever it was—was still indistinct, but I thought for sure that it was getting closer. Still, maybe it *was* just a dust devil or—

—or maybe it was something moving so quickly that it was kicking up a plume of dust behind it.

Ernie's conciliatory comments had been directed toward Lakshmi—after all, she was the lady holding a gun—but it was Reiko who answered. Not many women could still look pretty while sneering, but Denny's granddaughter pulled it off. "She double-crossed me," Reiko said. "No way she walks out of this with anything."

The Martian landscape was infuriatingly fractal: that crater there might be a meter across or a hundred; that rock might be man-sized or mountainous. It really was hard to gauge the size of the thing that was approaching—or how far away it still was. But it was getting nearer, I was sure of that, and it now filled enough of my vision that I could assign it a color: turquoise, a thoroughly un-Martian hue.

"Double-crosses happen all the time on Mars," I said to Reiko. "Ernie here calls me Mr. Double-X. Shrug it off."

"Really?" said Lakshmi. "I thought he called you that because you don't have any balls."

By now the turquoise object was even closer. It was still beyond my ability to resolve in detail—maybe I needed to see an optometrist, or maybe no one with biological eyes could have made it out—but it had moving parts, of that much I was certain.

I still wanted Lakshmi to go down for killing Diana, but with Huxley having presumably removed the body, I didn't see how to make that stick, at least not yet. I'd figure a way, though, if—*when*—I made it back to New Klondike. And getting there meant getting the writer-in-residence to lower her gun. "Lakshmi," I said, "what happens on the planitia stays on the planitia. Let Reiko go, then head back to Shopatsky House and work on your book—whatever it really is about."

The turquoise object was getting ever closer. It was . . . yes, yes! It was a person. But a biological couldn't run that fast; it had to be a transfer. I stole a glance at Ernie. His expression gave no hint that he'd seen anything, and, indeed, he seemed intent solely on the women in front of him.

The runner shifted his course slightly; he was now mostly eclipsed by Lakshmi and Reiko. I could have changed my own position or craned my neck, but Lakshmi would doubtless notice that; I now regretted having depolarized my helmet.

Of course, there was no reason to assume that whoever was barreling in was coming to rescue Ernie and me. Just as likely, he was coming to help Lakshmi, who perhaps had somehow managed to get a signal out that she'd been kidnapped, or to help Reiko—or maybe it was a free agent and would do us all in and seize the riches for himself. If any of us had been transfers, that might have been difficult without a broadband disruptor, but if the runner had a pump-action shotgun or a machine gun—not that I'd ever seen one of those on Mars—he could easily take all four of us out.

Ernie decided to weigh in. "Young lady, Mr. Lomax is right. I have connections that could make any difficulties disappear, and—"

And Ernie must have felt the ground shaking slightly beneath his feet; a guy like me doesn't have much that jiggles, but he was a walking distant-early-warning system, and Lakshmi had clearly seen something in his face. She suddenly turned around, swinging Reiko around with her. My view of the incoming transfer was restored—and my jaw dropped in astonishment.

Rushing toward us was a stunningly beautiful woman— a gorgeous transfer with a supermodel's face and long blonde hair bouncing behind her. I didn't recognize her, but she was wearing a turquoise tracksuit that hugged her curves. Her large breasts were bouncing delightfully as she ran, but there was no sign that her chest was heaving. She wasn't breathing hard; she wasn't breathing at all.

And perhaps in a few seconds, none of the rest of us would be, either.

FORTY-ONE

It was hard to tell while looking at Lakshmi from behind, but I think she'd pulled her out of Reiko's side and was now aiming it at the gorgeous apparition, who was sailing ten meters closer with each stride. I was all set to jump Lakshmi from the rear when the blonde transfer leapt, flying through the almost nonexistent air. She slammed into the writer, knocking her on her back. Reiko danced out of the way just in time to avoid being bowled over, too.

Lakshmi swore; it doubtless hurt to be knocked over, especially when wearing a backpack with oxygen tanks. She was flat on her back but still had her little gun. I kicked the hand that held it. The weapon went up, up, and up some more. Lakshmi was trying her best to throw the blonde bombshell off her, but the transfer had grabbed her wrists.

Blondie looked at Ernie even as she was struggling with Lakshmi, and she made some beckoning motions with her lovely head. Gargalian seemed baffled for a second, but then got it. It took some doing, but Blondie managed to get up, and Ernie managed to get down without Lakshmi escaping. He took the simple expedient of sitting on her chest. Lakshmi beat at him with gloved fists, but her suit didn't allow her arms to move fast enough for the blows to really hurt, I imagined.

Blondie smiled at me, but then her perfect mouth dropped open in surprise, showing the porcelain pearly whites within. It took me a second to realize she was now looking past me. I turned, and—

Damn. I really did need to do something about my eyes. Once again, there was something off in the distance. I squinted, and—yes: it was someone else running this way, this time coming in from the north.

Blondie's baby blues were wide. She probably had that bionic-vision thing going on; I wondered if there was a reticle over her retina. Reading a transfer's expression is hard, but I don't think she recognized whoever it was.

I didn't know if this interloper was friend or foe, but it pays to prepare for the worst. Since Blondie, at least, seemed to be an ally, I grabbed her hand—my glove in her naked plastiflesh—and led her perpendicular to the newcomer's travel, running west toward the Alpha, meaning he'd have to choose whether to come toward me and Blondie, or toward Lakshmi and Ernie. It was soon apparent that the newcomer had altered his trajectory to come after the two of us.

Blondie fell in next to me, matching my stride, and we continued on for a few hundred meters. Although the dust covering Isidis Planitia shifts over time, I could still make out two divots in the surface, and I maneuvered us between them. Then I scanned around for the automobile-shaped rock I'd dubbed Plymouth and the more jagged one I'd nicknamed Hudson. And so I figured stopping *here* was just right, with Plymouth at about ten o'clock and Hudson standing guard at 3:30.

The intruder was now just a hundred meters away. He was either wearing a beige surface suit, or was a transfer in beige clothes, or—less likely—a naked transfer with beige skin.

I was suddenly distracted by Ernie shouting into his helmet microphone. "Alex! Alex!"

I turned. Somehow, Lakshmi had managed to push Ernie

off, or—no, no, that wasn't it. Reiko had a gun pointed at
Ernie. Damn it! While I'd been busy maneuvering Blondie
and me to just the right spot, and Ernie had been busy trying
to flatten out all the appealing bumps on Lakshmi, Reiko
must have gone off to retrieve the piece I'd sent flying earlier.
Back on Earth, when people get surges of adrenaline, they
sometimes manage to lift cars off trapped pedestrians; the
sight of Reiko again packing heat must have been enough
to give Lakshmi the jolt she needed to heave Ernie off herself, and she now had hold of his rifle.

Blondie flexed her fingers, disengaging her hand from
mine, and in a blur of motion she scooped up a rock about
the size of a softball, hauled back, and let loose a pitch
worthy of the major leagues. The rock tore through the thin
air and made it a good fraction of the distance, but it fell
short, and I couldn't tell which of the three people she'd
been aiming at. Ernie was on his feet, and the two women
were facing off against each other, perhaps a dozen meters
between them, Reiko aiming her pistol at Lakshmi, and
Lakshmi pointing Ernie's rifle at Reiko.

If this had been the Old West, I would have heard the shot
ring out, but the air was too thin for that, and instead all I
heard was a feminine *"Oomph!"* over the radio as one of
the women was hit, and I waited breathlessly to see which
of them would crumple to the ground.

And, after about three seconds, one of them did, with
graceful Martian indolence: the shorter of the two, the lady
in dark green, the heiress who seemed to have inherited
nothing but her grandfather's obsession with wealth.

Blondie suddenly sprang into action, running toward
them. She'd yet to say a word, and I had no reason to think
she was listening to the same frequency I was using, but I
shouted anyway: "No! Stop! Go back the way we came!"

And either she *was* tuned into that channel, or else she
had bionic ears in addition to bionic eyes, because she skidded to a halt, changed direction, and followed the precise
path out that we'd taken in.

Meanwhile, the beige intruder was still coming straight

or me. If I moved, he'd alter his course—and so I stood my round.

Blondie was damn near flying, yellow hair a cloud around er head as she hurried toward Reiko and Lakshmi. Lakhmi aimed the rifle at Blondie, and I guess Blondie and I vere thinking the same thing—that perhaps a gun that big vould do real damage to a transfer; the blonde goddess tarted bobbing and weaving as she continued to race in. .akshmi's first shot was a clean miss. The second got 3londie somewhere in the torso—hard to tell exactly where vhen watching from the rear—but it didn't slow her down.

I turned back to the intruder. It was a male transfer in haki slacks and a khaki long-sleeved shirt, and he was still oming straight at me. As his shoulders worked up and lown, I glimpsed that he had on a backpack—surely not air anks, but rather a rucksack with equipment. Ah, and at last e was close enough that I could make out his face, and—

God, no!

I shouted, even though he almost certainly couldn't hear ne through my helmet in this thin atmosphere. *"Rory, top!"*

I hadn't seen the bootleg Pickover since shortly after I'd escued him from the torture room aboard the *Skookum Jim,* ut I had no doubt that this was him; the face was the one he bootleg had adopted to take on the identity of Joshua Vilkins. He was now just thirty meters from the line of land nines—and closing.

Even in a surface suit, I should be able to do at least as ;ood a long jump as I could have back on Earth. I started unning straight for him—meaning I was also running traight for the buried mines. When I got close to the line, kicked off with all my strength and went sailing horizonally toward him, arms outstretched. He had the most asonished expression I'd ever seen on a transfer's face as I ;ailed closer, and—

—and, *damn!*, my Smith & Wesson flew out of my hol-ter and dropped behind me. It must have hit one of the nines, because I was suddenly propelled forward by more than just the strength of my initial kick. The explosion was deafening even in the thin air. Something tore into my right leg as I collided with the bootleg Pickover and knocked him on his stainless-steel butt.

It took me a second to recover from the impact, but then I pushed myself to my feet and reached down to give Pickover a hand. As I pulled him up, I felt a stabbing in my calf. Land-mine shrapnel had sliced through my suit and the jeans beneath. A piece of skin about as long and wide as a banana was exposed to the subzero air, and blood was flowing down the suit's leg, although it would soon either freeze or boil off. I opened the suit-repair kit on my belt, pulled out the largest adhesive patch, and positioned it over the cut. Pickover and I were so close now that I could hear him speak. "My God!" he exclaimed. "Someone's booby-trapped the Alpha!"

I nodded as much to myself as to him; the legit Pickover had discovered that only after this bootleg had been spun off. I changed my radio's channel. "Channel twenty-two," I shouted. The transfer nodded, but didn't do anything visibly to indicate he'd selected that radio frequency. I went on at a normal volume. "What are you doing here?"

The bootleg's voice—which didn't sound anything like that of the real Rory—came through my helmet speakers. "I've been working a bed twenty kilometers north of here," he said. "I saw an airplane fly by, and it looked like the damn thing was coming down near the Alpha. I thought I should investigate—and then I caught sight of you."

"Good to see you, Rory. Some of those people over there want to steal fossils from here. Are you up for a fight?"

His eyes narrowed. "Hells yes."

Lakshmi, Reiko, Blondie, and Ernie were fifty meters east of us. Blondie was now kneeling next to the fallen Reiko. "The woman on the ground is the granddaughter of Denny O'Reilly."

"Oh, really?" he said, just as the other Pickover had when I'd first told him.

I wasn't in the mood for the "No, O'Reilly" schtick, although it *is* rare that you get to use a joke twice on more or ess the same person. "Yes," I said. "The woman in red is ᴌakshmi Chatterjee. She's a writer, and has tried to kill me more than once. As for the transfer babe in turquoise, I have no idea who she is, but she seems to be on our side, or at ᴇast not actively against us. And the big guy is—"

"Ernie Gargalian." Sneering is more effective with a British accent, but even without it, Rory's contempt was plain.

"Yes," I said, looking out at the tableau. I suppose it *was* debatable which of us was the Good and which the Bad, but here was no way Reiko, Lakshmi, or Blondie could qualify as the Ugly—which left Ernie, Rory, and me to vie for that title. "But that's Ernie's airplane. He brought me here. The real threat to the Alpha, at least right now, is Lakshmi."

"I—I don't want to kill to protect the secret," Pickover said.

"I don't see another way," I replied. "Lakshmi is certainly willing to kill us." As soon as I said it, I realized that Ms. Chatterjee really wasn't much of a threat to Rory. Indeed, he could just run off—he could move faster than Lakshmi; for all I knew, he could even outrun her in the buggy, if she ever got it going again. But I'd saved him from that torture room, and I'd saved him again when I hid his identity from the legitimate Pickover, who, had he known of this one's continued existence, would have demanded he be terminated. I doubted he was going to take off on me. And, after a moment, he confirmed that. "All right. What now?"

"See those two pits, there? That's where your, ah, brother and I removed two of the land mines. You can safely move in and out if you go between those pits." The bootleg nodded, and I went on. "So, let's go. Our first order of business: disarm Lakshmi."

"Okay," said Pickover. "But how?"

"Improvise," I replied as I started running toward the others: sailing forward, kicking off, sailing forward again. Pickover must have hesitated for a moment, but he soon fell in beside me.

It didn't take long for Lakshmi to react. She assumed a marksman's spread-legged stance and aimed her gun at me, which was precisely what I was hoping for, because it meant she could no longer cover Ernie. As soon as she swung the gun away from the big man, Ernie did the best leap he could manage. He might have weighed only a third as much here as he would have on Earth—a fact that let him clear the ground by half a meter and come forward a meter and a half—but he *massed* exactly the same, and he slammed into Lakshmi from behind with a lot of inertia. While Pickover and I continued to close the distance, Lakshmi pitched forward, legs still splayed. Ernie landed on her suit's backpack, and although my view was bouncing as I ran, it looked like he was trying to disengage her air tanks.

Pickover suddenly surged in front of me, his artificial legs pistoning in a way mine never could. Despite doubtless having the wind knocked out of her, Lakshmi was struggling to lift her head and get the gun up again, and she squeezed off a shot at Pickover. I thought the paleontologist was hit—he did a headfirst roll into the ground—but then I realized it was a deliberate evasion tactic, and he somersaulted perfectly, Lakshmi's bullet flying above him while he rolled. He sprang back into a running posture and continued in.

I was now close enough to make out more detail. Blondie was still kneeling, and—no, no. That wasn't it. She wasn't kneeling; she was sitting cross-legged on the sand, and Reiko Takahashi's helmeted head was cradled in her lap.

Ernie was still doing things on Lakshmi's back, and—yes!—he managed to disengage her tanks and toss them aside. Doubtless there was still some air in her helmet, but the writer couldn't have more than a couple of minutes left to live.

Suddenly my own helmet exploded around me. Lakshmi had shifted her aim from Pickover to me and had squeezed off another shot. I couldn't see for a moment—the atmosphere that had been in my fishbowl turned into a white cloud of condensation—but as I continued running forward, I left the cloud behind. The tanks on my back were still working, though, and oxygen was being pumped though the tube from them. I stopped running for a moment, hoping that Lakshmi had shot her last, and yanked on the tube, pulling it farther up; they were designed to have some play for just such emergencies.

I felt the skin on my face freezing, my eyes hurt from the cold and the exposure to near vacuum, and my sinuses were seizing up. But there was warm air coming through the tube, which I'd now stuck in my mouth and was clamping onto with my teeth. I continued to run because I didn't know what else to do. I think I was bleeding from my scalp; shards from the fishbowl must have sliced into it.

I needed another helmet and fast. Ernie was clearly conscious of my plight: he was trying to undog Lakshmi's fishbowl. I was having trouble seeing now—I think my eyeballs were freezing in place, and—

And everything went dark and I went plowing face first into the ground. I managed to lift my chin and spit out the oxygen tube just in time to keep it from bashing my front teeth out. And then I felt the weight of someone on my back, and strong hands grabbed the sides of my neck and squeezed, strangling the life out of me.

FORTY-TWO

S till face down in the dirt, I brought my own hands up and tried to yank away the constricting ones, which were—

—which were naked, gloveless, exposed to the elements, and . . .

. . . and my vision *hadn't* failed. Rather, someone had thrown some sort of bag over my head, then tackled me, driving me to the ground, and now these strong artificial hands were sealing the bag as tightly as possible around my neck.

I felt the bag inflating, filling out like a balloon, as air continued to flow through the tube from my backpack tanks. Pickover must have taken a fabric specimen bag out of his rucksack and thrown it over my head to create a makeshift helmet; it was him on my back now. "Alex!" he shouted, so that I could hear him without the radio, the headset for which had fallen away with the shards of my fishbowl. "For Christ's sake, stop fighting me!"

I hadn't been aware that I still was—but I guess panic had taken over. I took a deep breath in the darkness and was delighted that I could actually *smell* the musty bag. And although I couldn't see anything, I could feel my eyeballs swiveling in their sockets again.

Pickover released his too-tight grip on my neck. The bag loosened, and I felt a blast of cold air, which was actually refreshing by this point. I brought my hands back to my neck, one to each side, and took over holding the bag in place.

"I'll be back!" Pickover shouted, or at least I think that's what he said; it was quite faint and muffled.

My cheeks felt like they were burning; I suspected they were getting frostbitten. And the sack did seem to be sticking to the top of my head, lending credence to my theory that I was bleeding there. It didn't seem likely that any of the damage was life-threatening, but I wasn't happy being out of the action. I lifted my neck and tried to pull the bag tight to my face, in hopes that I might be able to see through its weave, but there was no way to do so and maintain the air seal, and so I finally risked pulling the bag up off my face for a second and—

—and Pickover had run to Juan's white-with-green-trim buggy. He was now in the driver's seat, the canopy still up, and I saw him pound the dash, probably with balled fists, in frustration; the damn thing wouldn't start.

I brought my left forearm up into the bag and spoke to my phone, telling it to transmit the ON sequence. Nothing happened; the bag had all but emptied of air, and my phone couldn't hear me speaking, or, if it did, it didn't recognize my voice. I tried with my one free hand to keep the bag's mouth reasonably tight around my neck and wrist, and I waited for enough oxygen to be pumped out of the tube for the fabric to puff out a bit, and then I tried again. "Send the ON code to Juan's buggy!"

I hoped I was close enough. I was still lying on the ground, and would have a devil of a time getting to my feet without using my hands. "Send the ON code to Juan's buggy!" I shouted again.

The ground shook a bit beneath my chest. I thought perhaps Ernie was running—and that's a sight I'd have paid to see—but then I heard the Mars buggy's horn. I arched my neck and risked pulling the bag up enough to see out for a second. Again, there was a cloud of condensation and a blast of arctic air, but through the cloud, I made out Pickover in Juan's buggy, about a dozen meters in front of me. He still had the canopy up. I pulled the bag down, held it around my neck again, and stumbled toward the vehicle.

I soon felt Pickover's hands on me—he must have exited the buggy—and he helped me into its driver's seat, and then he slammed the canopy down from the outside. I emptied my lungs, then pulled the bag up—tugging hard to separate it from the frozen blood on the top of my head—reached forward, hit the switch labeled "Pressurize Cabin," and waited to breathe until I could feel and hear that there was enough air in the little chamber for me to do so.

I looked through the canopy and tried to take in everything that was happening. The situation had definitely changed: Ernie was standing with his hands held over his head. Lakshmi was back on her feet, air tanks attached and fishbowl securely on, and she had Ernie's rifle aimed at him. Blondie, meanwhile, was still tending to the fallen Reiko—which I presume meant that Reiko was alive, even if she wasn't moving.

Pickover was now standing beside the Mars buggy. He waved to catch my attention, then pointed straight ahead. I nodded and floored it, sending the buggy hurtling toward Lakshmi. It was three seconds before she realized what was happening, and when she did, she swung the rifle to fire at me. She managed to hit the windshield three times, each impact sending spider webs of cracks throughout the allo-quartz, but she soon realized that she wasn't going to be able to stop me that way. She bolted in the opposite direction.

I already had the accelerator flush with the floor and just kept going, confident I could mow her down. She was weaving left and right, and I had to yank repeatedly on the steering wheel to keep her dead ahead, but at last the inevitable happened: I was upon her, and—

And she did indeed still have Earthly muscles. She leapt up, up, up just as I was about to run her over, and came down feet first on the little hood of the buggy, her back to me. The springy front wheels compressed as she hit.

We were still speeding forward; I slammed on the brakes in hopes of dislodging her, but she leapt up again as I did so, did a neat half twist in the air, and came down once more, this time with her calves bent back so that she landed on her knees facing me, denting the hood. The buggy had stopped, and she placed the rifle's muzzle against the center of one of the spider-web patterns her previous shots had made and she swiveled the barrel so she was aiming at my chest. Lakshmi was betting that a point-blank shot at a weak spot would go right through the alloquartz and into me—and that was a bet I didn't want to take.

Suddenly there was an impact behind me and the car was rocking up and down. I swung my head around to discover that Pickover had jumped onto the trunk, and now was leaping up onto the top of the canopy. He leapt again, this time landing on the hood right in front of Lakshmi, her rifle barrel between his legs. She pulled the gun away from the alloquartz so she could shoot up at him.

There wasn't room between the canopy and Lakshmi for Pickover to get enough leverage for a decent kick, but he brought his hands down, grabbing her arms just below the shoulders. His left arm worked its way down her right one until it was over the hand holding the rifle, and he tore it from her. He then maneuvered the gun around so that it was aimed at her face, and I waited for her own fishbowl— not to mention the gorgeous head within—to explode.

But Pickover couldn't bring himself to shoot, and after a few seconds the terror ebbed from Lakshmi's exquisite features as she realized that. She rolled backward onto her rump, her spine flat against the buggy's hood, and kicked her legs up into Rory's armpits, flipping him into the air and sending him sailing over so he came down headfirst toward the planitia. The fall was slow enough that he managed to break it by getting his hands splayed out, but that meant dropping the rifle. Lakshmi spun around on her butt, vaulted from the hood, and scooped up the rifle once more. She didn't aim it at Rory, but rather at me, and although the canopy might protect me, it also might not, and given that I didn't have a helmet, Rory clearly decided not to chance rushing her.

Lakshmi hurried around the side of the buggy. I was all set to gun it in reverse, but she stopped before she got behind the vehicle, and—

—and, crap, she reached into the side battery compartment and disconnected the excimer pack. The car's electrical systems—including life support—shut down just as surely as if I'd sent the OFF code again. Lakshmi then hauled back and threw the battery with all her might as far behind the buggy as she could—which was pretty damn far, thanks to her Earthly muscles, the almost nonexistent air drag, and the feeble Martian gravity.

There was enough oxygen in the canopy to keep me alive for some time, I supposed, but if I cracked the lid to go retrieve the battery, I'd lose it. Lakshmi took off running in the opposite direction from where she'd thrown the excimer pack, and Rory hesitated, trying to decide whether to go after the battery or after her. I guess he decided it was more important to get my air circulating again, and he ran toward the rear.

A movement to the right caught my eye. It was Ernie Gargalian, making a beeline for his airplane. He wasn't running, but he was walking fast, his arms working back and forth at his sides as he did so. He'd clearly decided to get away, and, in good Simon Weingarten fashion, apparently was content to maroon his partner here at the Alpha Deposit.

FORTY-THREE

Lakshmi, having apparently noticed what Ernie was up to, took off after him, presumably with an eye on the plane's passenger seat.

The bootleg Pickover hadn't seen precisely where Lakshmi tossed the excimer pack, and he was now searching around for it. With the buggy's power off and my fishbowl radio wrecked, I couldn't give him verbal instructions, although if he would just look back at me, I could at least point in the right direction.

I swiveled my head again to the front. Ernie was standing beside the plane now, turning it around by pulling on the tip of its port wing.

Blondie suddenly picked Reiko up and cradled her in bent arms. Reiko's body was limp; it reminded me of the poster for *Forbidden Planet* with Robby the robot holding Altaira. Blondie began running, carrying Reiko. The Amazonian transfer clearly had her sights set on the airplane, too, doubtless realizing it would be the quickest way to get the injured Reiko to the dome.

I turned the other way, and Rory finally looked back at me. I pointed emphatically, and he at last started looking in the right spot. Excimer packs don't get warm, so I guess his infrared vision was of no help, but—

Finally! He scooped the pack up and jogged back toward the buggy. Lakshmi had left the battery-compartment door open, but it took Rory a while to get the pack seated properly—one of the leads must have gotten bent. When he finally got it in place, I hit the power switch, and the dashboard indicators came to life. I then put my foot on the accelerator. I didn't want to ram the plane, but I could at least prevent Ernie from immediately taking off. I drove directly into the middle of the bit of open terrain he and I had used as a landing strip. Ernie had finished rotating the airplane to his satisfaction but now saw that I was in his way.

Blondie had covered most of the distance to the plane already, and Lakshmi had arrived at it. Ernie and Lakshmi started arguing, both gesticulating wildly. But the lady *did* have the rifle, and after a moment, he waved a hand resignedly at the cockpit, and she clambered into the rear passenger seat.

Ernie was getting in, too, although that took some doing in his eggplant suit. When he was aboard, the teardrop-shaped canopy slid shut over him and Lakshmi, and he started revving his engines; I could see the turbines spinning to life. I moved the buggy even closer, blocking him in. But he seemed willing to try taking off anyway—and, who knows, carbon nanofibers are pretty much indestructible; maybe the plane *could* survive ramming into the buggy.

The blonde goddess still had a few dozen meters to go. I couldn't imagine all the bouncing up and down was good for Reiko. The transfer bent down and gently laid Reiko on the ground again. She then did precisely what Ernie had done earlier: she grabbed the tip of the port wing and started rotating the airplane, turning it to face some nasty boulders. The two people aboard probably doubled the weight of the craft, but Blondie seemed to have no trouble with the task. Ernie might have thought his plane could take plowing into a buggy, but he had to realize that having a transfer hanging off the wing would screw up the aerodynamics that were already chancy in this meager atmosphere. He cut the engine and, rather than have Blondie rip the canopy open, he cracked the seal himself and let it slide to the rear.

Ernie knew he didn't have to get out—he was the trained pilot, after all—but Lakshmi looked like she wasn't going to budge, either. Blondie had her hands on her hips, annoyed. After about five seconds, she started moving toward the cockpit.

Pickover had now run up to the plane, and was on the opposite side of it from Blondie. Lakshmi's gun couldn't do much against either of their artificial bodies, and she at last seemed to think better of being stubborn; after all, if Pickover grabbed her on the left and Blondie on the right, the two transfers could probably rip her in half. Lakshmi lifted herself up out of the rear passenger seat and dropped to the ground. Blondie gestured for Pickover to come around to her side of the plane, and the two of them gently got Reiko into the vacated passenger seat.

I drove the buggy off to one side, Blondie realigned the airplane with the makeshift runway, Ernie gave a jaunty thumbs-up from the pilot's seat and he set the plane rolling along, the preposterously long wings bouncing up and down a bit as it did so, almost as if they thought flapping might help.

At last, the bird lifted off, climbing into the sky and heading east. I had served as navigator on the way out, but I supposed New Klondike couldn't be that hard to spot from the air, and soon enough Ernie would be able to lock in on the town's homing beacon.

That left two transfers and two biologicals here by the Alpha: Pickover and Blondie from Team Silicon and me and Lakshmi on the Carbon side. While I'd been getting the buggy out of the way, Lakshmi had given up her gun. This time, I think she had simply handed it to Rory rather than have him wrench it from her grip; a writer with a broken wrist was going to have a hard time typing, after all.

Rory then came over to the buggy. He and I exchanged discreet hand signs to agree on a frequency so we could have a private chat; I used the buggy's dashboard radio.

"I guess that's it for me," he said.

"Aren't you coming back to the dome?"

He shook his head. "I won't go back until I need to re-charge; there's nothing for me there."

I blew out air. There were things we had to discuss, but this wasn't the time. "Come see me tomorrow, would you?" I said. "Maybe 2:00 p.m. at my office? There are a few, um, interesting developments you should know about."

"Not tomorrow. I'm in the middle of excavating a delicate specimen."

"The day after, then?"

"Fine." And then he walked the dozen or so meters over to Blondie, gave her Lakshmi's gun, and headed off, his back to me, walking slowly toward the northern horizon. I watched him go for a bit, thinking.

But my thoughts were interrupted by Blondie rapping knuckles on the canopy. She had propelled Lakshmi over to the other side of the buggy. I figured now that she was unarmed, I could easily take the writer, if need be. Except of course that I was confined to the interior of this buggy by my lack of a helmet. And, it seemed, Blondie wanted Lakshmi to be confined here, too. She was gesturing for me to open the canopy. I'd be just as happy to leave Lakshmi out here to eventually asphyxiate, but Blondie was pretty much in charge now; she had both guns and could force the canopy open from the outside—which might prevent it from ever sealing properly again. I complied with her wish and swung the transparent cover back. The interior atmosphere escaped. I didn't want to put the sack back on my head—I had my dignity!—and this should only take a second.

The blonde transfer shoved Lakshmi toward the car. Lakshmi glared defiantly for a moment but then acquiesced and pulled herself into the passenger seat. I immediately lowered the canopy and hit the "Pressurize Cabin" button.

"Might as well take off your helmet," I shouted once the interior was filled with air again. "We've got a long ride ahead of us."

Lakshmi made a small nod. She undogged then pulled off her fishbowl and shook out her glorious hair. She held the helmet firmly on her lap rather than putting it in the little storage space behind her; she clearly didn't trust me not to grab it then crack open the canopy again. Smart girl.

Outside, Blondie slapped a palm against my side of the buggy, urging me to get going. I pressed my foot down, and we began moving forward. The blonde bombshell started running, and I drove behind, letting her set the pace as we headed into the darkness.

FORTY-FOUR

The buggy continued to roll through the night. I looked over at Lakshmi, dimly illuminated by the dashboard. A couple of times her chin dropped toward her chest, but she shook herself awake; she was probably as exhausted as I was but terrified of falling asleep.

"You're going to have plenty of time to sleep, sister," I said. "Icing Diana—that wasn't right."

"I told you before, I didn't kill her," she said, looking at me.

"If you didn't, who did?"

"I don't know. She was dead when I got there."

"I need something better than that. Your phone call from inside Weingarten and O'Reilly's descent stage was overheard by the ship's computer. You said Diana was your insurance policy."

"Exactly!" Lakshmi exclaimed "She was no good to me dead. But, as I said to Reiko in that conversation, if I had Diana alive, I could control you."

"But then you discovered that Diana was planting a bug for me at your place, and so you let her have it."

"I didn't, I swear."

"I don't have a lot of reasons to trust you."

"Maybe not. But look at it this way: if I'm lying, fine—

you've got her killer. But if I'm not, then somebody who wanted Diana dead is still out there—and you could be their next target."

"I can take care of myself," I said.

"The way you took care of her?"

That stung, but I refused to let it show. More kilometers passed by.

. . . .

At last, we reached the vicinity of the dome. Blondie had effortlessly run the whole way. We headed to the north airlock station, since that was the one Lakshmi had logged the buggy out through, and, sure enough, Ernie's ungainly airplane was parked near there, safe and sound.

Normally, I'd have left the buggy outside, but I still didn't have a helmet, and so I drove it into the airlock tunnel. The outer door closed behind us, and we waited while the tube was brought up to one standard atmosphere; Blondie, meanwhile, went through the personnel airlock, which cycled much more quickly. By the time the door in front of me slid up, she was already on the other side waiting, along with, I was surprised to see, Dougal McCrae.

I swung back the buggy's canopy and clambered out of the vehicle. Mac moved quickly to the passenger side. "Lakshmi Chatterjee?" he said.

"Yes?"

"You're under arrest."

"What for?"

"One of our leading citizens, Mr. Ernest Gargalian, says you pulled a gun on him."

Lakshmi gestured dismissively. "What if I did? If it happened at all, it was outside your jurisdiction."

Mac stood firm. "You'll come with me," he said. I was grinning. Lakshmi probably had thought herself clever buying Huxley's support, but Ernie could afford to buy himself the top dog. The writer protested a bit more, but there really wasn't anything she could do, and Mac soon had her cuffed. He turned to me. "Alex, I'll expect a full report on everything."

"Of course, Mac. I'll drop by the station later."

"You do that," he said, and he led Lakshmi away—which left just me and Blondie alone here. The gorgeous transfer rushed over to me, and—

Wow!

She threw her arms around me and drew me close, and with that lovely mouth of hers, she planted a long, hard kiss on my lips. There was no doubt I deserved some thanks after all of this, and if this was to be the payment, I couldn't really complain, but—

But the kiss went on and on, and when Blondie finally drew away, a giant grin spread across her stunning features. And now that we were in real air again, she could speak. I didn't recognize the voice at all; it was sultry, sexy, and totally captivating. "Thank you so much!" she said. "As soon as we got close enough to phone, I contacted Ernie. He said Reiko went into surgery hours ago and is already out and in recovery; she's going to be fine." She gave me another kiss on the lips, then added, "Thank you, Alex!"

I noted, in good detective fashion, that she was on a first-name basis with Gargantuan, not to mention with me—but I still had no idea who this blonde goddess was. "You're welcome," I said. "But you have me at a disadvantage, Miss, um . . ."

I'd never seen a transfer's eyes twinkle before, but hers seemed to just then. "Oh, Alex! It's *me.*"

I shook my head slightly, baffled, and she took a half step back to appraise me. "Look at you! You're a mess! Cut, frostbitten, filthy. Go off and get yourself fixed up, get some sleep, and be ready to go by 6:00 p.m."

"Go where?" I said.

"Dinner, silly. You still owe me dinner at Bleaney's."

My jaw dropped, and it was a few moments before I could get it working again. "Diana?"

Her smile was a mile wide. "The one and only."

My heart was pounding, and I'm sure I was grinning, too, but there'd been enough twists and turns in this case that I had to be sure. "Prove it," I said.

"Your left testicle—"

"Fine! Fine. Fine. Diana! But—no, no. I saw your dead body."

"You saw my *discarded* body."

"With a bullet hole in the middle of its forehead."

She waited for me to get it, and I did. "A frame-up," I said. "You were framing Lakshmi for murder." I thought about it. "Her gun, doubtless with her fingerprints, the body at her place—well, at Shopatsky House." I nodded. "But why? And how? You couldn't possibly afford to transfer."

"It pays to have friends in the right places," Diana said.

I'd been aware that she'd been seeing someone else of late, of course, but . . . well, well, well. "I didn't even know you knew Reiko Takahashi."

"Isn't she adorable?" Diana gushed. "I fell for her the first night she came into The Bent Chisel."

"But why frame Lakshmi?"

"She and Reiko were working together at first," Diana said. "You knew that: Reiko willingly loaned Lakshmi her grandfather's diary because Lakshmi supposedly had made a study of the Weingarten and O'Reilly expeditions; if there was a coded reference to the location of the Alpha in the diary, Lakshmi said she'd figure it out and split the riches with Reiko. But Lakshmi wasn't going to do that at all; she had learned where the Alpha was, but kept telling Reiko she didn't know its location—a double-cross. We had to get Lakshmi out of the picture, and, well, we *did* have a spare biological body that we had to dispose of somehow . . ."

"But if Lakshmi knew where the Alpha was, why frame her for murder before you'd found the location?"

"Because, my darling Alex, I knew that *you* knew where it was."

"How?" But then it came to me. "Dirk. The switchblade. You figured if Rory Pickover was back to being my client, I was bound to eventually learn where the Alpha was, and so you arranged for me to acquire something that had a tracking chip in it."

Diana nodded. "Sorry, baby, but, well, it *was* Reiko's rightful claim, not yours and not Dr. Pickover's. Lakshmi was already working with Dirk, and every time you returned to the dome, the tracking chip uploaded its data to the Shop-atsky House computer—so Reiko and I took it when we planted the body."

"Clever," I said.

"Yes, but Lakshmi must have been anticipating some-thing, because by the time we got it, she'd wiped the data from the computer. And, of course, by that point you'd fig-ured out about the tracking chip and destroyed it."

"Ah, and so you decided it would be easier to just force Lakshmi to show Reiko where the Alpha was than it would be to get the secret from me—and so you kidnapped her."

"I didn't; Reiko did. But I *did* tail them, running a couple of kilometers behind, just in case Reiko needed help—which, of course, it turned out she did."

My head was spinning. She'd betrayed me, she'd used me, she'd outsmarted me. I took a step back and looked at her, absolutely stunned.

"You . . ." I said, my voice quavering, and I raised my right hand, pointing a finger at her. "You are . . ."

The blue eyes blinked. "Yes?"

"You are *amazing*," I said.

"I am that," she replied, and smiled. "Sorry, honey."

"So what happens now?"

She lifted her blonde eyebrows and grinned lasciviously. "Now? Why, we go to Bleaney's, of course."

"But you don't need to eat."

"No, of course not. But I love to dance."

"And after?"

She indicated her amazing new body with a sweeping motion of her hands. "A night we'll both remember."

FORTY-FIVE

Transfers weren't supposed to die. I'd never heard of a funeral for one, and, anyway, there couldn't be much of a funeral for Rory Pickover here on Mars. Whatever family he had was back on Earth, and he had few friends here. In fact, I think he had only one.

Dougal McCrae had released the dead transfer bodies, including that of the legitimate Rory Pickover, to NewYou. After the bootleg had come to see me at my office, as promised, he and I headed over there. We came through the front door, and that must have triggered a signal, because Horatio Fernandez immediately appeared from the workroom. His eyes went wide the moment he saw the bootleg Pickover. "Joshua!"

I scratched my ear. "Ah, yes. Um, this is going to take a little explaining. This isn't actually Joshua Wilkins. It's a bootleg copy of Dr. Rory Pickover."

"Good God," said Horatio. "Seriously?"

"Yes," I said.

"Then—then where's Joshua?"

"He's dead," I said. "He was mixed up in some bad stuff, and the police fried him with their disruptor."

"My . . . God. Really?"

"Yes," I said. Then: "Is Reiko in?"

"No," replied Horatio. "No, and she won't be coming back. I had to let her go. She was performing unauthorized transfers after hours."

"Transfers, plural?"

"Well, at least one."

"Are you going to bring charges?"

Horatio lifted his massive shoulders. "No cameras upstairs, remember. Hard to make an airtight case against her. And, besides, I've got a business to run. Going after the granddaughter of Denny O'Reilly isn't going to make me popular."

"Ah."

Horatio was looking at the bootleg. "I guess lots of things were going on here that I didn't know about."

"Yeah," I said. "I understand the body of the legitimate Pickover is here?"

"In the back room. Along with *three* bodies that look like Dazzling Don Hutchison, and one that looks like Krikor Ajemian." Horatio shook his head. "I honestly don't know what to do with them all."

Rory spoke for the first time since we'd come into the shop. "May I—can I—have a moment with . . . with the other me?"

Horatio nodded, and he led us into the workroom. Uno, Dos, and Tres—not necessarily in that order—were on their backs on the floor by the far wall. Stuart Berling was up on one worktable, his chest open; fiber-optic cables were running from the cavity to some equipment. And on the other table, the body of Professor Rory Pickover, Ph.D., was lying on his back, face up. His mouth was slightly ajar, revealing a strip of artificial dentition, and his acrylic eyes were open. They weren't staring straight ahead, though. Rather, they were looking to the right, frozen in a sideways glance.

As I've said, it's hard to read a transfer's expression, and so all I could do was guess at what the bootleg Pickover was thinking as he regarded his dead brother. It couldn't have made things any easier that the legitimate Pickover had opted to keep his original face. Oh, he'd had it cleaned up a bit, and he'd taken a lot of the gray out of his hair and had most of the wrinkles erased, but it was still recognizably Rory Pickover, mousy paleontologist.

The bootleg Pickover stood over him, unblinking. I'd have thought blinks were autonomic even for a transfer. Maybe he was trying not to cry—not that he *could*—and that was keeping his eyelids from moving.

"Give us a minute, won't you, Horatio?" I said.

Fernandez nodded and returned to the showroom. When he was gone, the bootleg lifted his head and looked at me, while indicating the dead transfer. "He knew about me, didn't he?"

"He didn't know you were still around, but, yes, he knew you'd been created."

"What did he say about me?"

What the legit Pickover had said was, "If you find another me, erase it. Destroy it. I never want to see the damned thing." Looking now at the bootleg, I found it hard to give voice to those words. "What would you have said in the same position?"

More silence, then the slightest of nods. "I don't blame him."

We stood quietly for a while, then the bootleg Rory said, "Okay. I'm ready."

We went back into the showroom. Horatio was at his cash station. We approached him and when he looked up, I said, "I ask for *fal-tor-pan,* the refusion."

If it had been my fellow old-movie-buff Lakshmi, I might have gotten the response, "What you seek has not been done since ages past—and then, only in legend." But all Horatio managed was, "Excuse me?"

"Let's go upstairs."

At least that generated a smile from Horatio. "I thought you'd never ask." He headed for the staircase, and I followed, with the bootleg Pickover making up the rear. Once upstairs, I pointed at the scanning room, Horatio opened the door, and we all went in. "You said there were no security cameras up here," I said. "Was that the truth?"

Horatio nodded.

"Good," I said. "We want you to open up this bootleg's skull, take out the artificial brain, and transplant it into the legitimate Rory's body."

Horatio looked stunned for a moment, but then he slowly nodded. "Yes, I guess—yes, I can do that. Of course, there are a bunch of systems in the body that will have to be re-calibrated, but—"

"Whatever it takes," I said. "Do it."

"But . . . but Pickover is officially dead now."

"Only the cops know that—the cops and you. It does your business no good to have word getting spread around that transfers aren't in fact immortal, so I know you'll keep your trap shut. And the cops are in Ernie Gargalian's back pocket—or, at least the top cop is. Ernie owes me a favor; he'll get the report about Pickover to disappear."

We went back down to the workroom. Horatio and I moved Stuart Berling's dead husk to the floor to clear a worktable, then Horatio set about examining the corpse of the legitimate Pickover.

Soon enough, the top was off the legit Pickover's head, and Horatio removed the disruptor-fried and slightly squished brain. Apparently a transfer brain was normally spherical, rather than the, well, brain shape of a biological brain. It was about the size of a softball, but was teal in color and seemed completely rigid. At the bottom was a complex connector that I guess plugged into the artificial spinal cord. Horatio put that dead brain on the tabletop, the spine-plug keeping it from rolling away, and then he took a moment to hammer out the dents in the metal skull.

When he was satisfied, he turned to the bootleg Rory and said, "Okay, take your shirt off and have a seat on the edge of this table."

The bootleg unbuttoned and removed his khaki work shirt, then boosted himself up. I couldn't see any jack on Pickover's side, but Horatio managed to attach a fiber-optic cable terminating in a metal plug there, ninety degrees to the right of his plastic belly button; maybe it clamped on magnetically. "All right," he said. "First things first. I'm going to dial down your pain response."

"You can do that?" Rory replied. "Where were you when I needed you?"

Horatio, I'm sure, didn't understand, but he smiled anyway and turned to a control console. "Okay. That should do it; this shouldn't hurt. Tell me if it does." He picked up a laser cutter and sliced through the plastiskin above the bootleg's eyebrows; there was indeed no sign of discomfort from Rory. Horatio continued right around the head. The incision separated, just like a cut in real flesh would, but there was no blood. The metal skull it revealed had a seam around it, not unlike the ones you sometimes saw on anatomy-class skeletons.

It was strange watching surgery with the surgeon using bare hands and not wearing a facemask. The top of the skull came neatly off after Horatio did something to unseat it, and he placed it upside down on the table—a titanium cranium covered with artificial hair; it looked like half of a bionic coconut.

"Wait," said Pickover. "Give me a second." He tilted his head down—and I was afraid his teal brain might roll out of his skull as he did so, but it seemed to still be firmly attached. I guess he just wanted one last look at this body. I knew how he felt. Every time I'd left an apartment for the last time, I'd had one final look around, committing the place to memory—and saying my farewell.

"Okay," Rory said softly. "I'm ready."

Horatio made a couple more adjustments on his console then he placed his hand on the top of the brain and gave it a quarter twist, which disengaged it. He then pulled it up and out, and moved over to the other worktable, where the corpse of the legitimate Dr. Pickover was still lying on its back. There must have been an orientation mark on the brain that I couldn't see, because he rotated it until he had it facing a particular way. And then he placed it in the vacant skull, gave it a ninety-degree twist, and—

And the transfer's eyes, which had been stuck looking askance, shifted left and right a few times, taking in the scene, and then the mouth opened all the way, and the only remaining Dr. Rory Pickover in all the world said, in his inimitable fashion, "Thanks so much, old chap!"

I imagine the first time you transferred from a biological existence to an electronic one there was some disorientation. But Pickover was already used to what it was like to be a transfer, and he seemed comfortable. He sat up with ease, swinging his legs over the edge of the table.

"Your arms are four centimeters longer in this body," Horatio said, "so pay attention for a day or two while you reach for things. Oh, and you'll have to relearn how to activate your telescopic and infrared vision. These eyes are from a different manufacturer and operate slightly differently."

Pickover nodded—effortlessly, it seemed. And then he tipped his head down and looked at the back of his hand; I guess he figured he should get to know it. "The colors are a bit different," Rory said, looking up. "Your skin, Alex's hair."

"Oh?" said Fernandez.

"They're all a little more . . . golden."

"We can adjust that easily enough."

"It's kind of nice, actually." He brought his hands up and patted his chest. I thought he was exploring his body, but that wasn't it. "And it's so good to be wearing my own clothes again!" When he'd died, the legitimate Pickover had been wearing a dark blue work shirt with a silhouette of a dinosaur on one of the pockets.

Fernandez picked up the top of the skull and set about reattaching it. While he was doing that, I said, "Now, there's just one more task." I jerked my thumb at the empty form on the other table. "The world thinks that's Joshua Wilkins, who, of course, has really been dead for months. We've got to dispose of the corpse."

"I—he—was supposed to be hunting fossils," offered Pickover, as Horatio used a tool to lay down new plastiskin, sealing the skullcap in place. "You could just dump the body out on the planitia—make it look like he malfunctioned and expired out there."

"No," said Horatio, stopping in his work. "Absolutely not."

I looked at him.

"I've got a business to run here," he said, "and, like you

said, it's based on the notion that I'm selling immortality—or, at the very least, durability. It can't be that his body just failed—not under anything approaching normal circumstances. You owe me that much."

"Okay," I said. "We'll find another way."

FORTY-SIX

Rory wanted to go home, and I could hardly blame him for being anxious to finally get there. After all, this version of him hadn't been to his own place since he'd been created. He had woken up in a primitive robotic body, had endured torture aboard the *Skookum Jim,* had upgraded that body to assume the identity of Joshua Wilkins, and had retreated for the past couple of months out onto the planitia to look for fossils, all without ever once seeing his own place. And so we parted company at NewYou. I headed to Gully's for a workout, then went to my apartment—and slept clear through to 10:00 a.m. the next morning.

When I awoke, there was voice mail from Ernie Gargalian, requesting my presence for a noon meeting at Ye Olde Fossil Shoppe.

I got there bang on time; one doesn't keep Mars's Mister Big waiting. I was surprised to find two other people already inside: Reiko Takahashi and Dr. Rory Pickover. Reiko was leaning against one of the display tables but looked no worse for wear; Ernie, of course, had gotten her the best medical treatment when his plane had arrived back at the dome—no Windermere Clinic butchery for Denny O'Reilly's grand-daughter.

"Ah, Alex, my dear boy, good to see you!" Ernie said. "Come in, come in!" He gestured expansively. "Can I get you something? I have a hundred-year-old Scotch you might like."

"Maybe later," I replied.

"Later," agreed Ernie. "Yes, yes—propriety, my boy! One doesn't start business with alcohol; one concludes it. We'll save it for a toast."

Ernie's showroom didn't have any seats in it, but he led us to his opulent office, a room I'd never been in before. It had three wine red chairs that I imagined were upholstered with real leather. Ernie took the one behind the wide, ornately carved desk. Reiko took another, crossing her lovely legs. I took the final one. Rory, of course, could stand comfortably for hours.

"Alex, you've created a problem for me," Ernie said, "and we need to sort it out."

"A problem?" I repeated.

"Yes, my boy, yes. You've led me to the promised land; you've shown me Denny and Simon's mother lode. Riches beyond imagining, one might think."

"And that's a problem how?"

"Back on Earth," Ernie said, pointing vaguely at the sky, "they synthesize gold, they manufacture diamonds, they replicate rubies. Those things have no value—virtually no material object does. But actual fossils of extraterrestrial life—ah, *those* collectors will pay dearly for! And why, my dear Alex, why?"

"Their provenance," I said.

Ernie's fat face exploded in laughter. He looked at Pickover. "Did you hear him, my good professor? 'Provenance,' he said. Such a highfalutin word for him to know!" He turned his attention back to me. "Yes, absolutely—the fact that they're demonstrably genuine, that they haven't been synthesized or replicated, yes, indeed, my boy, that's one reason they're so valuable. But there's another criterion. After all, you can't make any money selling genuine moon rocks anymore, even though their provenance is easy to establish; it's hard to even give them away. But in days of yore, they used to be the most valuable stones on Earth. And do you know why that was?"

I had an idea, but you learn more by letting people tell stories their way rather than trying to beat them to the punch. "No."

"Because between 1972, when the last *Apollo* astronaut walked on the moon, until humans finally returned there, there were only 382 kilograms of moon rocks on Earth. Scarcity, my boy! Supply and demand! There were *tons* of diamonds then, but—well, my lad, I'll say it because I know you're thinking it! You know that surface suit of mine? The purple one? You could fit *all* the *Apollo* booty into it. And so of course those stones were highly valued."

"Right," I said. "Okay."

"But it's *not* okay, dear Alex. Not at all. I now know where a huge cache of wonderfully preserved Martian fossils is located—the best of the best, and not just quality, but quantity! I simply can't reveal that fact to the public. Oh, if I started selling a lot of material from there, yes, for a short time, I might realize spectacular prices, but soon Alpha fossils would be ubiquitous, and not just directly via me but on the secondary market, too. Alphas will be a drug on the market—everybody selling alphas; there will be alphas everywhere."

"So what are you going to do?" I asked.

Ernie smiled, his grapefruit cheeks moving up as he did so. "That's the question! And the answer is this, my boy: we're going to *curate* the Alpha. Dr. Pickover here will get to select the specimens to work on, studying them, scanning them, learning from them, describing them for science. He works at a slow pace; I know that, and that's fine. And when he's finally done with each specimen, he'll release it to me, and I will bring it to market; we'll find an appreciative buyer. And Miss Takahashi, here, the descendant of my dear old friend Denny, will share in the profits; I will send her a cut from every sale."

"But . . . but that could take years."

"By Gad, Alex, yes, it might! But so what? We not only live in an age of material abundance, my boy, we live in an age of immortality! Dr. Pickover has already made the transition, and surely none of the rest of us intend to ultimately join his fossils in the ground! I'm the oldest one in this room by a good piece, but I've just barely begun my life! And, as any good businessperson knows, an asset that pays steady dividends over time is far more valuable than one consumed quickly."

I looked up at Pickover. "And you're okay with this, Rory?"

Rory shrugged a bit. "It's not ideal; not even close. But I've got the site map that Weingarten and O'Reilly made, and Ernie here has been plugged into the black market for fossils since the very beginning; he's going to help me locate the collectors who have those old specimens. Now that Willem Van Dyke is gone, Ernie is just about the only lead I have for ever getting access to those fossils and describing them in the scientific literature. And I *do* get to scan and describe every new specimen that's excavated."

I turned to Reiko Takahashi. "And what about you? This works for you?"

She nodded her lovely head. "It'll do."

"But what about Lakshmi?" I said. "She knows where the Alpha is, too."

"My dear boy, please don't worry about that. She's no longer a problem."

"She's going back to Earth?" I asked.

Ernie's eyebrows climbed toward his slicked-back hair. "So unfortunate. She really shouldn't have resisted arrest."

I frowned; she hadn't.

"Of course, the *body* will be shipped back," he said. He tilted his fat head. "I hear our next writer-in-residence will be a playwright."

I looked over at Pickover, but it *was* hard to read a transfer's expression.

"And so that just leaves you, Mr. Double-X." Ernie shook his massive head. "I knew Stuart Berling, as you know—he was selling his fossils through me. Found some fabulous specimens not that long ago, and they made him a rich man, but he couldn't bring himself to return to Earth—that nasty business aboard the *B. Traven* had scarred him for life. And you're in much the same situation, aren't you, my boy? Berling couldn't return to Earth and neither can you; his reasons were psychological and yours are legal, but the effect is the same, isn't it?"

I crossed my arms in front of my chest. "And your point is?"

"My point is that for all this to work, the Alpha will still need protection—and nothing so clumsy as land mines. It will need someone to look after it. And that someone can be you. Insane wealth will do you no good, not here, not on Mars, but you'll make enough to have your life-support tax always paid, and your tab at The Bent Chisel always settled, and, when the time comes, you'll be able to afford to have yourself transferred into the finest of bodies." He raised a beefy hand. "It won't be full-time work, of course; you'll still have plenty of opportunities to ply your usual trade. But it will keep you nicely in the black for many mears to come."

"And you think that'll be enough for me?" I asked.

"My dear Mr. Double-X, I would not presume to speak for you. But it strikes me as win-win all around. What do you say?"

I thought about the four fossil slabs I'd jackhammered out of the Alpha and then hidden outside the dome. But my own little pieces of the stuff that dreams are made of had waited billions of years—they could wait a while longer . . . perhaps, even, until the day when I might be able to go back home.

And so I looked at each of the faces in turn: at the broad countenance of Gargantuan Gargalian, who had always known how to get what he wanted; at the exquisite, delicate features of Reiko Takahashi, who had perhaps gotten what I had wanted; and at the inquisitive visage of Rory Pickover, who would walk naked into a live volcano if he thought he could learn something that no other man knew.

I turned back to Ernie. "I want my own Mars buggy. My own surface suit."

"Of course," said Ernie. "Consider it done."

"And I need a new gun."

"Naturally."

"And my own broadband disruptor."

Ernie laughed heartily. "Alex, my boy, that's thinking ahead, by Gad, it is. Yes, certainly, we'll get you one of those, too."

"All right," I said, nodding slowly. "We'll drink on it. Get that Scotch."

. . . .

Because of speed-of-light delays, it's impossible to interact in real time with people on Earth. You can't chat with them by video; you can't speak with them on the phone; you can't swap instant messages. And so I hadn't spoken to Wanda—really spoken to her—in the ten years I'd been on Mars.

I didn't regret my choice, I didn't regret it at all. Wanda had done the only thing she *could* do. That abusing bastard had to be stopped, and she had stopped him, simply, cleanly, and for all time. But when you love someone, you look after them—and I looked after her. I took the rap for her, and, rather than face decades in jail, I escaped to a sealed dome on a red, barren rock; sometimes, it was hard to tell the difference.

Despite everything that had gone down these last few days, a man needs routines in his life, he needs order, he needs something to hold on to. Every week—every seven Earth days—I would record a video message for Wanda and pay to have it transmitted to Earth: Howard Slapcoff got his fee whether you were coming or going, whether you were living or dying, or whether you were just one of the living dead. I always found it awkward making the videos; it wasn't like me to talk about what was going on in my life. But a few days after she received mine, she'd send one of her own in reply, and when I got those, when I saw how happy she was, how at peace, how full of joy, it made everything worthwhile; it made me, at least for a time, feel alive.

And so I sat in the chair in my office, the wallpaper displaying the alternating green and caramel stripes of our house from all those years ago, and I straightened my collar, patted down my hair, cleared my throat, activated my camera, and spoke to it. "Hello, sis . . ."

FORTY-SEVEN

Diana, with her gorgeous new body, drove by my place to pick me up in Juan's buggy.

"How'd seeing Juan go?" I asked.

She smiled, and although it wasn't the smile of hers I was used to, it was still very pleasant. "He's such a sweetheart," she said. "He was so relieved that I was still alive."

"I bet."

"But—funny. I knew he liked me; I mean—come on—it was painfully obvious. But he didn't look at me the same way this time. I know I'm ten times better-looking now than I was before, but . . ." She shrugged a little. "Maybe there *is* something to be said for people who like you just the way you are . . . or were."

"Maybe," I said softly.

We drove to NewYou and collected the dead transfer body that had housed the bootleg Rory. Horatio Fernandez, per my instructions, had put the fried brain of the legitimate Pickover into the empty skull. In good mobster fashion, Diana and I stuffed the cybercorpse into the trunk. We then headed to the western airlock and drove through the tunnel there and out onto the surface.

I'd said before that newcomers to Mars sometimes hurt

themselves because they feel invincible in the low gravity. I imagined something similar could happen with transfers: the combination of enhanced strength and feeble gravity makes them feel like comic-book superheroes. And Joshua Wilkins—poor, grieving Joshua Wilkins, who had recently lost his doting wife Cassandra—would quite plausibly have felt more reckless than most.

There were amazing places on Mars, and if a tourist industry ever develops here, I'm sure the brochures will feature Valles Marineris and Olympus Mons—respectively, the solar system's longest canyon and its largest volcano. Either of those would have done well for our purpose, but unfortunately they were both clear around the globe from Isidis Planitia. But Rory—who, of course, knew his geology—suggested a suitable spot closer to home. There was a dried lava flow extending thirteen kilometers from a mountain peak in Nili Patera. The sides of the flow were steep, and in some places featured an eighty-meter sheer drop.

Diana and I had brought along some climbing gear—carbon-fiber rope, a piton gun, and so forth—to make it look like old Joshua-never-Josh had decided to try his luck rappelling down the lava flow. We found the steepest edge we could along its length, opened the trunk, and carried the body to the precipice. I took one leg, Diana took the other, and we dangled it headfirst over the edge. "Count of three," I said. "One, two, three."

We let it go and watched it fall in that wonderful Martian slow motion, down, down, down, descending a height equal to that of a twenty-seven-story office tower. Mars, being Mars, served up a Wile E. Coyote falling-off-the-cliff-style puff of dust when the body hit.

It might be years or mears, or decades or mecades, until the body was found, but, when it was, I'm sure the coroner's report will read "death by misadventure." If my time ever comes, I'd like the same thing, I think—beats all hell out of being gunned down by an ex-wife, strangled by a creditor, or knifed by a disgruntled client.

The trip back to the dome took the better part of a day, and that gave Diana and me plenty of time to talk. And, after several hours, with the sun low behind us and the sky ahead purpling, I decided to pop the question—the one that had been swirling at the back of my mind ever since I discovered that she was still alive. But getting to it required some setup, so, as we continued east, I said, "I think it's time to change things around a little."

"Oh?" replied Diana, turning her lovely head to look at me.

"Yeah. I'm tired of being the only private detective on Mars."

"What would you do instead?"

"No, no, no. I'm not talking about quitting. I love my work; to quote one of my predecessors, this is my métier. But I'm thinking about taking on a partner."

"Maybe Dougal McCrae would like to join you," Diana offered. "I imagine he gets tired of all the paperwork that goes with being a cop."

"No, not him." I took one hand off the steering wheel and swept it back and forth in front of me, as if indicating lines of text. "Can't you just see it? Light streaming through a window with two names painted on it, and the names visible as shadows on the floor: 'Lomax and Connally, Private Investigators.'"

She looked surprised, but whether at the vocational suggestion or at the discovery that I knew her last name, I wasn't sure.

"Well?" I said. "You certainly can't keep working at The Bent Chisel. No one wants to be served booze by a transfer; it's like having a Mormon bartender—the vibe is all wrong. And, sure, I know you don't need to pay the life-support tax anymore, but surely you still want to make some money."

She looked at me with lustrous acrylic eyes, and her voice was soft. "Oh, Alex . . ."

"Yes?"

"Alex, baby, don't you get it? I transferred for a reason."

"Of course. Immortality. Eternal youth."

"Not that; none of that matters to me. But, honey, I've been here twelve years, and, unlike you, I haven't been going to the gym. I wanted strength."

"You've certainly got that," I said. "That's one of the reasons you'd make a great partner."

She shook her head gently, the blonde hair glistening as she did so. "Stop for a second."

I did, and she turned around in her seat and pointed through the clear canopy. At first I thought she was referring to the body we'd disposed of—as if *that* was an impediment to being a private eye—but then I realized she was indicating the evening star, a sapphire glowing low in the western sky.

"Earth?" I said.

"Earth. I'm going home, and I'll weigh three times there what I weighed here. I could never have managed it in my old body. But in *this* body, I'll do just fine."

"But what's Earth got that Mars doesn't?"

The question was facetious, of course; the list was almost endless. But, still, her answer surprised me. "Reiko."

"She's here."

"For now. But she wants to go home; she never intended to settle here permanently—and, frankly, neither did I; it just sort of happened. Reiko and I are booked on the return flight of the *Kathryn Denning.*"

"But Reiko's still biological, no? And she'll weigh three times as much there, too."

"Sure. But she's only been on Mars for a couple of months, and she's been working out. She'll have no trouble readjusting to a full gee."

"I've never seen her at Gully's."

"That dump? Alex, she works out at the Amsterdam."

"I'm going to miss you," I said.

"Come see me. Surely that's why *you've* been working out, right? So you could go home someday?"

"Someday," I said quietly. "Maybe." I looked again at the blue planet, slowly setting behind us, then turned and started the buggy up. We drove in silence for the next hour or more, and when we did start talking again, it was about nothing of consequence.

Finally, we made it back to the New Klondike dome. We parked Juan's buggy, and I returned my rented surface suit, and, of course, I escorted Diana back to her place; it was, after all, almost 4:00 a.m.—although, realistically, she was in a better position now to protect me than I was to protect her. I wondered if she was going to invite me to spend what little was left of the night, but, as we headed up the rickety stairs to her apartment, she said, "Reiko's staying over, although I'm sure she's sound asleep by now."

I nodded, accepting that.

"But if you can wait for just a minute . . ." She unlocked her door and went in without turning on the lights; perhaps she was using infrared vision to do whatever she wanted to do. She came out again carrying a plain white bag, and she moved in and gave me a hug—a gentle one, as if she still wasn't sure of her own strength. "It's been fun, Alex."

She then reached into the white bag and pulled out another bag, one with a shiny rainbow-sheen finish and U-shaped handles secured by a red satiny ribbon. "I got you a little gift," she said. "Something to remember me by." She handed it to me. "Go ahead. Open it."

I was no better with the knot in the ribbon than Dr. Pickover had been with the knot in Lakshmi's lasso. Diana, who had longer fingernails, laughed a little and took the package back briefly to undo the bow. She then handed it to me, and I opened up the bag and pulled out its contents—a crisp gray fedora.

"Now you've got a real hat to tip at people," she said.

I picked it up by the crown and positioned it carefully on the top of my head. The fit was perfect. I lifted it and gave its inaugural tip to Diana.

"Thank you, sweetheart," I said, and I leaned in and kissed her on the lips one last time.

"My pleasure," Diana replied. "Take care of yourself, won't you, Alex?"

"Always have," I said. "Always will."

I walked down the stairs and out into the lonely night.

ABOUT THE AUTHOR

Robert J. Sawyer's novel *FlashForward* was the basis for the ABC TV series of the same name, and he was a scriptwriter for that program.

Rob is a lifelong space buff. In 2007, he participated in the invitation-only workshop The Future of Intelligence in the Cosmos at the NASA Ames Research Center. In 2010 and again in 2012, he was the only science-fiction writer invited to speak at the SETI Institute's first two SETIcon conferences on the search for extraterrestrial intelligence. In 2011, he became an invited contributor to the 100 Year Starship initiative, sponsored by the US Defense Advanced Research Projects Agency (DARPA). A thirty-year member of the Royal Astronomical Society of Canada, a member of both The Planetary Society and The Mars Society, and a graduate of the NASA-sponsored Launch Pad Astronomy Workshop, Rob has published in *Archaeology, Nature, Science,* and *Sky & Telescope,* and has done science commentary on-air for both the CBC and the BBC.

Rob is one of only eight writers ever to win all three of the world's top awards for best science-fiction novel of the year: the Hugo (which he won in 2003 for *Hominids),* the Nebula (which he won in 1996 for *The Terminal Experiment),* and the John W. Campbell Memorial Award (which he won in 2006 for *Mindscan).* According to *The Locus Index to Science Fiction Awards,* he has won more awards for his novels than anyone else in the history of the science-fiction and fantasy fields.

He's also won an Arthur Ellis Award from Crime Writers of Canada, and *The Globe and Mail: Canada's National News-*

paper named his previous SF/mystery crossover *Illegal Alien* "the best Canadian mystery novel of the year."

Rob hosts the Canadian skeptical television series *Supernatural Investigator.* He has been writer-in-residence at The Merril Collection of Science Fiction, Speculation and Fantasy in Toronto; at the Canadian Light Source, Canada's national synchrotron research facility, in Saskatoon (a position created specifically for him); and at Berton House in Dawson City.

Rob has received an honorary doctorate from Laurentian University and the Alumni Award of Distinction from Ryerson University, and he was the first-ever recipient of Humanist Canada's Humanism in the Arts Award. *Quill & Quire,* the Canadian publishing trade journal, calls him "one of the thirty most influential, innovative, and just plain powerful people in Canadian publishing." His website and blog are at **sfwriter. com**, and on Twitter and Facebook he's **RobertJSawyer**.